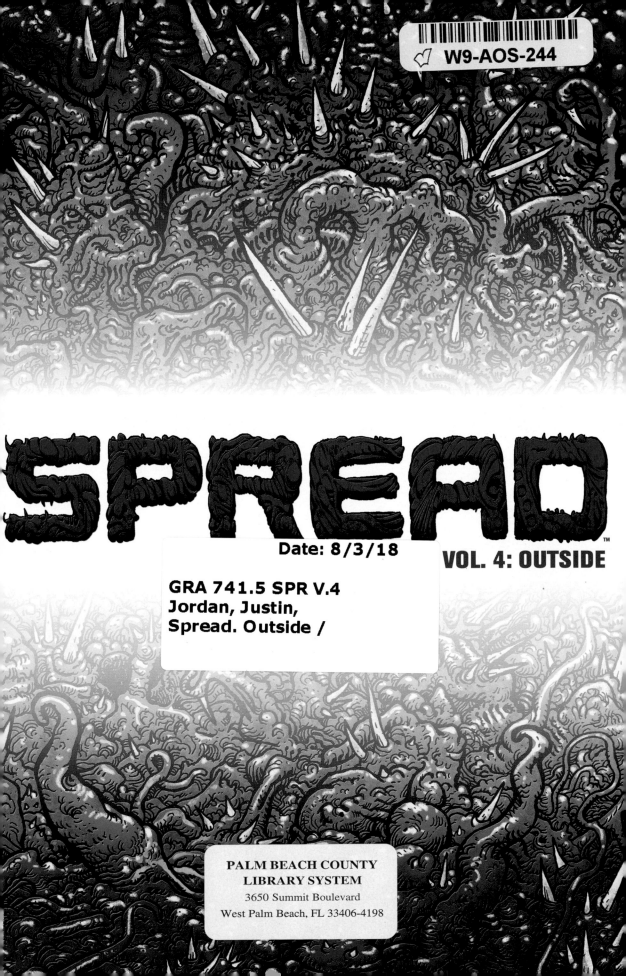

SPREAD™

VOL. 4: OUTSIDE

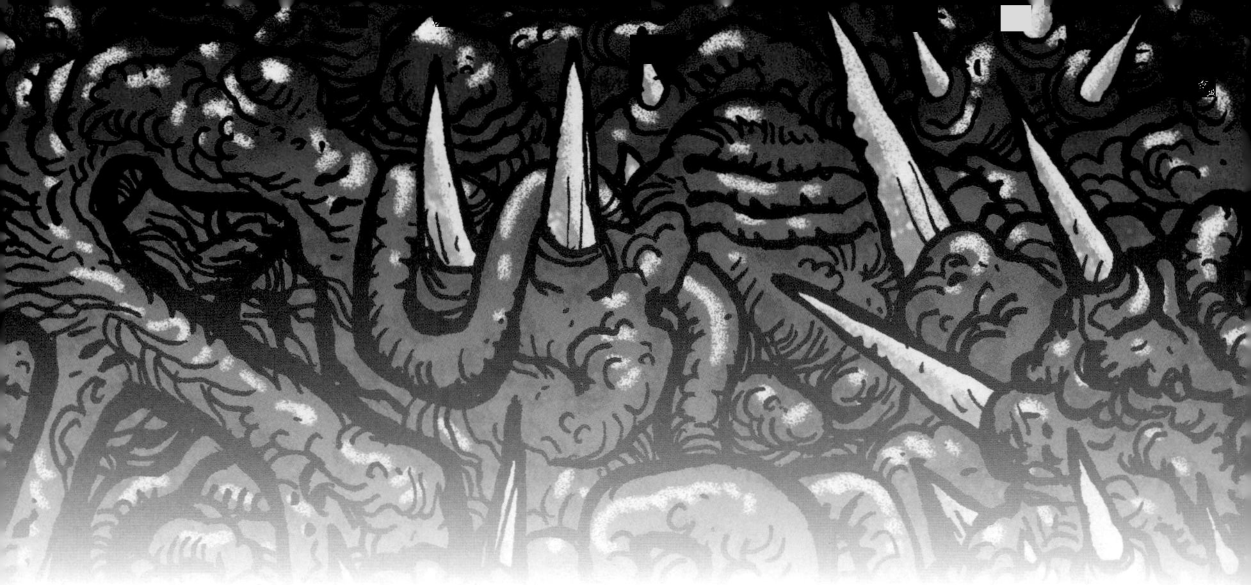

SPREAD VOL. 4: OUTSIDE. FIRST PRINTING. JULY 2017.
ISBN# 978-1-5343-0184-9

Published by Image Comics, Inc. Office of publication: 2701 NW Vaughn St., Ste. 780, Portland, OR 97210. **PRINTED IN THE U.S.A. For information regarding the CPSIA on this printed material call: 203-595-3636 and provide reference # RICH – 747530.**

For international rights, contact:
foreignlicensing@imagecomics.com

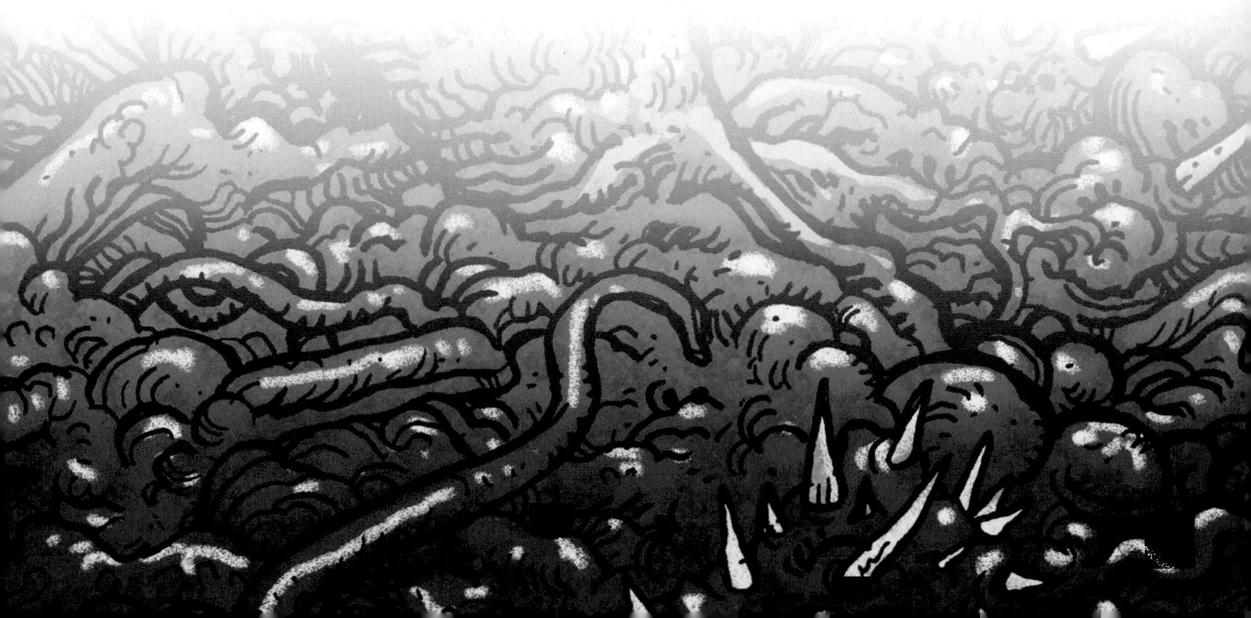

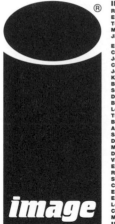

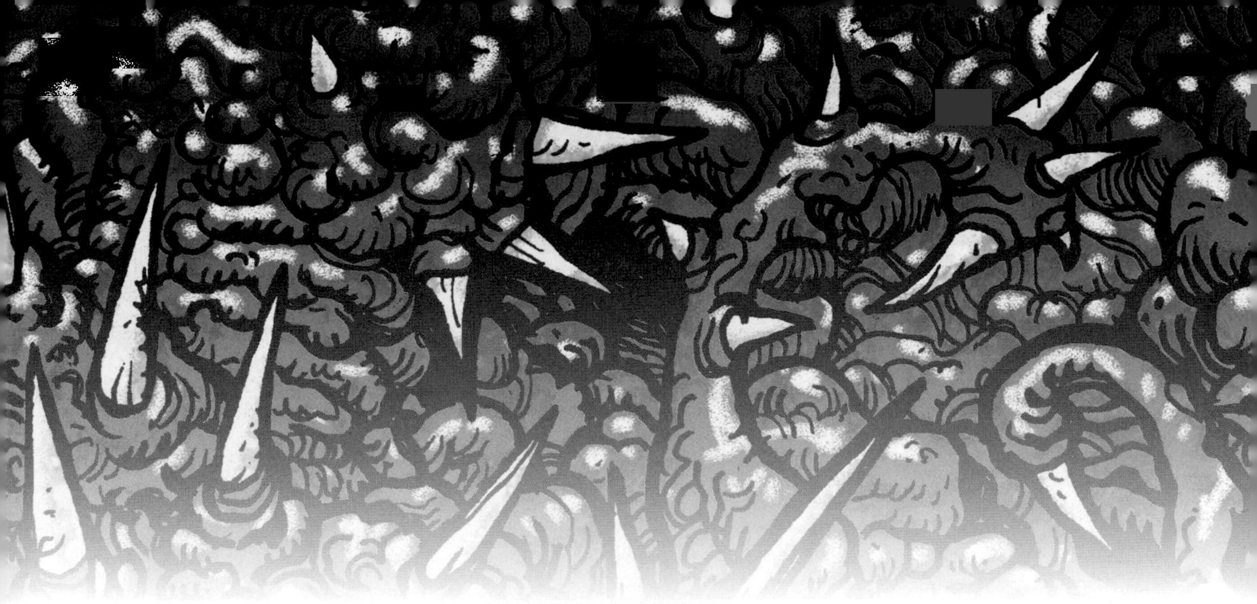

CO-CREATED BY

JUSTIN JORDAN and KYLE STRAHM

WRITTEN BY

JUSTIN JORDAN

ART BY

JOHN BIVENS

COLORS BY

FELIPE SOBREIRO

LETTERS BY

CRANK!

EDITED BY

SEBASTIAN GIRNER

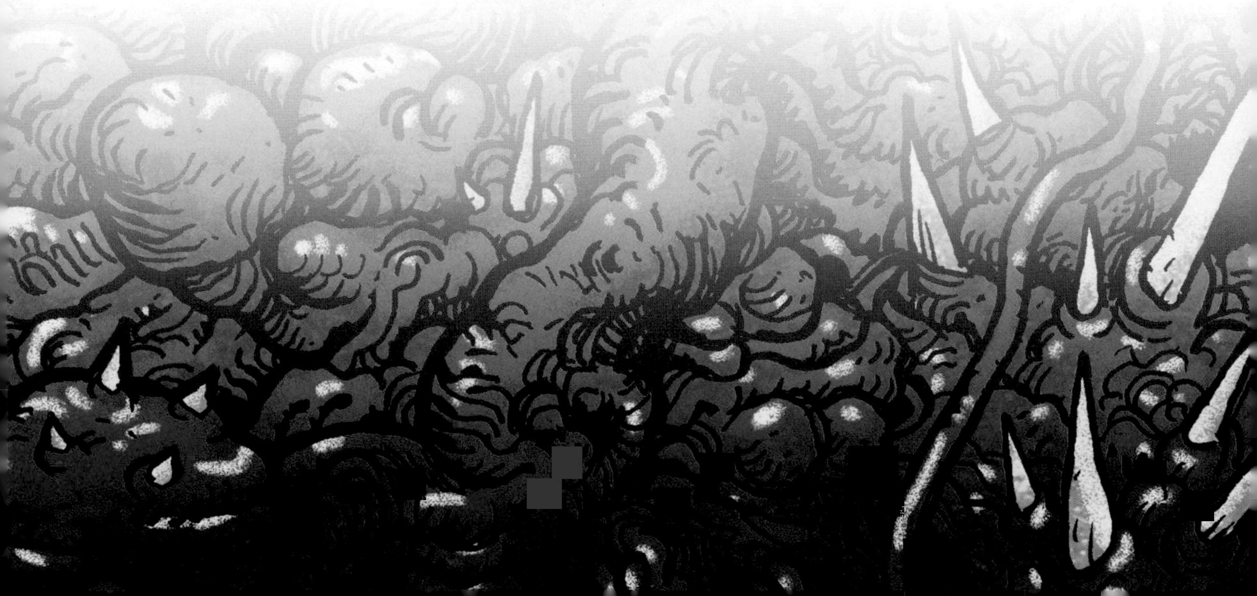

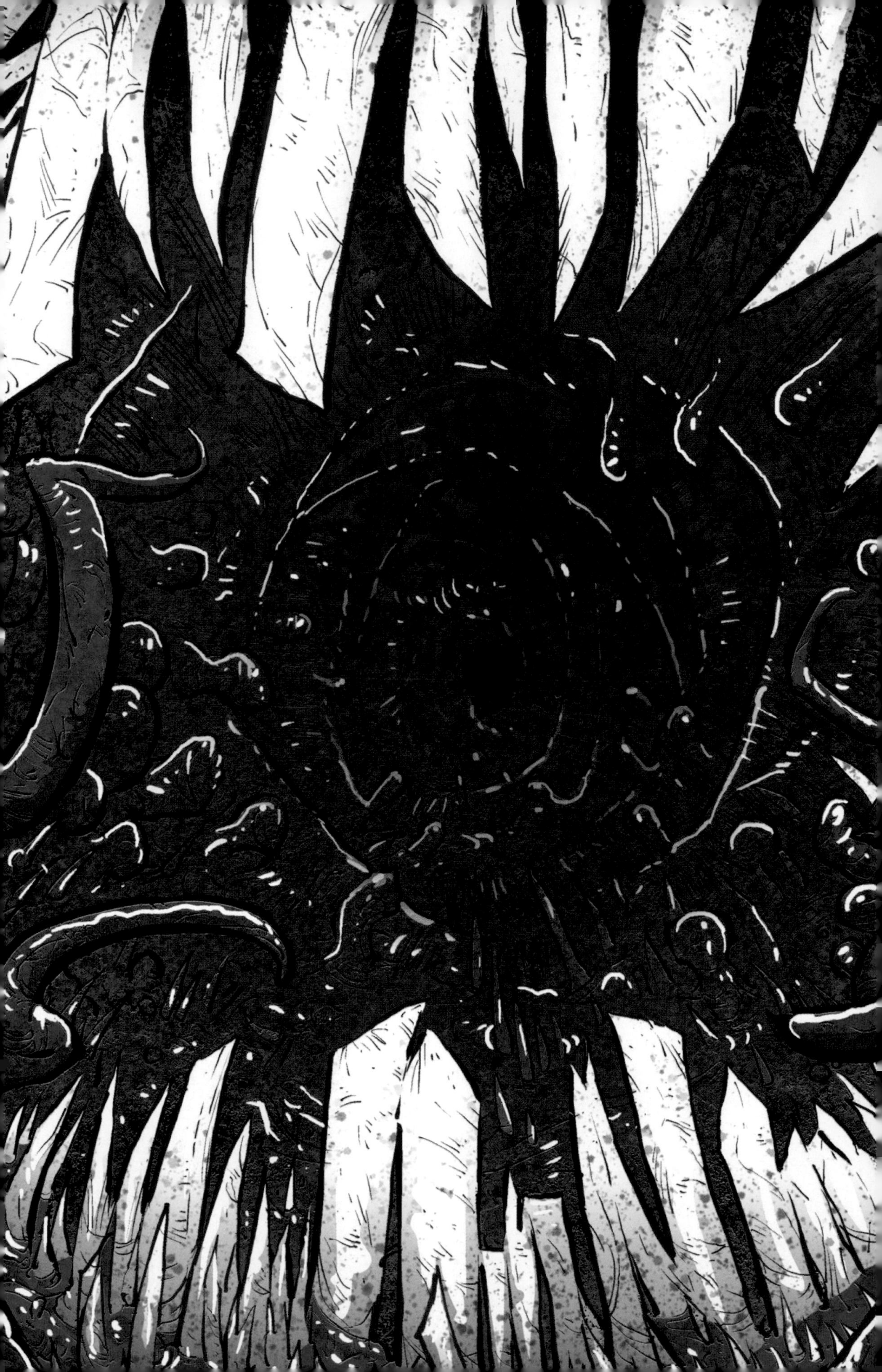

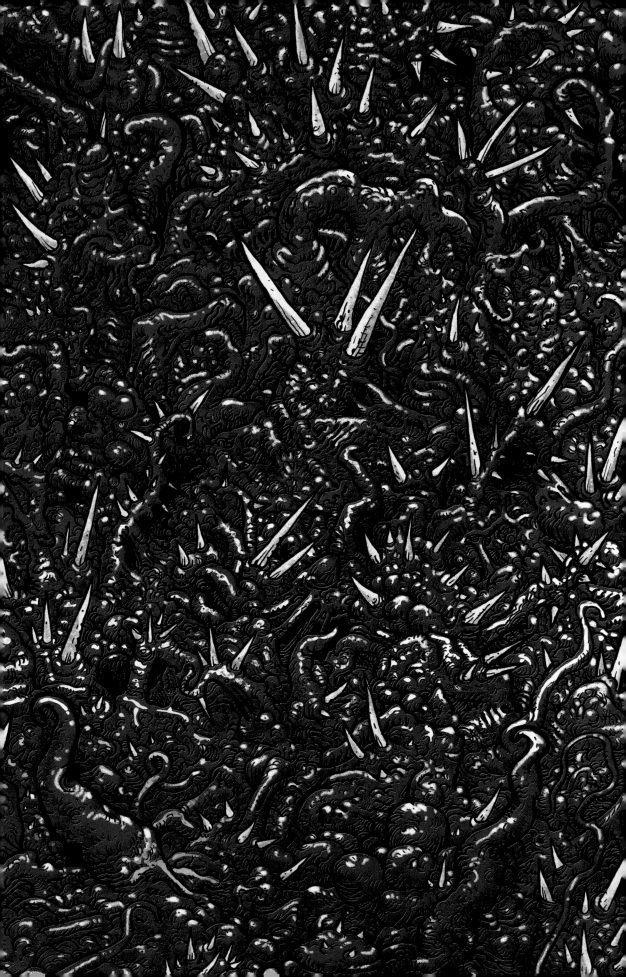

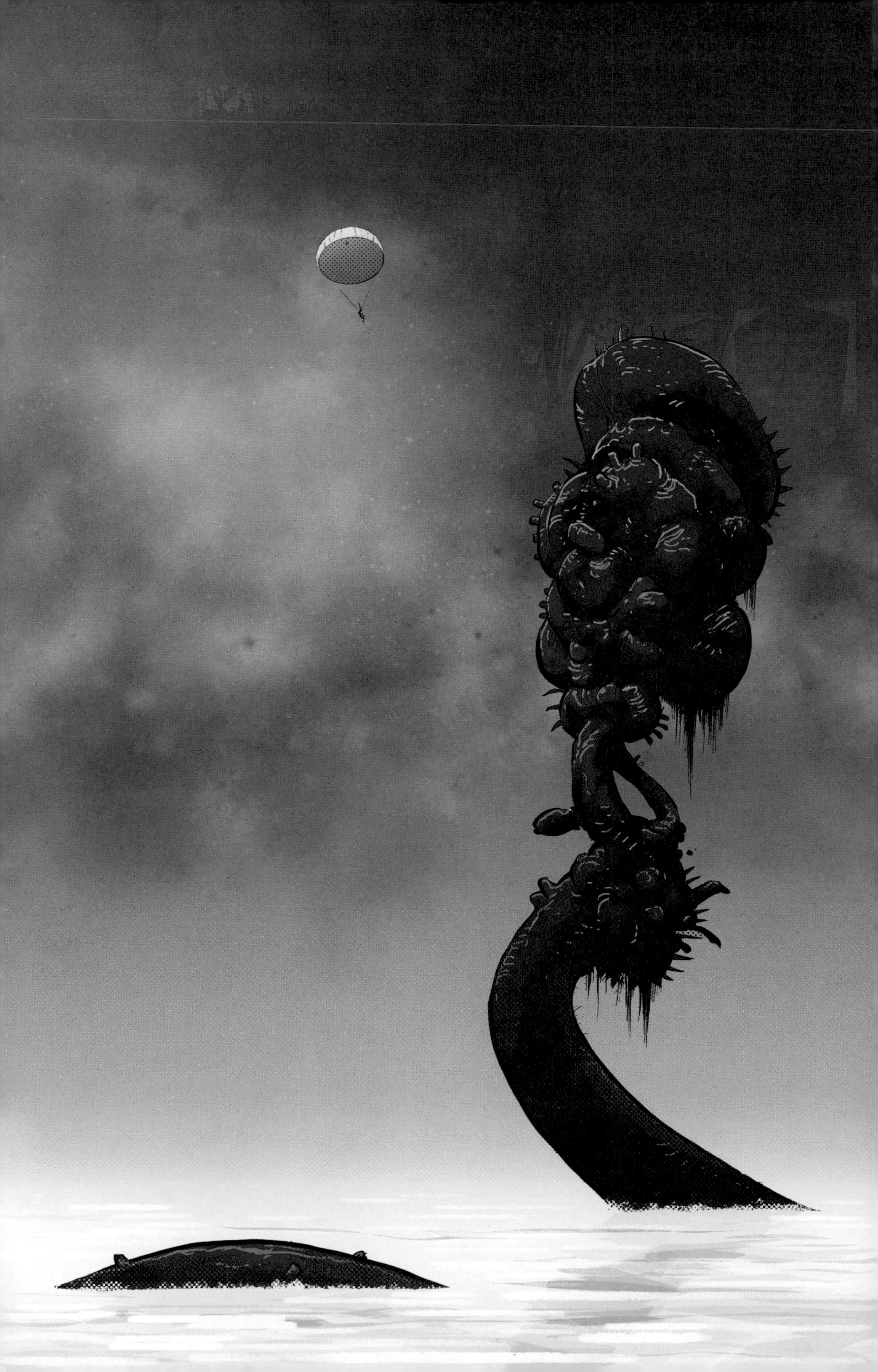

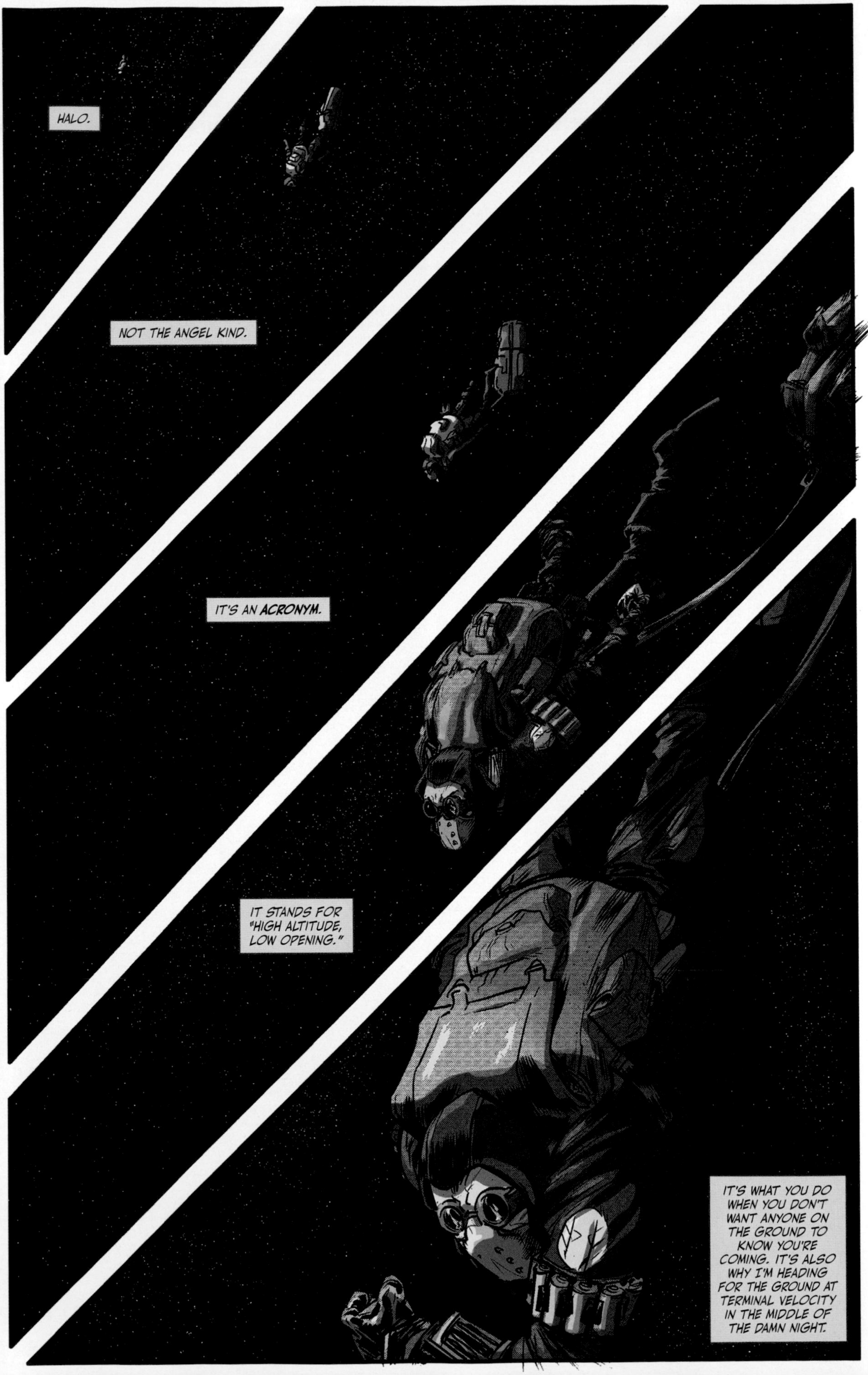
HALO.
NOT THE ANGEL KIND.
IT'S AN ACRONYM.
IT STANDS FOR "HIGH ALTITUDE, LOW OPENING."
IT'S WHAT YOU DO WHEN YOU DON'T WANT ANYONE ON THE GROUND TO KNOW YOU'RE COMING. IT'S ALSO WHY I'M HEADING FOR THE GROUND AT TERMINAL VELOCITY IN THE MIDDLE OF THE DAMN NIGHT.

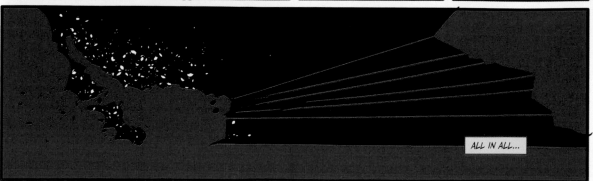

I STARTED THIS JUMP ON THE EDGE OF SPACE, FLYING AS HIGH AS A STEALTH JET COULD GO.

I PULL THE CHUTE AT FIVE HUNDRED FEET.

IT'S NERVE-WRACKING.

AND MAYBE **BONE-WRECKING**.

ALL IN ALL...

...I'VE HAD **WORSE** LANDINGS.

EQUIPMENT SEEMS TO HAVE MADE IT, TOO.

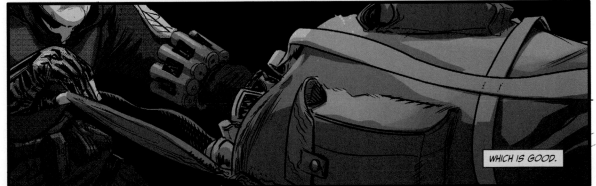

WHICH IS GOOD.

BECAUSE THAT JUMP?

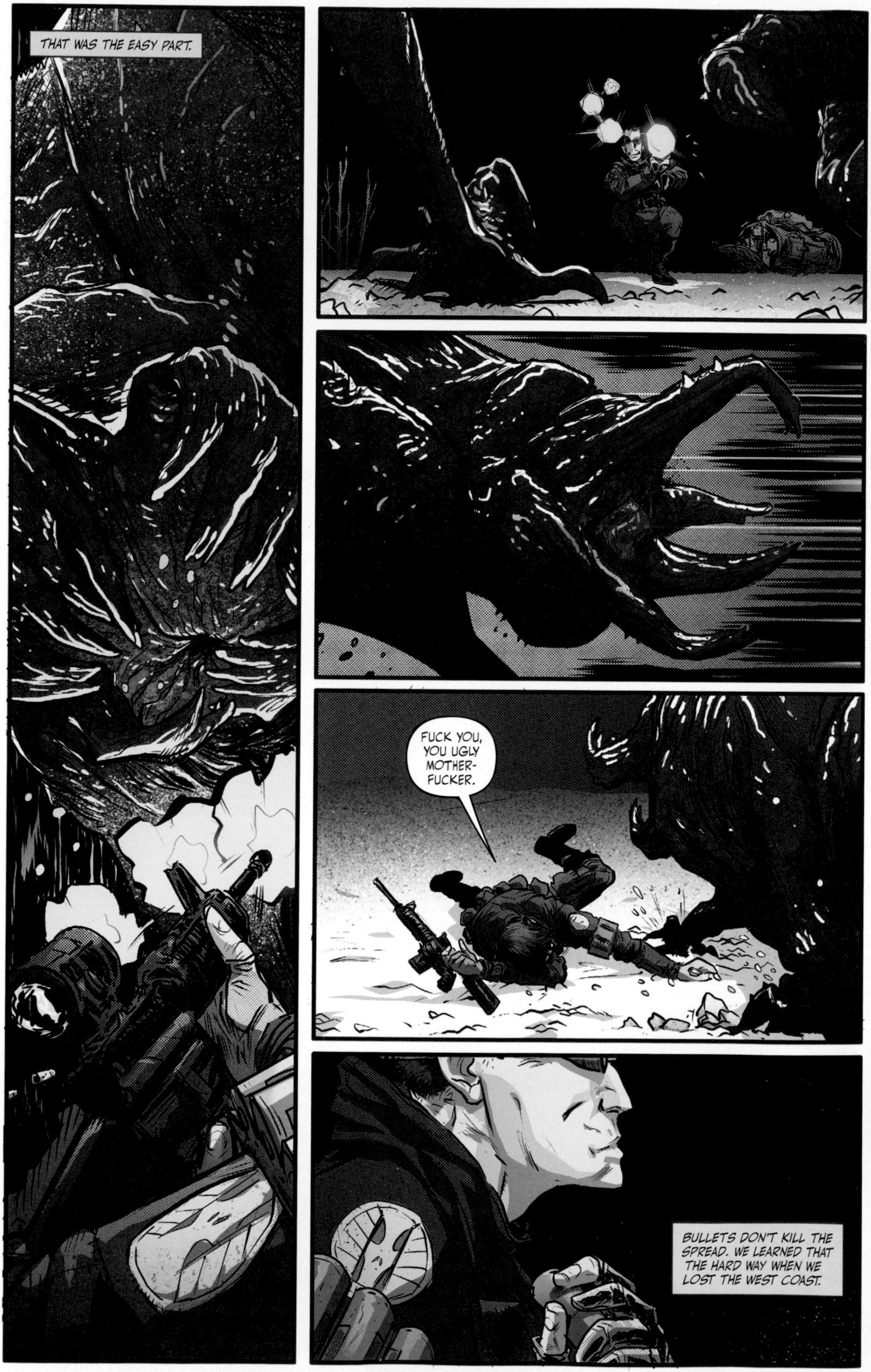
THAT WAS THE EASY PART.
FUCK YOU, YOU UGLY MOTHER-FUCKER.
BULLETS DON'T KILL THE SPREAD. WE LEARNED THAT THE HARD WAY WHEN WE LOST THE WEST COAST.

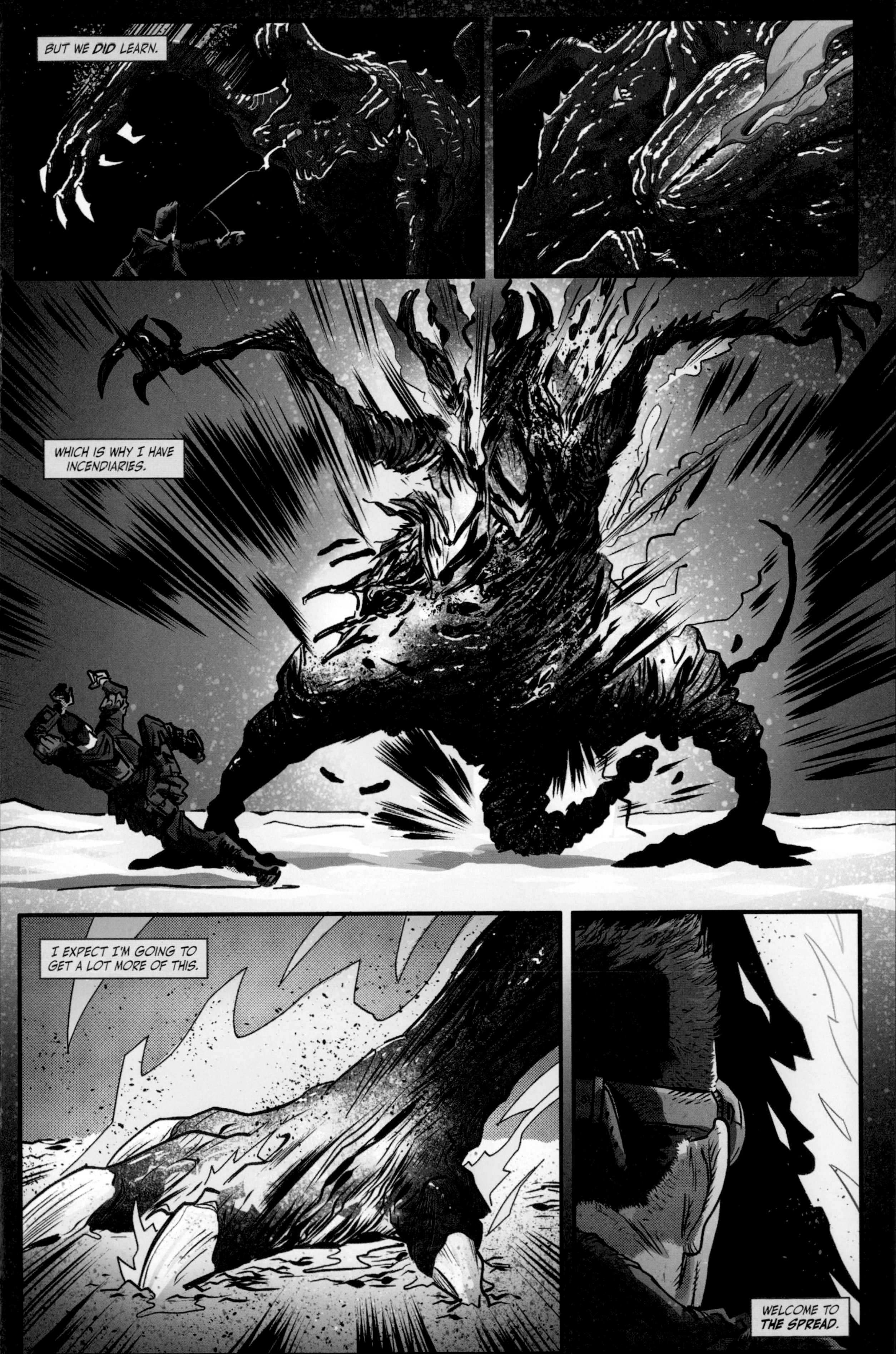
BUT WE DID LEARN.
WHICH IS WHY I HAVE INCENDIARIES.
I EXPECT I'M GOING TO GET A LOT MORE OF THIS.
WELCOME TO THE SPREAD.

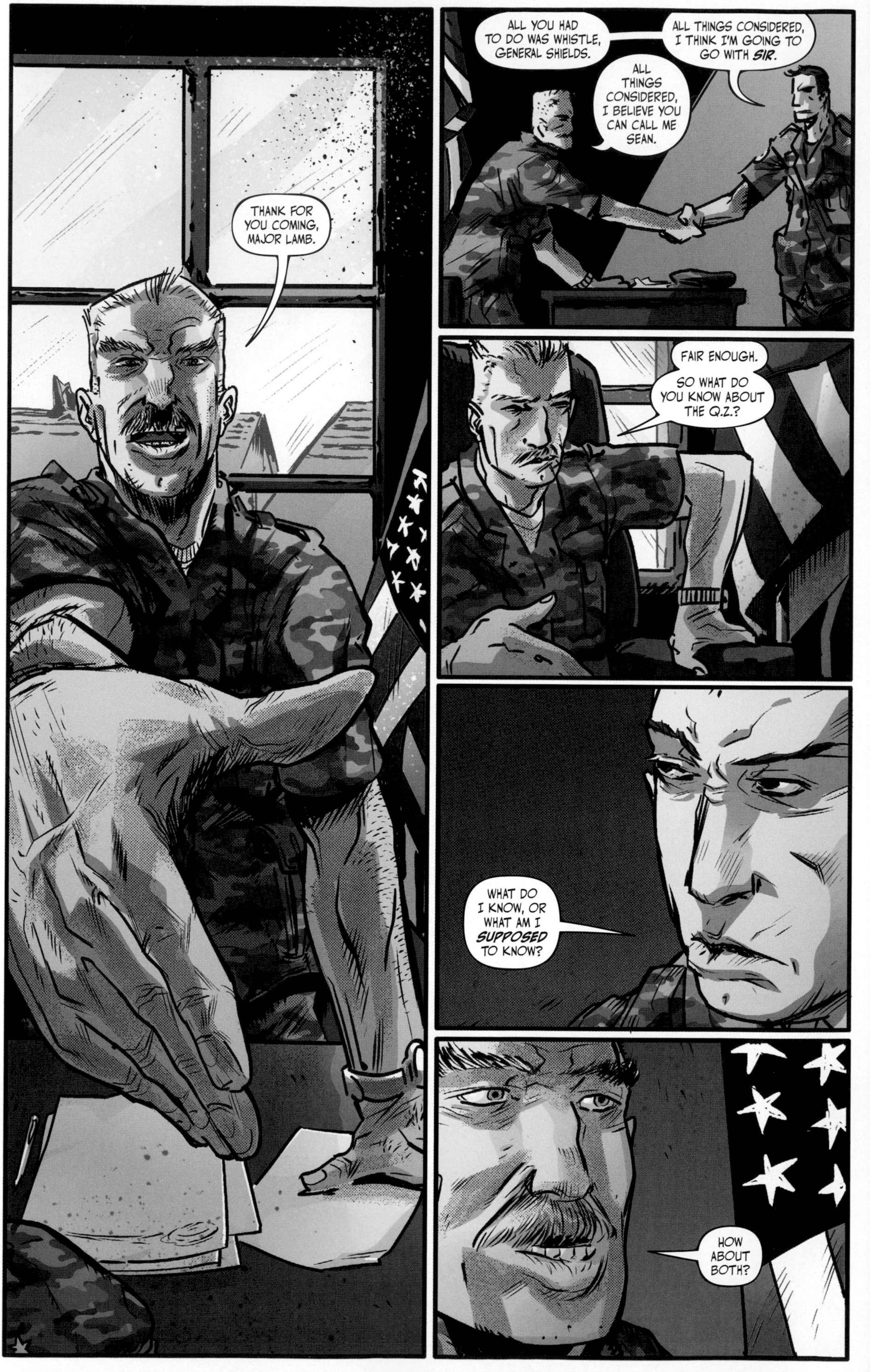
THANK FOR YOU COMING, MAJOR LAMB.
ALL YOU HAD TO DO WAS WHISTLE, GENERAL SHIELDS.
ALL THINGS CONSIDERED, I BELIEVE YOU CAN CALL ME SEAN.
ALL THINGS CONSIDERED, I THINK I'M GOING TO GO WITH *SIR*.
FAIR ENOUGH.
SO WHAT DO YOU KNOW ABOUT THE Q.Z.?
WHAT DO I KNOW, OR WHAT AM I *SUPPOSED* TO KNOW?
HOW ABOUT BOTH?

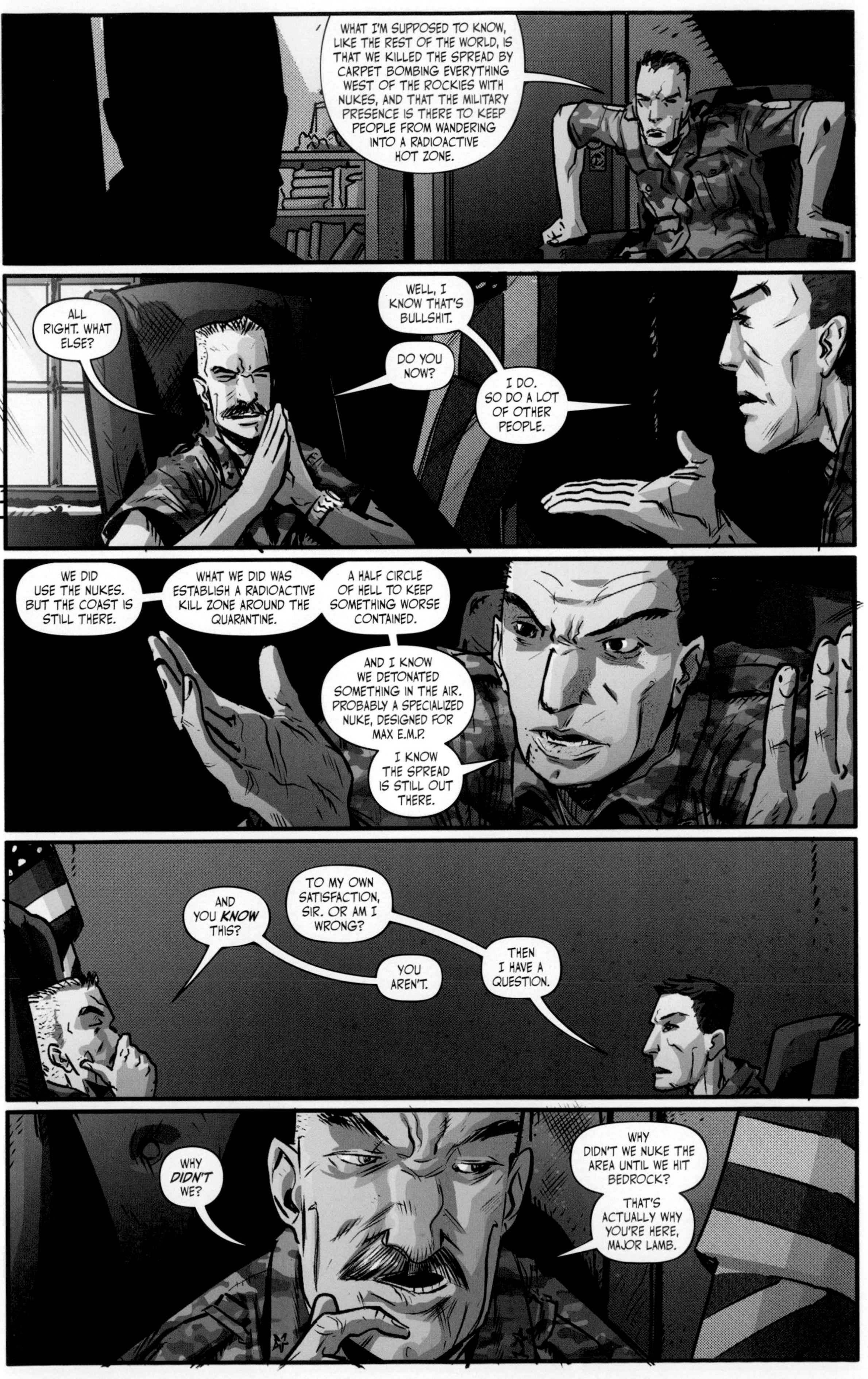
WHAT I'M SUPPOSED TO KNOW, LIKE THE REST OF THE WORLD, IS THAT WE KILLED THE SPREAD BY CARPET BOMBING EVERYTHING WEST OF THE ROCKIES WITH NUKES, AND THAT THE MILITARY PRESENCE IS THERE TO KEEP PEOPLE FROM WANDERING INTO A RADIOACTIVE HOT ZONE.
ALL RIGHT. WHAT ELSE?
WELL, I KNOW THAT'S BULLSHIT.
DO YOU NOW?
I DO. SO DO A LOT OF OTHER PEOPLE.
WE DID USE THE NUKES. BUT THE COAST IS STILL THERE.
WHAT WE DID WAS ESTABLISH A RADIOACTIVE KILL ZONE AROUND THE QUARANTINE.
A HALF CIRCLE OF HELL TO KEEP SOMETHING WORSE CONTAINED.
AND I KNOW WE DETONATED SOMETHING IN THE AIR. PROBABLY A SPECIALIZED NUKE, DESIGNED FOR MAX E.M.P.
I KNOW THE SPREAD IS STILL OUT THERE.
AND YOU *KNOW* THIS?
TO MY OWN SATISFACTION, SIR. OR AM I WRONG?
YOU AREN'T.
THEN I HAVE A QUESTION.
WHY DIDN'T WE NUKE THE AREA UNTIL WE HIT BEDROCK?
WHY *DIDN'T* WE?
THAT'S ACTUALLY WHY YOU'RE HERE, MAJOR LAMB.

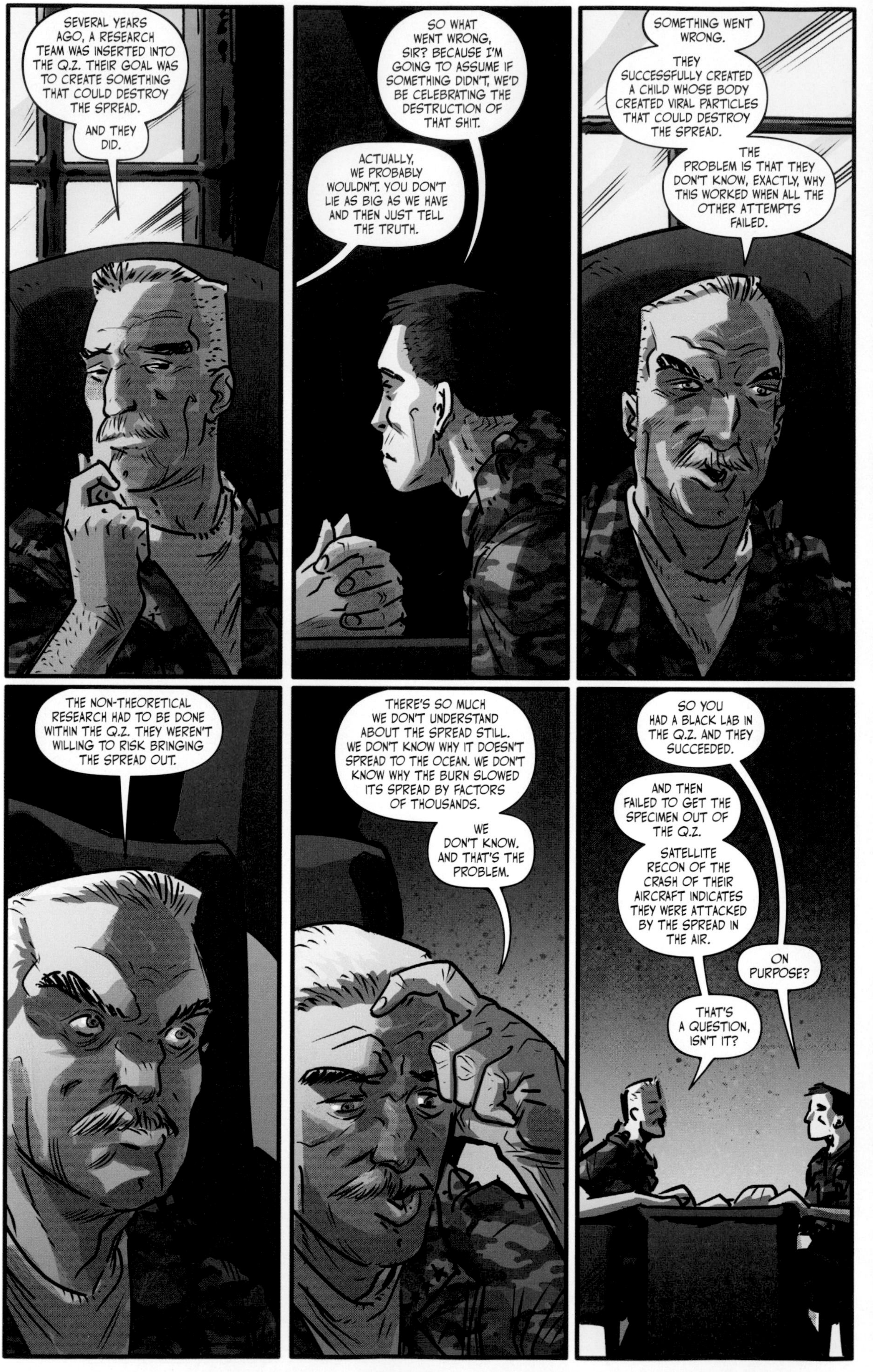
SEVERAL YEARS AGO, A RESEARCH TEAM WAS INSERTED INTO THE Q.Z. THEIR GOAL WAS TO CREATE SOMETHING THAT COULD DESTROY THE SPREAD.
AND THEY DID.
SO WHAT WENT WRONG, SIR? BECAUSE I'M GOING TO ASSUME IF SOMETHING DIDN'T, WE'D BE CELEBRATING THE DESTRUCTION OF THAT SHIT.
ACTUALLY, WE PROBABLY WOULDN'T. YOU DON'T LIE AS BIG AS WE HAVE AND THEN JUST TELL THE TRUTH.
SOMETHING WENT WRONG.
THEY SUCCESSFULLY CREATED A CHILD WHOSE BODY CREATED VIRAL PARTICLES THAT COULD DESTROY THE SPREAD.
THE PROBLEM IS THAT THEY DON'T KNOW, EXACTLY, WHY THIS WORKED WHEN ALL THE OTHER ATTEMPTS FAILED.
THE NON-THEORETICAL RESEARCH HAD TO BE DONE WITHIN THE Q.Z. THEY WEREN'T WILLING TO RISK BRINGING THE SPREAD OUT.
THERE'S SO MUCH WE DON'T UNDERSTAND ABOUT THE SPREAD STILL. WE DON'T KNOW WHY IT DOESN'T SPREAD TO THE OCEAN. WE DON'T KNOW WHY THE BURN SLOWED ITS SPREAD BY FACTORS OF THOUSANDS.
WE DON'T KNOW. AND THAT'S THE PROBLEM.
SO YOU HAD A BLACK LAB IN THE Q.Z. AND THEY SUCCEEDED.
AND THEN FAILED TO GET THE SPECIMEN OUT OF THE Q.Z.
SATELLITE RECON OF THE CRASH OF THEIR AIRCRAFT INDICATES THEY WERE ATTACKED BY THE SPREAD IN THE AIR.
ON PURPOSE?
THAT'S A QUESTION, ISN'T IT?

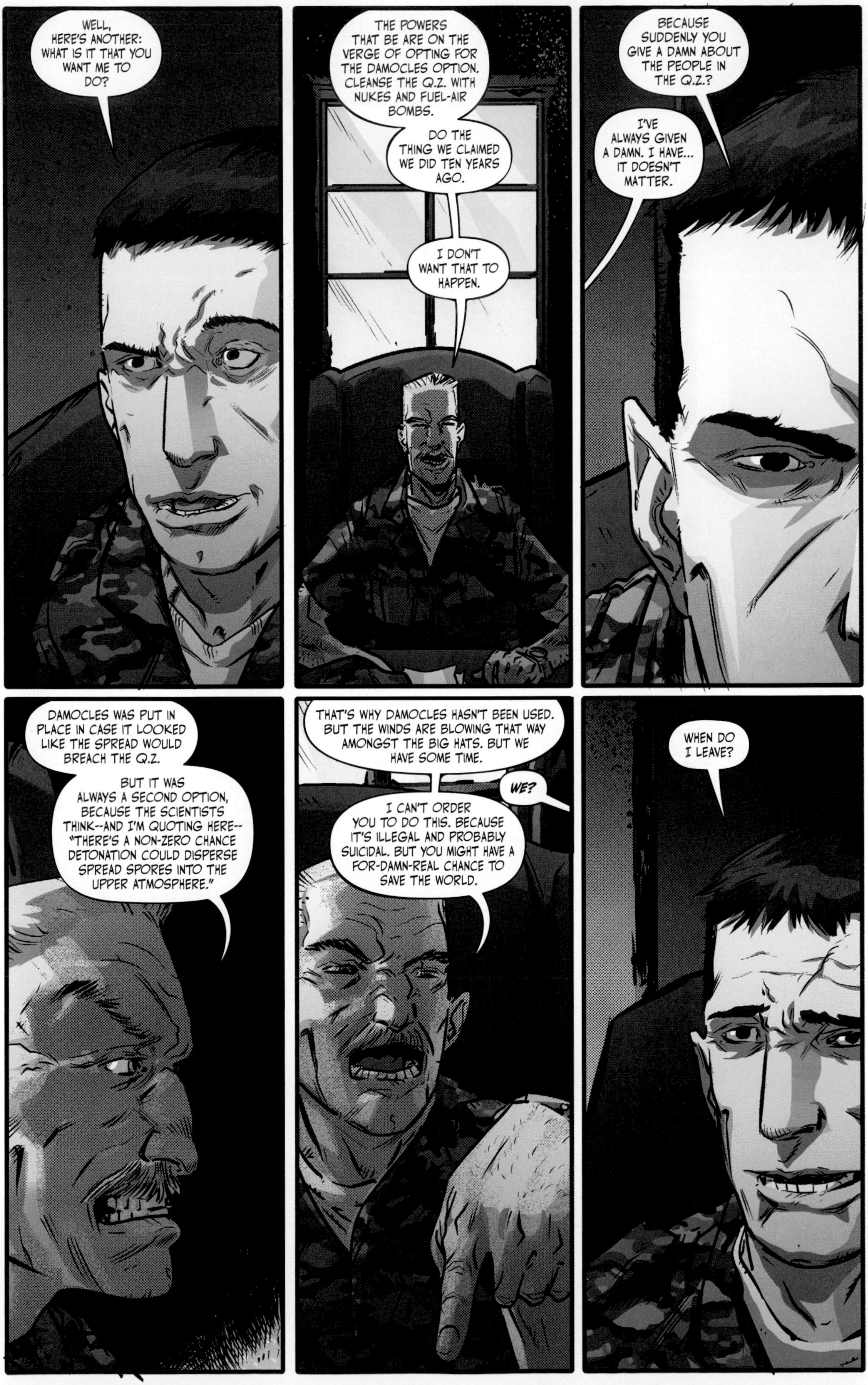
WELL, HERE'S ANOTHER: WHAT IS IT THAT YOU WANT ME TO DO?
THE POWERS THAT BE ARE ON THE VERGE OF OPTING FOR THE DAMOCLES OPTION. CLEANSE THE Q.Z. WITH NUKES AND FUEL-AIR BOMBS.
DO THE THING WE CLAIMED WE DID TEN YEARS AGO.
I DON'T WANT THAT TO HAPPEN.
BECAUSE SUDDENLY YOU GIVE A DAMN ABOUT THE PEOPLE IN THE Q.Z.?
I'VE ALWAYS GIVEN A DAMN. I HAVE... IT DOESN'T MATTER.
DAMOCLES WAS PUT IN PLACE IN CASE IT LOOKED LIKE THE SPREAD WOULD BREACH THE Q.Z.
BUT IT WAS ALWAYS A SECOND OPTION, BECAUSE THE SCIENTISTS THINK--AND I'M QUOTING HERE--"THERE'S A NON-ZERO CHANCE DETONATION COULD DISPERSE SPREAD SPORES INTO THE UPPER ATMOSPHERE."
THAT'S WHY DAMOCLES HASN'T BEEN USED. BUT THE WINDS ARE BLOWING THAT WAY AMONGST THE BIG HATS. BUT WE HAVE SOME TIME.
WE?
I CAN'T ORDER YOU TO DO THIS. BECAUSE IT'S ILLEGAL AND PROBABLY SUICIDAL. BUT YOU MIGHT HAVE A FOR-DAMN-REAL CHANCE TO SAVE THE WORLD.
WHEN DO I LEAVE?

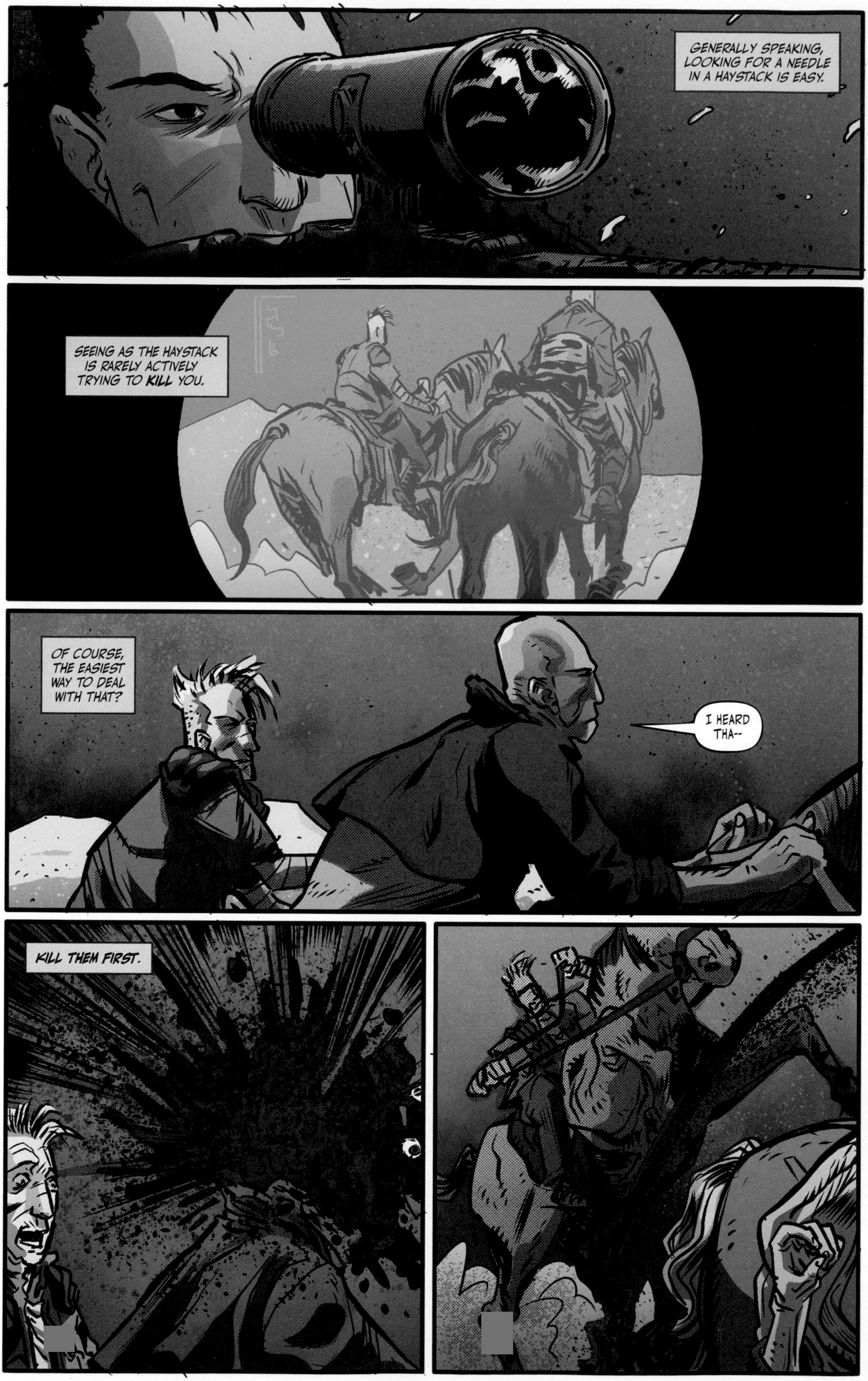
GENERALLY SPEAKING, LOOKING FOR A NEEDLE IN A HAYSTACK IS EASY.
SEEING AS THE HAYSTACK IS RARELY ACTIVELY TRYING TO KILL YOU.
OF COURSE, THE EASIEST WAY TO DEAL WITH THAT?
I HEARD THA--
KILL THEM FIRST.

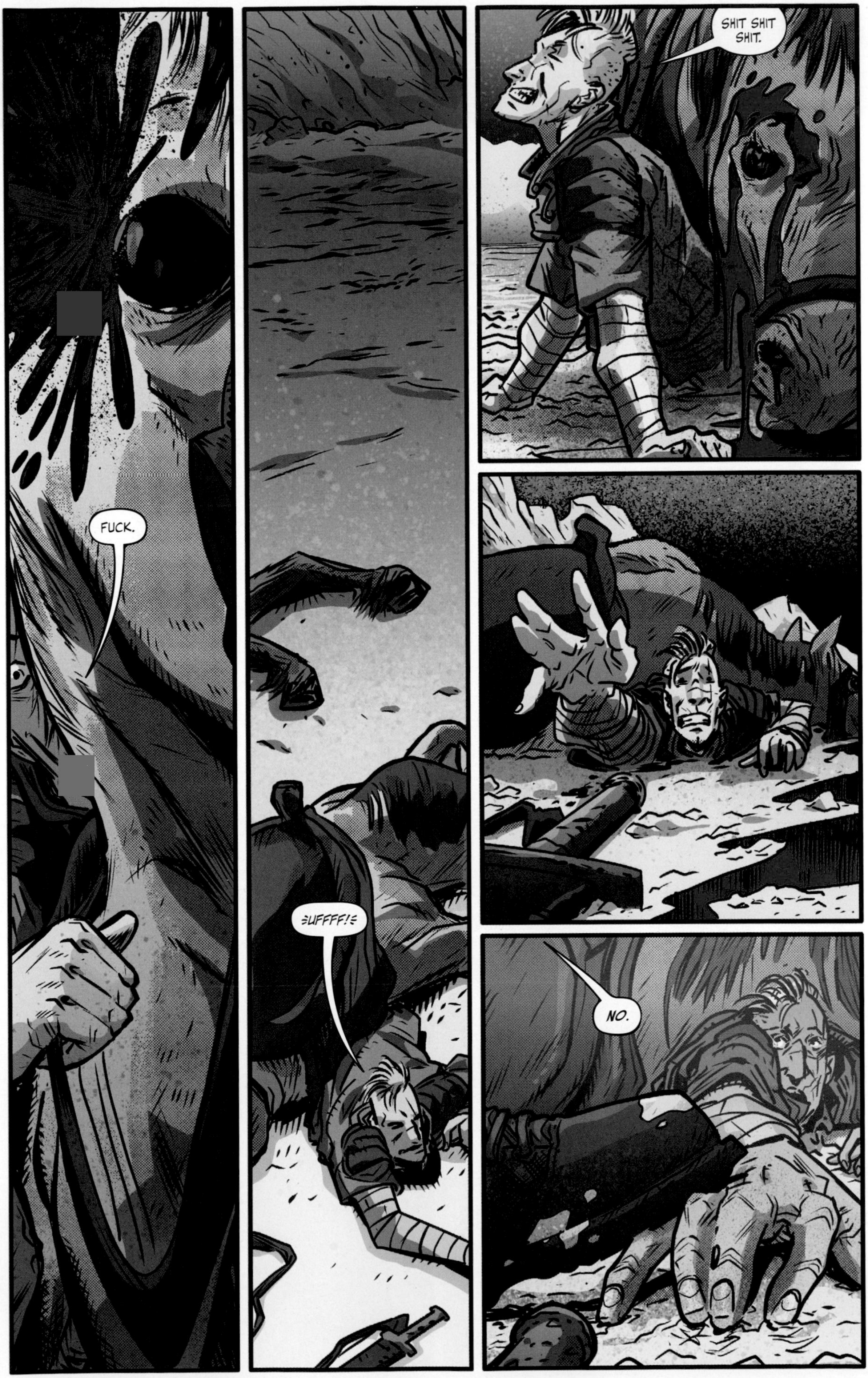
FUCK.
UFFFF!
SHIT SHIT SHIT.
NO.

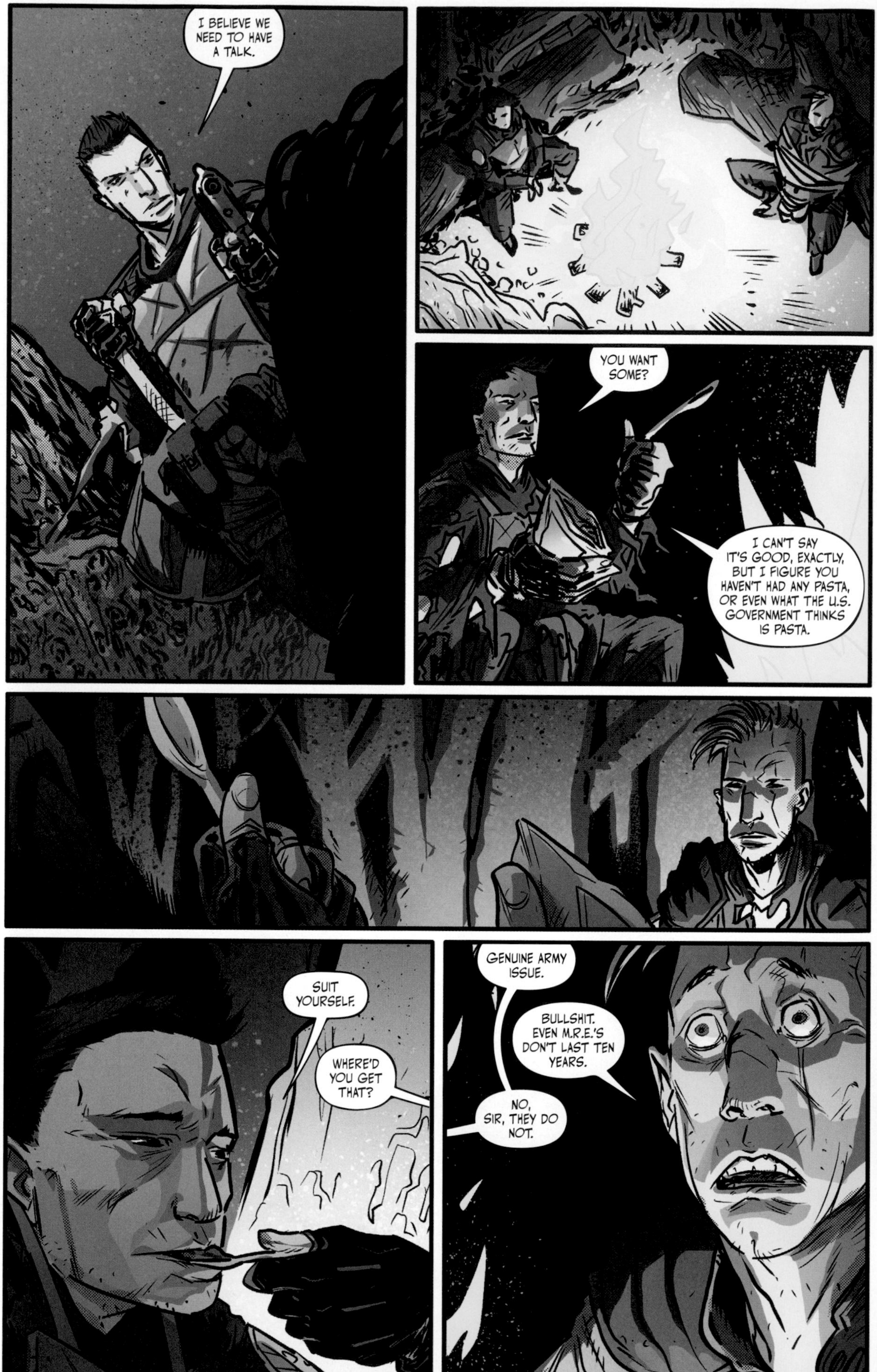
I BELIEVE WE NEED TO HAVE A TALK.
YOU WANT SOME?
I CAN'T SAY IT'S GOOD, EXACTLY, BUT I FIGURE YOU HAVEN'T HAD ANY PASTA, OR EVEN WHAT THE U.S. GOVERNMENT THINKS IS PASTA.
SUIT YOURSELF.
WHERE'D YOU GET THAT?
GENUINE ARMY ISSUE.
BULLSHIT. EVEN M.R.E.'S DON'T LAST TEN YEARS.
NO, SIR, THEY DO NOT.

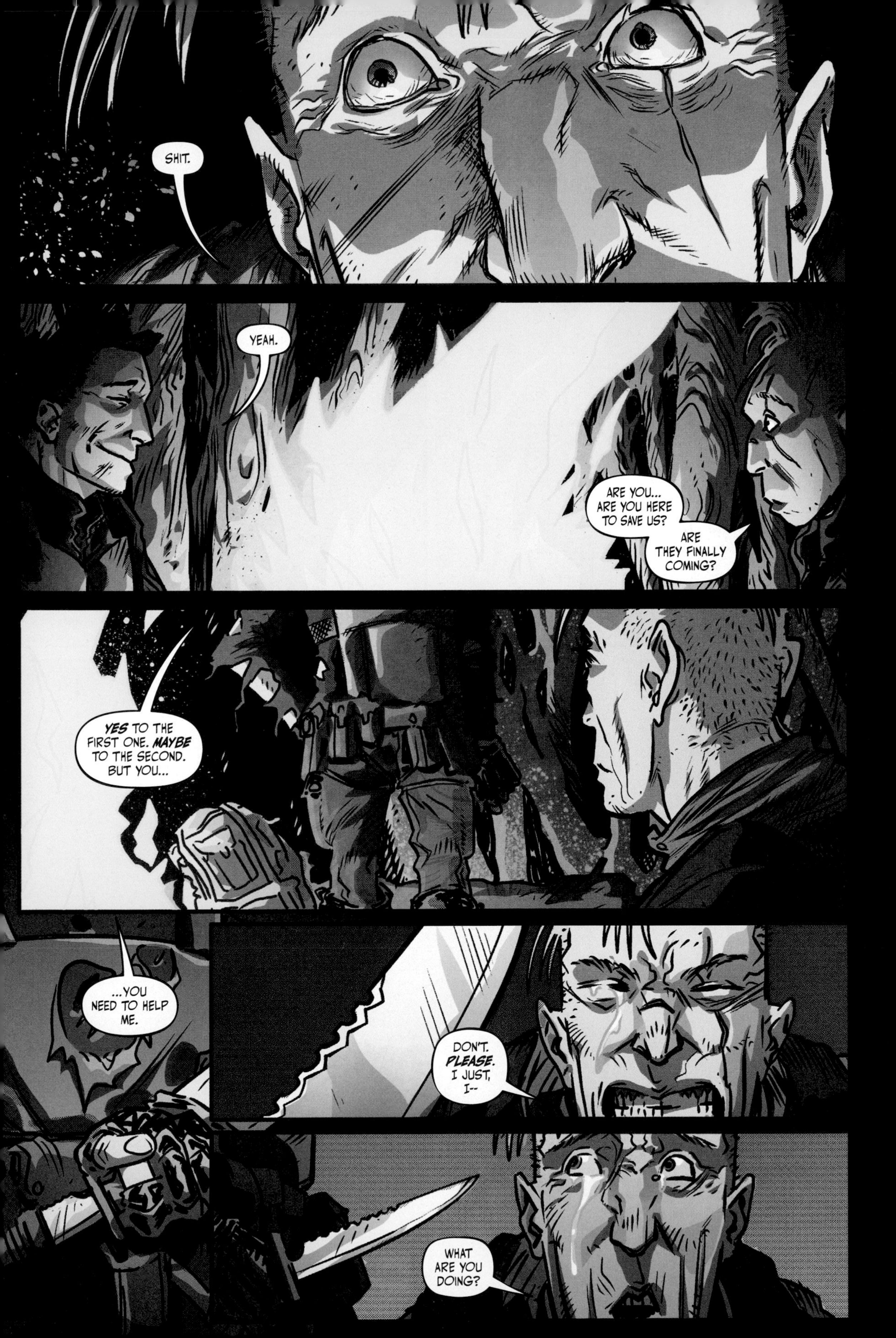
SHIT.
YEAH.
ARE YOU... ARE YOU HERE TO SAVE US?
ARE THEY FINALLY COMING?
YES TO THE FIRST ONE. MAYBE TO THE SECOND. BUT YOU...
...YOU NEED TO HELP ME.
DON'T. PLEASE. I JUST, I--
WHAT ARE YOU DOING?

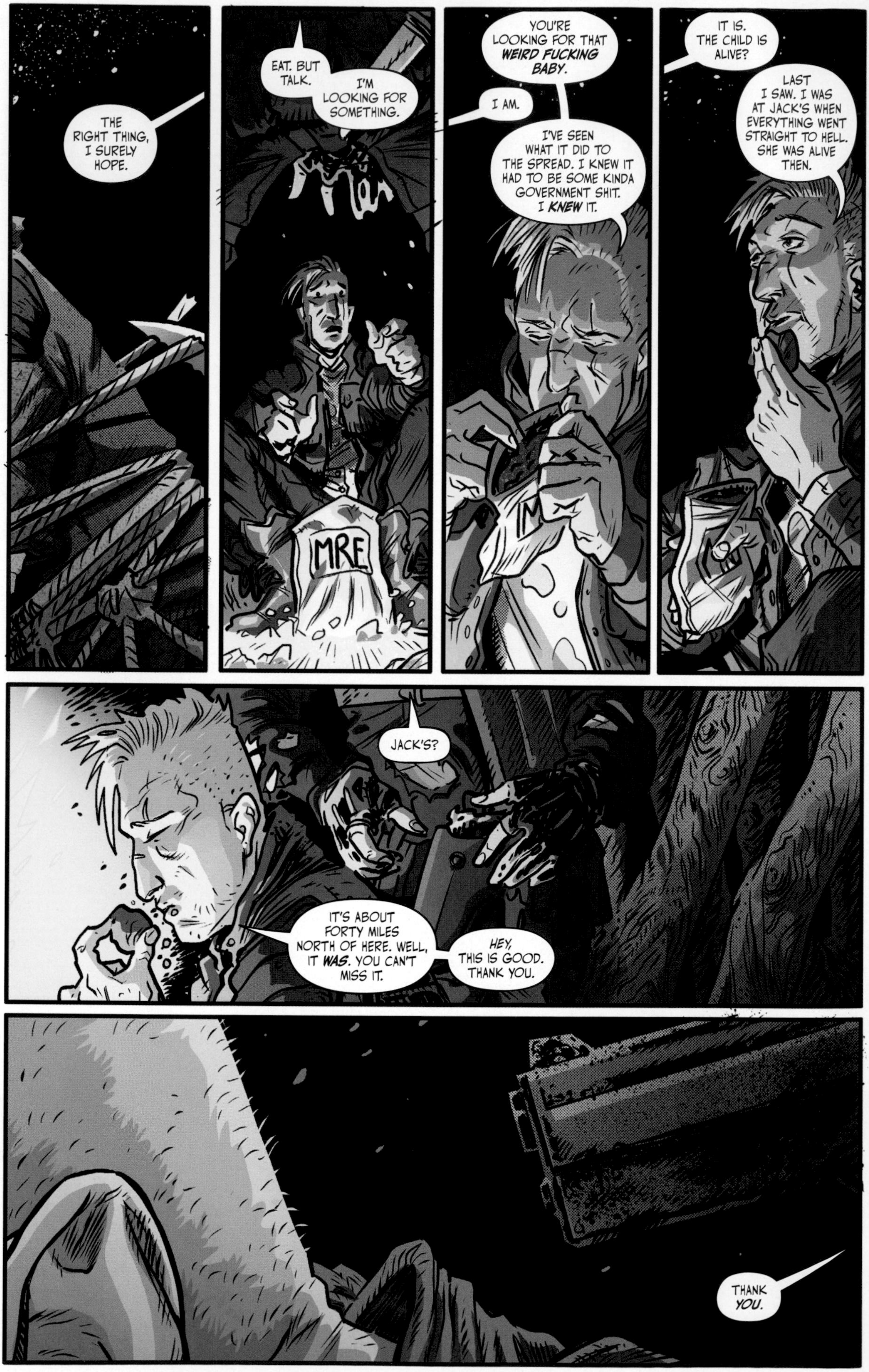
THE RIGHT THING, I SURELY HOPE.
EAT. BUT TALK.
I'M LOOKING FOR SOMETHING.
YOU'RE LOOKING FOR THAT *WEIRD FUCKING BABY*.
I AM.
I'VE SEEN WHAT IT DID TO THE SPREAD. I KNEW IT HAD TO BE SOME KINDA GOVERNMENT SHIT. I *KNEW* IT.
IT IS. THE CHILD IS ALIVE?
LAST I SAW. I WAS AT JACK'S WHEN EVERYTHING WENT STRAIGHT TO HELL. SHE WAS ALIVE THEN.
JACK'S?
IT'S ABOUT FORTY MILES NORTH OF HERE. WELL, IT *WAS*. YOU CAN'T MISS IT.
HEY, THIS IS GOOD. THANK YOU.
THANK *YOU*.

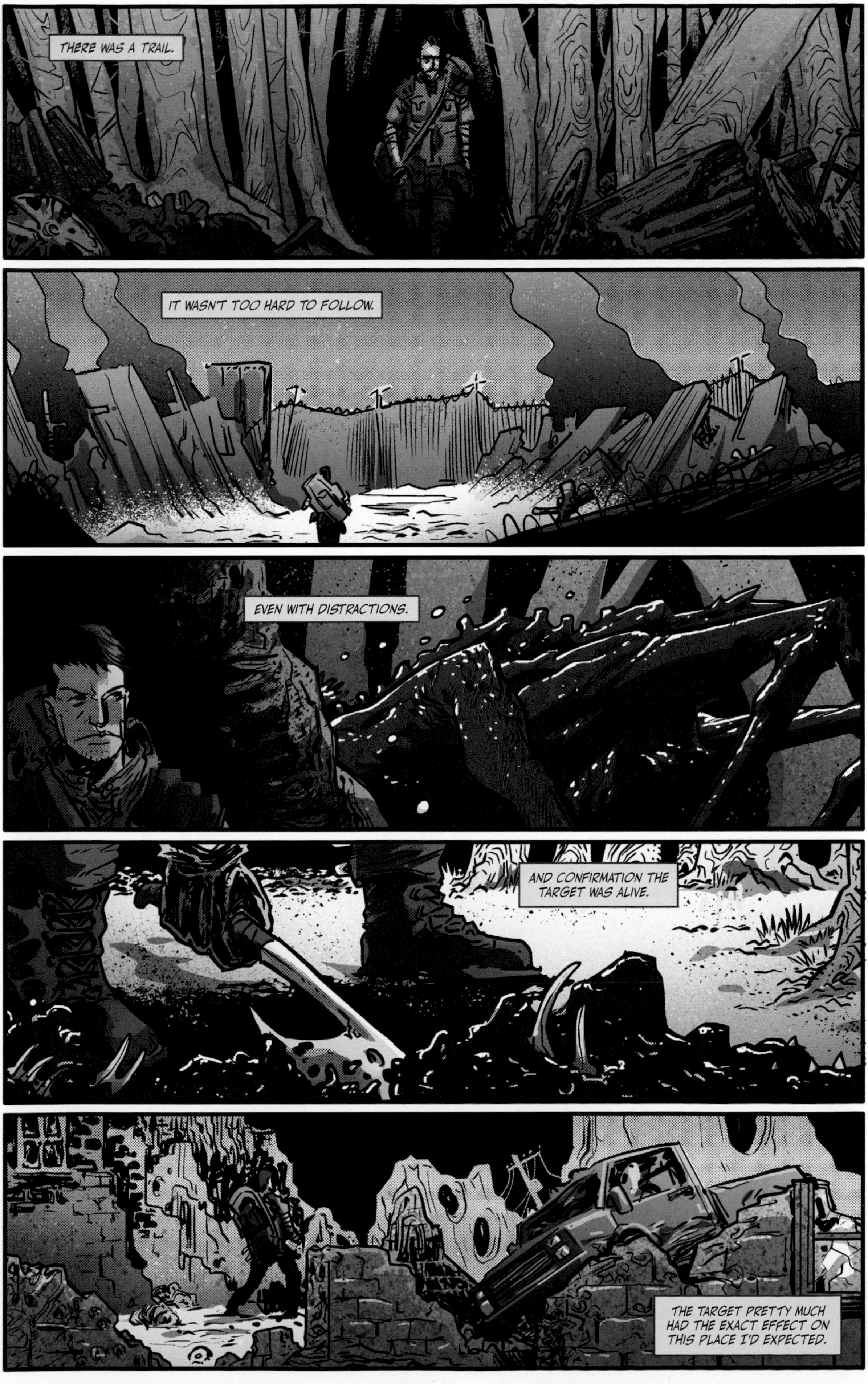
THERE WAS A TRAIL.
IT WASN'T TOO HARD TO FOLLOW.
EVEN WITH DISTRACTIONS.
AND CONFIRMATION THE TARGET WAS ALIVE.
THE TARGET PRETTY MUCH HAD THE EXACT EFFECT ON THIS PLACE I'D EXPECTED.

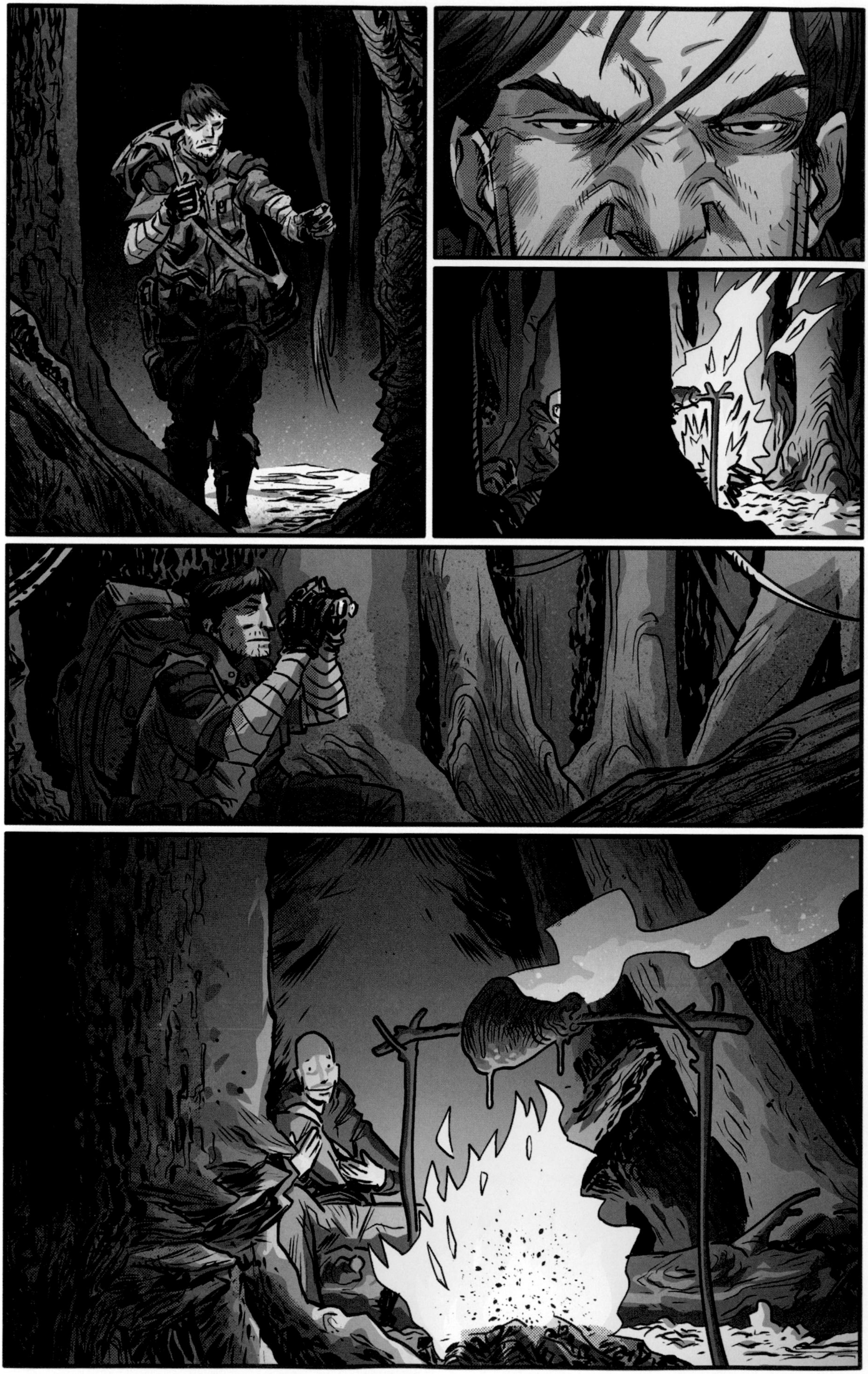

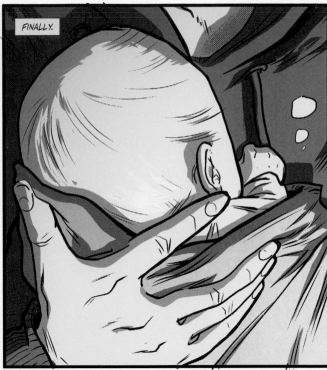

FINALLY.

KRCH

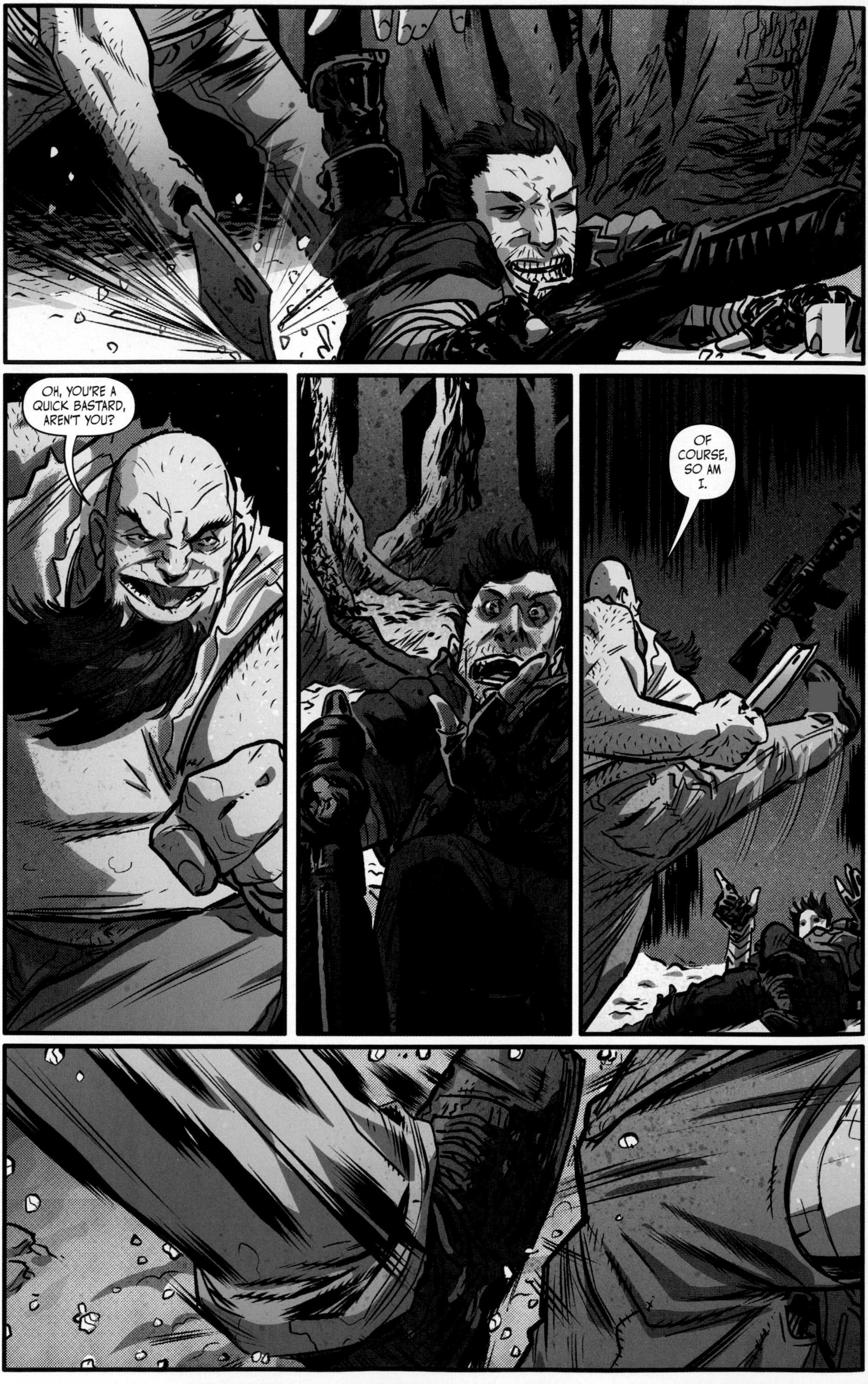
OH, YOU'RE A QUICK BASTARD, AREN'T YOU?
OF COURSE, SO AM I.

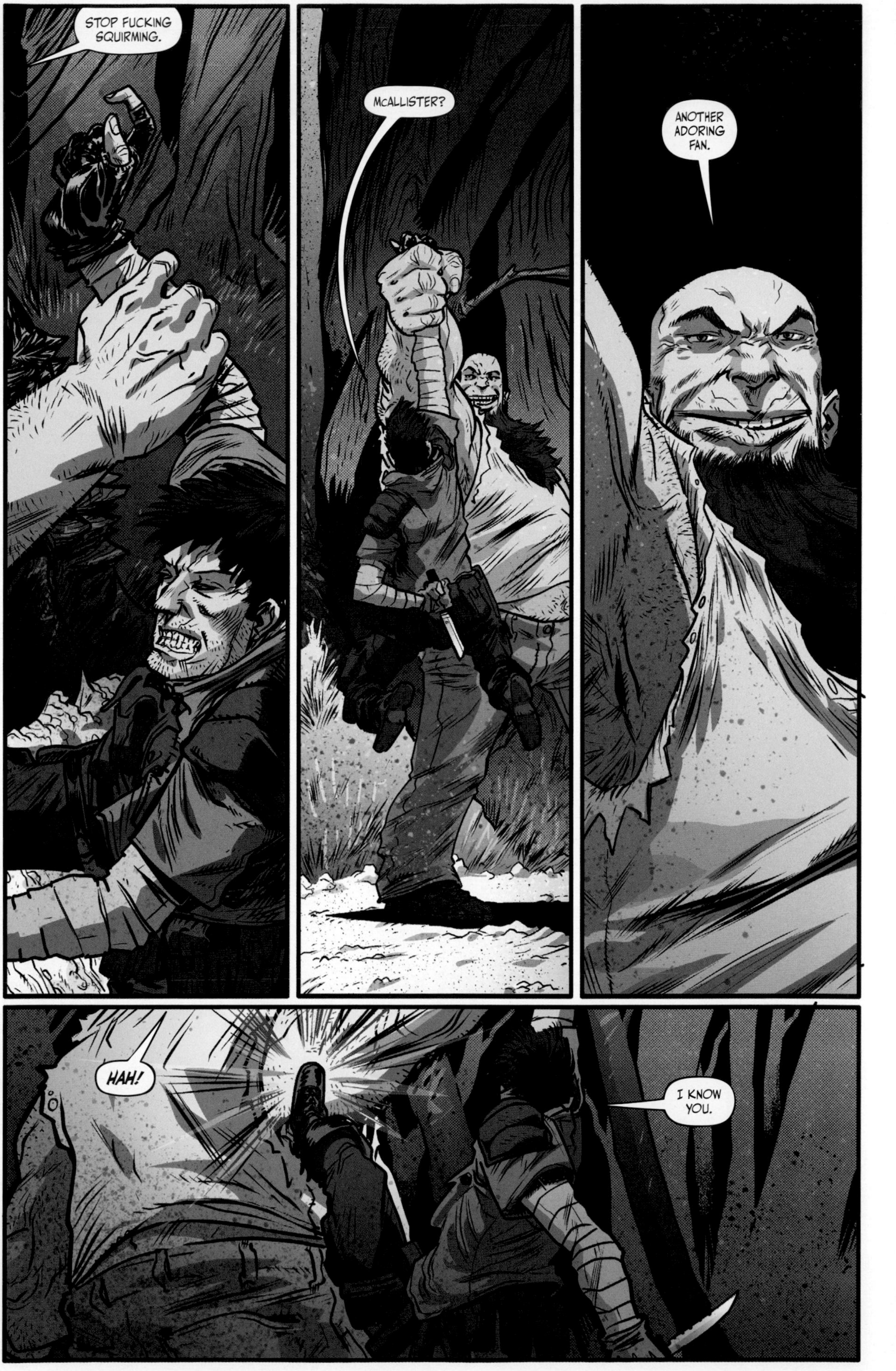
STOP FUCKING SQUIRMING.
McALLISTER?
ANOTHER ADORING FAN.
HAH!
I KNOW YOU.

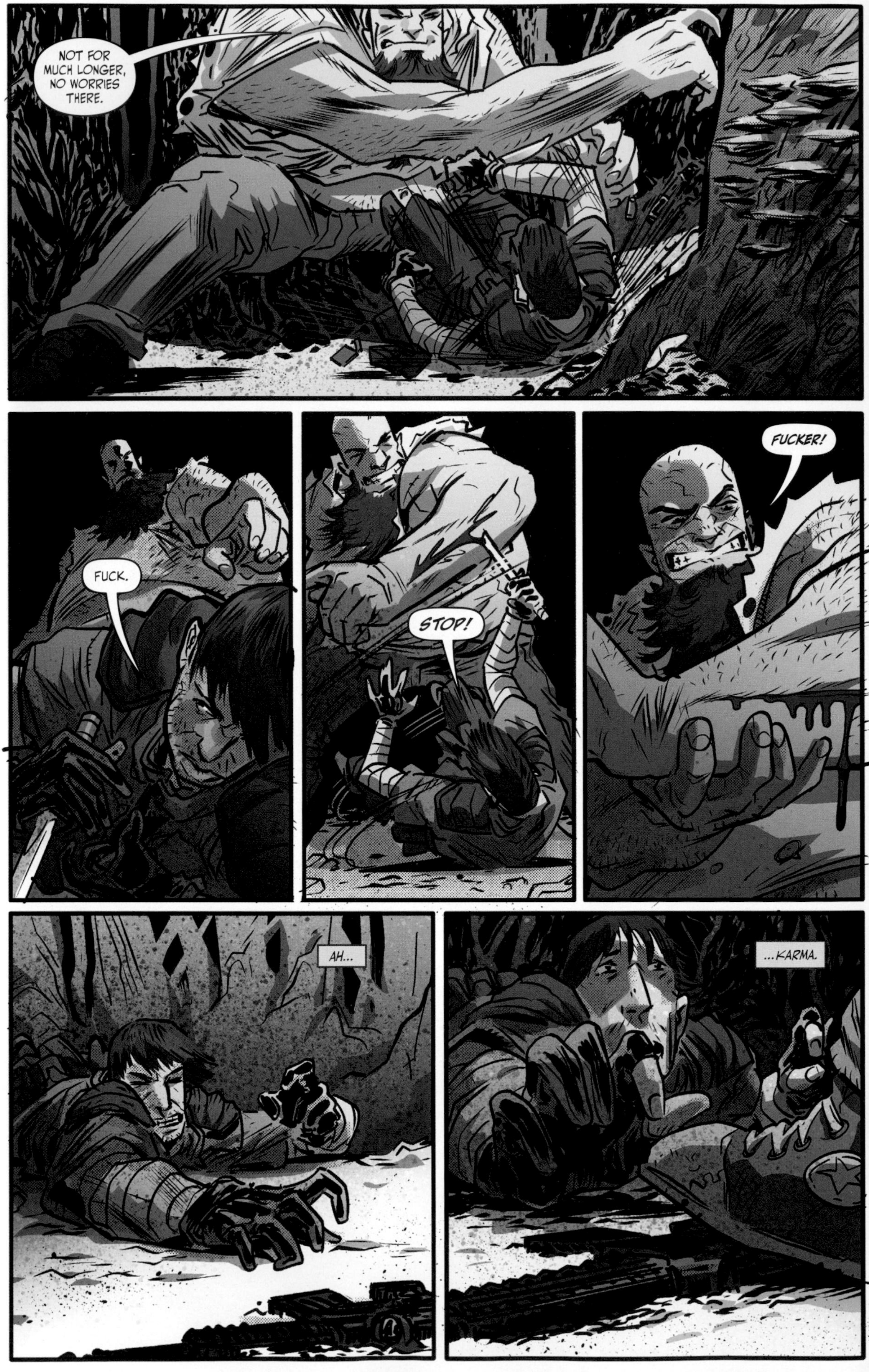
NOT FOR MUCH LONGER, NO WORRIES THERE.
FUCK.
STOP!
FUCKER!
AH...
...KARMA.

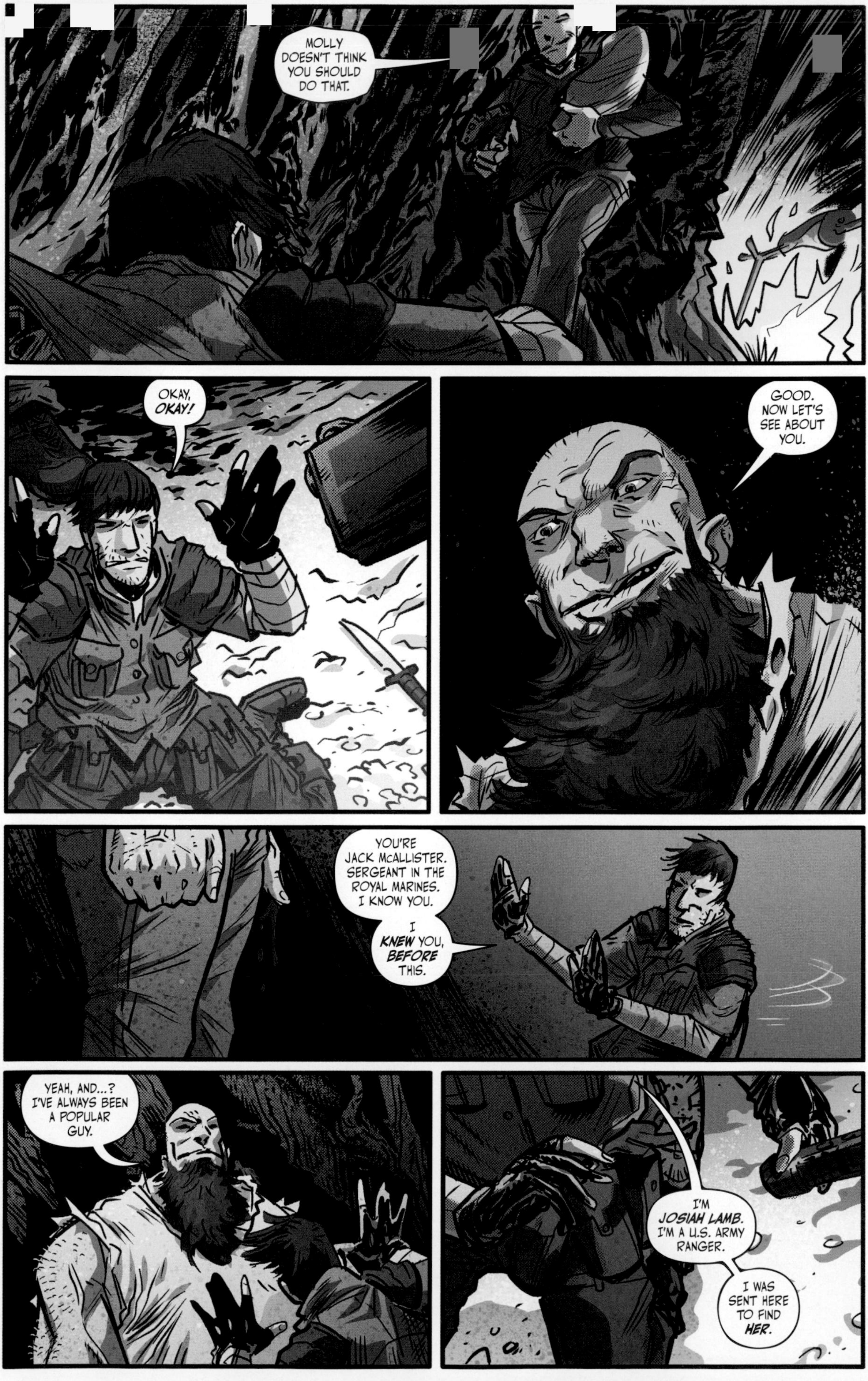
MOLLY DOESN'T THINK YOU SHOULD DO THAT.
OKAY, *OKAY!*
GOOD. NOW LET'S SEE ABOUT YOU.
YOU'RE JACK McALLISTER. SERGEANT IN THE ROYAL MARINES. I KNOW YOU.
I *KNEW* YOU, *BEFORE* THIS.
YEAH, AND...? I'VE ALWAYS BEEN A POPULAR GUY.
I'M *JOSIAH LAMB.* I'M A U.S. ARMY RANGER.
I WAS SENT HERE TO FIND *HER.*

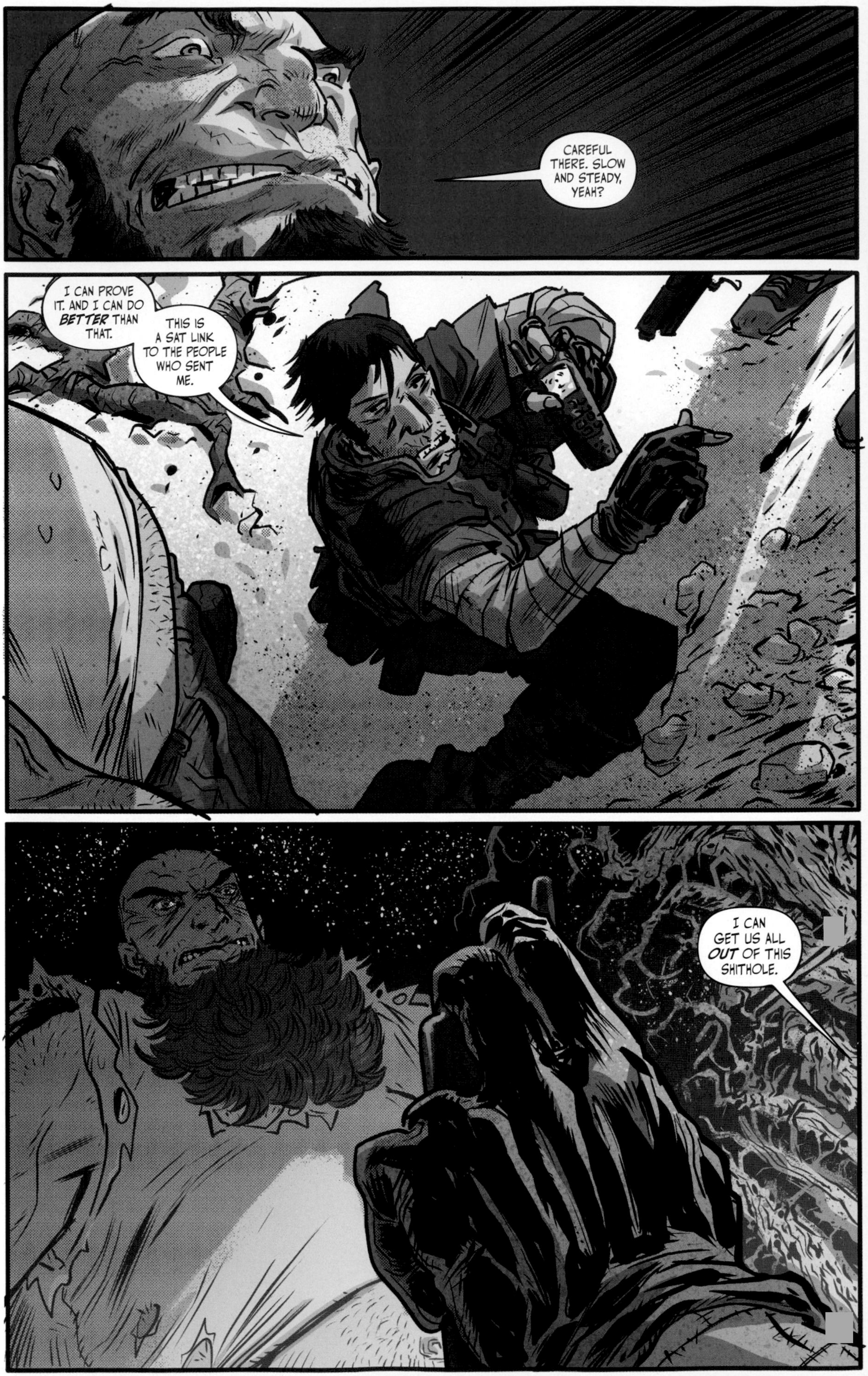
CAREFUL THERE. SLOW AND STEADY, YEAH?
I CAN PROVE IT. AND I CAN DO BETTER THAN THAT.
THIS IS A SAT LINK TO THE PEOPLE WHO SENT ME.
I CAN GET US ALL OUT OF THIS SHITHOLE.

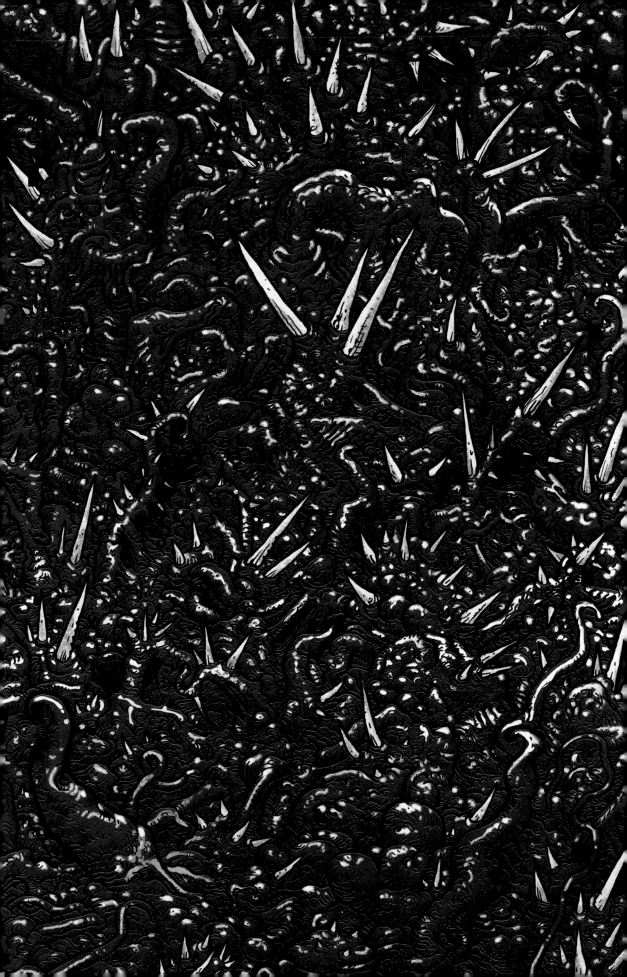

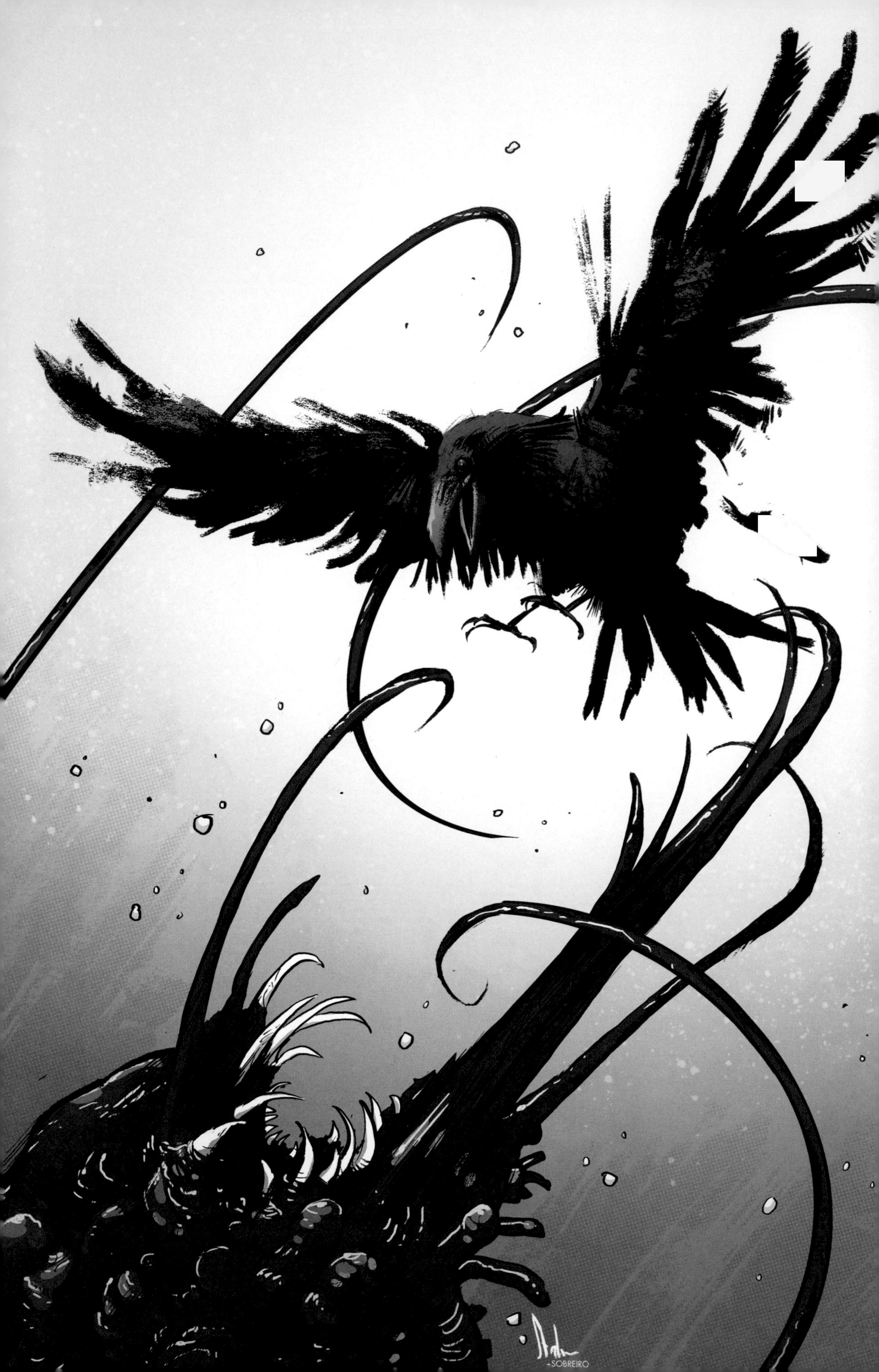
+SOBREIRO

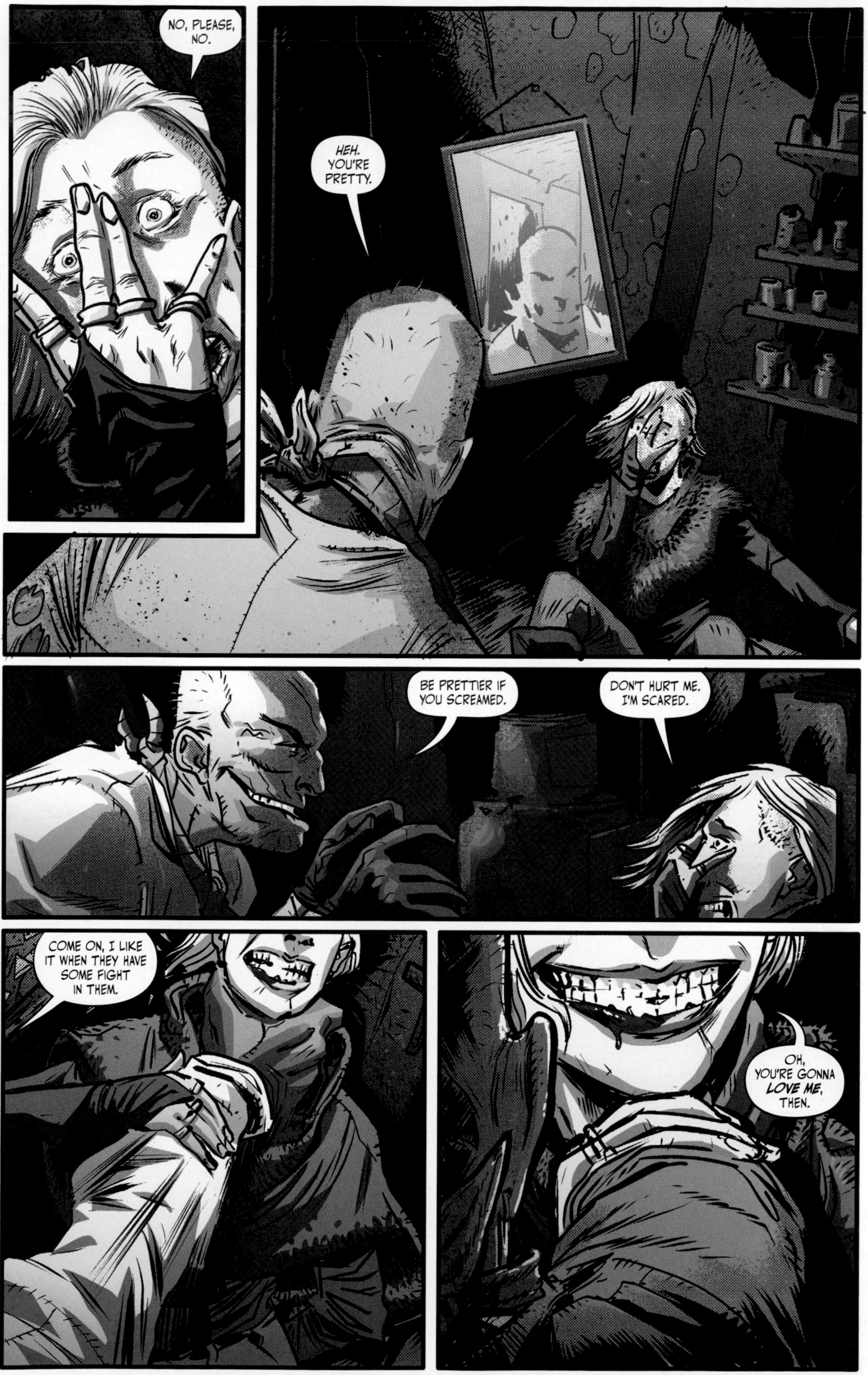
NO, PLEASE, NO.
HEH. YOU'RE PRETTY.
BE PRETTIER IF YOU SCREAMED.
DON'T HURT ME. I'M SCARED.
COME ON, I LIKE IT WHEN THEY HAVE SOME FIGHT IN THEM.
OH, YOU'RE GONNA *LOVE ME*, THEN.

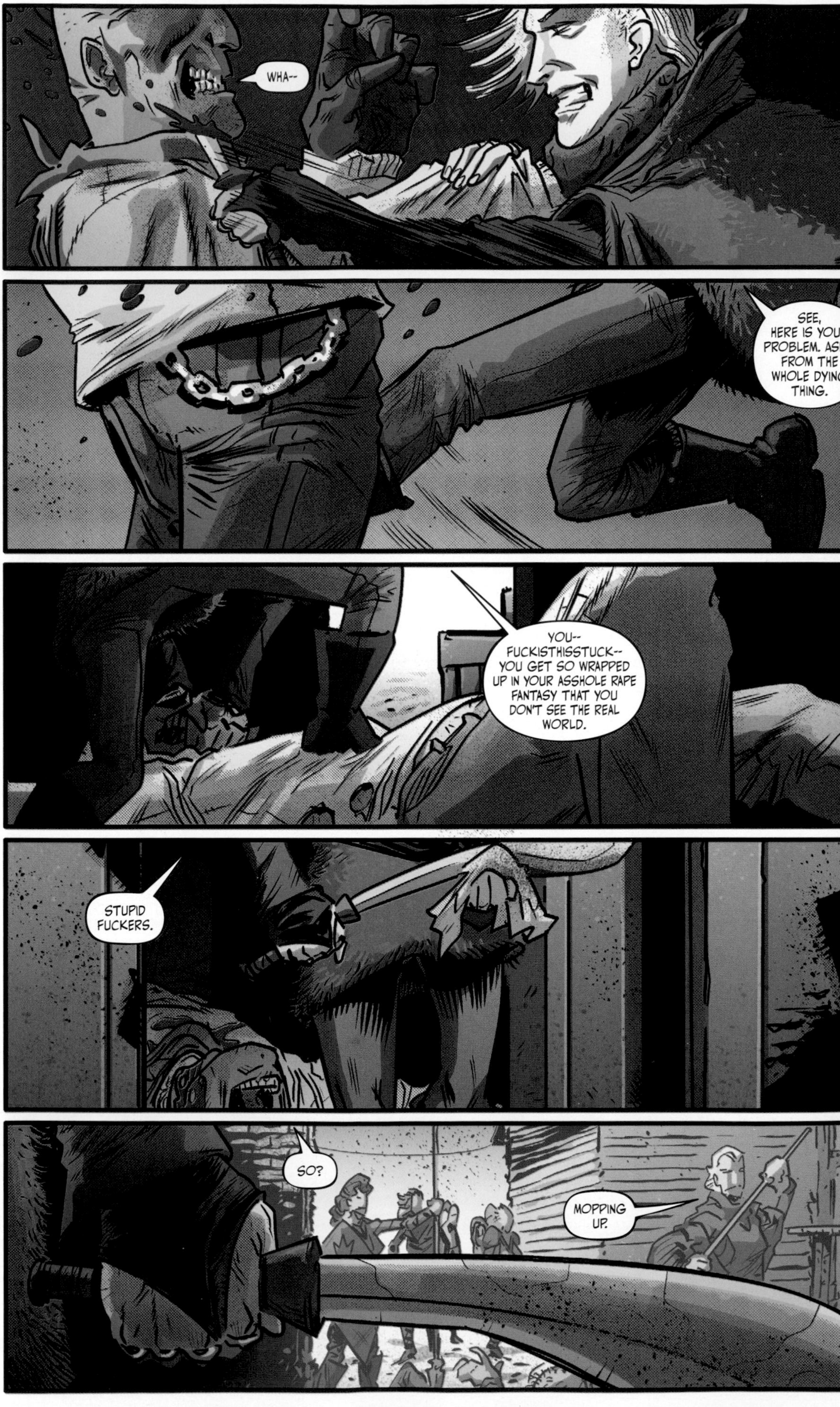
WHA--
SEE, HERE IS YOUR PROBLEM. ASIDE FROM THE WHOLE DYING THING.
YOU-- FUCKISTHISSTUCK-- YOU GET SO WRAPPED UP IN YOUR ASSHOLE RAPE FANTASY THAT YOU DON'T SEE THE REAL WORLD.
STUPID FUCKERS.
SO?
MOPPING UP.

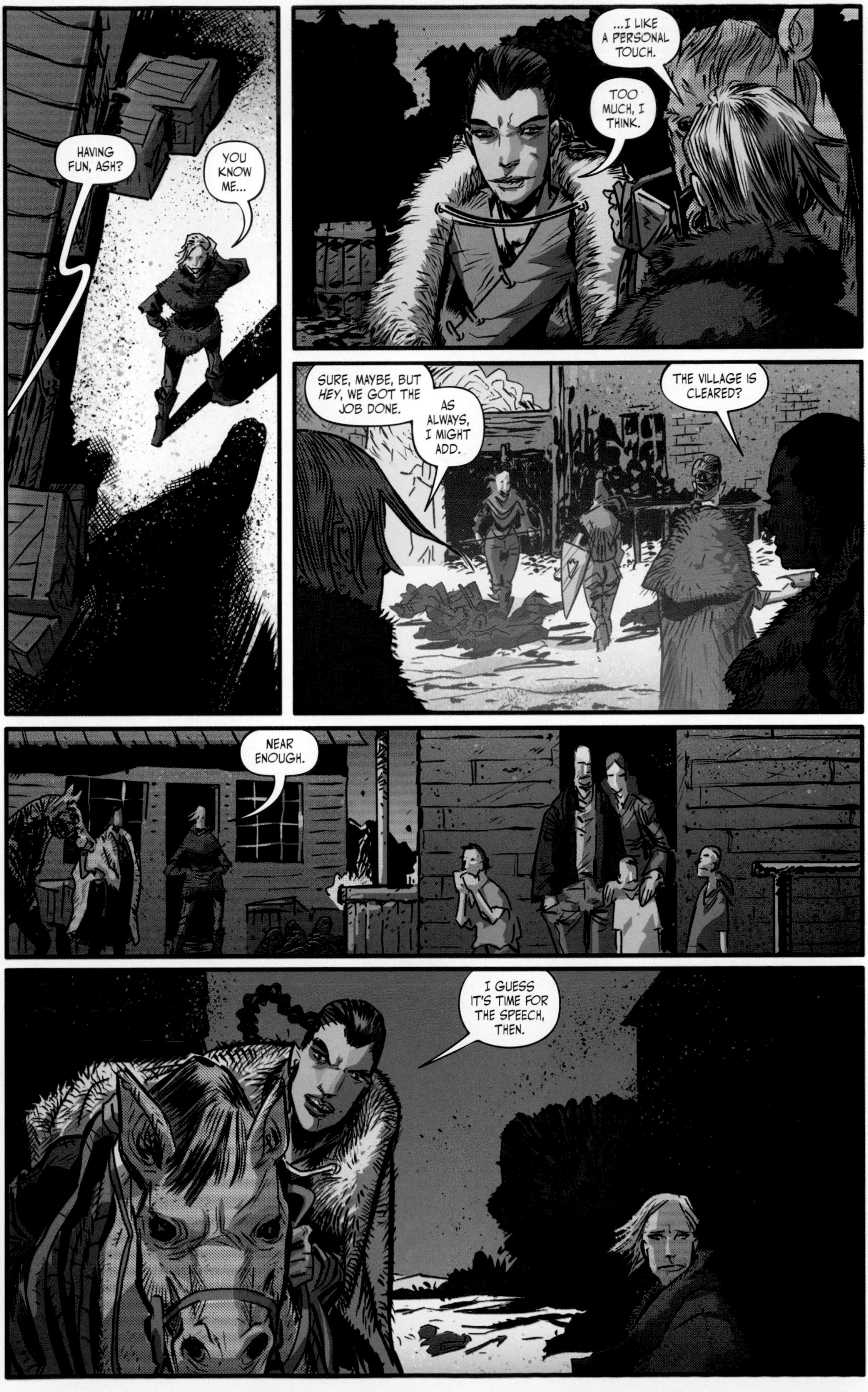
HAVING FUN, ASH?
YOU KNOW ME...
...I LIKE A PERSONAL TOUCH.
TOO MUCH, I THINK.
SURE, MAYBE, BUT HEY, WE GOT THE JOB DONE.
AS ALWAYS, I MIGHT ADD.
THE VILLAGE IS CLEARED?
NEAR ENOUGH.
I GUESS IT'S TIME FOR THE SPEECH, THEN.

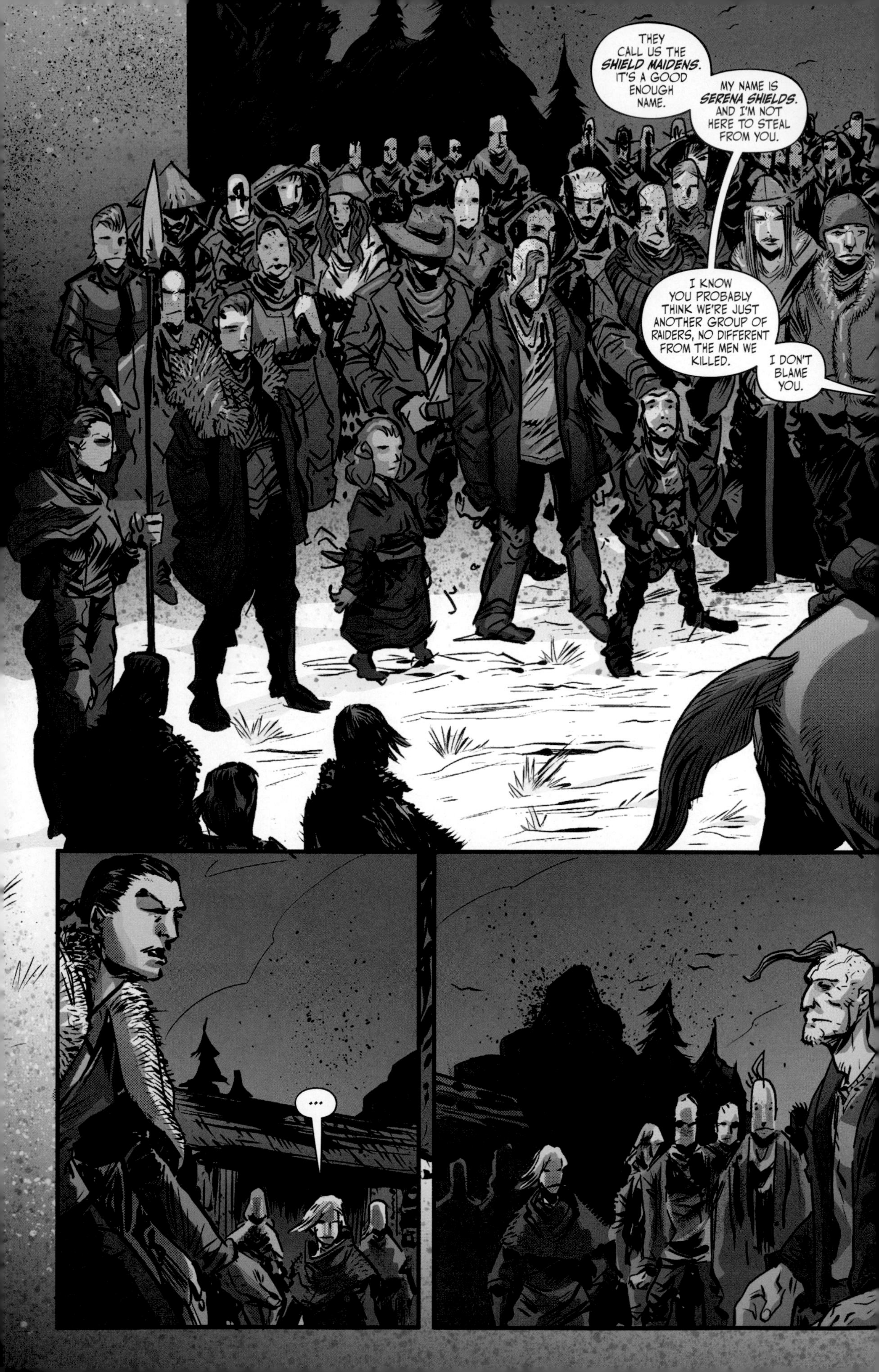
THEY CALL US THE SHIELD MAIDENS. IT'S A GOOD ENOUGH NAME.
MY NAME IS SERENA SHIELDS. AND I'M NOT HERE TO STEAL FROM YOU.
I KNOW YOU PROBABLY THINK WE'RE JUST ANOTHER GROUP OF RAIDERS, NO DIFFERENT FROM THE MEN WE KILLED.
I DON'T BLAME YOU.
...

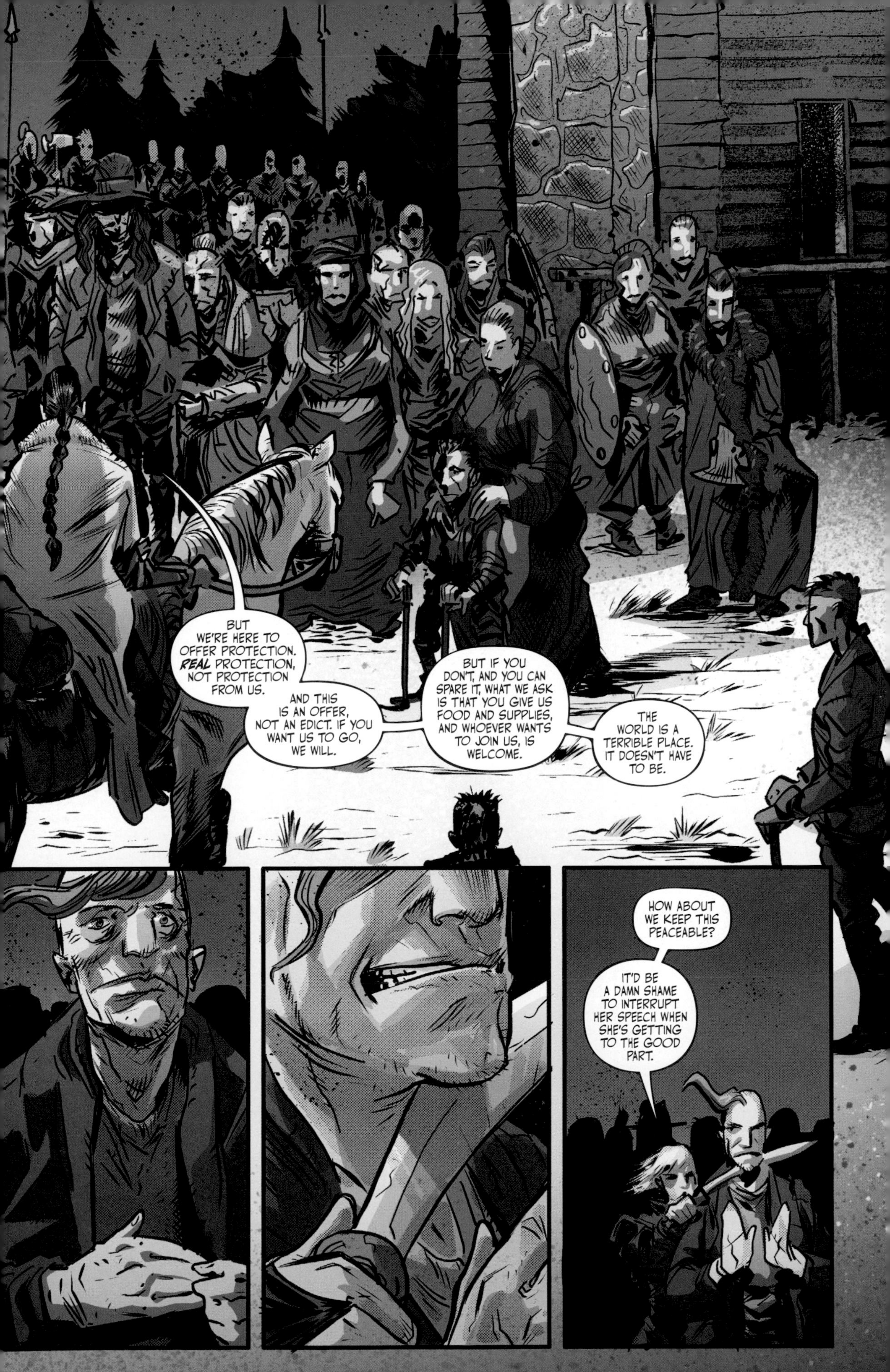
BUT WE'RE HERE TO OFFER PROTECTION. REAL PROTECTION, NOT PROTECTION FROM US.
AND THIS IS AN OFFER, NOT AN EDICT. IF YOU WANT US TO GO, WE WILL.
BUT IF YOU DON'T, AND YOU CAN SPARE IT, WHAT WE ASK IS THAT YOU GIVE US FOOD AND SUPPLIES, AND WHOEVER WANTS TO JOIN US, IS WELCOME.
THE WORLD IS A TERRIBLE PLACE. IT DOESN'T HAVE TO BE.
HOW ABOUT WE KEEP THIS PEACEABLE?
IT'D BE A DAMN SHAME TO INTERRUPT HER SPEECH WHEN SHE'S GETTING TO THE GOOD PART.

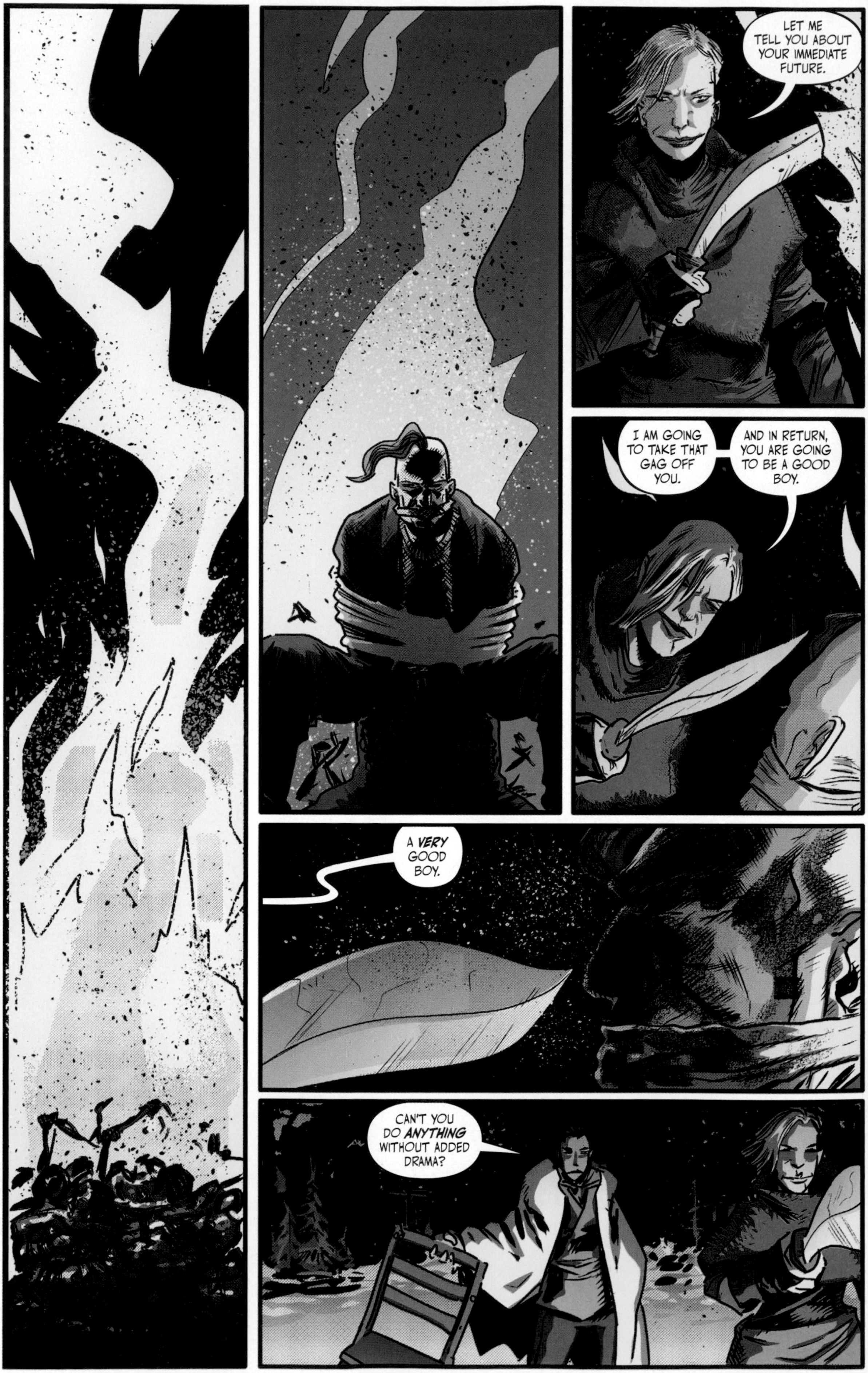
LET ME TELL YOU ABOUT YOUR IMMEDIATE FUTURE.
I AM GOING TO TAKE THAT GAG OFF YOU.
AND IN RETURN, YOU ARE GOING TO BE A GOOD BOY.
A VERY GOOD BOY.
CAN'T YOU DO ANYTHING WITHOUT ADDED DRAMA?

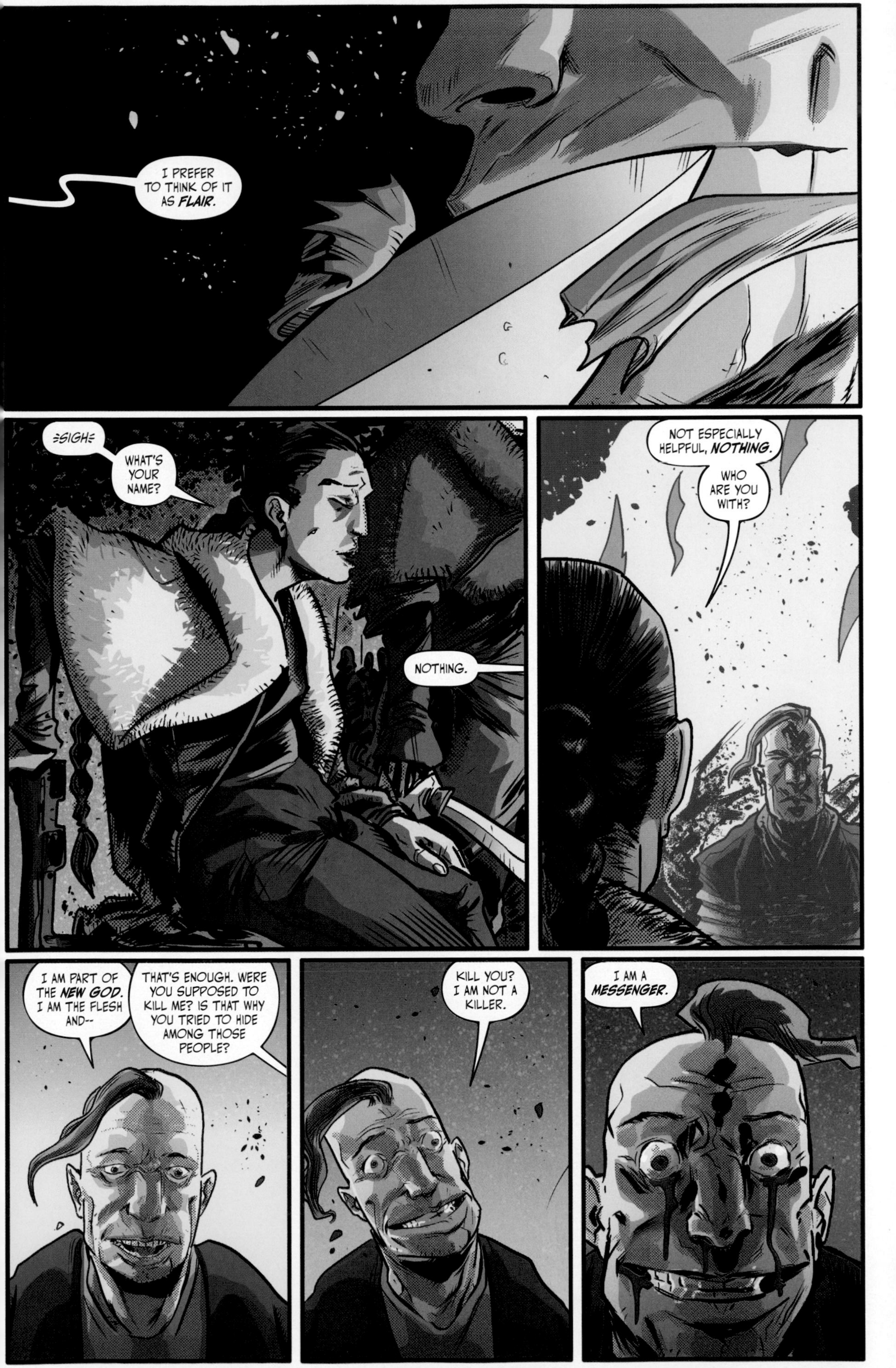
I PREFER TO THINK OF IT AS FLAIR.
=SIGH=
WHAT'S YOUR NAME?
NOTHING.
NOT ESPECIALLY HELPFUL, NOTHING.
WHO ARE YOU WITH?
I AM PART OF THE NEW GOD. I AM THE FLESH AND--
THAT'S ENOUGH. WERE YOU SUPPOSED TO KILL ME? IS THAT WHY YOU TRIED TO HIDE AMONG THOSE PEOPLE?
KILL YOU? I AM NOT A KILLER.
I AM A MESSENGER.

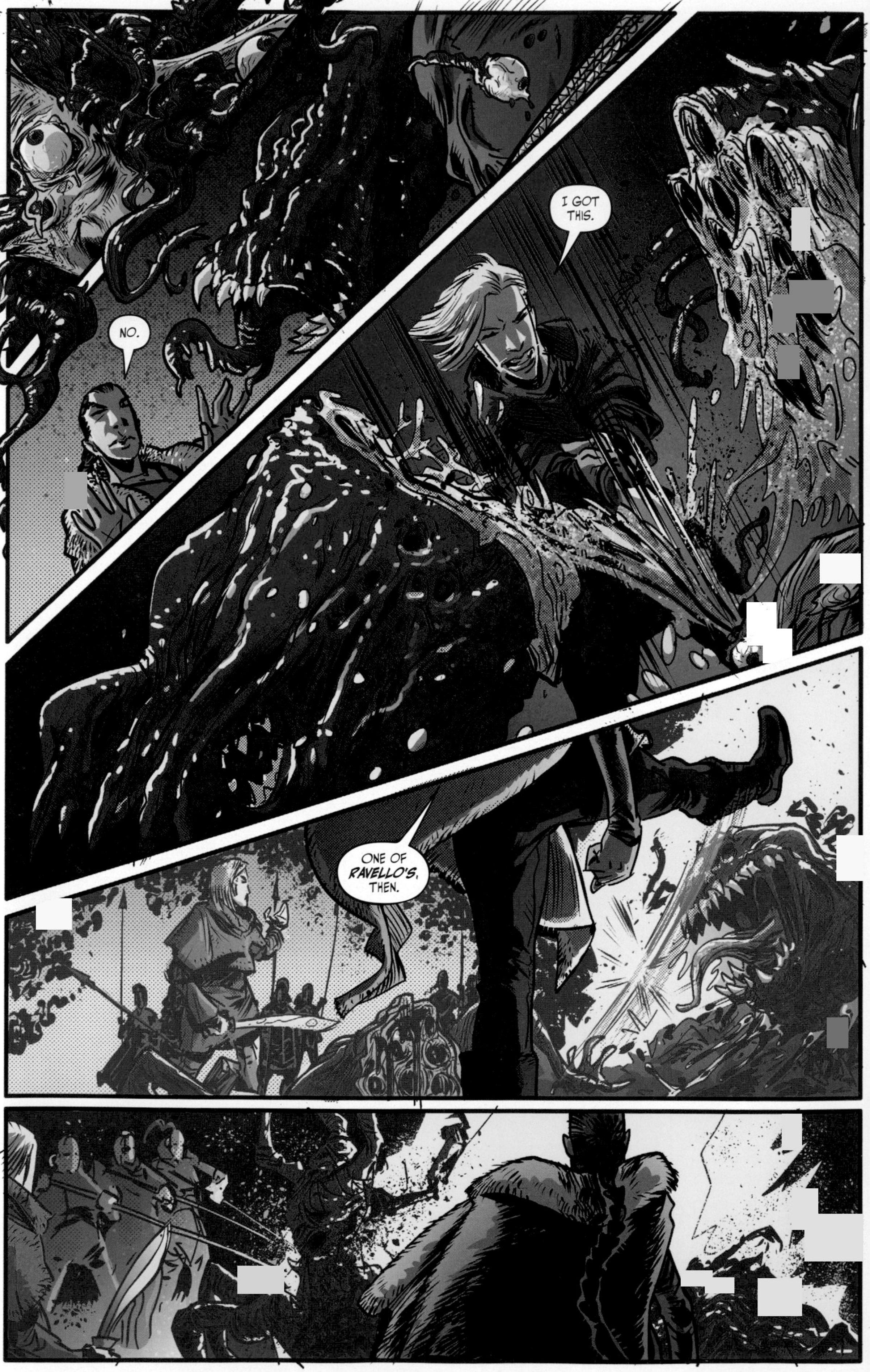
NO.
I GOT THIS.
ONE OF *RAVELLO'S*, THEN.

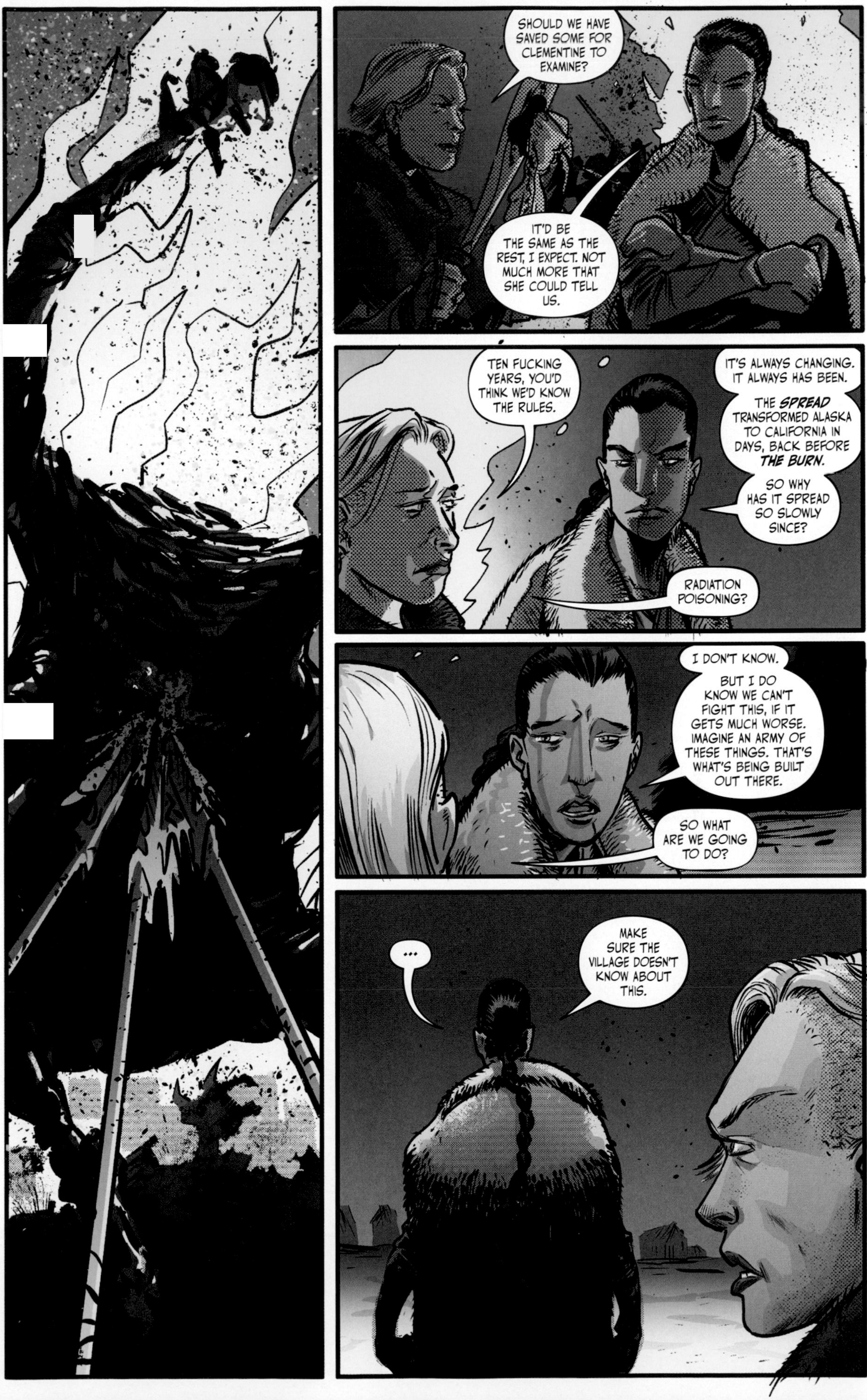
SHOULD WE HAVE SAVED SOME FOR CLEMENTINE TO EXAMINE?
IT'D BE THE SAME AS THE REST, I EXPECT. NOT MUCH MORE THAT SHE COULD TELL US.
TEN FUCKING YEARS, YOU'D THINK WE'D KNOW THE RULES.
IT'S ALWAYS CHANGING. IT ALWAYS HAS BEEN.
THE SPREAD TRANSFORMED ALASKA TO CALIFORNIA IN DAYS, BACK BEFORE THE BURN.
SO WHY HAS IT SPREAD SO SLOWLY SINCE?
RADIATION POISONING?
I DON'T KNOW.
BUT I DO KNOW WE CAN'T FIGHT THIS, IF IT GETS MUCH WORSE. IMAGINE AN ARMY OF THESE THINGS. THAT'S WHAT'S BEING BUILT OUT THERE.
SO WHAT ARE WE GOING TO DO?
...
MAKE SURE THE VILLAGE DOESN'T KNOW ABOUT THIS.

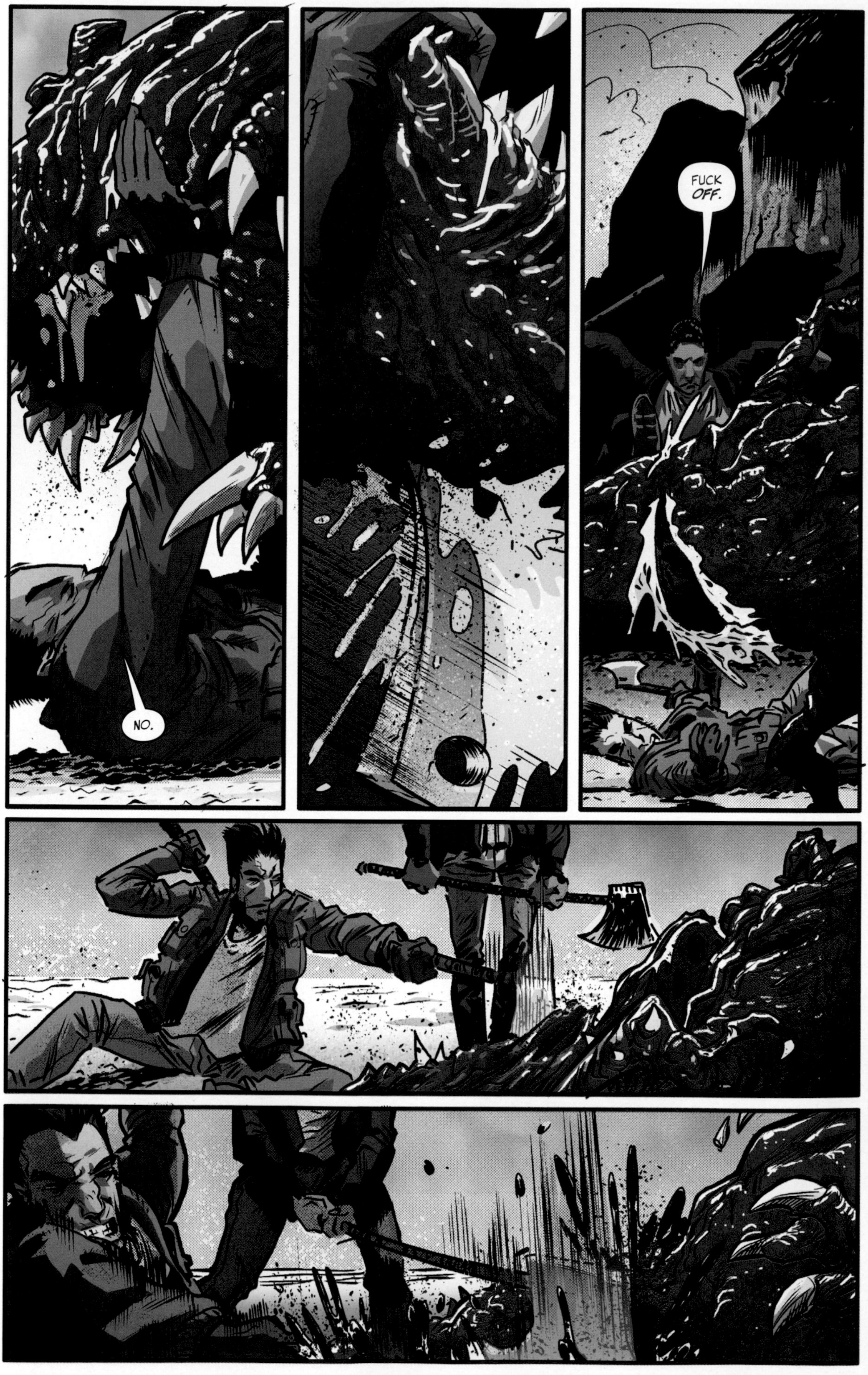
NO.
FUCK OFF.

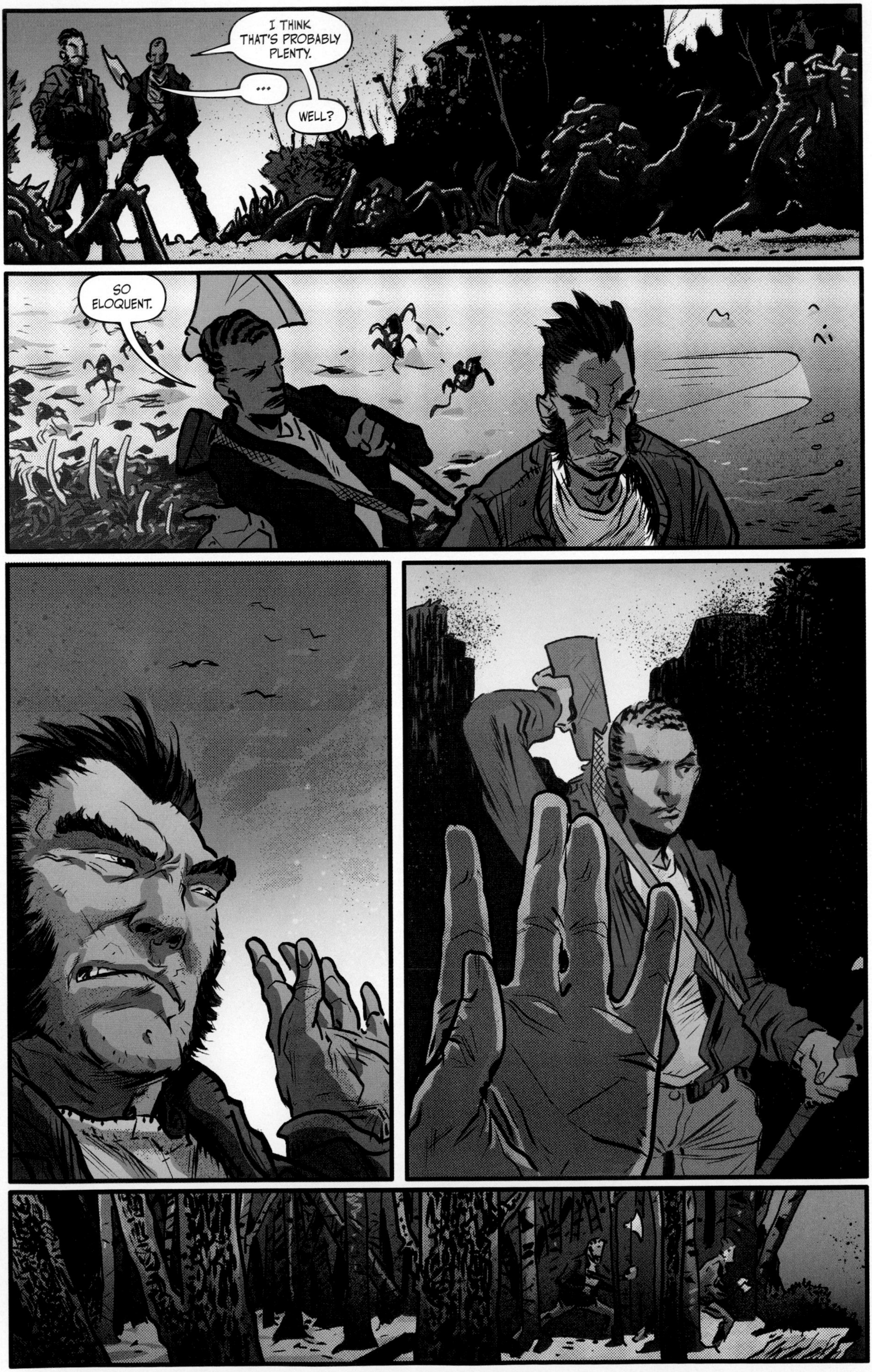
I THINK THAT'S PROBABLY PLENTY.
...
WELL?
SO ELOQUENT.

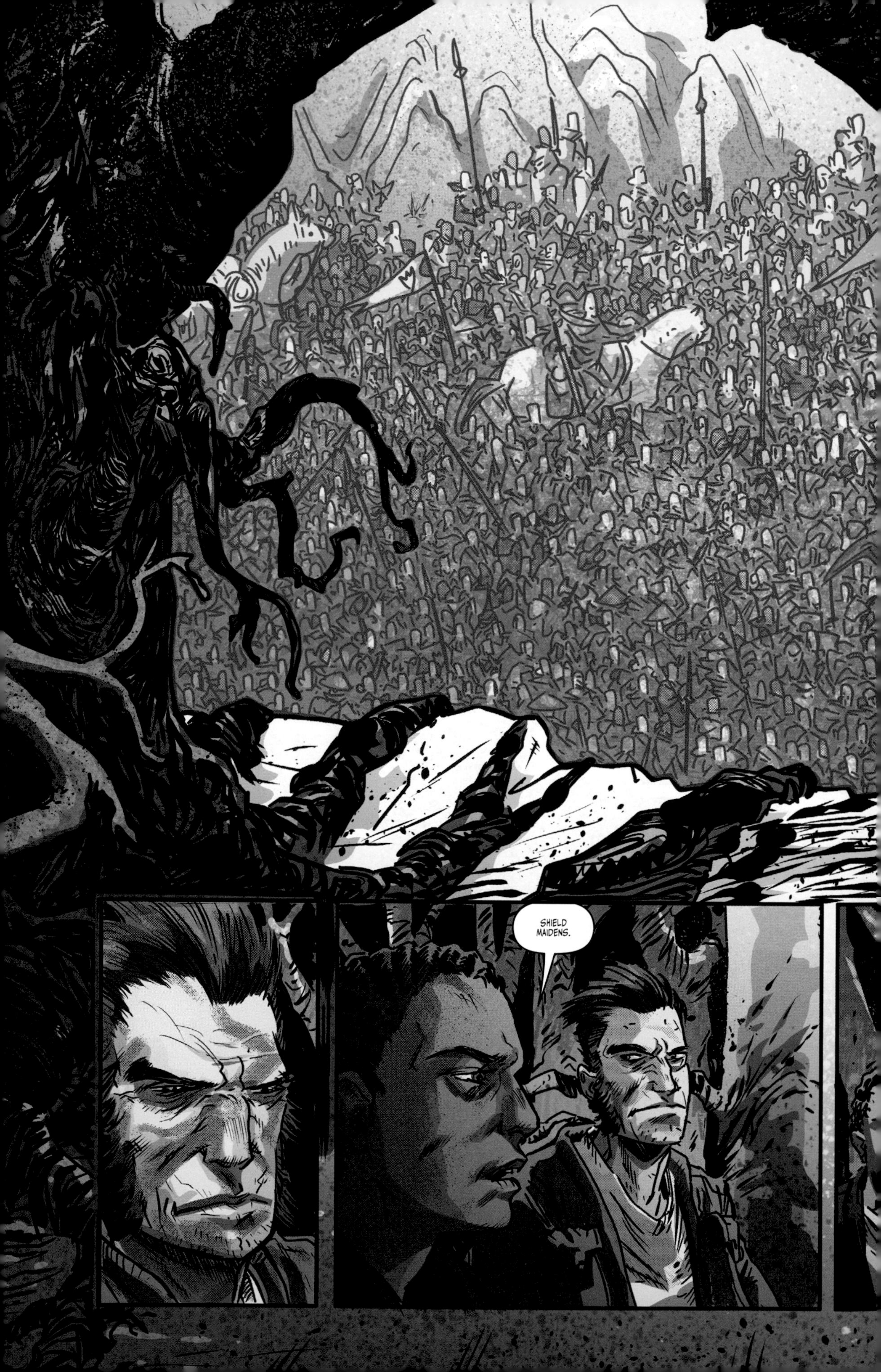
SHIELD MAIDENS.

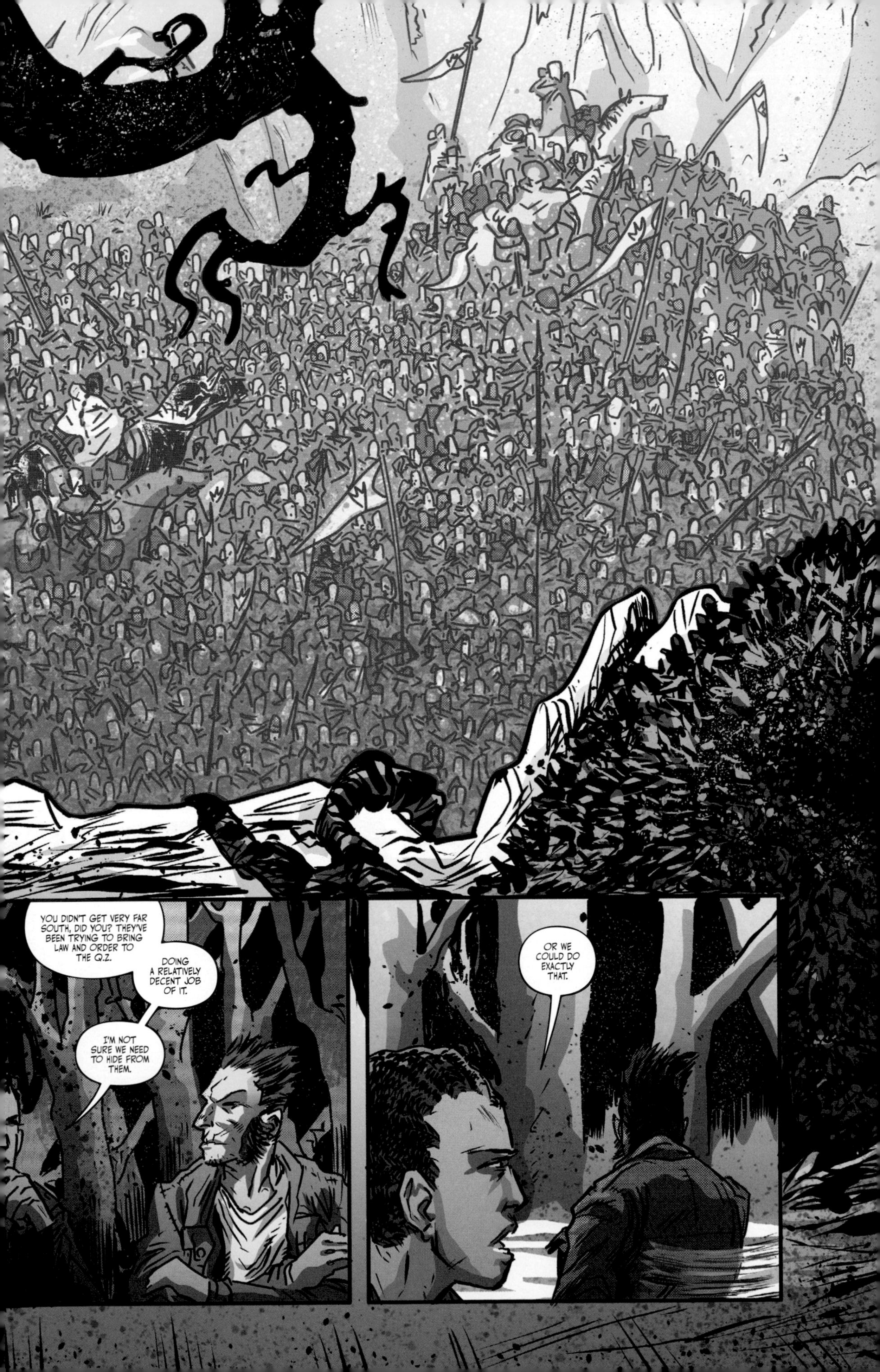
YOU DIDN'T GET VERY FAR SOUTH, DID YOU? THEY'VE BEEN TRYING TO BRING LAW AND ORDER TO THE Q.Z.
DOING A RELATIVELY DECENT JOB OF IT.
I'M NOT SURE WE NEED TO HIDE FROM THEM.
OR WE COULD DO EXACTLY THAT.

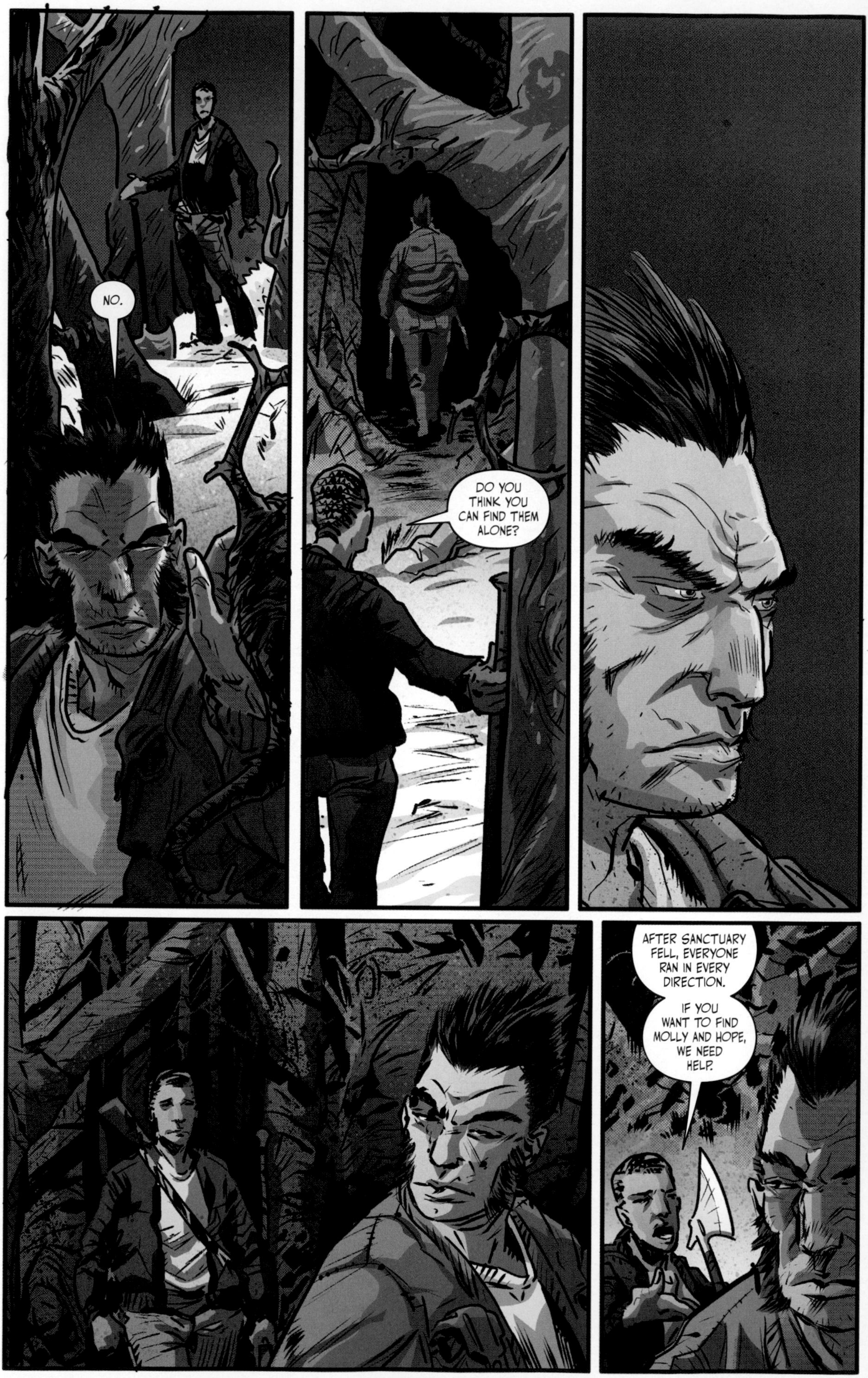
NO.
DO YOU THINK YOU CAN FIND THEM ALONE?
AFTER SANCTUARY FELL, EVERYONE RAN IN EVERY DIRECTION.
IF YOU WANT TO FIND MOLLY AND HOPE, WE NEED HELP.

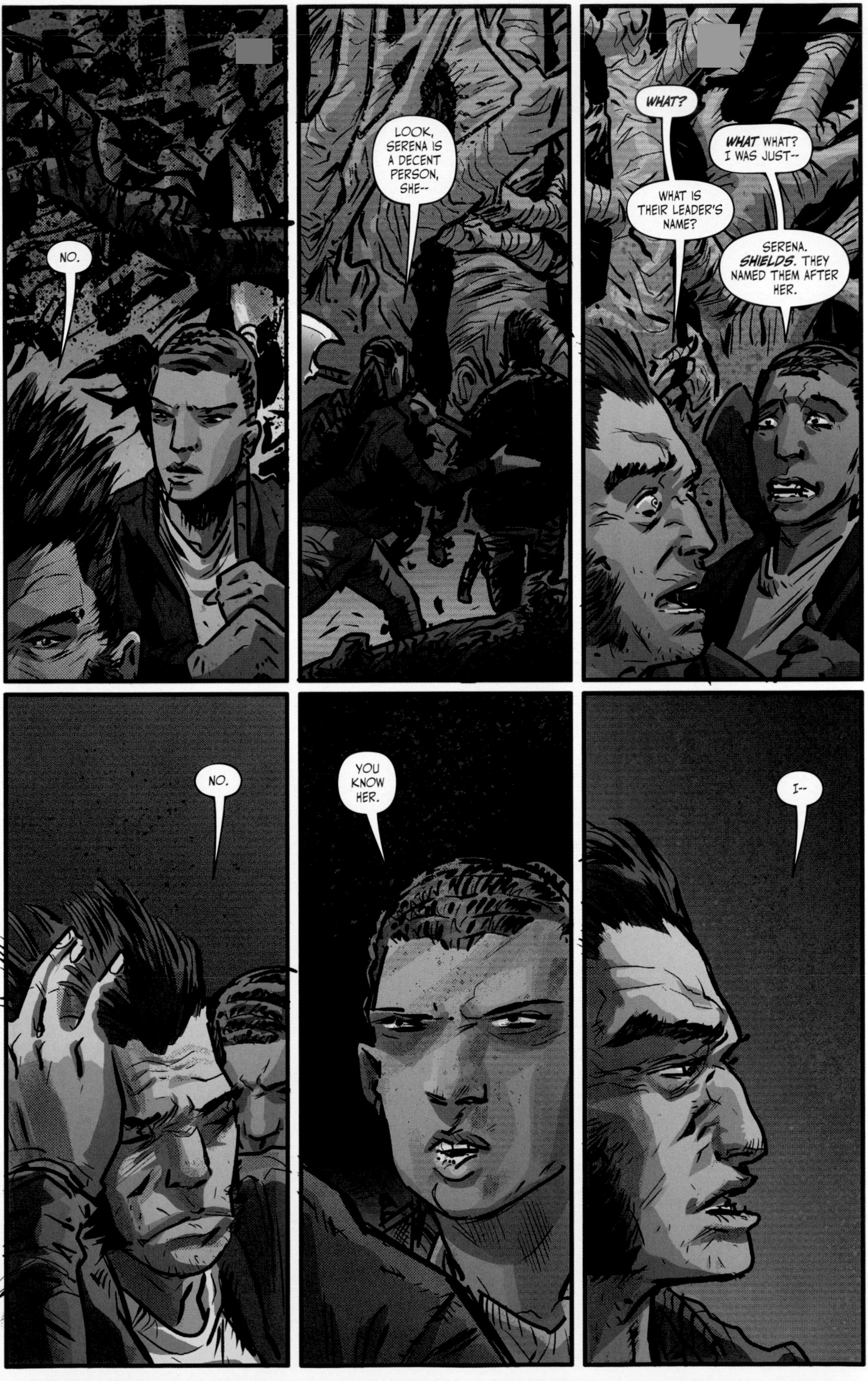
NO.
LOOK, SERENA IS A DECENT PERSON, SHE--
WHAT?
WHAT WHAT? I WAS JUST--
WHAT IS THEIR LEADER'S NAME?
SERENA. SHIELDS. THEY NAMED THEM AFTER HER.
NO.
YOU KNOW HER.
I--

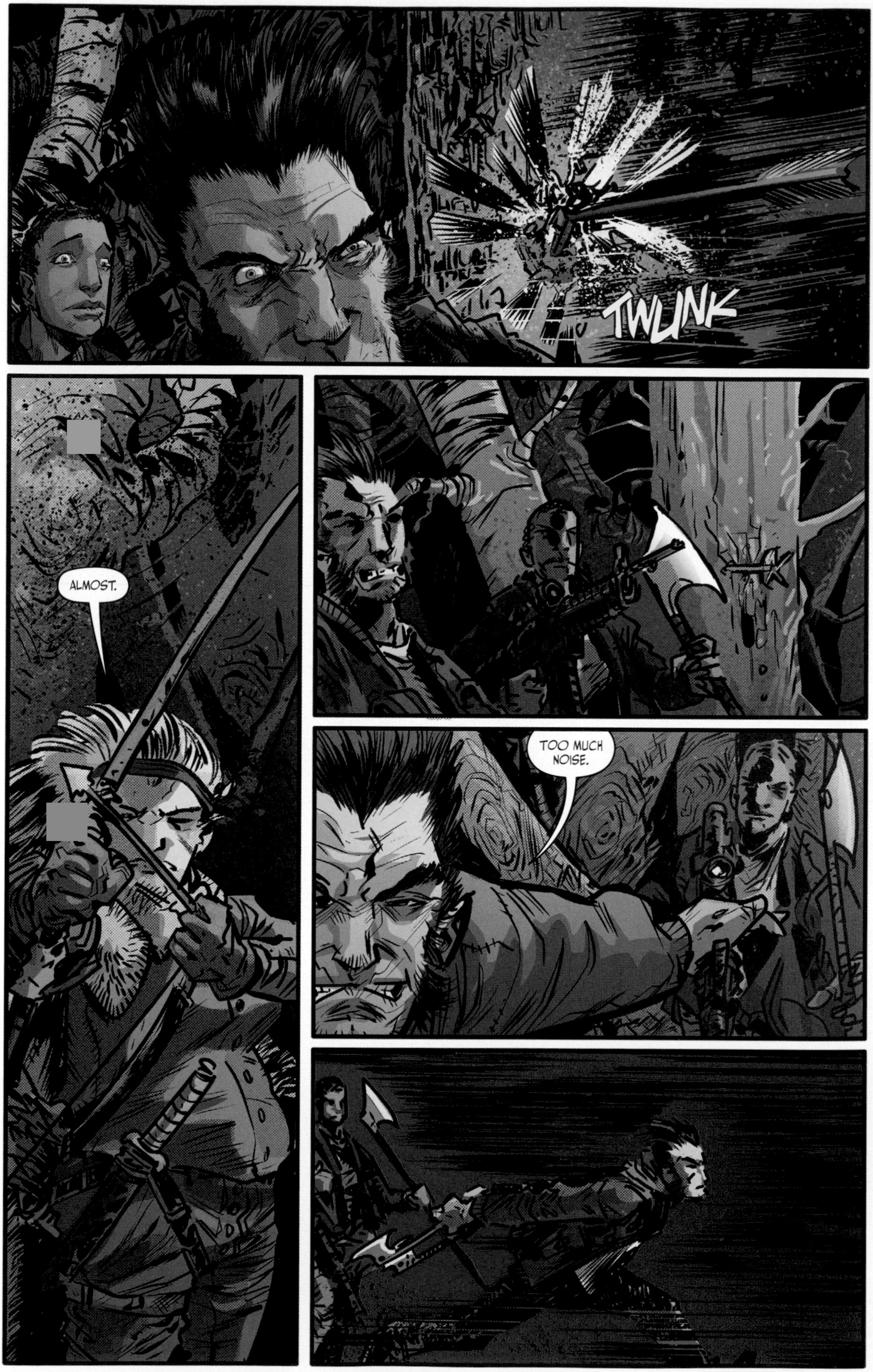
TWUNK
ALMOST.
TOO MUCH NOISE.

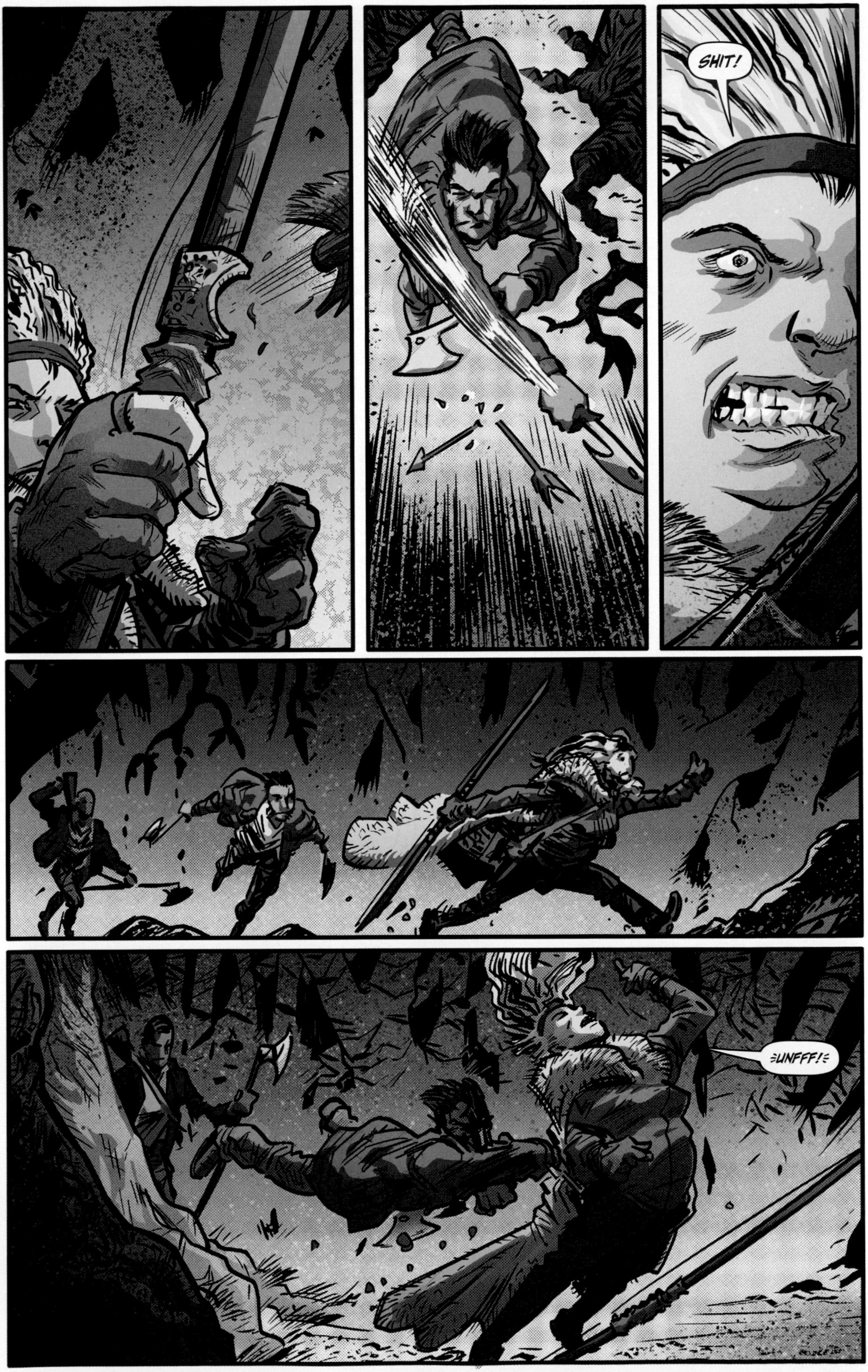
SHIT!
UNFFF!

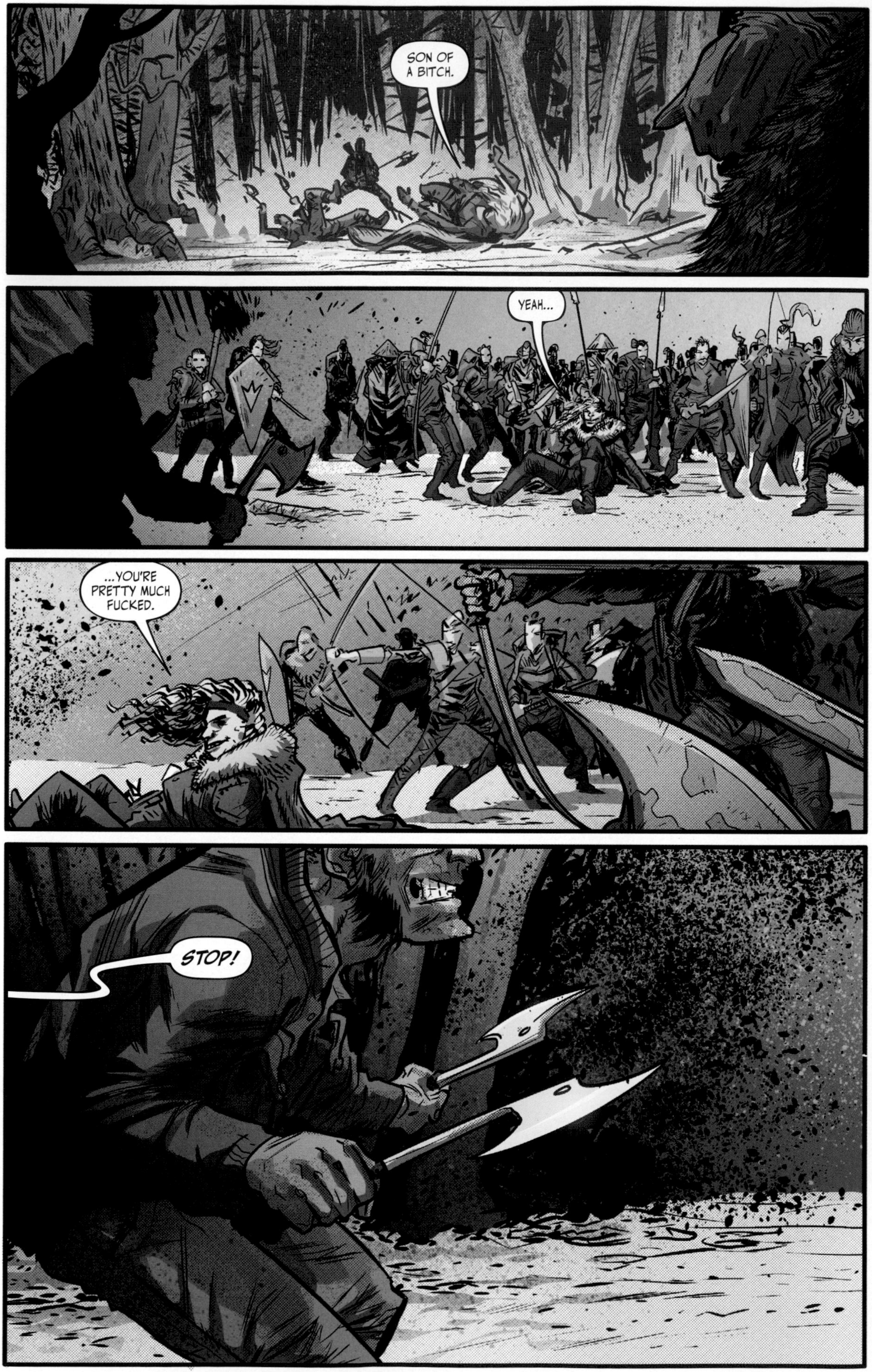
SON OF A BITCH.
YEAH...
...YOU'RE PRETTY MUCH FUCKED.
STOP!

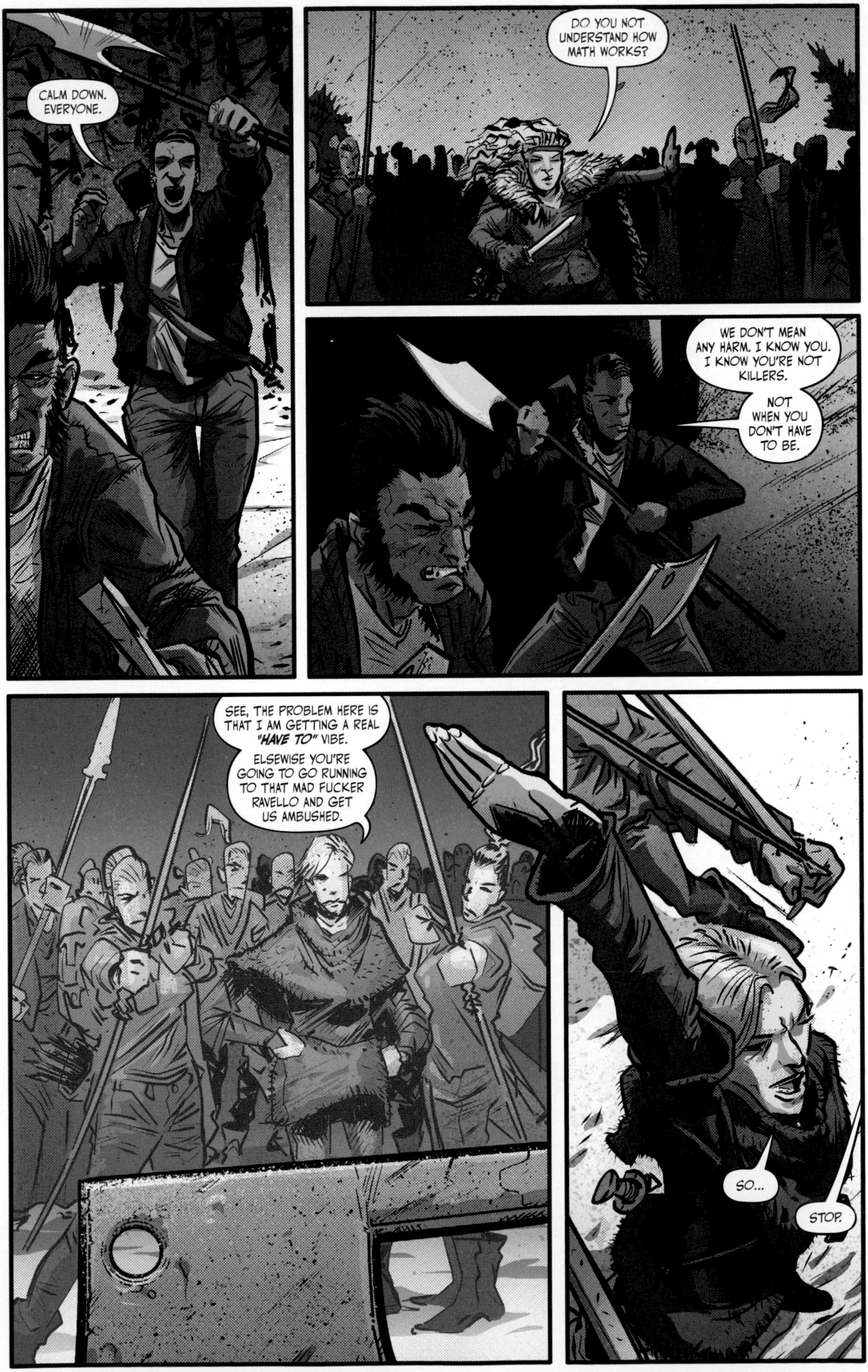
CALM DOWN. EVERYONE.
DO YOU NOT UNDERSTAND HOW MATH WORKS?
WE DON'T MEAN ANY HARM. I KNOW YOU. I KNOW YOU'RE NOT KILLERS.
NOT WHEN YOU DON'T HAVE TO BE.
SEE, THE PROBLEM HERE IS THAT I AM GETTING A REAL "HAVE TO" VIBE.
ELSEWISE YOU'RE GOING TO GO RUNNING TO THAT MAD FUCKER RAVELLO AND GET US AMBUSHED.
SO...
STOP.

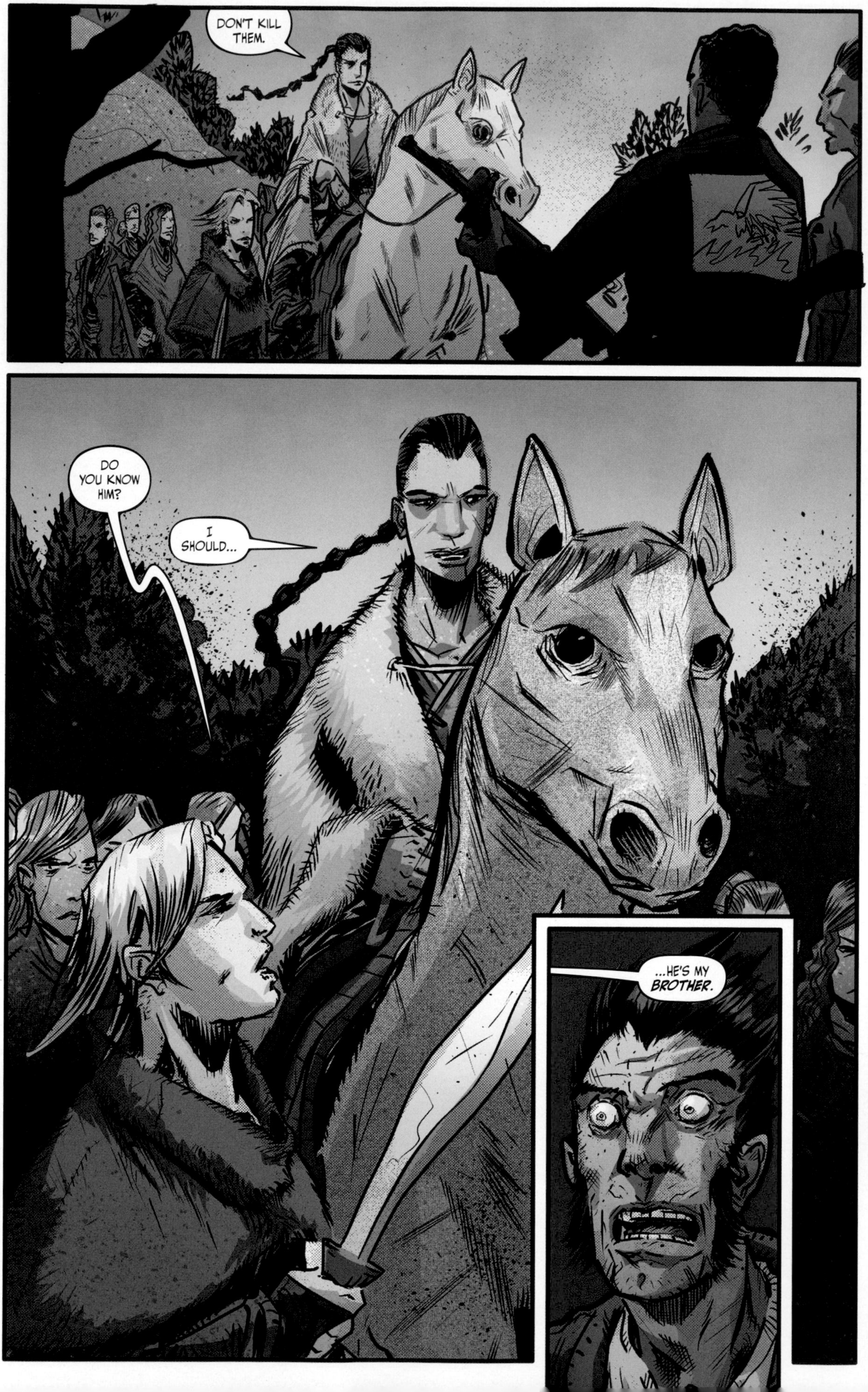
DON'T KILL THEM.
DO YOU KNOW HIM?
I SHOULD...
...HE'S MY *BROTHER*.

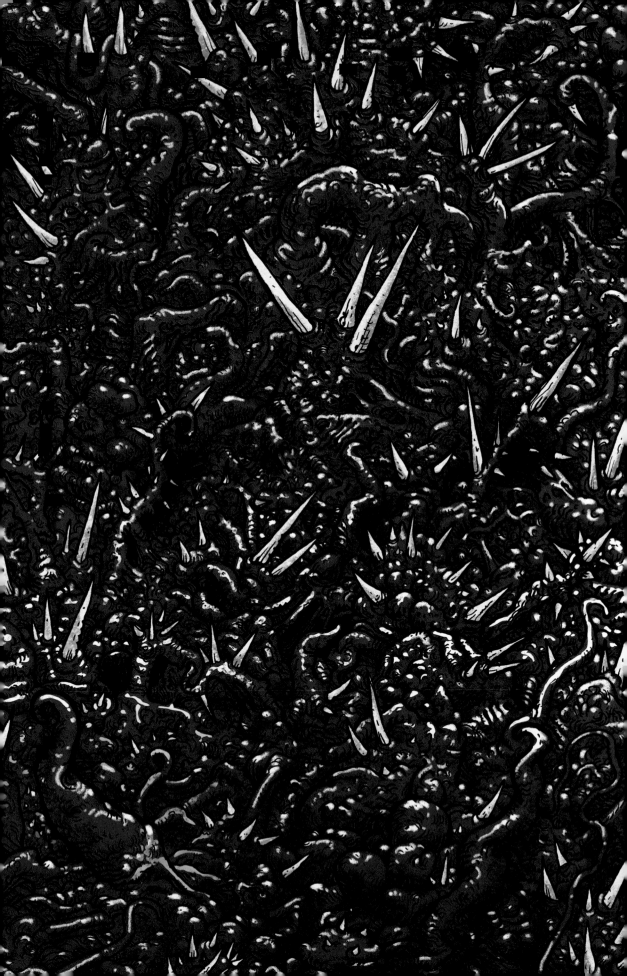

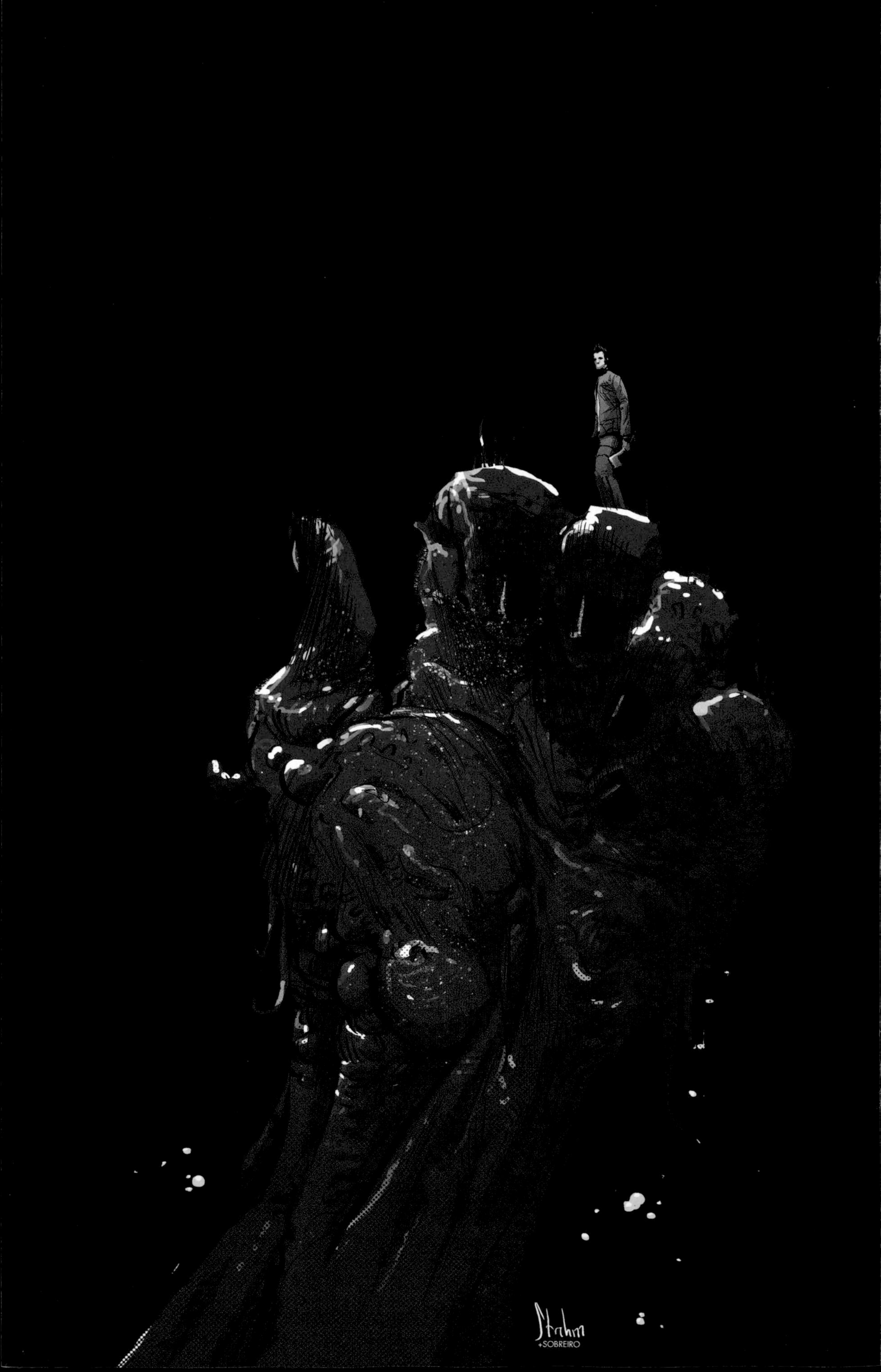
+SOBREIRO

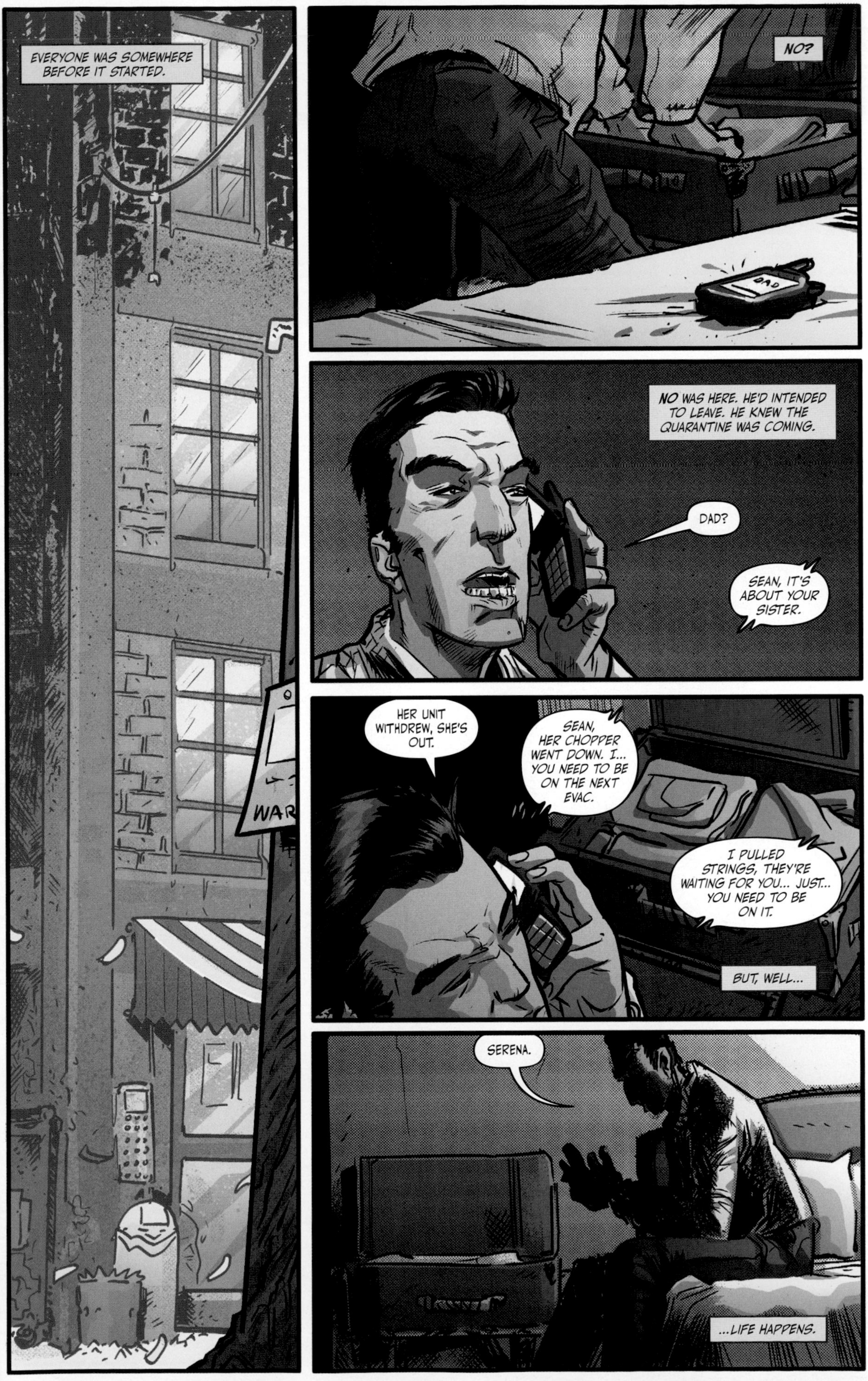
EVERYONE WAS SOMEWHERE BEFORE IT STARTED.
NO?
DAD
NO WAS HERE. HE'D INTENDED TO LEAVE. HE KNEW THE QUARANTINE WAS COMING.
DAD?
SEAN, IT'S ABOUT YOUR SISTER.
HER UNIT WITHDREW, SHE'S OUT.
SEAN, HER CHOPPER WENT DOWN. I... YOU NEED TO BE ON THE NEXT EVAC.
I PULLED STRINGS, THEY'RE WAITING FOR YOU... JUST... YOU NEED TO BE ON IT.
BUT, WELL...
SERENA.
...LIFE HAPPENS.

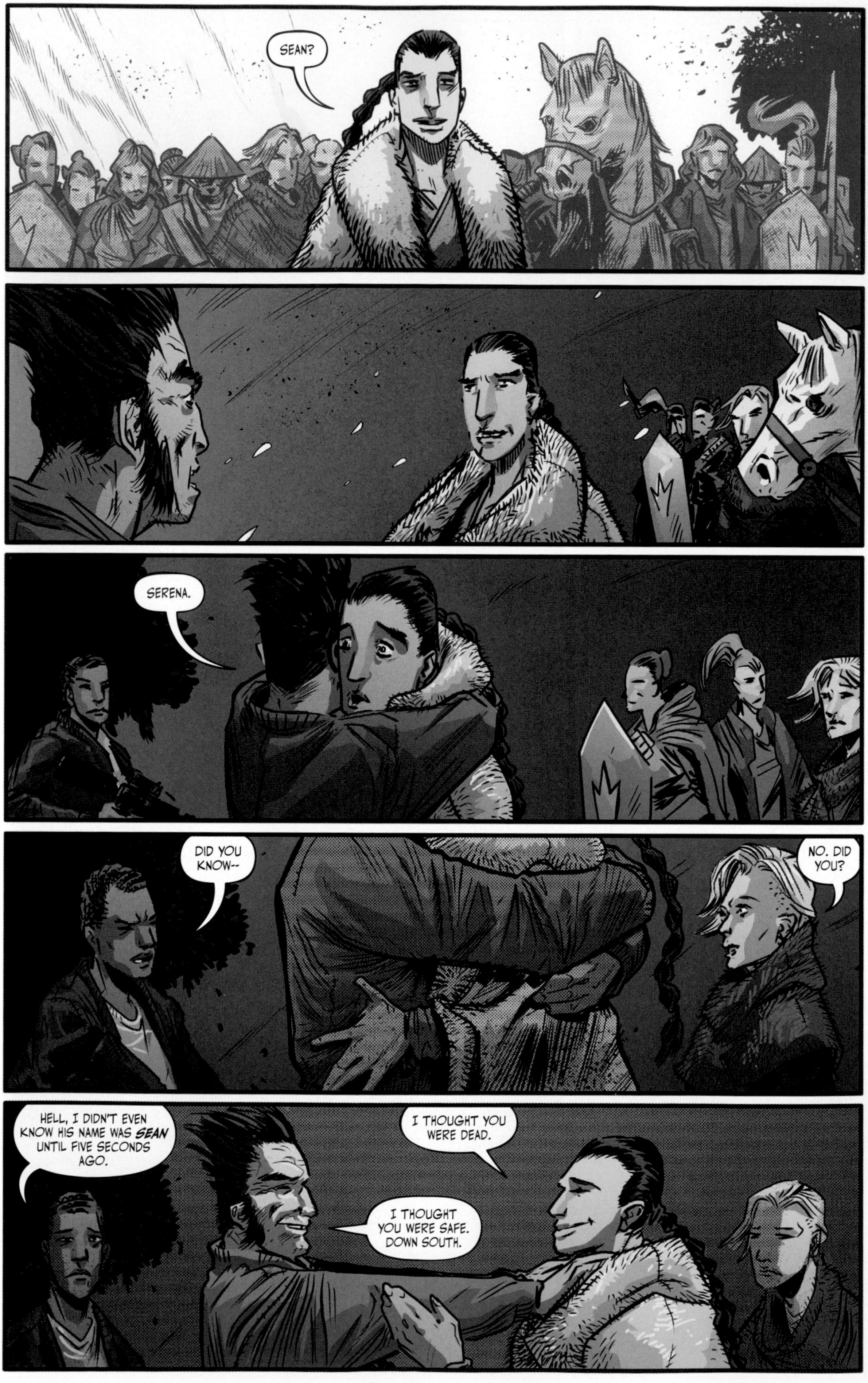
SEAN?
SERENA.
DID YOU KNOW--
NO. DID YOU?
HELL, I DIDN'T EVEN KNOW HIS NAME WAS *SEAN* UNTIL FIVE SECONDS AGO.
I THOUGHT YOU WERE DEAD.
I THOUGHT YOU WERE SAFE. DOWN SOUTH.

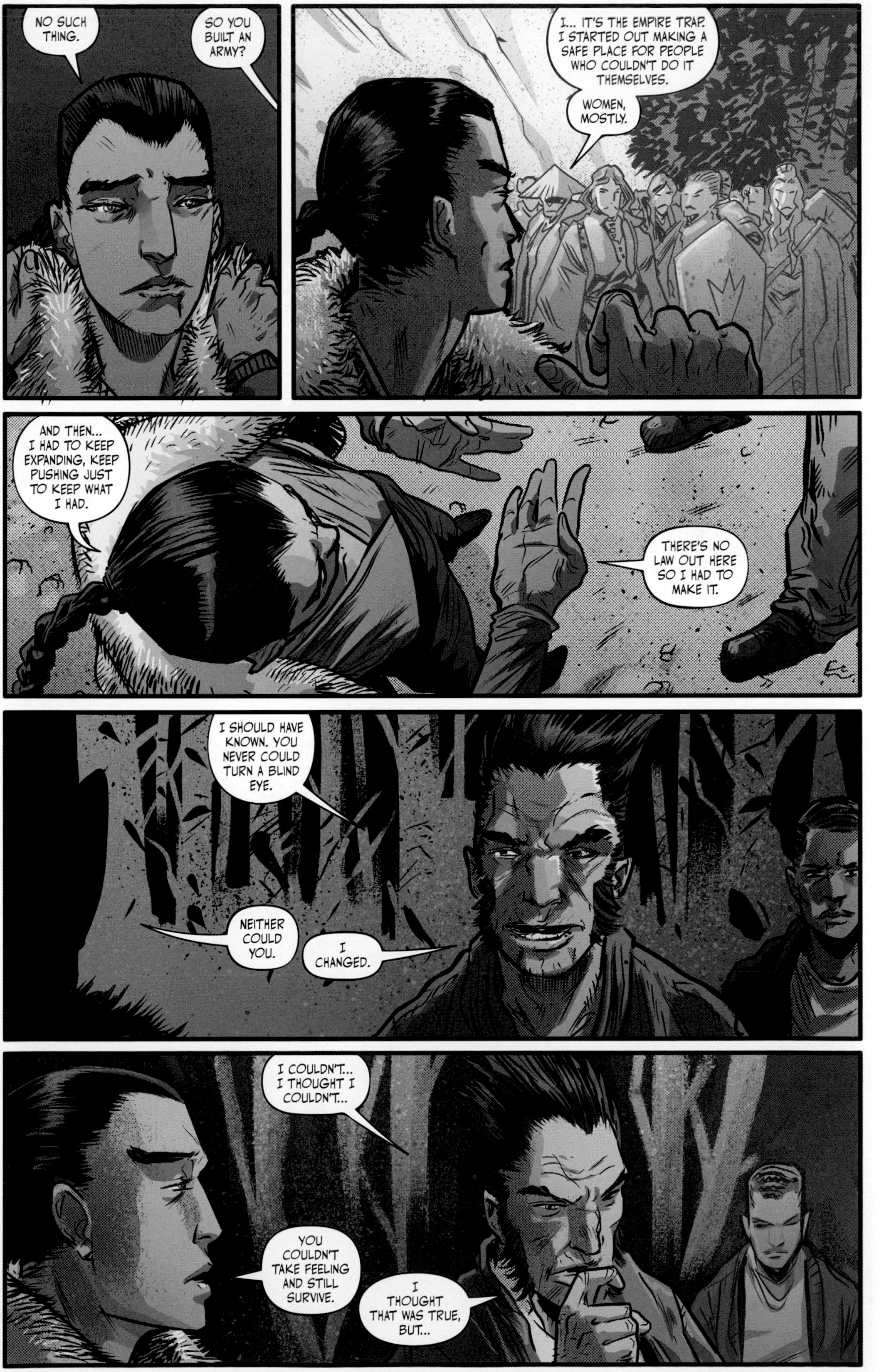
NO SUCH THING.
SO YOU BUILT AN ARMY?
I... IT'S THE EMPIRE TRAP. I STARTED OUT MAKING A SAFE PLACE FOR PEOPLE WHO COULDN'T DO IT THEMSELVES.
WOMEN, MOSTLY.
AND THEN... I HAD TO KEEP EXPANDING, KEEP PUSHING JUST TO KEEP WHAT I HAD.
THERE'S NO LAW OUT HERE SO I HAD TO MAKE IT.
I SHOULD HAVE KNOWN. YOU NEVER COULD TURN A BLIND EYE.
NEITHER COULD YOU.
I CHANGED.
I COULDN'T... I THOUGHT I COULDN'T...
YOU COULDN'T TAKE FEELING AND STILL SURVIVE.
I THOUGHT THAT WAS TRUE, BUT...

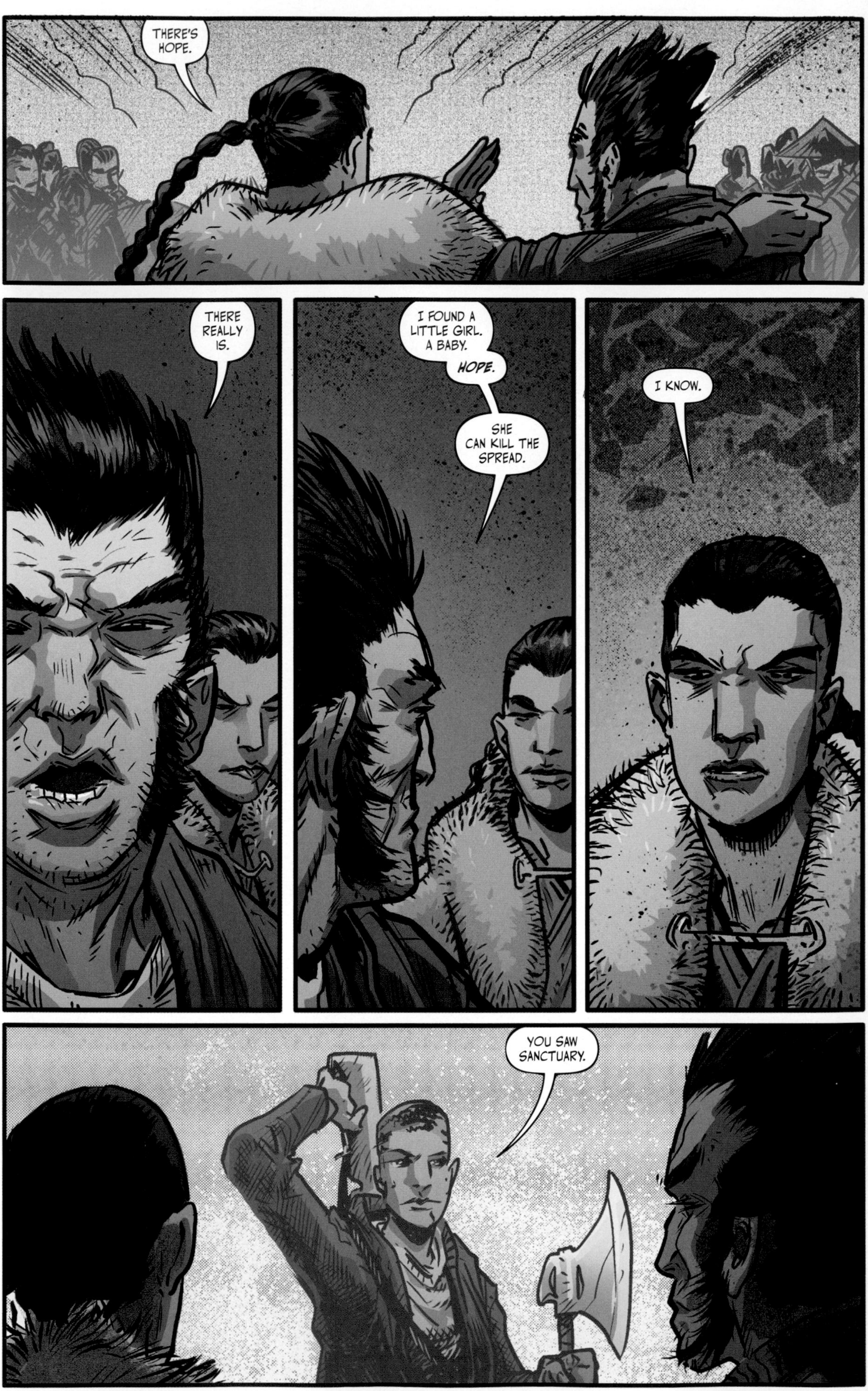
THERE'S HOPE.
THERE REALLY IS.
I FOUND A LITTLE GIRL. A BABY. HOPE.
SHE CAN KILL THE SPREAD.
I KNOW.
YOU SAW SANCTUARY.

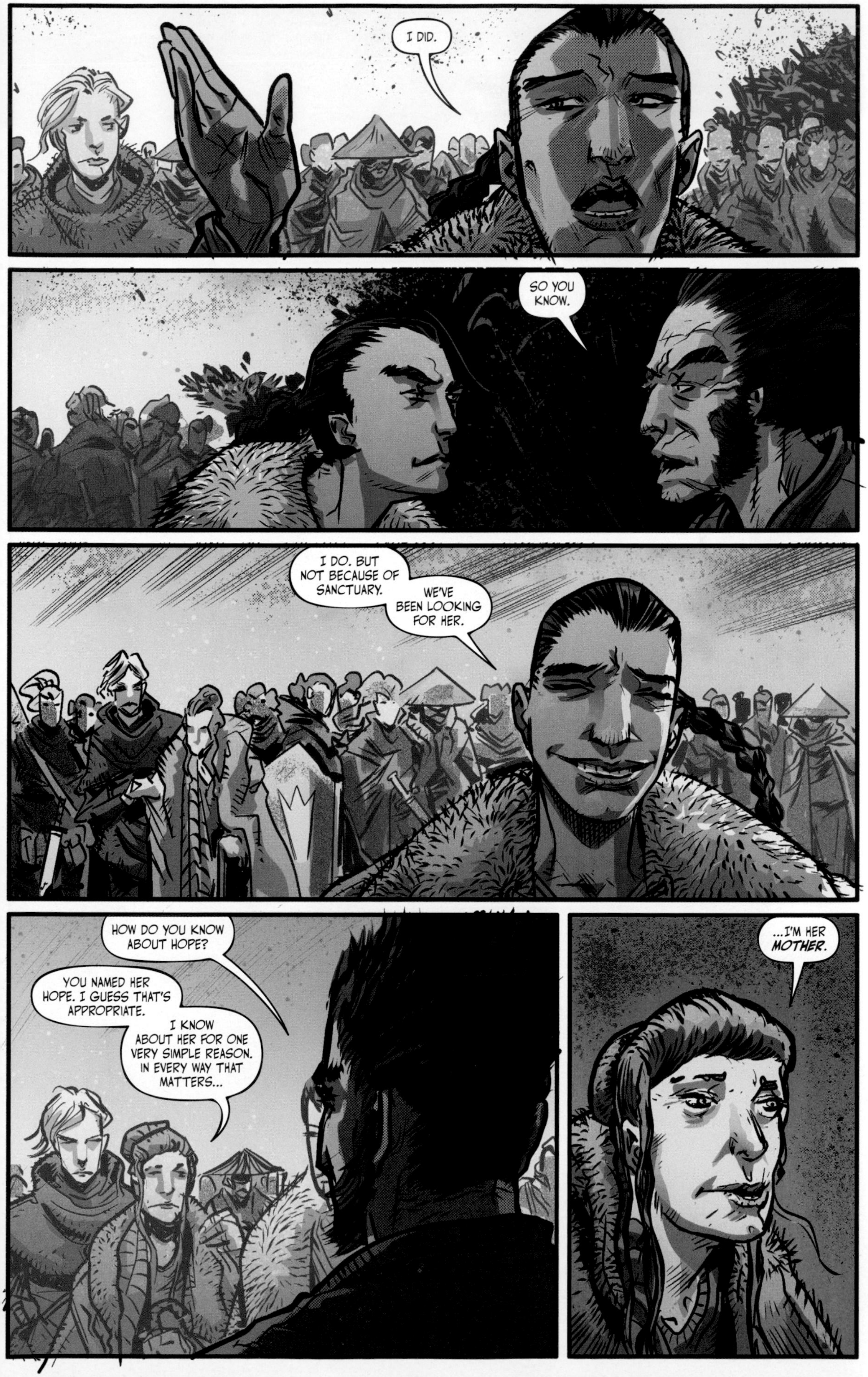
I DID.
SO YOU KNOW.
I DO. BUT NOT BECAUSE OF SANCTUARY.
WE'VE BEEN LOOKING FOR HER.
HOW DO YOU KNOW ABOUT HOPE?
YOU NAMED HER HOPE. I GUESS THAT'S APPROPRIATE.
I KNOW ABOUT HER FOR ONE VERY SIMPLE REASON. IN EVERY WAY THAT MATTERS...
...I'M HER *MOTHER*.

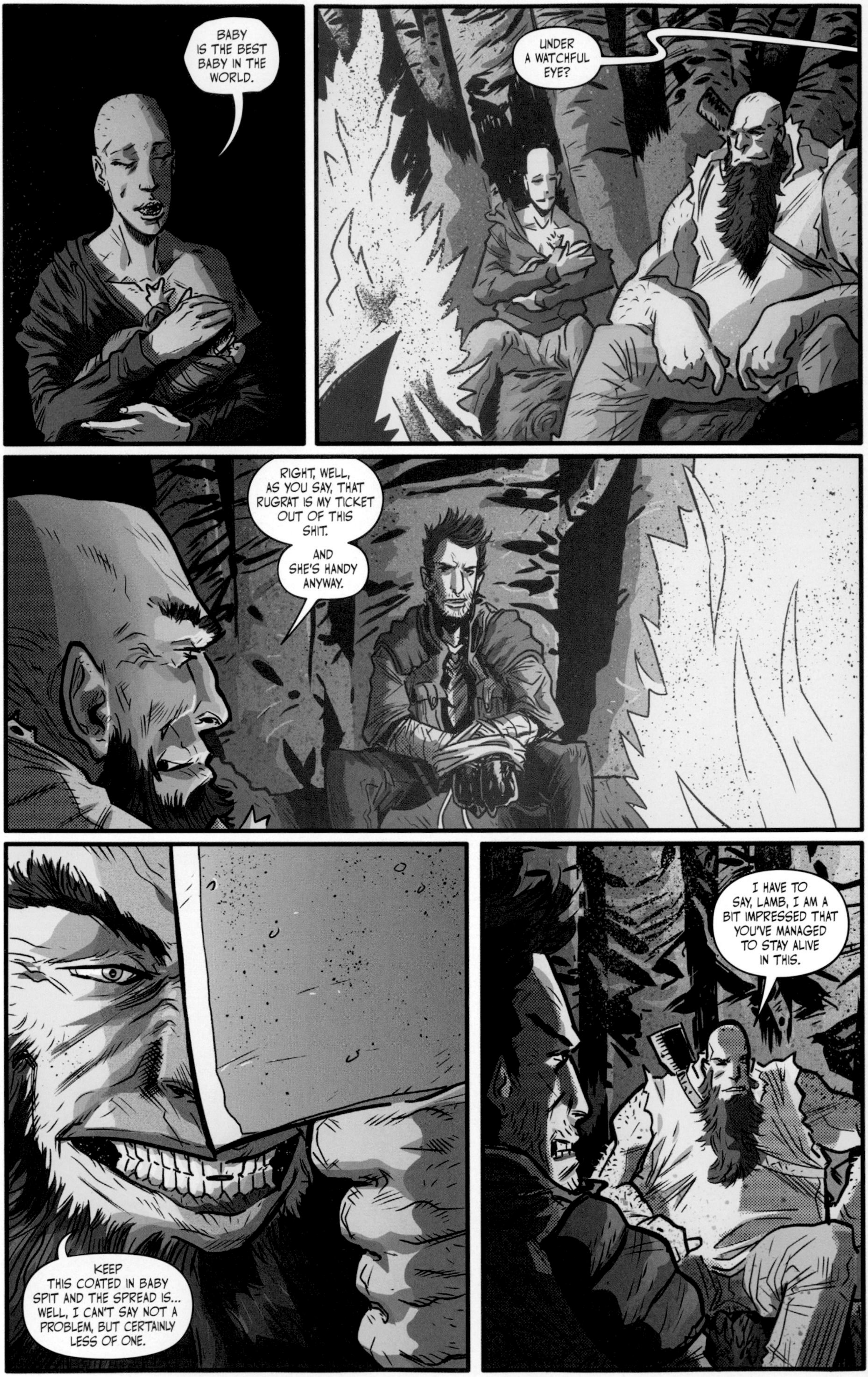
BABY IS THE BEST BABY IN THE WORLD.
UNDER A WATCHFUL EYE?
RIGHT, WELL, AS YOU SAY, THAT RUGRAT IS MY TICKET OUT OF THIS SHIT.
AND SHE'S HANDY ANYWAY.
KEEP THIS COATED IN BABY SPIT AND THE SPREAD IS... WELL, I CAN'T SAY NOT A PROBLEM, BUT CERTAINLY LESS OF ONE.
I HAVE TO SAY, LAMB, I AM A BIT IMPRESSED THAT YOU'VE MANAGED TO STAY ALIVE IN THIS.

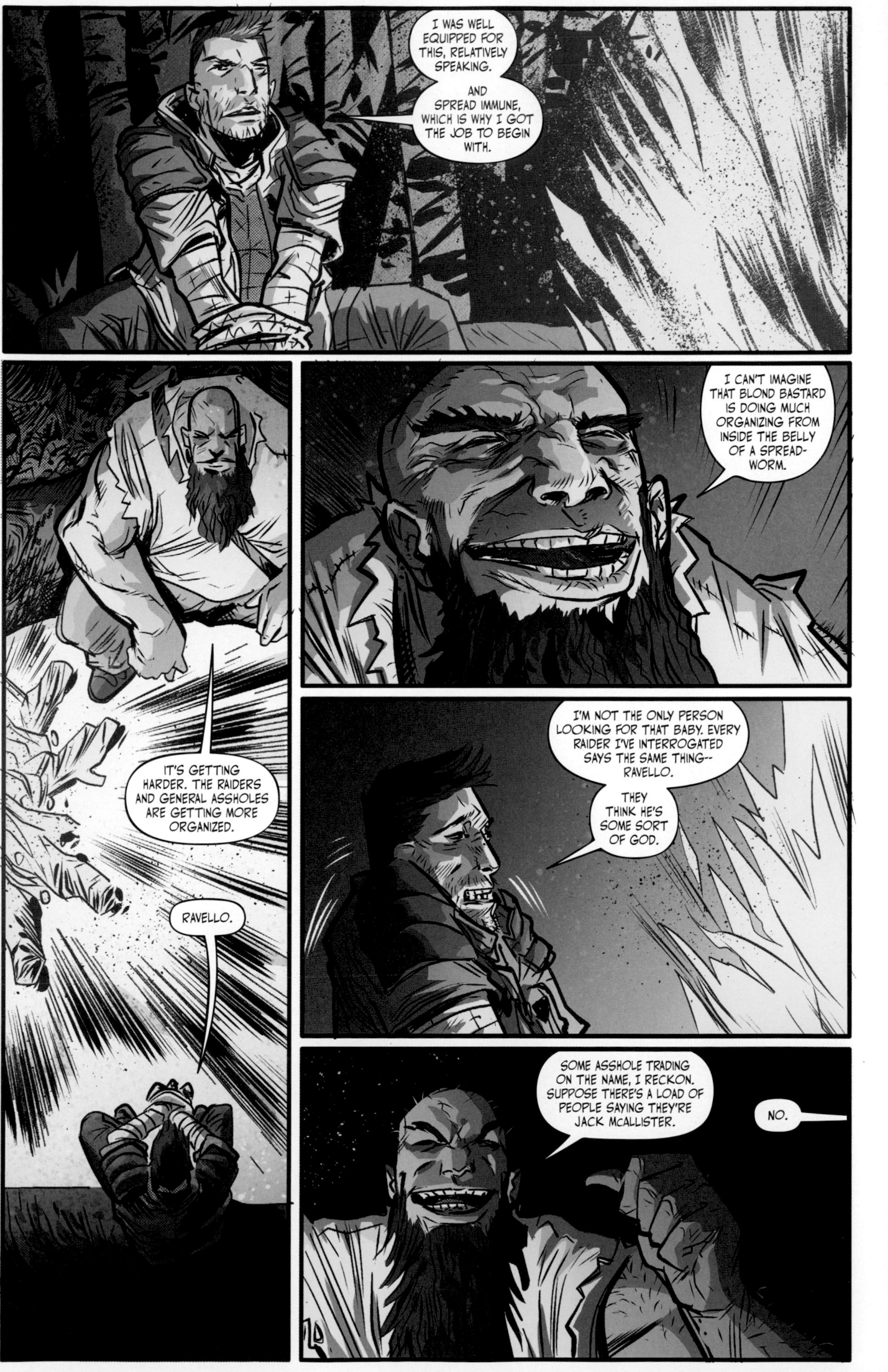
I WAS WELL EQUIPPED FOR THIS, RELATIVELY SPEAKING.
AND SPREAD IMMUNE, WHICH IS WHY I GOT THE JOB TO BEGIN WITH.
I CAN'T IMAGINE THAT BLOND BASTARD IS DOING MUCH ORGANIZING FROM INSIDE THE BELLY OF A SPREAD-WORM.
IT'S GETTING HARDER. THE RAIDERS AND GENERAL ASSHOLES ARE GETTING MORE ORGANIZED.
I'M NOT THE ONLY PERSON LOOKING FOR THAT BABY. EVERY RAIDER I'VE INTERROGATED SAYS THE SAME THING-- RAVELLO.
THEY THINK HE'S SOME SORT OF GOD.
RAVELLO.
SOME ASSHOLE TRADING ON THE NAME, I RECKON. SUPPOSE THERE'S A LOAD OF PEOPLE SAYING THEY'RE JACK McALLISTER.
NO.

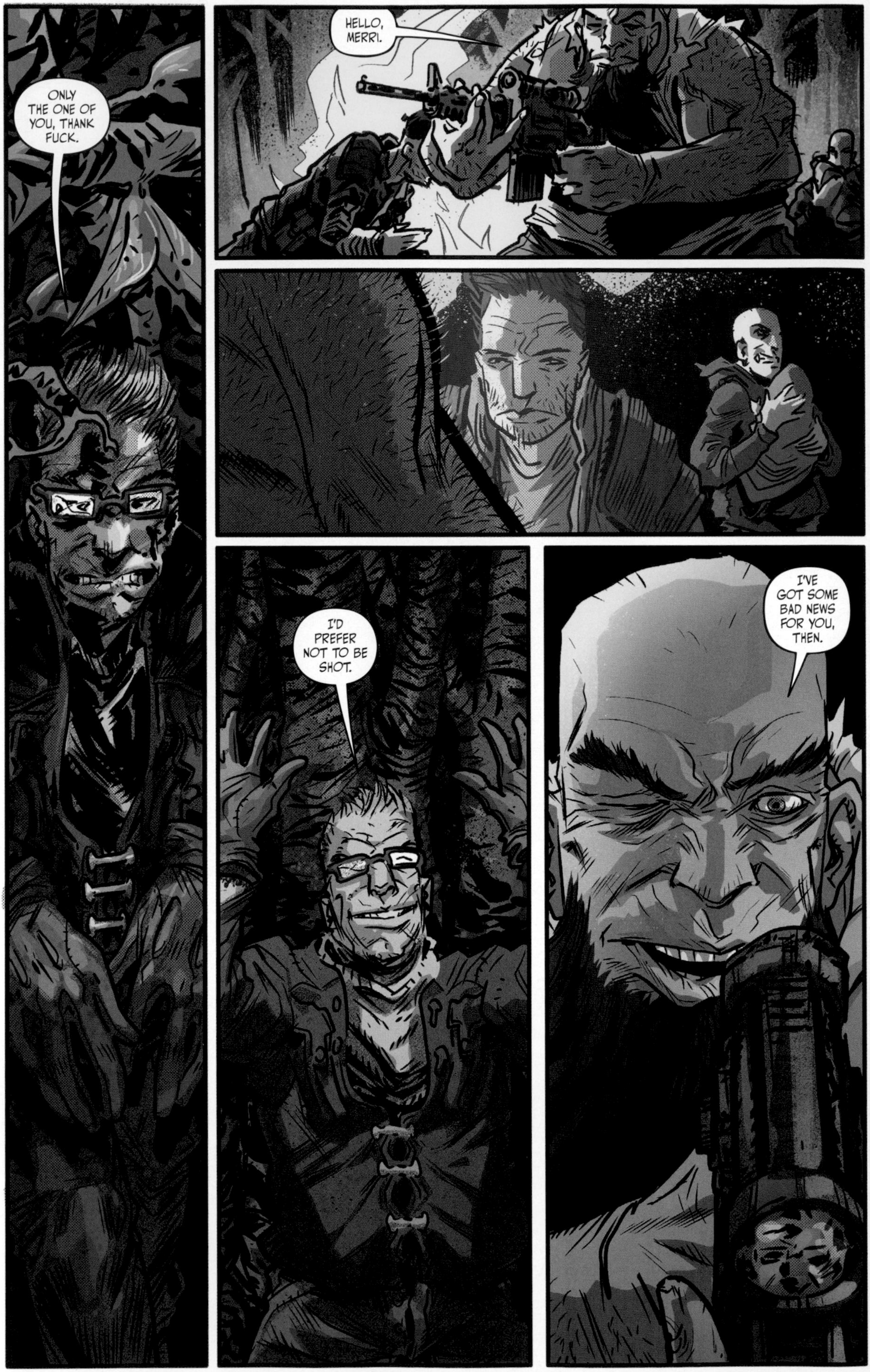
ONLY THE ONE OF YOU, THANK FUCK.
HELLO, MERRI.
I'D PREFER NOT TO BE SHOT.
I'VE GOT SOME BAD NEWS FOR YOU, THEN.

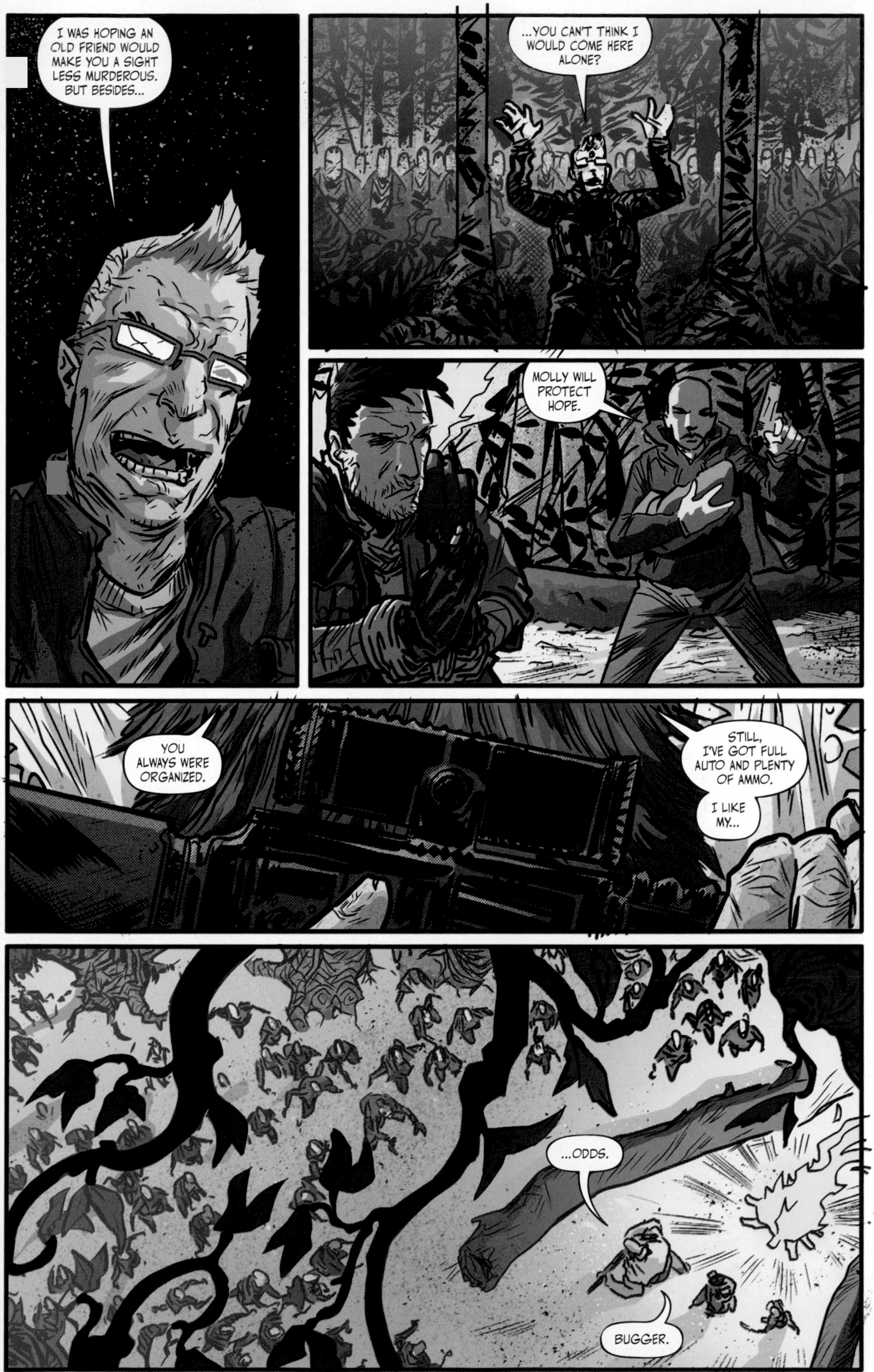

I WAS HOPING AN OLD FRIEND WOULD MAKE YOU A SIGHT LESS MURDEROUS. BUT BESIDES...
...YOU CAN'T THINK I WOULD COME HERE ALONE?
MOLLY WILL PROTECT HOPE.
YOU ALWAYS WERE ORGANIZED.
STILL, I'VE GOT FULL AUTO AND PLENTY OF AMMO.
I LIKE MY...
...ODDS.
BUGGER.

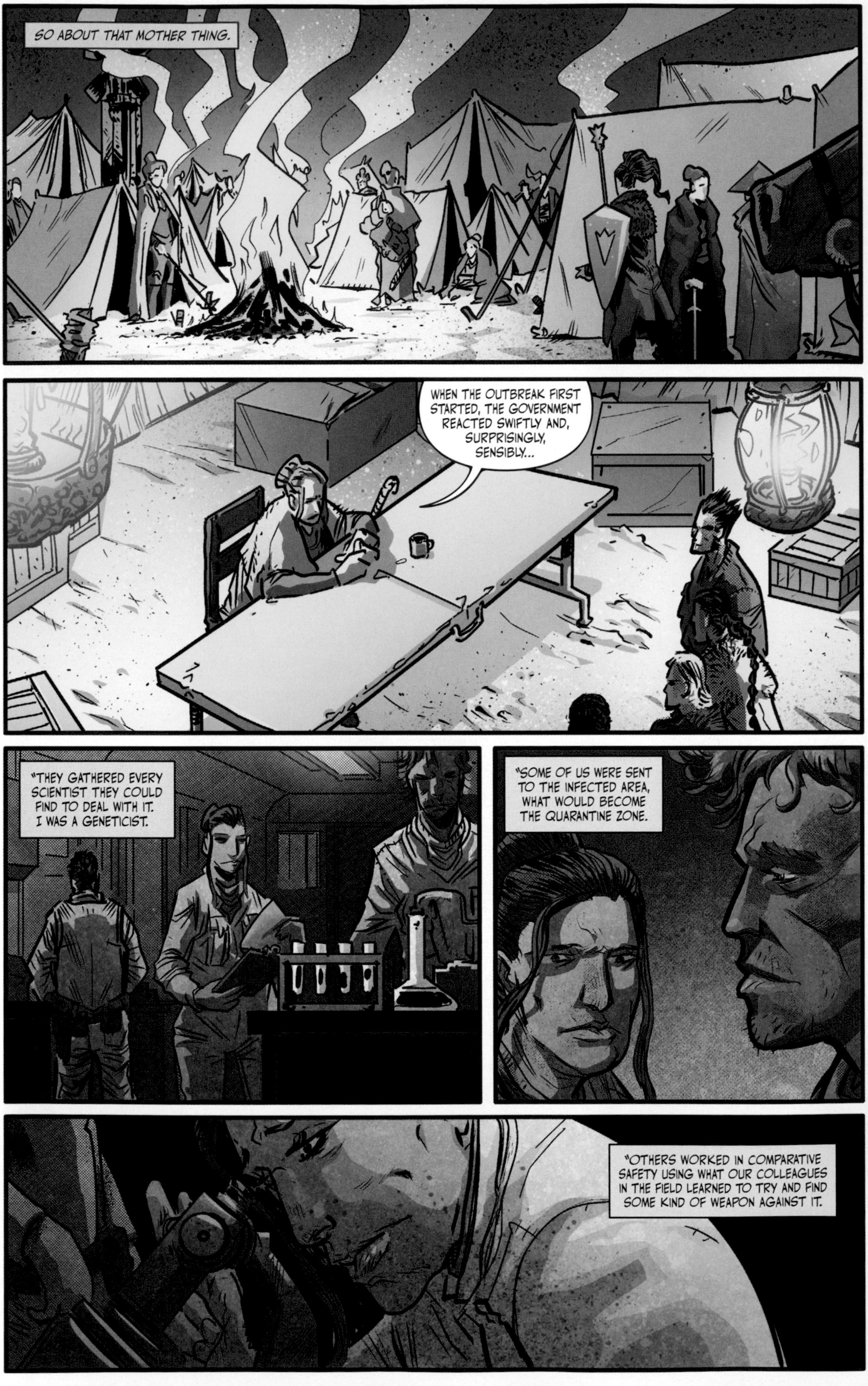
SO ABOUT THAT MOTHER THING.
WHEN THE OUTBREAK FIRST STARTED, THE GOVERNMENT REACTED SWIFTLY AND, SURPRISINGLY, SENSIBLY...
"THEY GATHERED EVERY SCIENTIST THEY COULD FIND TO DEAL WITH IT. I WAS A GENETICIST.
"SOME OF US WERE SENT TO THE INFECTED AREA, WHAT WOULD BECOME THE QUARANTINE ZONE.
"OTHERS WORKED IN COMPARATIVE SAFETY USING WHAT OUR COLLEAGUES IN THE FIELD LEARNED TO TRY AND FIND SOME KIND OF WEAPON AGAINST IT.

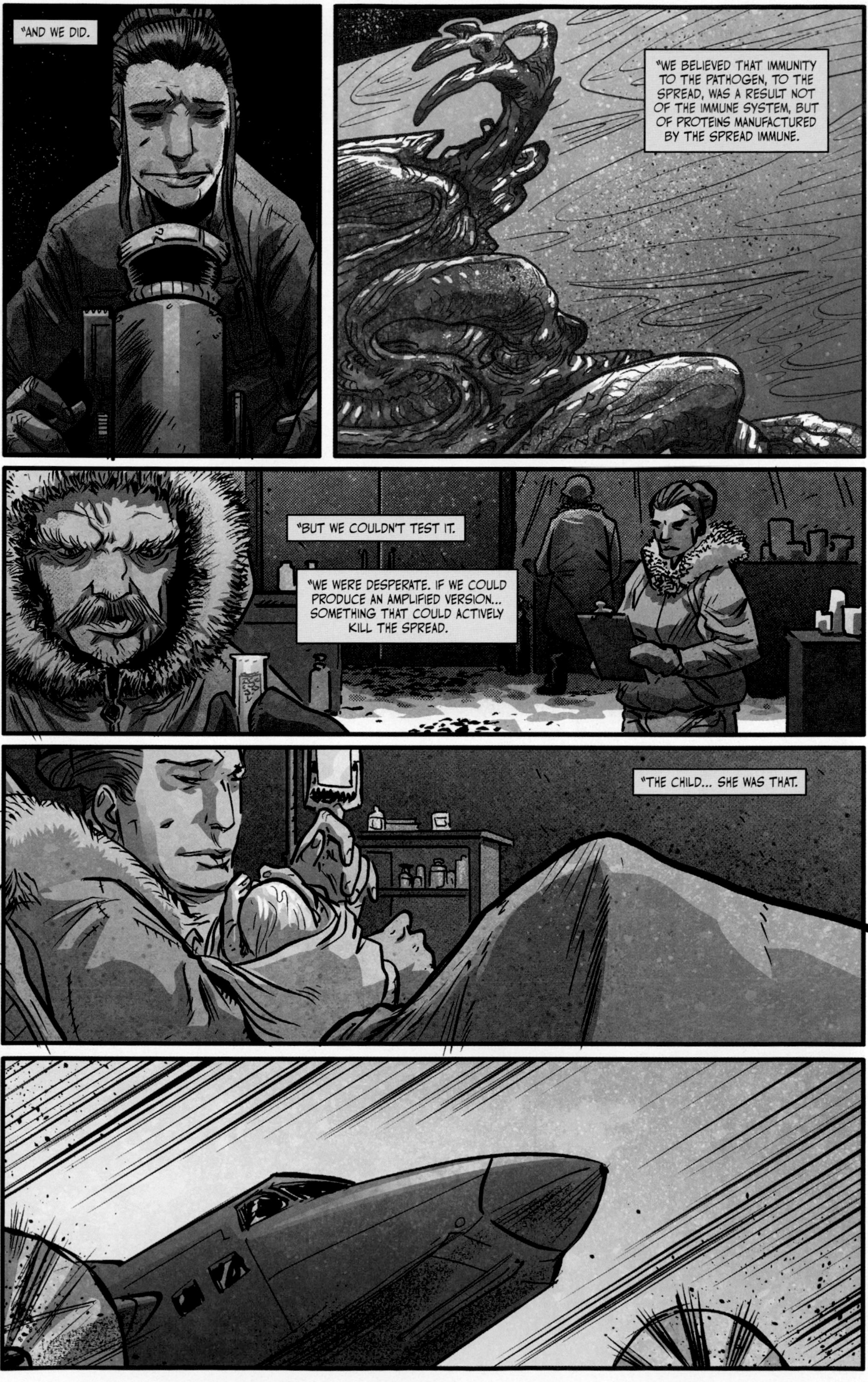
"AND WE DID.
"WE BELIEVED THAT IMMUNITY TO THE PATHOGEN, TO THE SPREAD, WAS A RESULT NOT OF THE IMMUNE SYSTEM, BUT OF PROTEINS MANUFACTURED BY THE SPREAD IMMUNE.
"BUT WE COULDN'T TEST IT.
"WE WERE DESPERATE. IF WE COULD PRODUCE AN AMPLIFIED VERSION... SOMETHING THAT COULD ACTIVELY KILL THE SPREAD.
"THE CHILD... SHE WAS THAT.

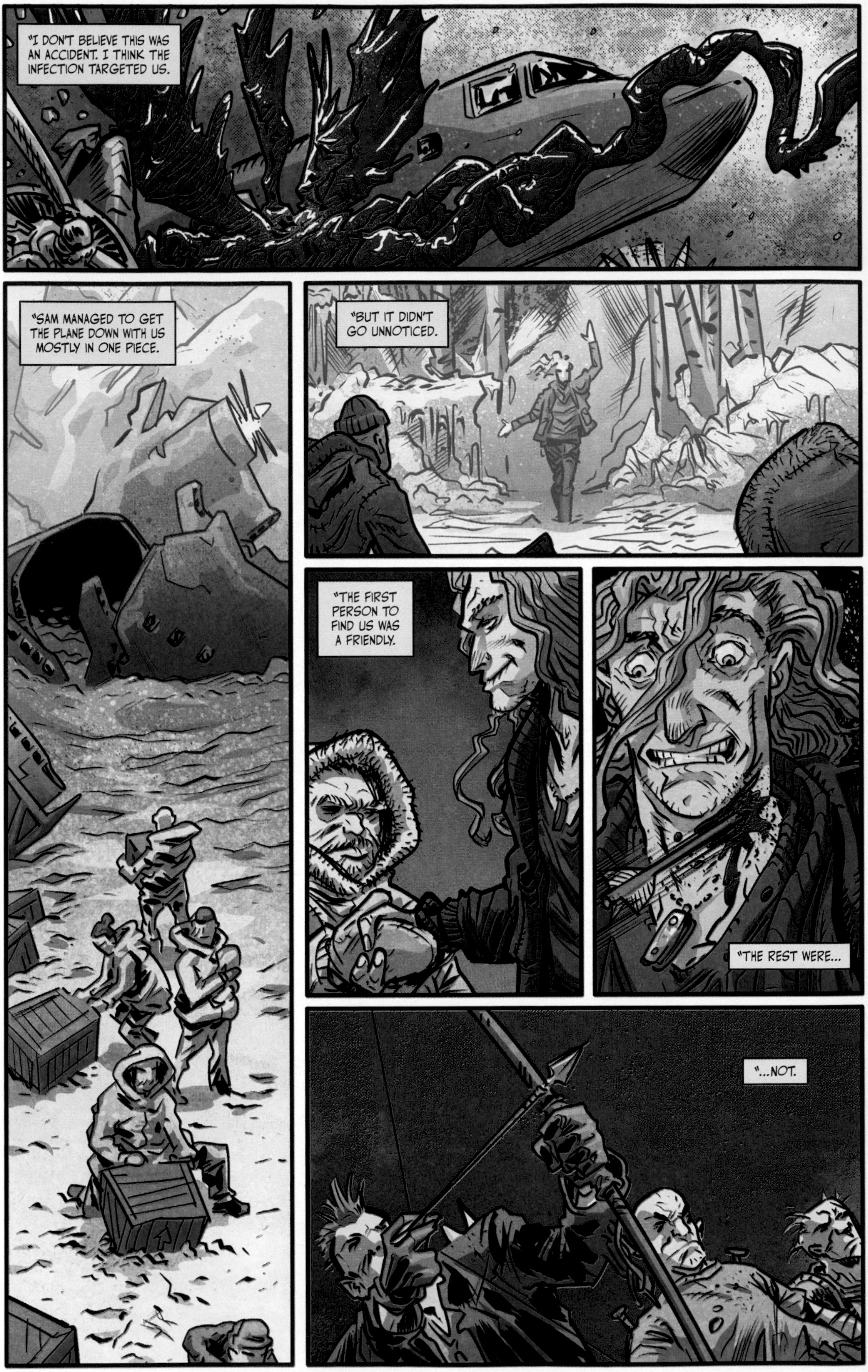
"I DON'T BELIEVE THIS WAS AN ACCIDENT. I THINK THE INFECTION TARGETED US.
"SAM MANAGED TO GET THE PLANE DOWN WITH US MOSTLY IN ONE PIECE.
"BUT IT DIDN'T GO UNNOTICED.
"THE FIRST PERSON TO FIND US WAS A FRIENDLY.
"THE REST WERE...
"...NOT.

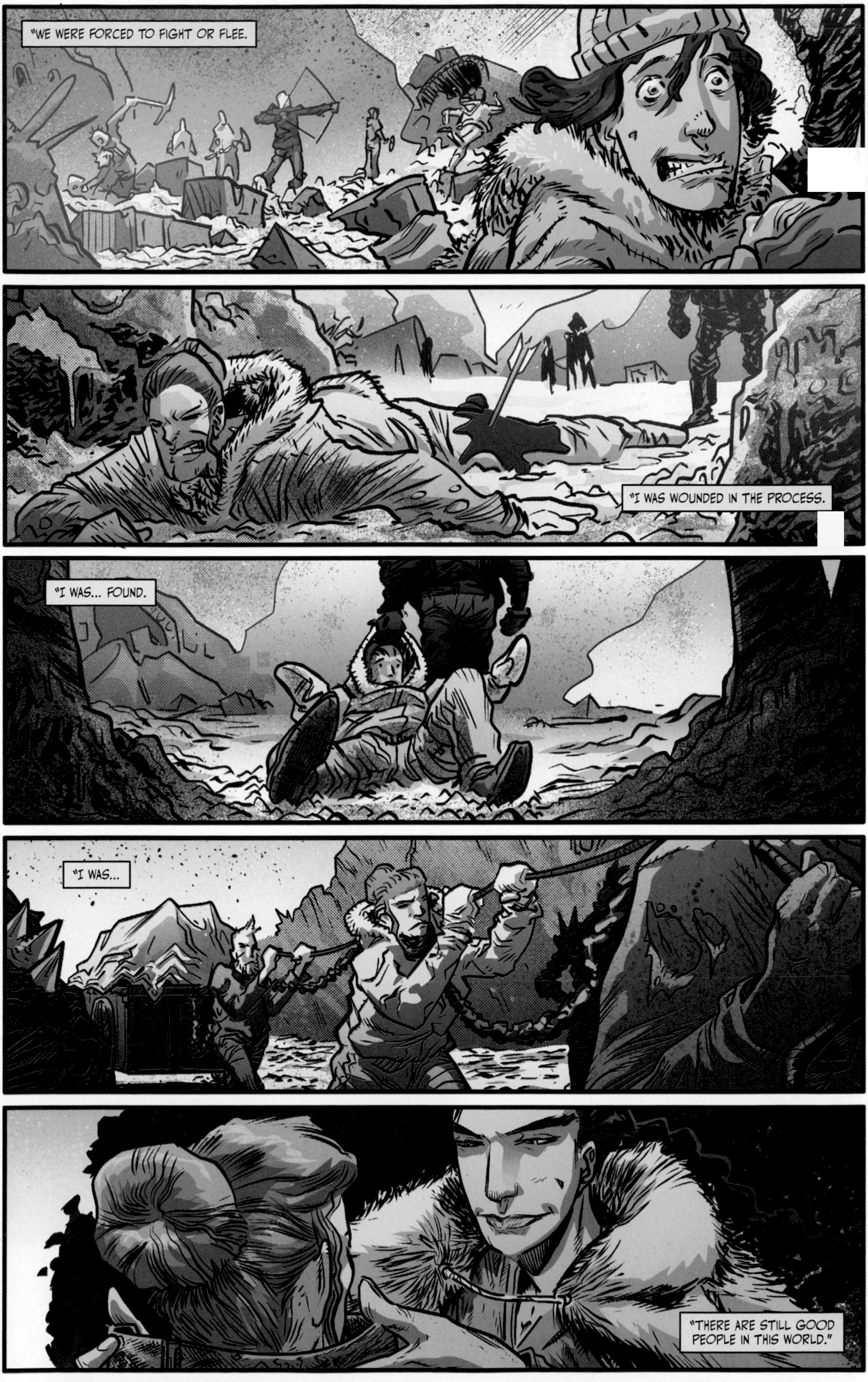
"WE WERE FORCED TO FIGHT OR FLEE.
"I WAS WOUNDED IN THE PROCESS.
"I WAS... FOUND.
"I WAS...
"THERE ARE STILL GOOD PEOPLE IN THIS WORLD."

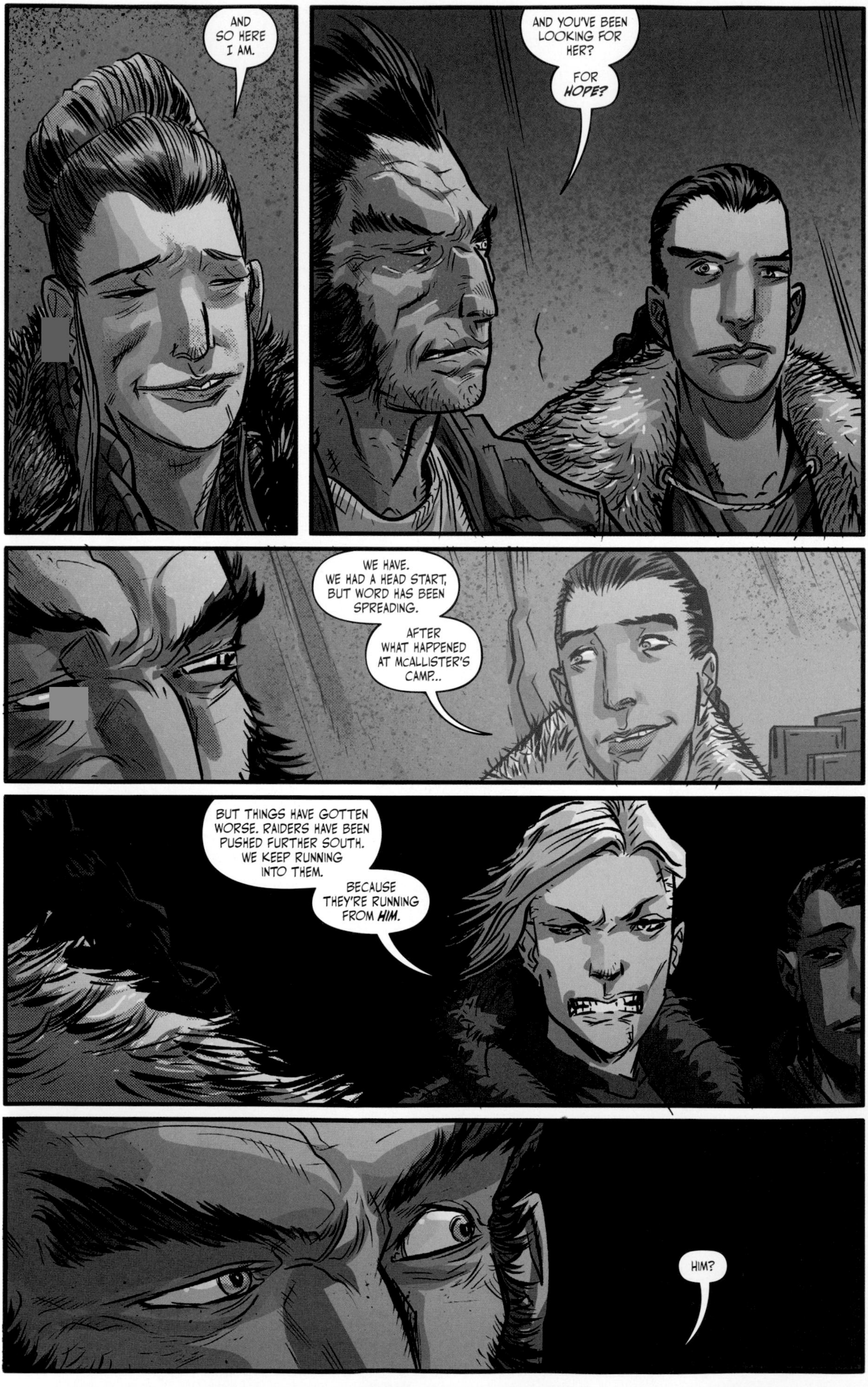
AND SO HERE I AM.
AND YOU'VE BEEN LOOKING FOR HER?
FOR HOPE?
WE HAVE. WE HAD A HEAD START, BUT WORD HAS BEEN SPREADING.
AFTER WHAT HAPPENED AT McALLISTER'S CAMP...
BUT THINGS HAVE GOTTEN WORSE. RAIDERS HAVE BEEN PUSHED FURTHER SOUTH. WE KEEP RUNNING INTO THEM.
BECAUSE THEY'RE RUNNING FROM HIM.
HIM?

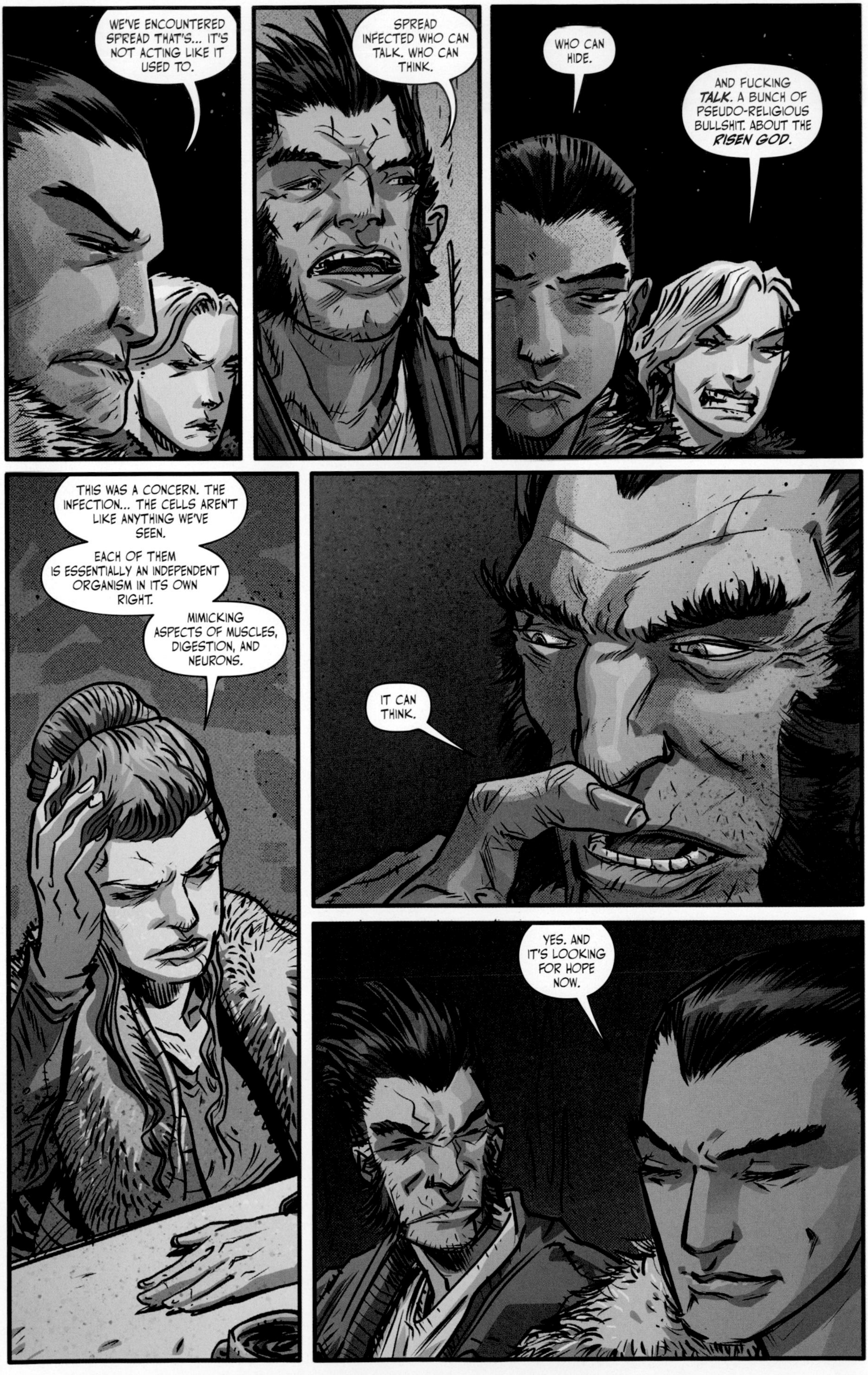
WE'VE ENCOUNTERED SPREAD THAT'S... IT'S NOT ACTING LIKE IT USED TO.
SPREAD INFECTED WHO CAN TALK. WHO CAN THINK.
WHO CAN HIDE.
AND FUCKING *TALK*. A BUNCH OF PSEUDO-RELIGIOUS BULLSHIT. ABOUT THE *RISEN GOD*.
THIS WAS A CONCERN. THE INFECTION... THE CELLS AREN'T LIKE ANYTHING WE'VE SEEN.
EACH OF THEM IS ESSENTIALLY AN INDEPENDENT ORGANISM IN ITS OWN RIGHT.
MIMICKING ASPECTS OF MUSCLES, DIGESTION, AND NEURONS.
IT CAN THINK.
YES. AND IT'S LOOKING FOR HOPE NOW.

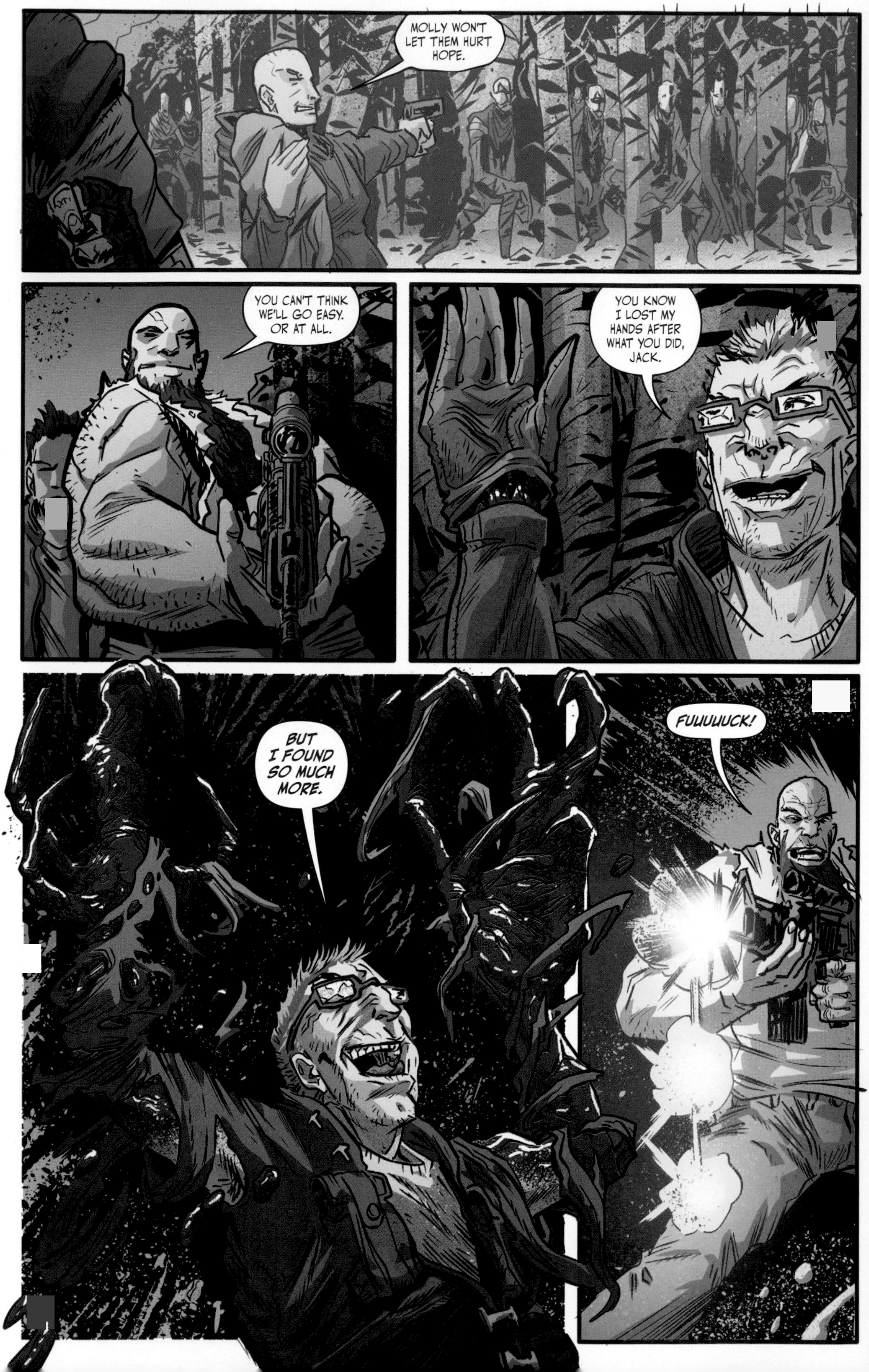
MOLLY WON'T LET THEM HURT HOPE.
YOU CAN'T THINK WE'LL GO EASY. OR AT ALL.
YOU KNOW I LOST MY HANDS AFTER WHAT YOU DID, JACK.
BUT I FOUND SO MUCH MORE.
FUUUUUCK!

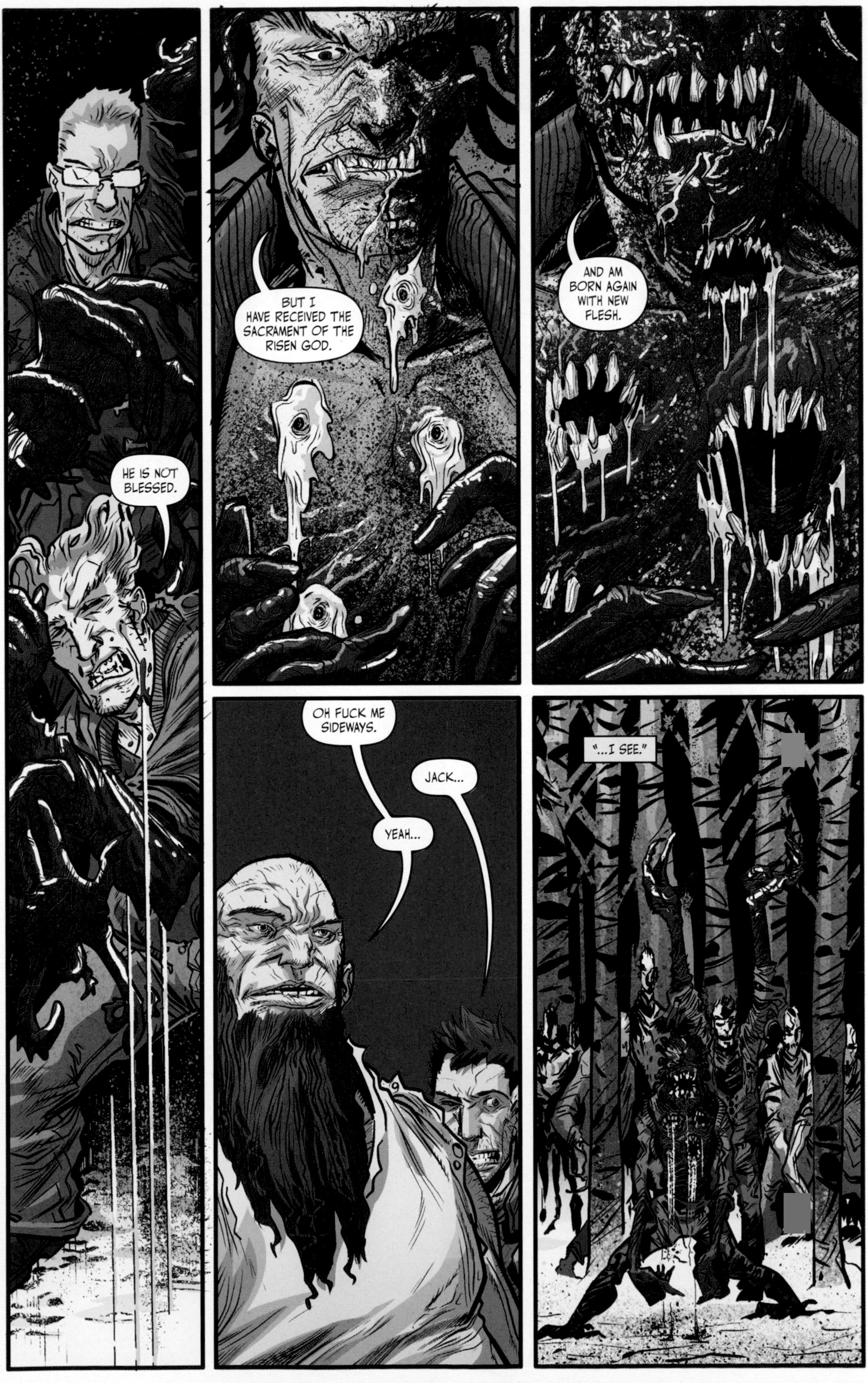
HE IS NOT BLESSED.
BUT I HAVE RECEIVED THE SACRAMENT OF THE RISEN GOD.
AND AM BORN AGAIN WITH NEW FLESH.
OH FUCK ME SIDEWAYS.
YEAH...
JACK...
"...I SEE."

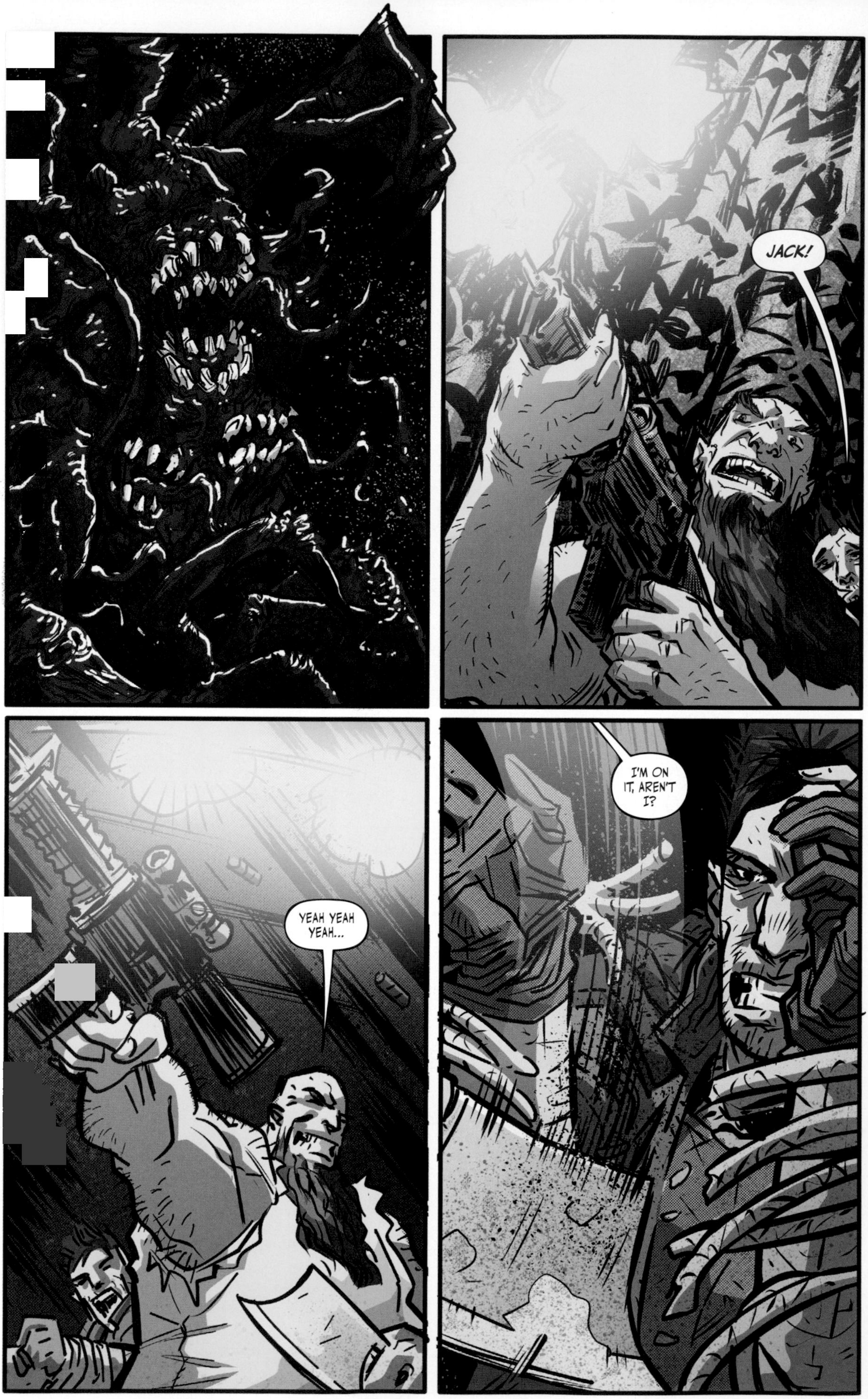
JACK!
YEAH YEAH YEAH...
I'M ON IT, AREN'T I?

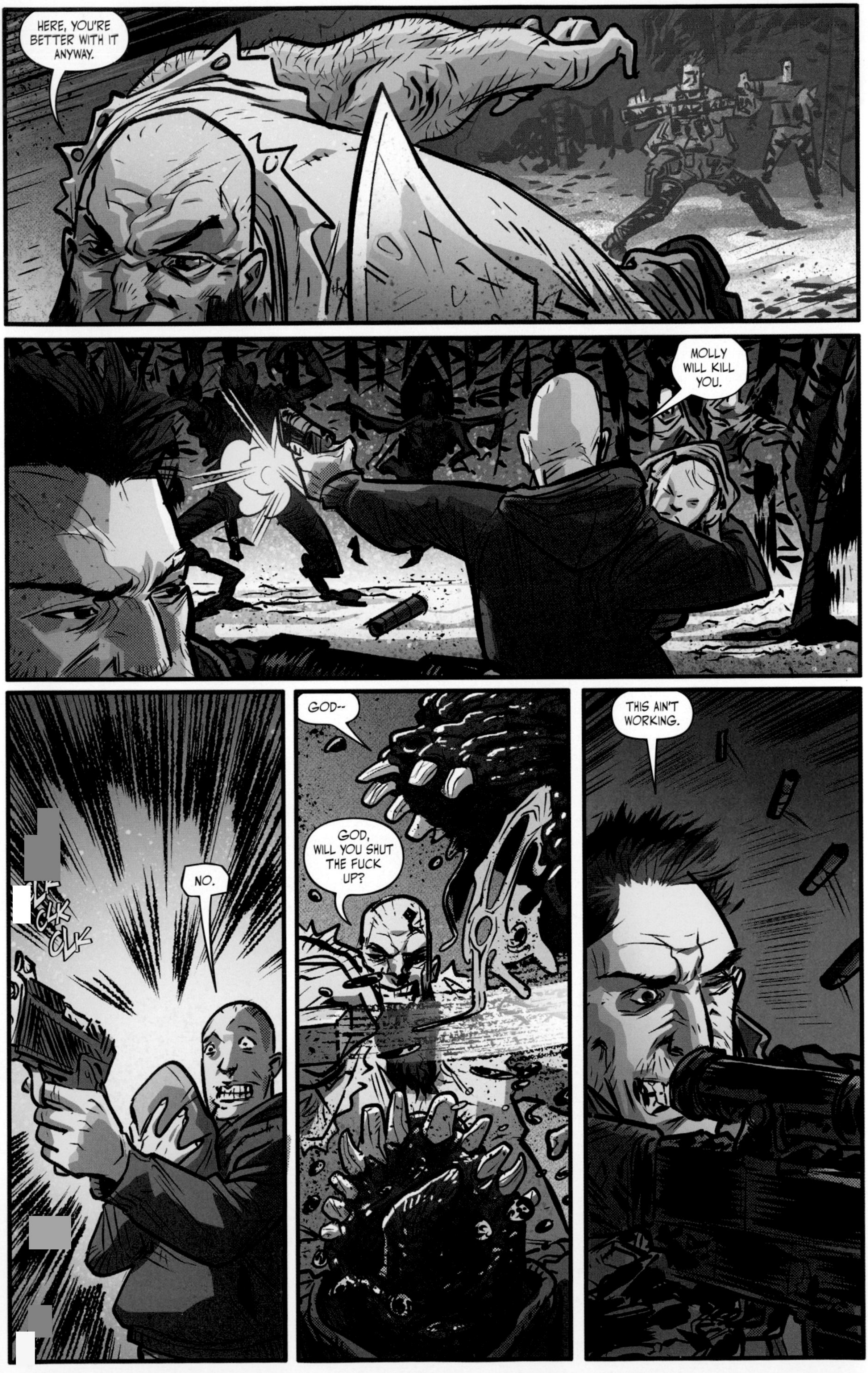
HERE, YOU'RE BETTER WITH IT ANYWAY.
MOLLY WILL KILL YOU.
NO.
GOD--
GOD, WILL YOU SHUT THE FUCK UP?
THIS AIN'T WORKING.

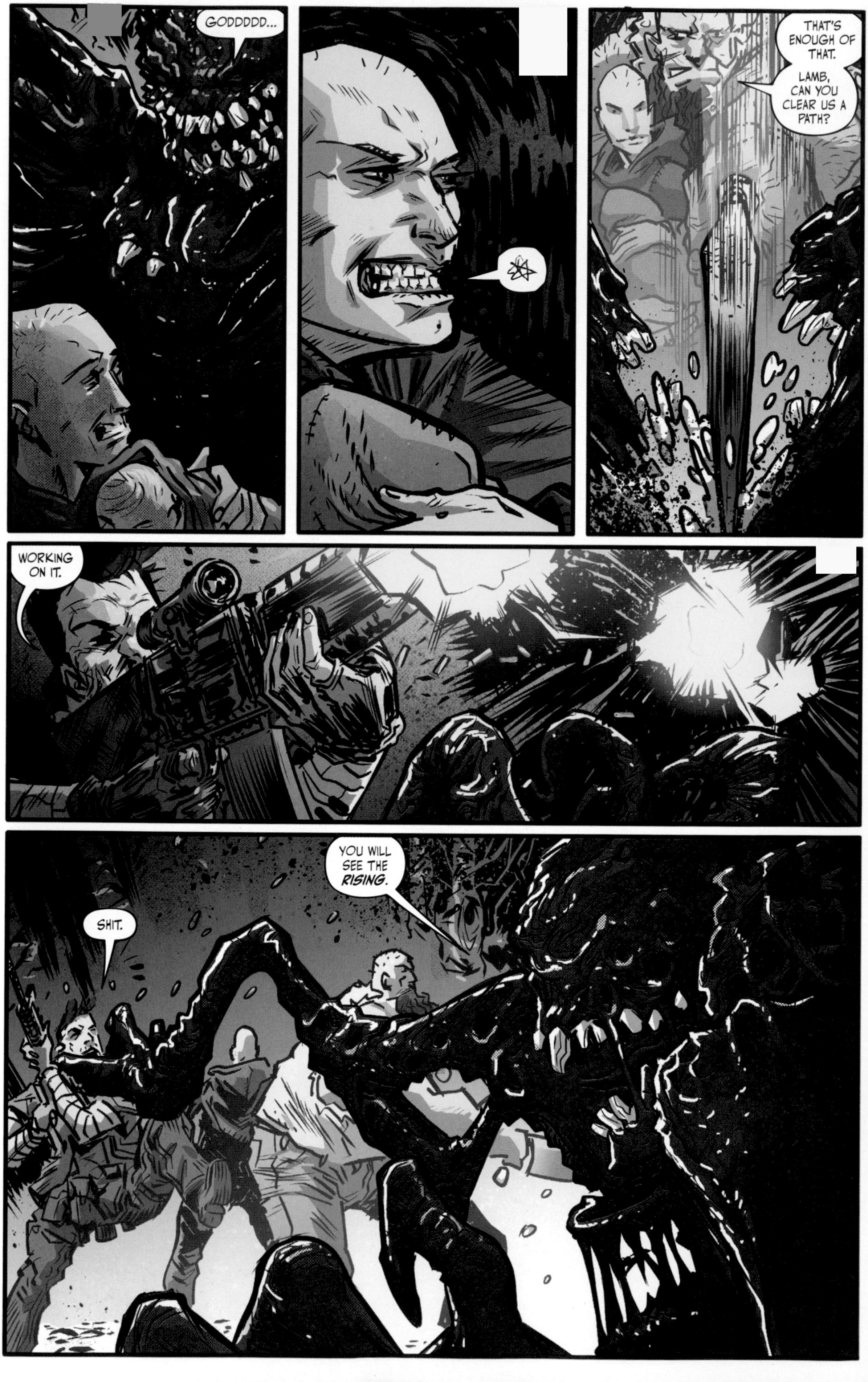
GODDDDD...
THAT'S ENOUGH OF THAT.
LAMB, CAN YOU CLEAR US A PATH?
WORKING ON IT.
YOU WILL SEE THE *RISING*.
SHIT.

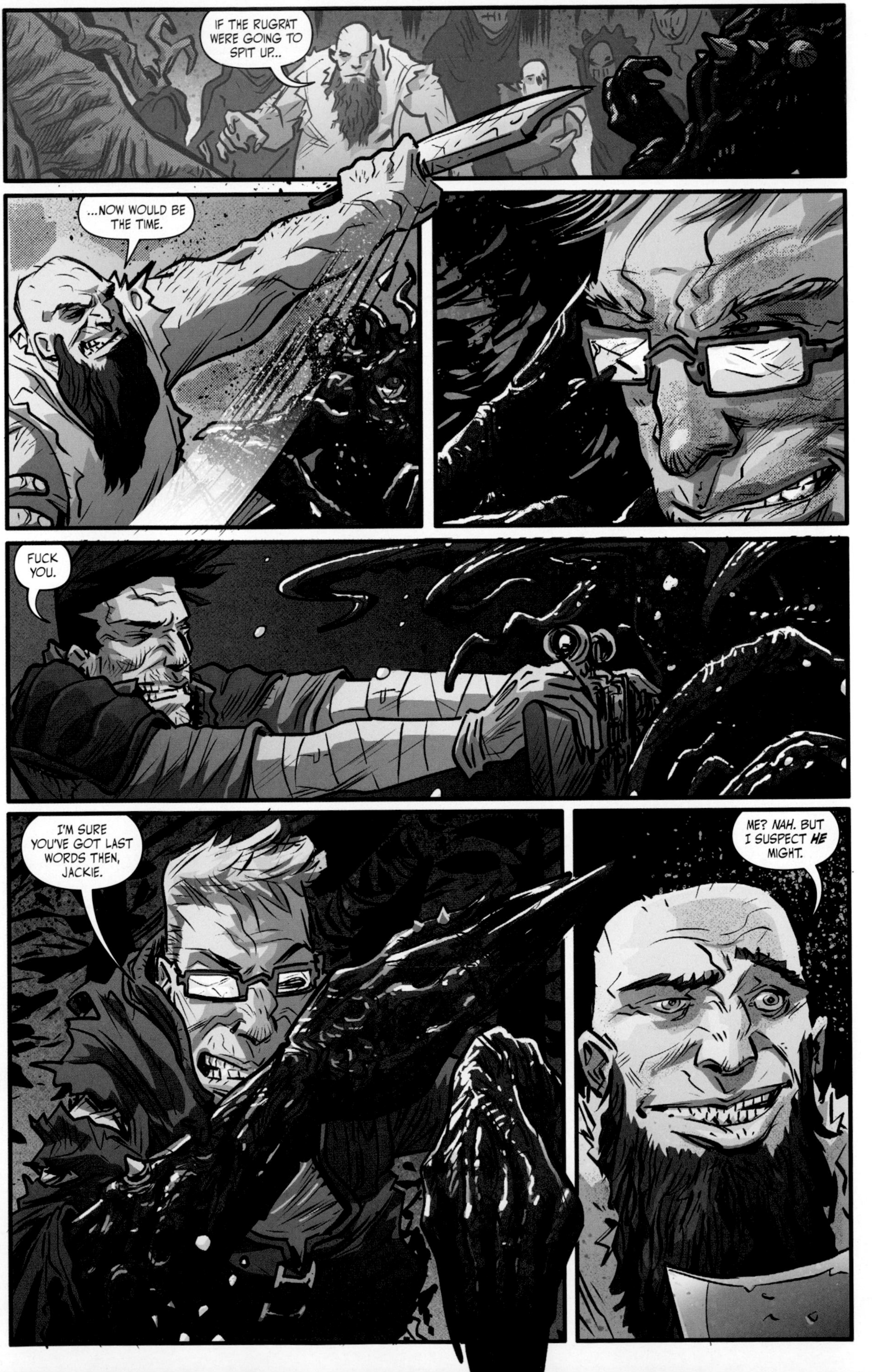
IF THE RUGRAT WERE GOING TO SPIT UP...
...NOW WOULD BE THE TIME.
FUCK YOU.
I'M SURE YOU'VE GOT LAST WORDS THEN, JACKIE.
ME? *NAH*. BUT I SUSPECT ***HE*** MIGHT.

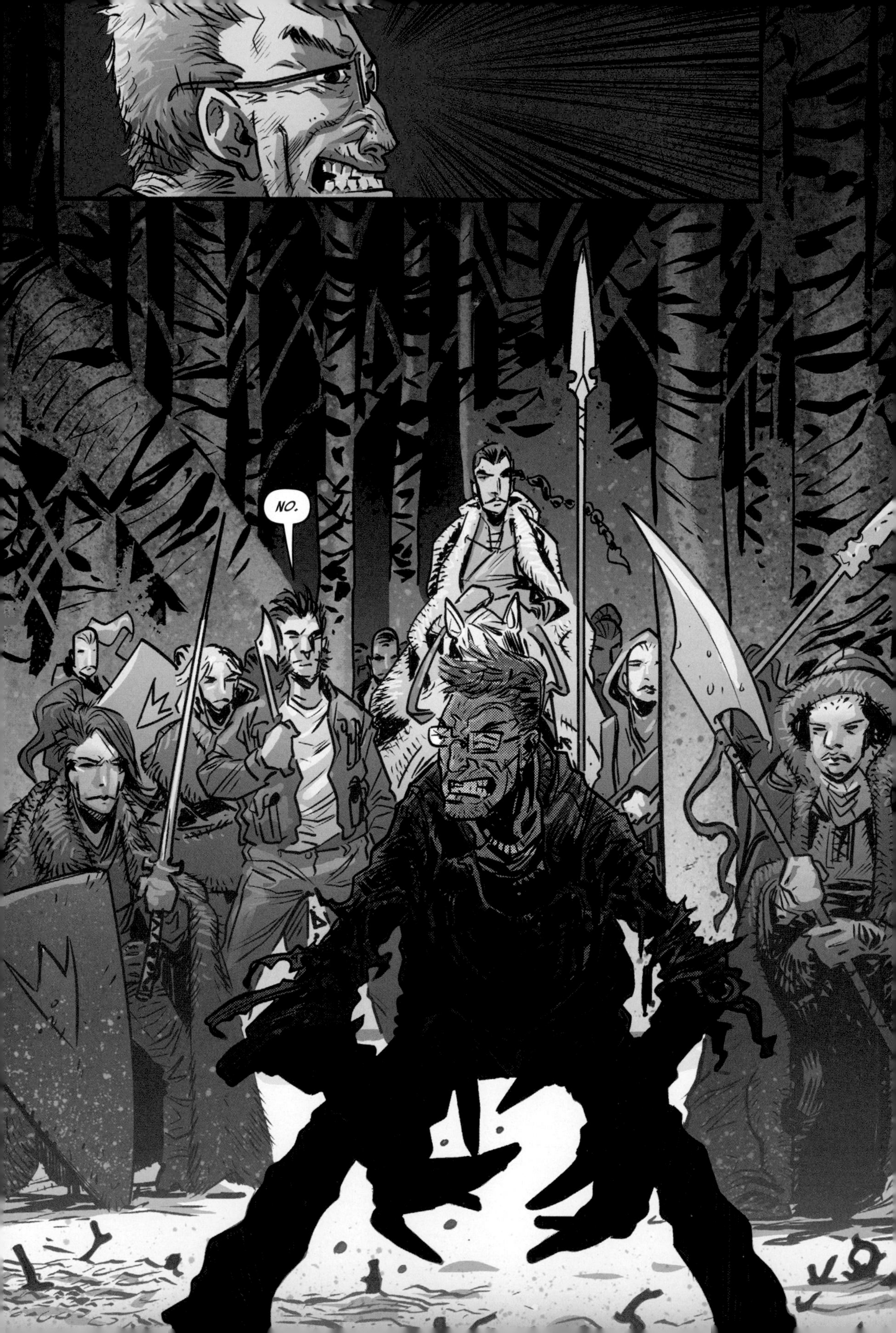
NO.

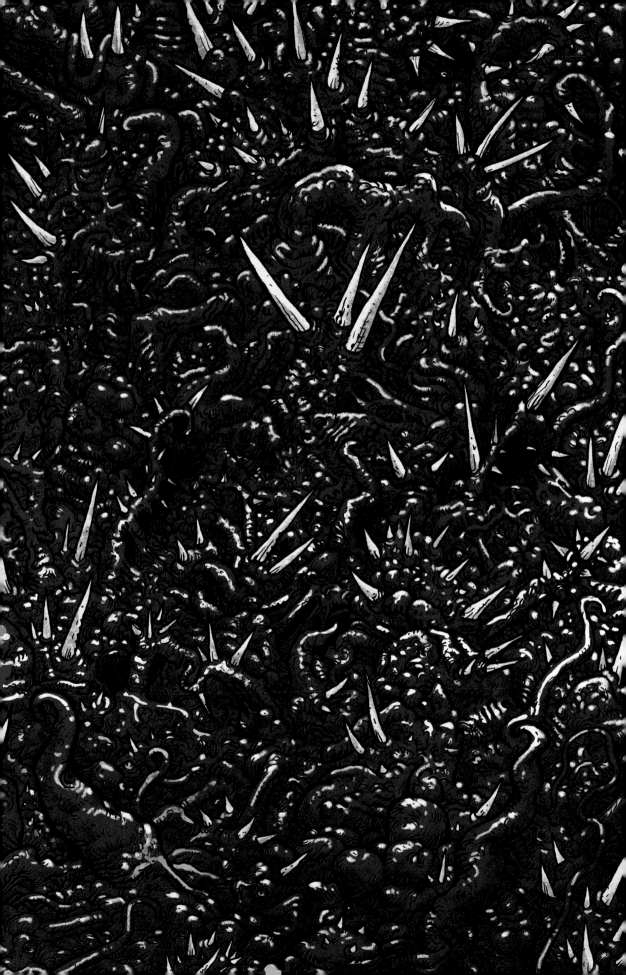

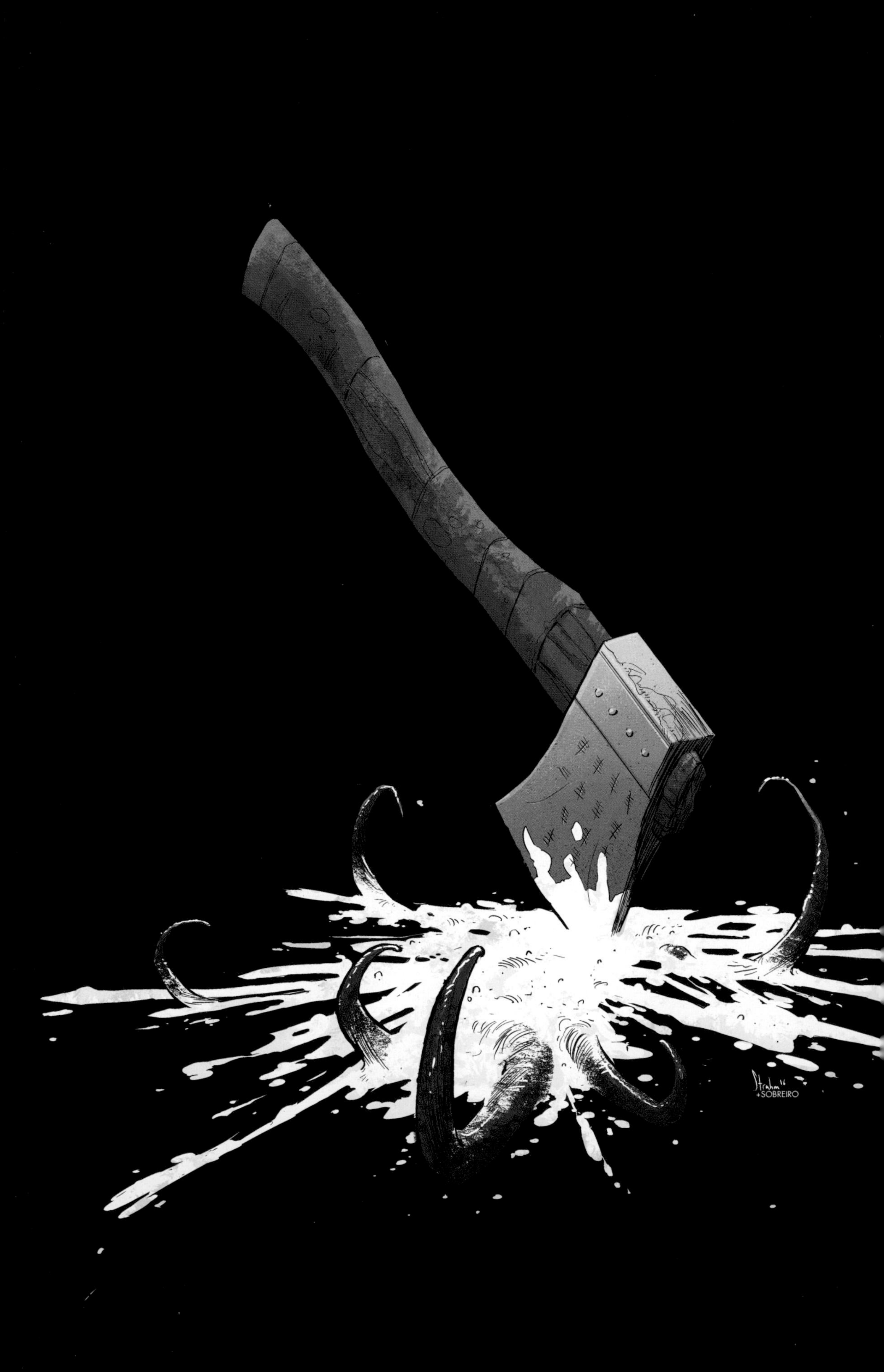
+SOBREIRO

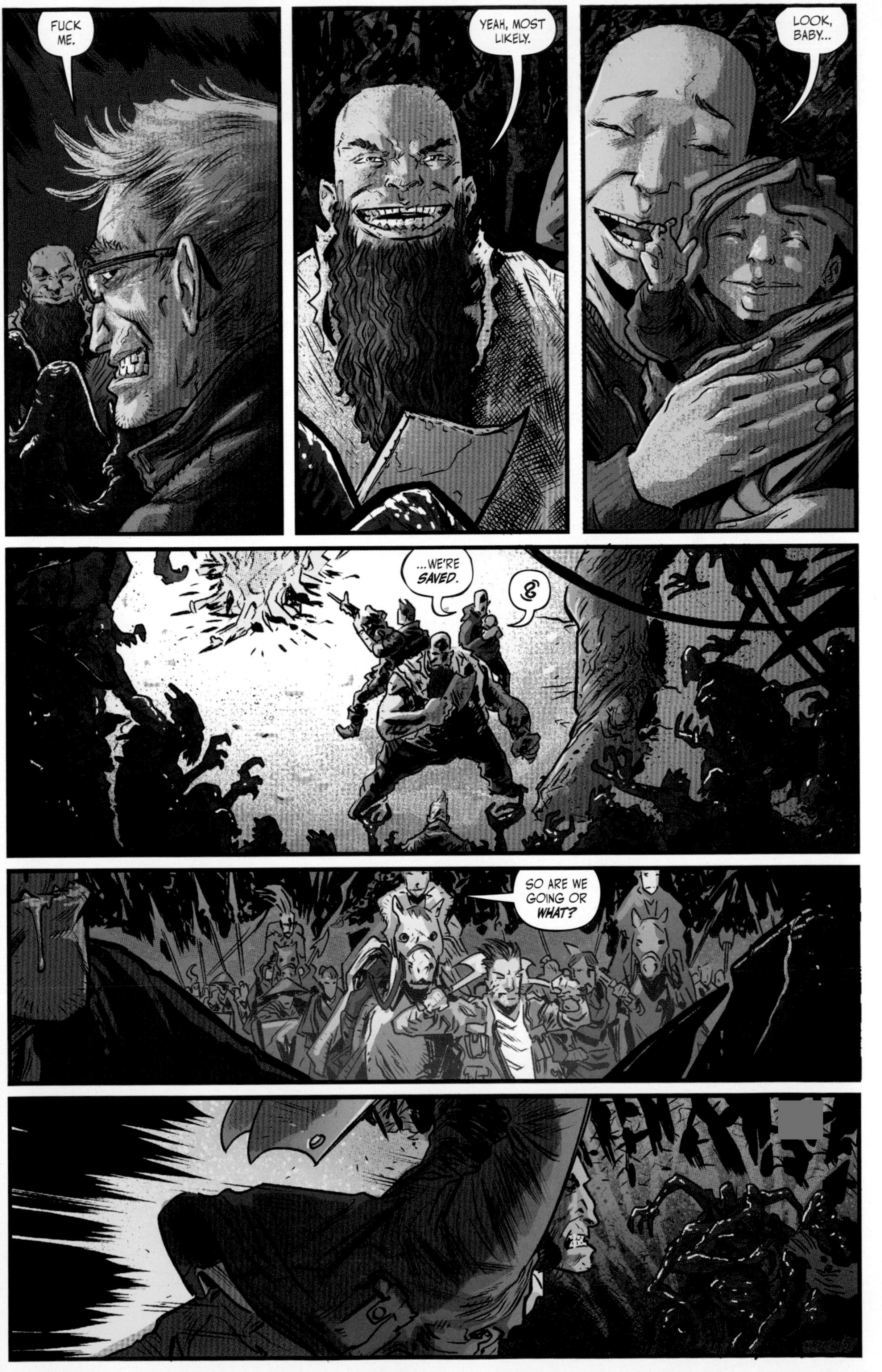
FUCK ME.
YEAH, MOST LIKELY.
LOOK, BABY...
...WE'RE SAVED.
&
SO ARE WE GOING OR WHAT?

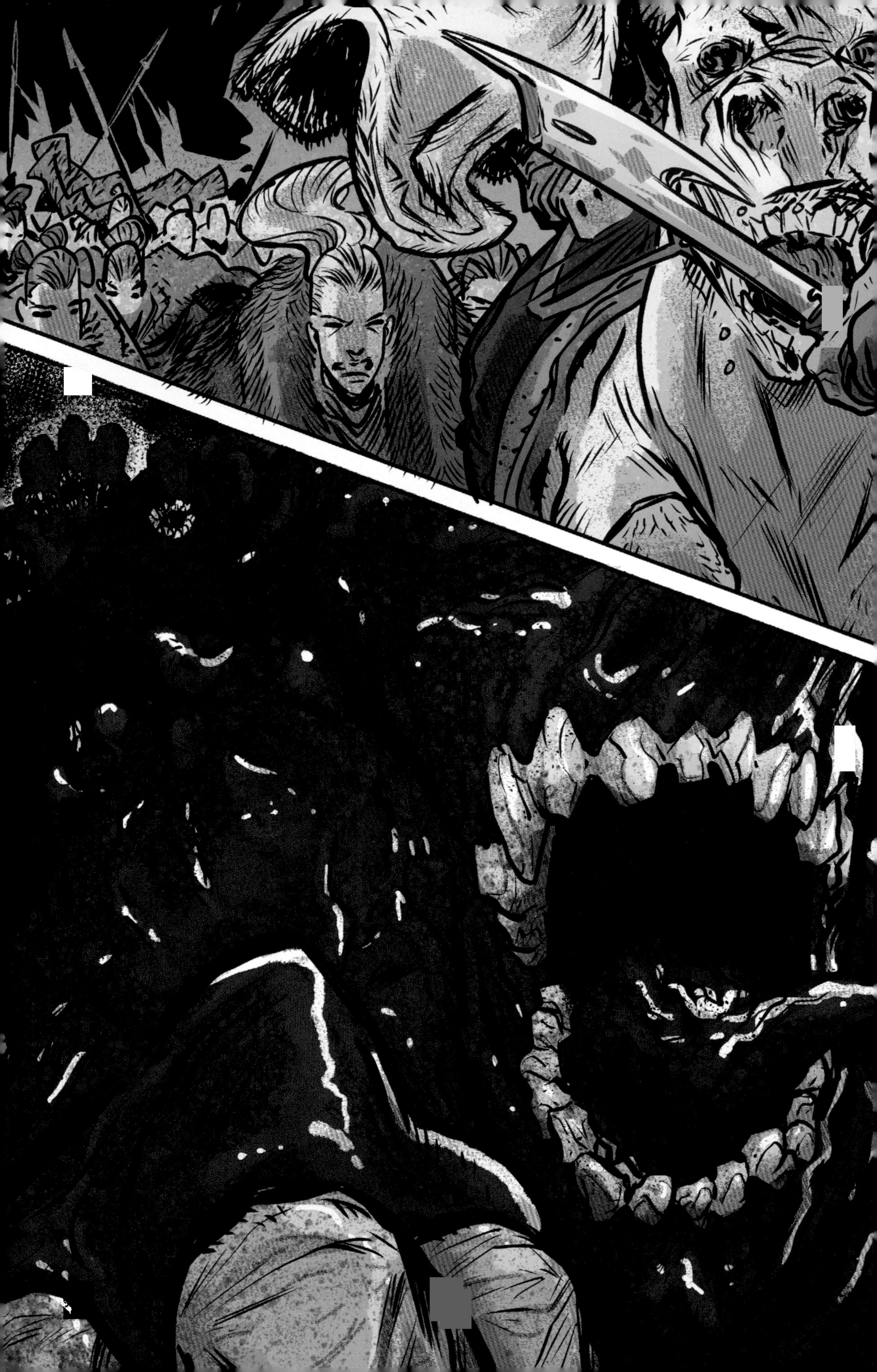

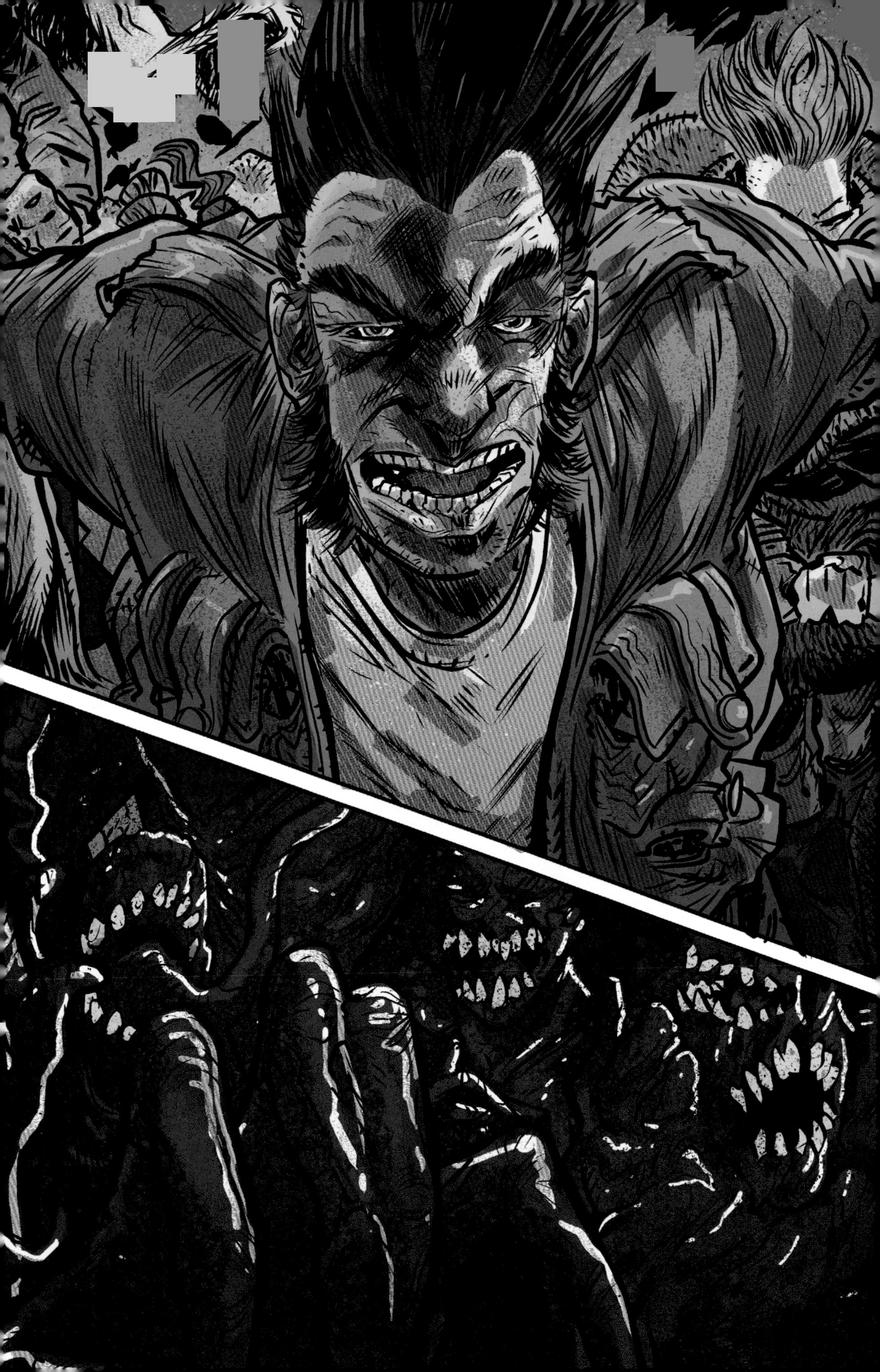

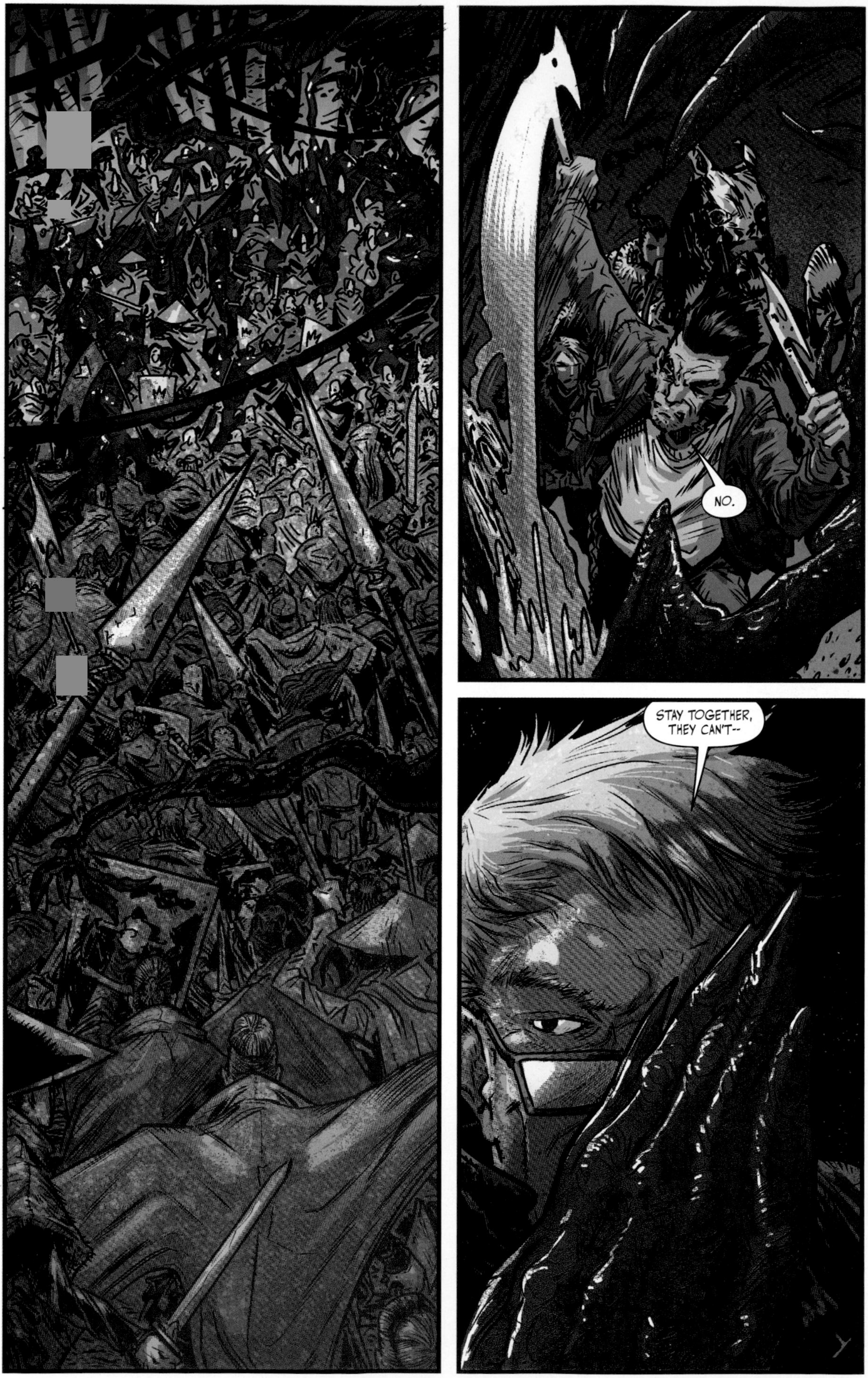
NO.
STAY TOGETHER, THEY CAN'T--

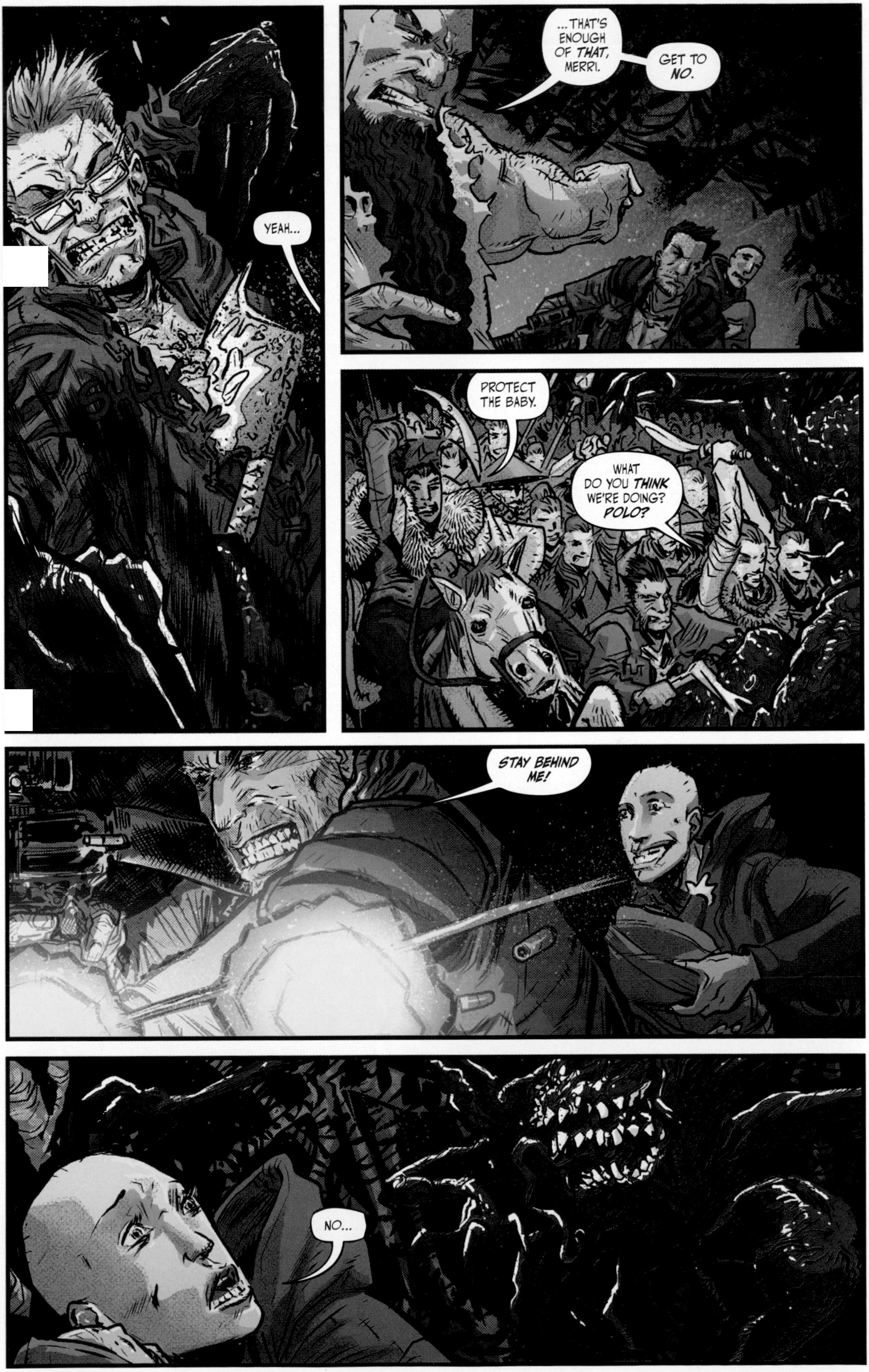
YEAH...
...THAT'S ENOUGH OF THAT, MERRI.
GET TO NO.
PROTECT THE BABY.
WHAT DO YOU THINK WE'RE DOING? POLO?
STAY BEHIND ME!
NO...

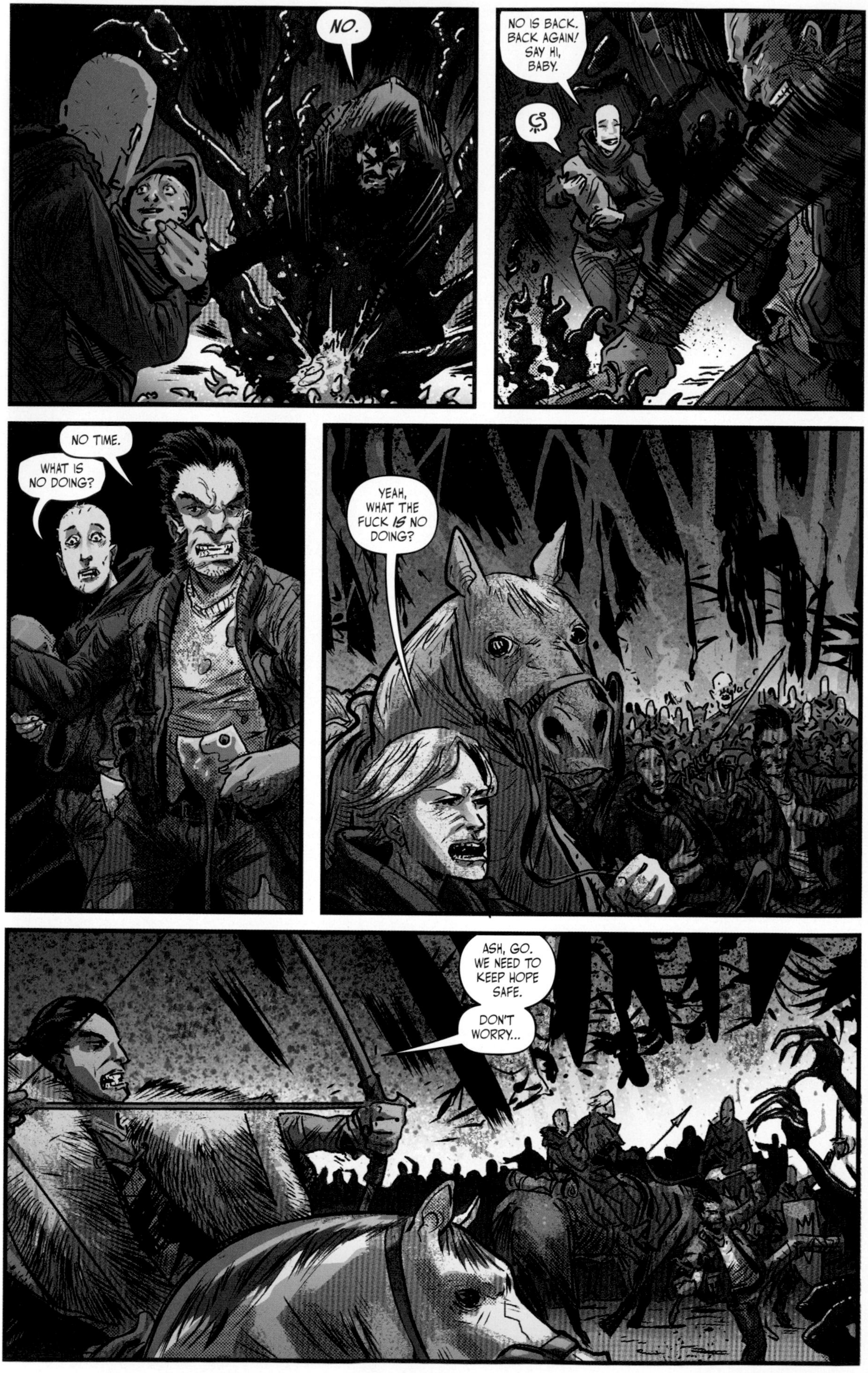
NO.
NO IS BACK. BACK AGAIN! SAY HI, BABY.
NO TIME.
WHAT IS NO DOING?
YEAH, WHAT THE FUCK *IS* NO DOING?
ASH, GO. WE NEED TO KEEP HOPE SAFE.
DON'T WORRY...

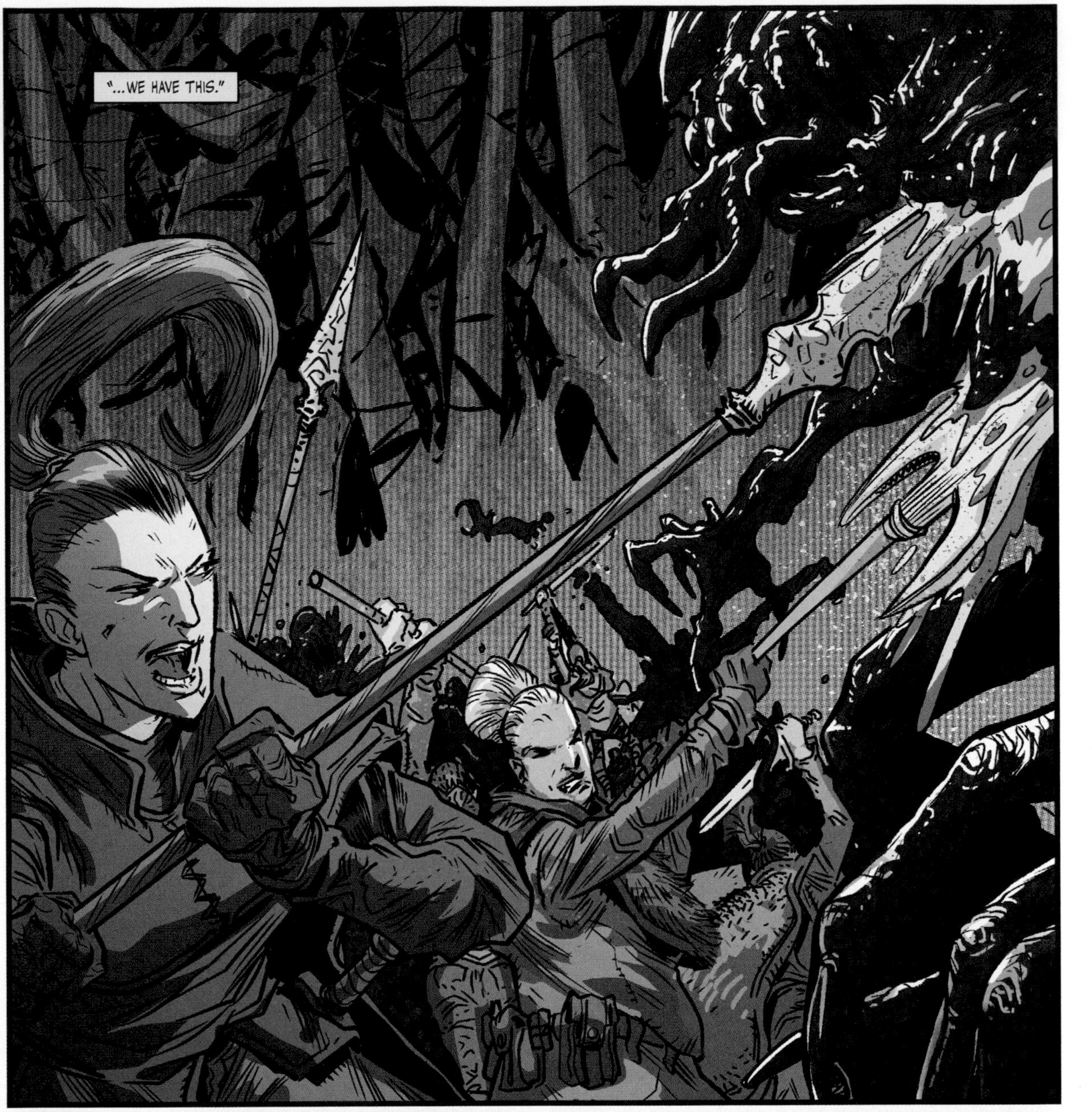
"...WE HAVE THIS."

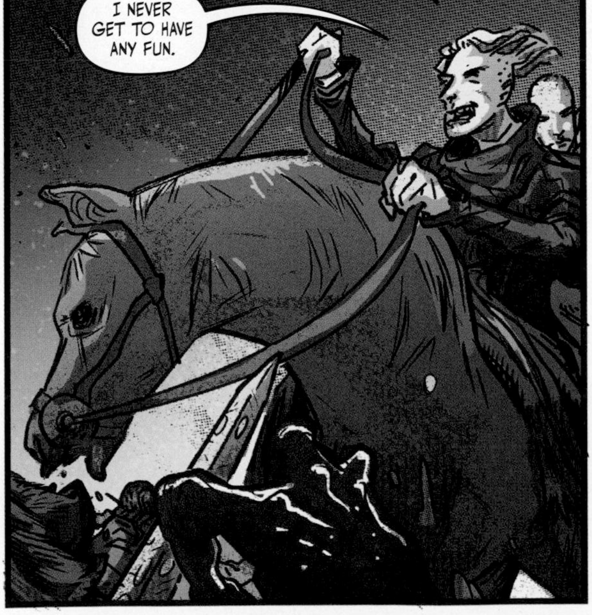
I NEVER GET TO HAVE ANY FUN.

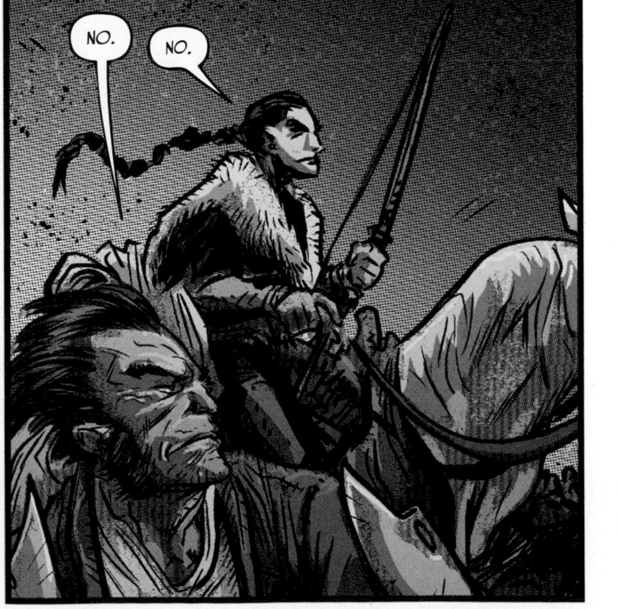
NO.
NO.

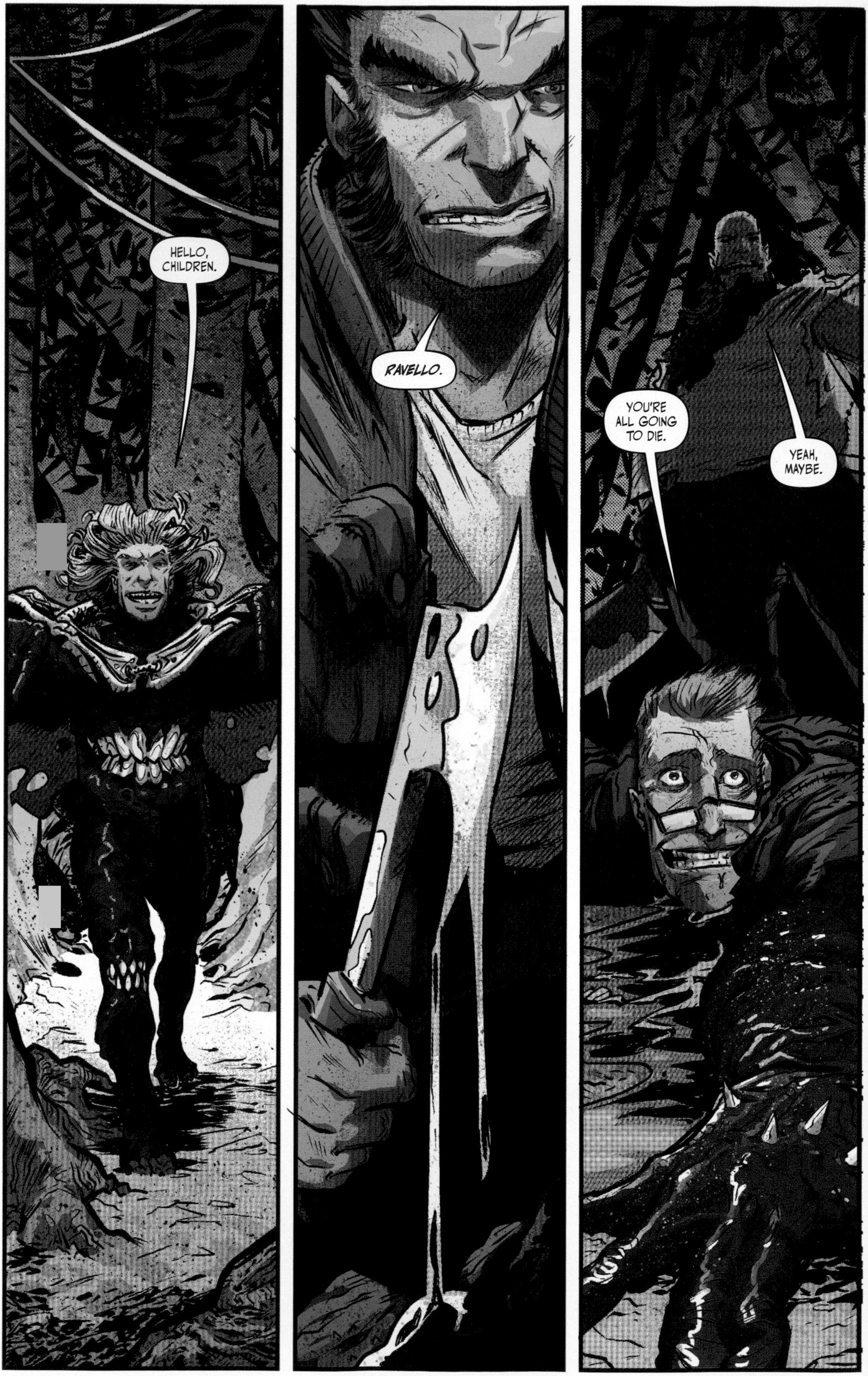
HELLO, CHILDREN.
RAVELLO.
YOU'RE ALL GOING TO DIE.
YEAH, MAYBE.

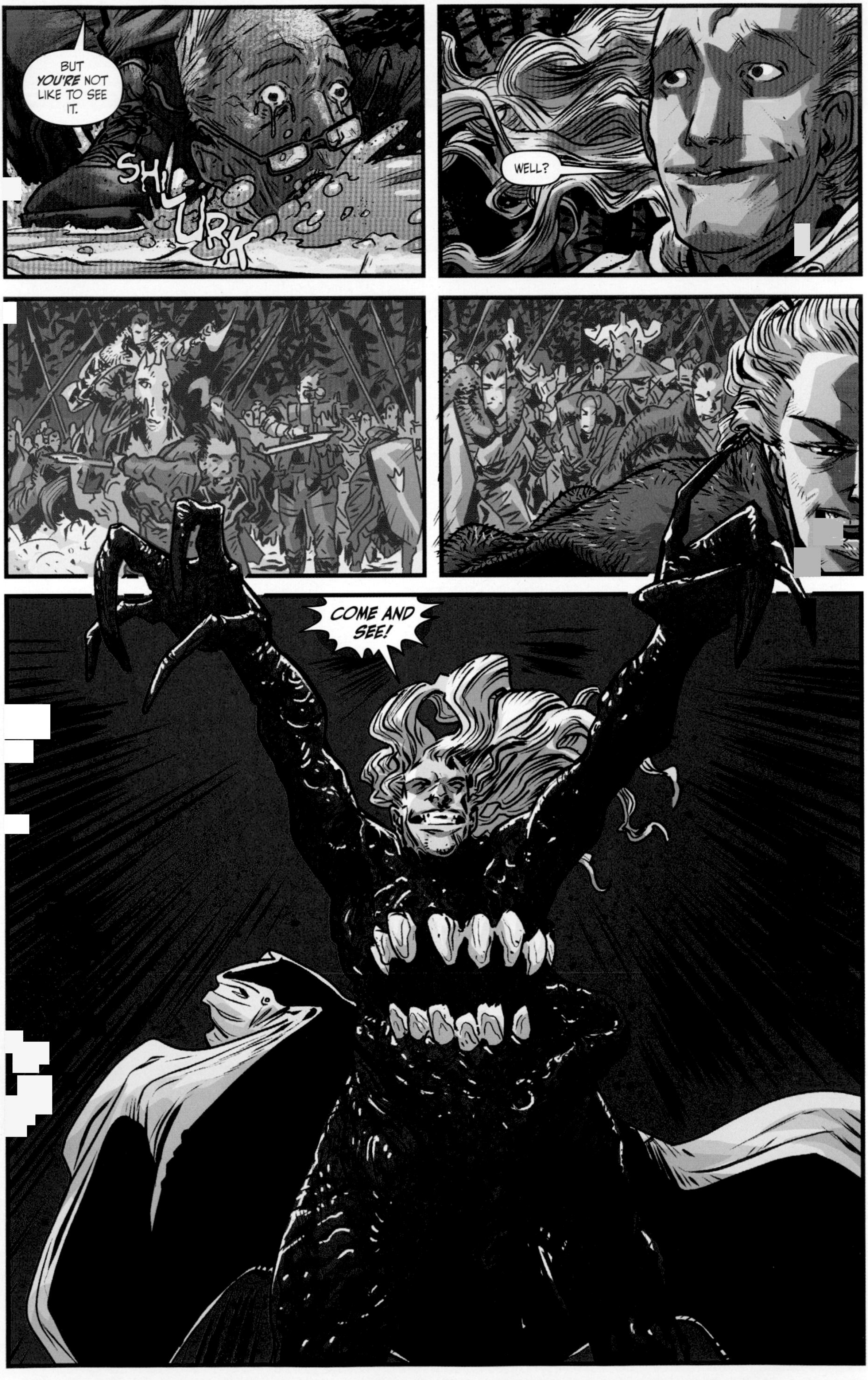
BUT YOU'RE NOT LIKE TO SEE IT.
SHLURK
WELL?
COME AND SEE!

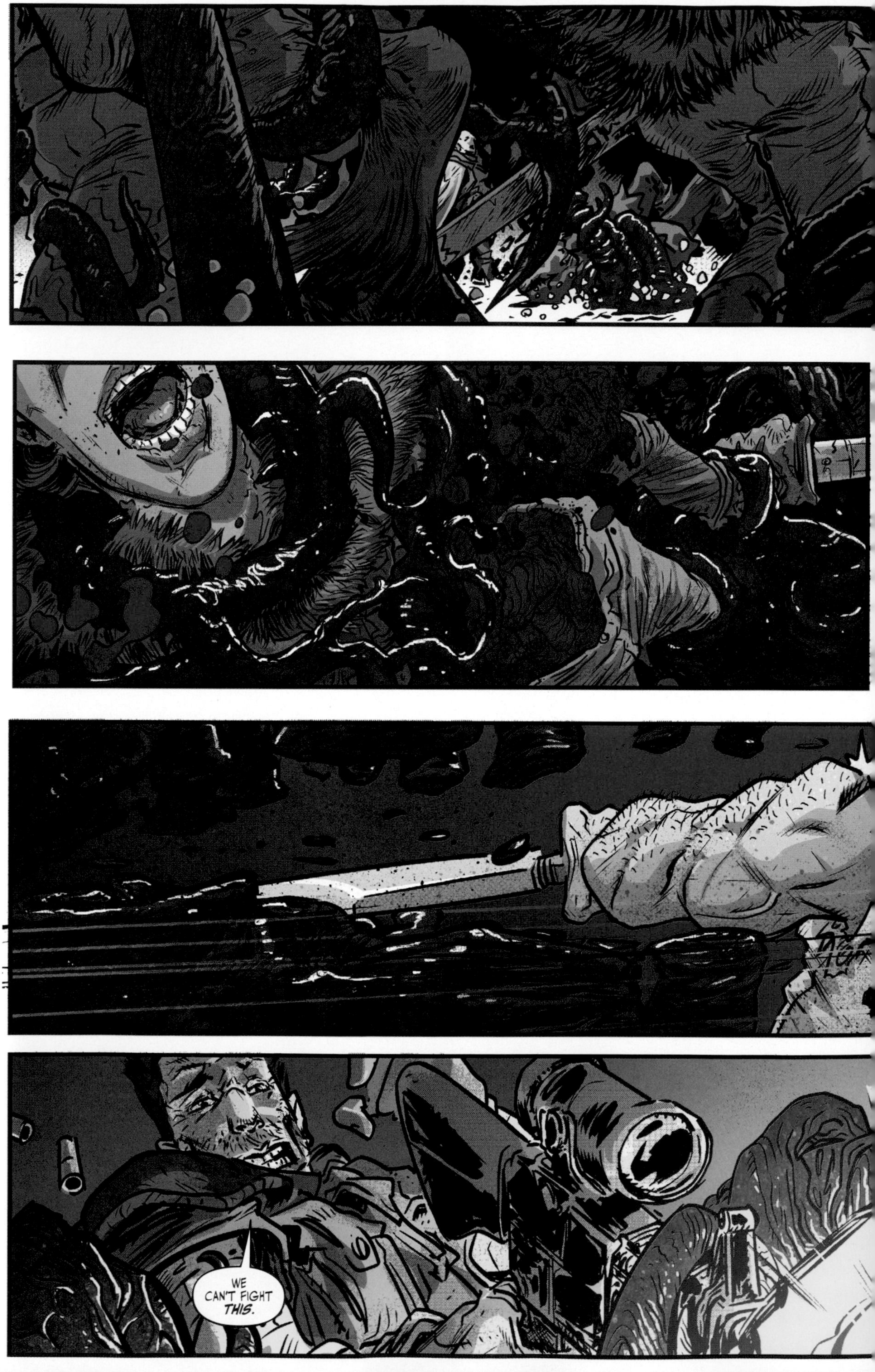
WE CAN'T FIGHT *THIS*.

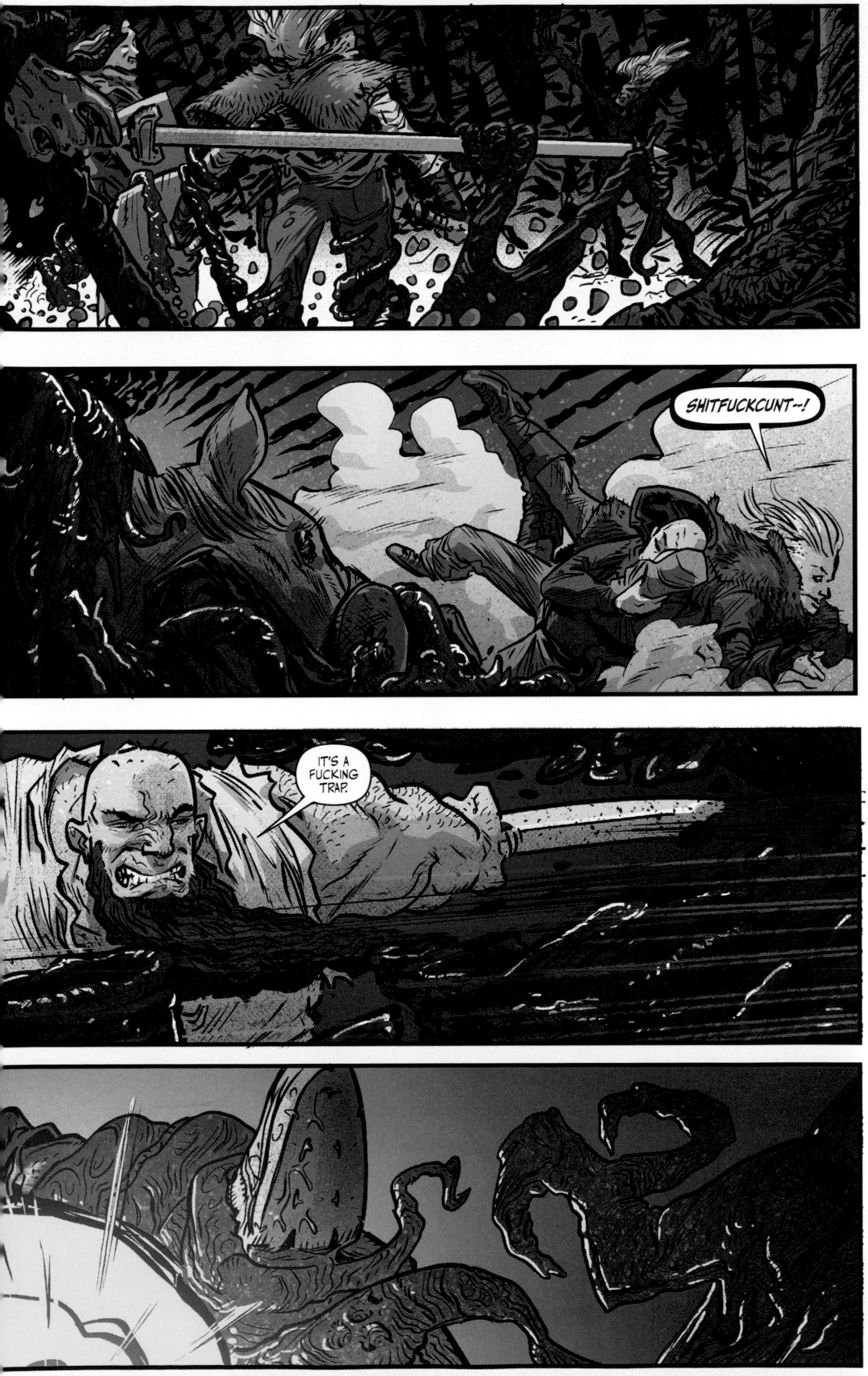
SHITFUCKCUNT--!
IT'S A FUCKING TRAP.

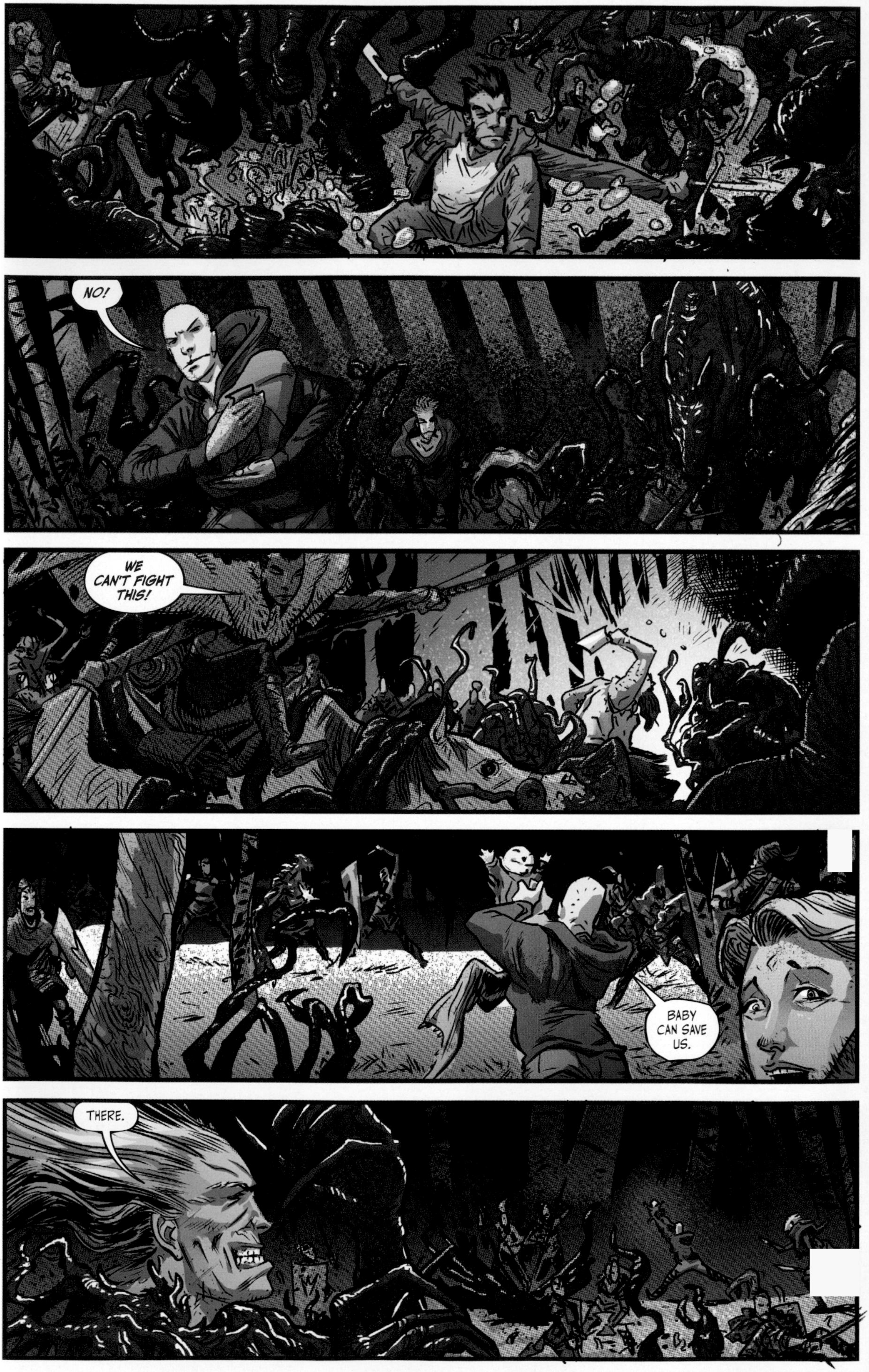
NO!
WE CAN'T FIGHT THIS!
BABY CAN SAVE US.
THERE.

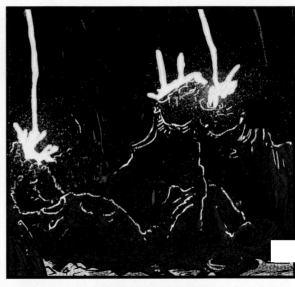

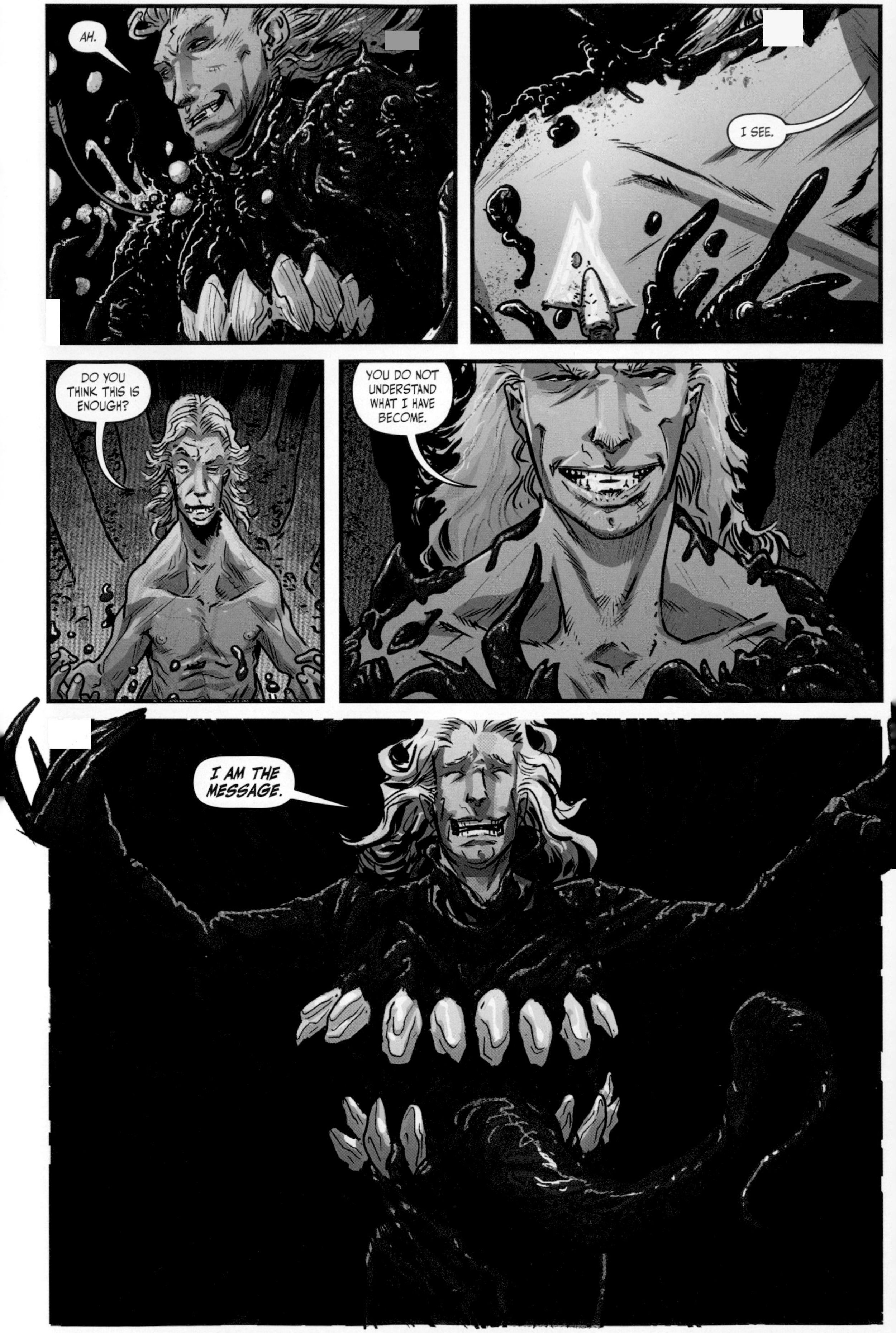
AH.
I SEE.
DO YOU THINK THIS IS ENOUGH?
YOU DO NOT UNDERSTAND WHAT I HAVE BECOME.
I AM THE MESSAGE.

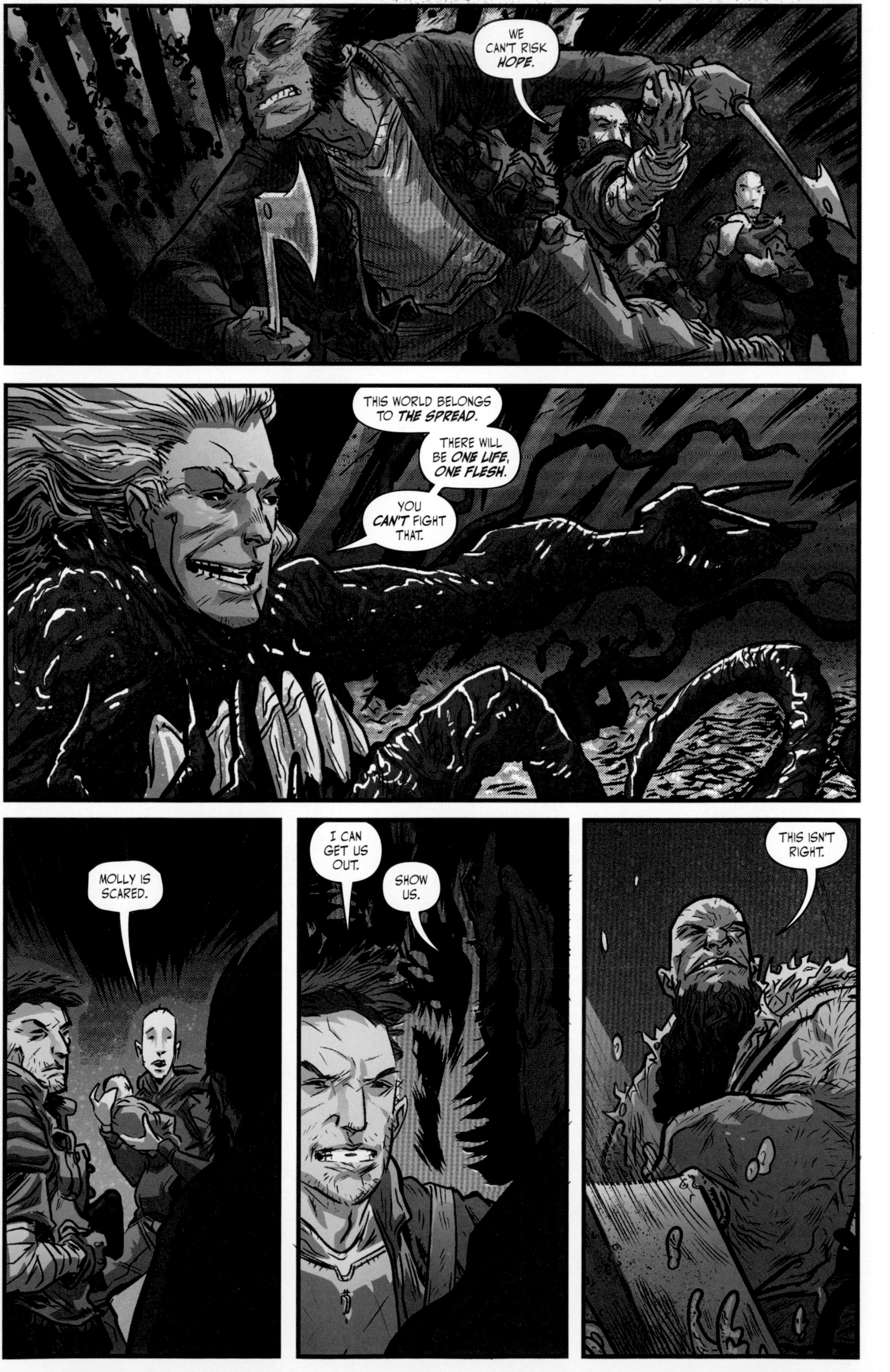
WE CAN'T RISK HOPE.
THIS WORLD BELONGS TO THE SPREAD.
THERE WILL BE ONE LIFE, ONE FLESH.
YOU CAN'T FIGHT THAT.
MOLLY IS SCARED.
I CAN GET US OUT.
SHOW US.
THIS ISN'T RIGHT.

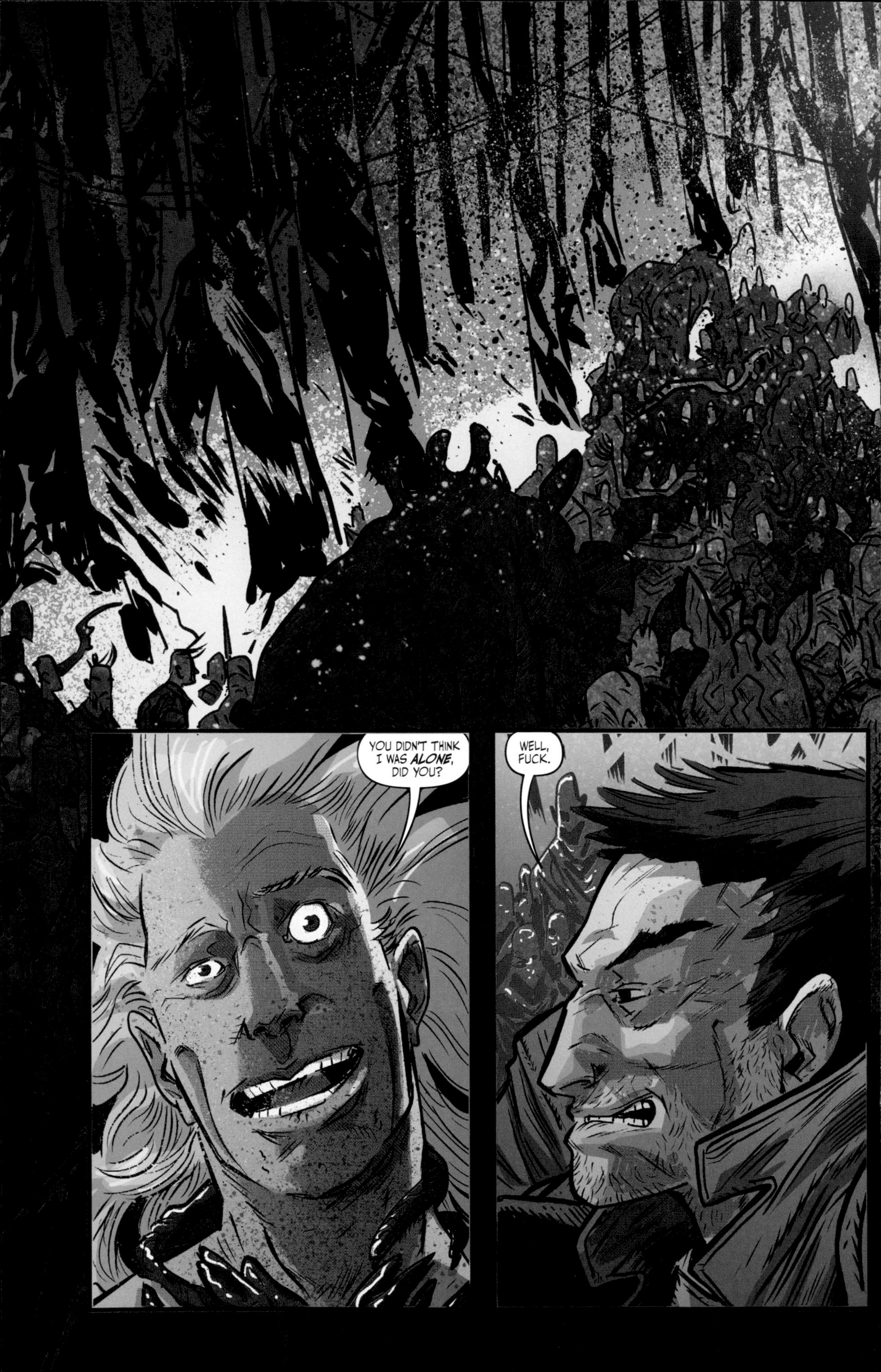

YOU DIDN'T THINK I WAS ALONE, DID YOU?
WELL, FUCK.

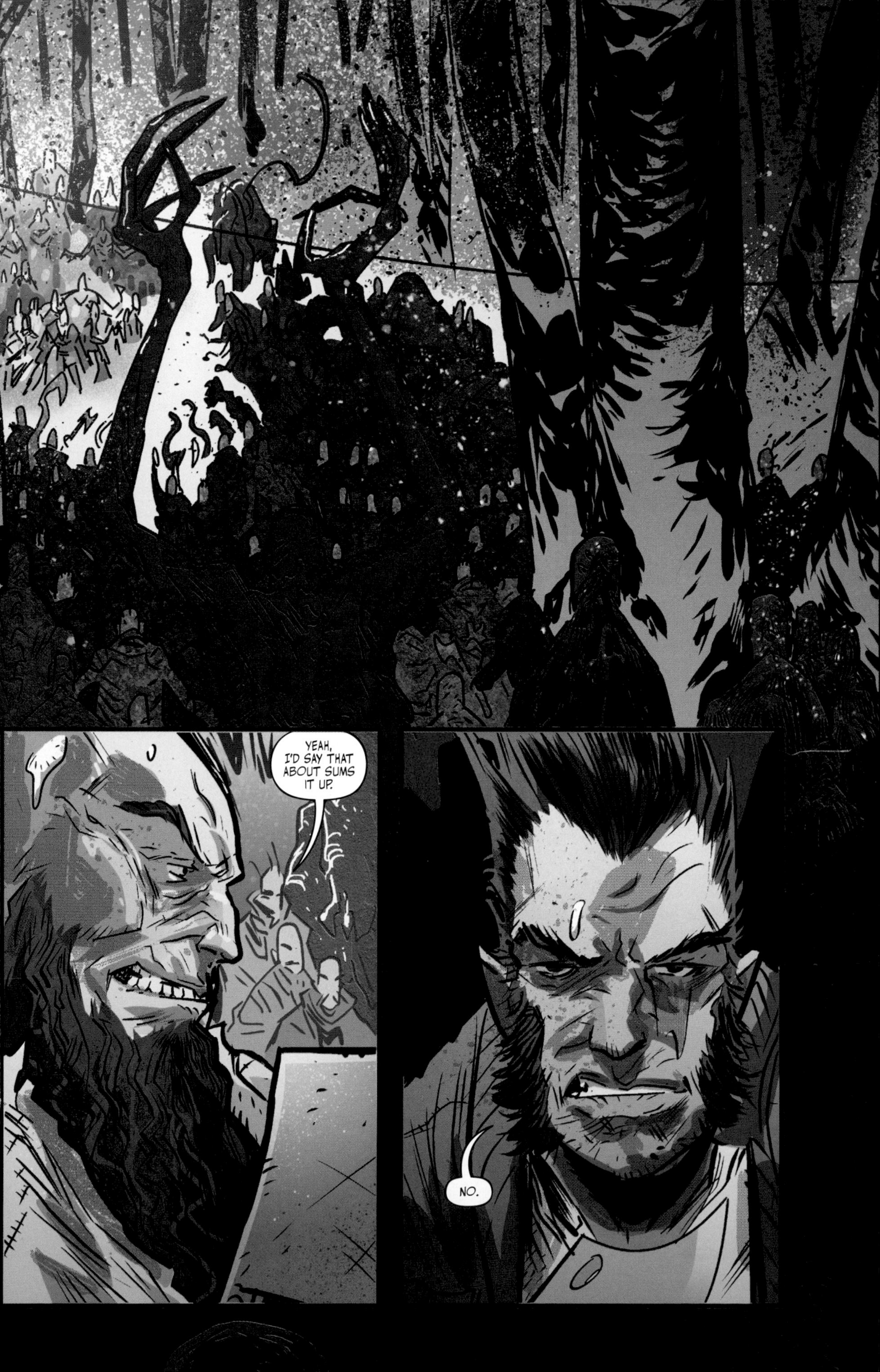
YEAH, I'D SAY THAT ABOUT SUMS IT UP.
NO.

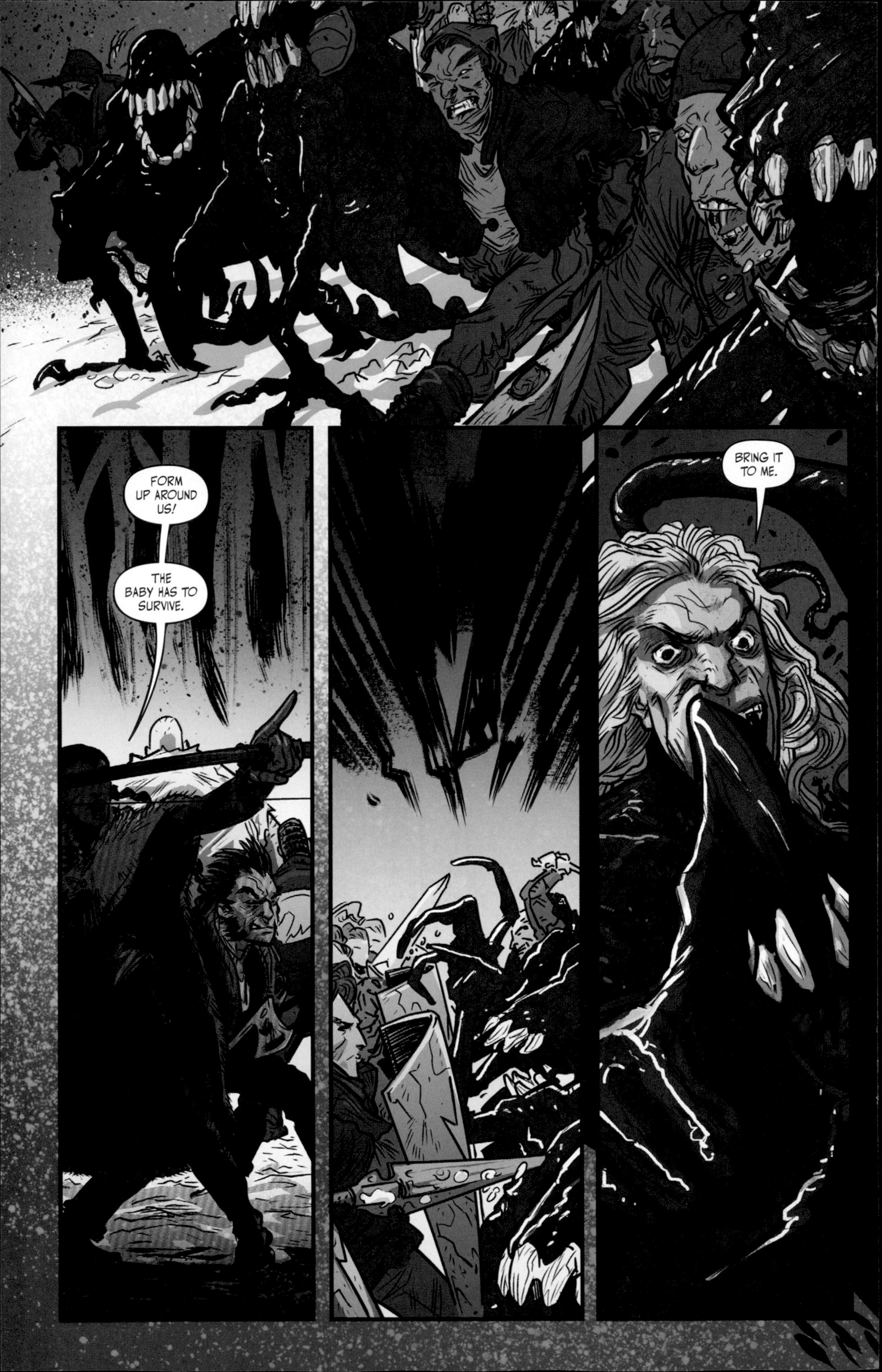
FORM UP AROUND US!
THE BABY HAS TO SURVIVE.
BRING IT TO ME.

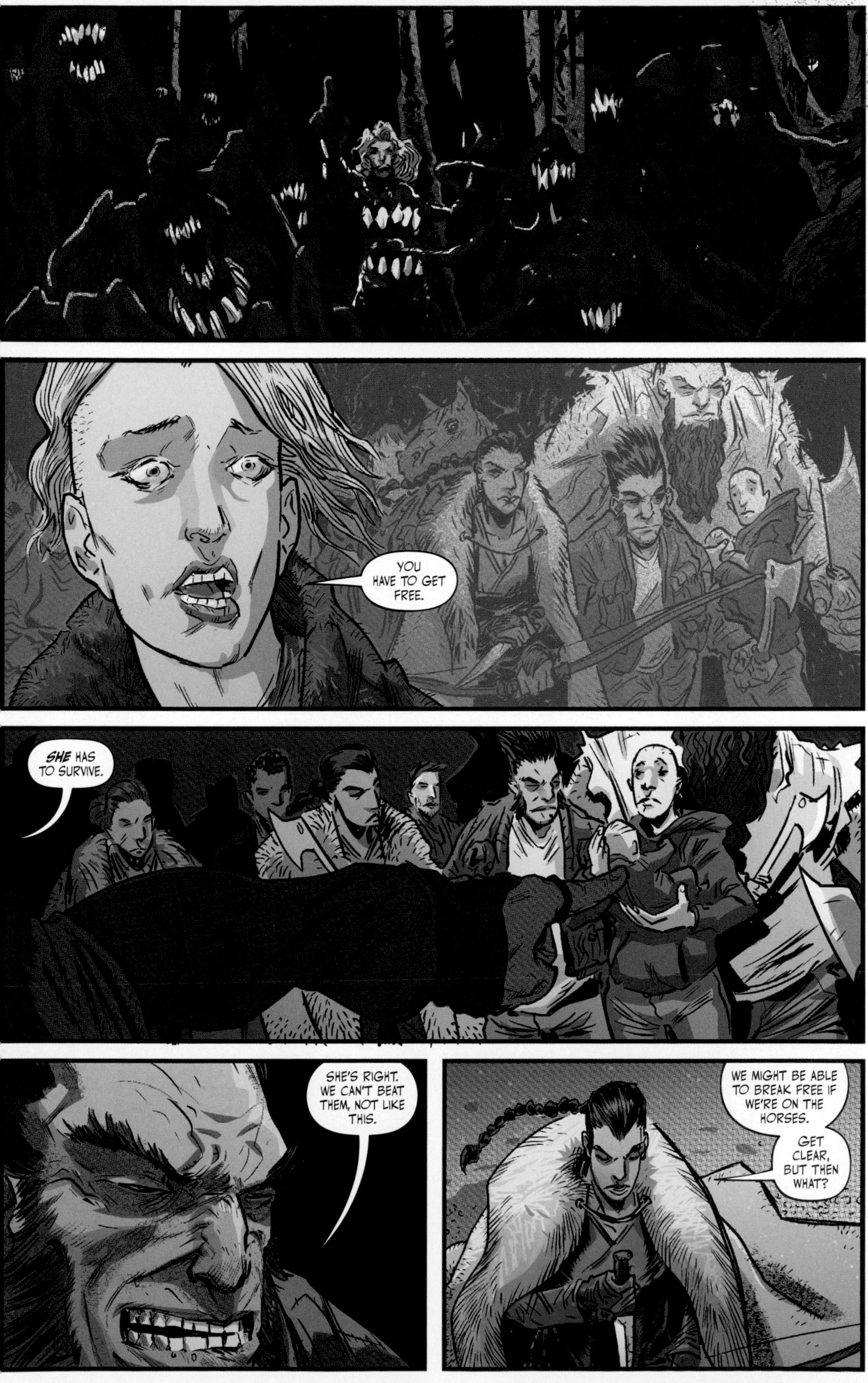
YOU HAVE TO GET FREE.
SHE HAS TO SURVIVE.
SHE'S RIGHT. WE CAN'T BEAT THEM, NOT LIKE THIS.
WE MIGHT BE ABLE TO BREAK FREE IF WE'RE ON THE HORSES.
GET CLEAR, BUT THEN WHAT?

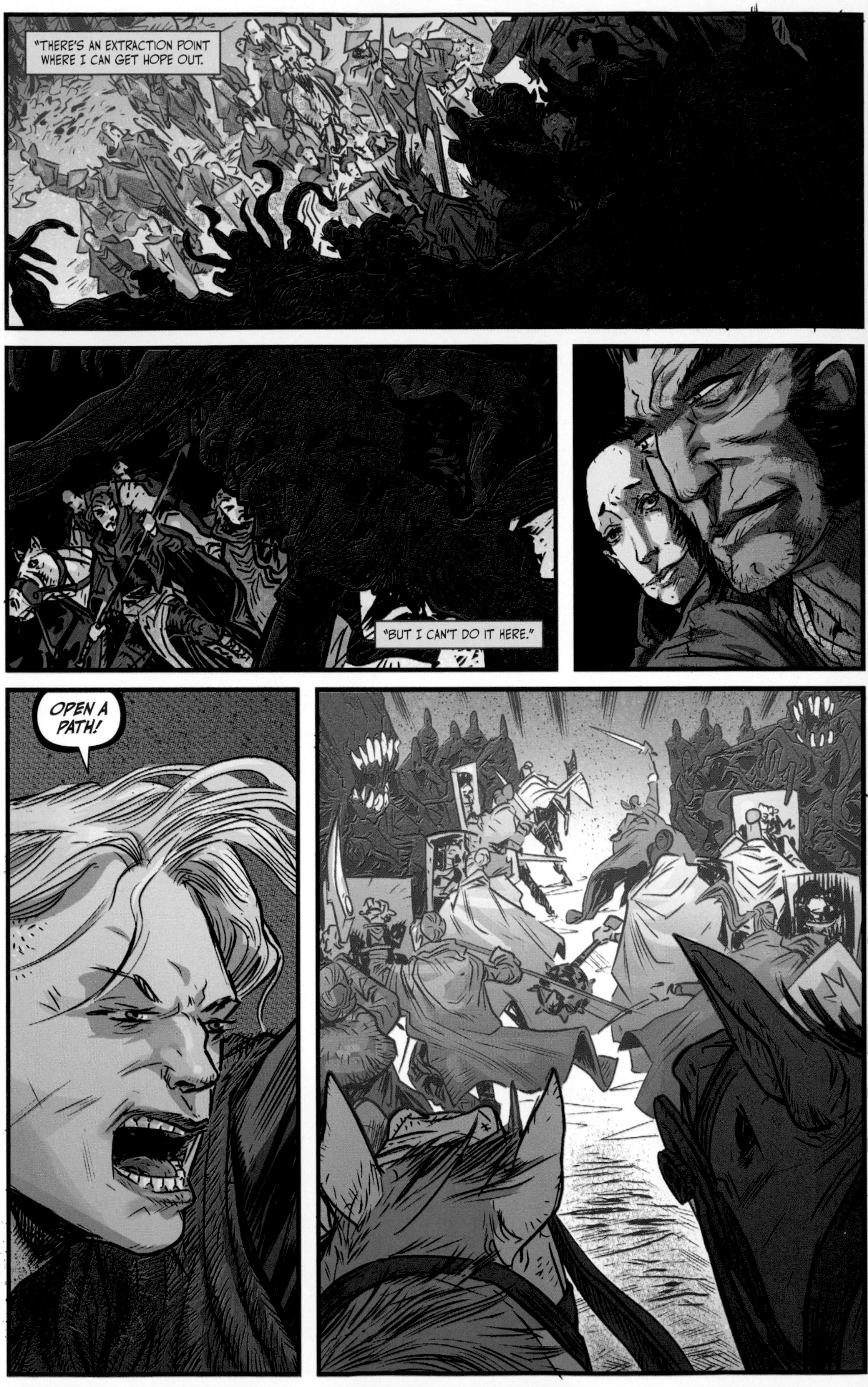
"THERE'S AN EXTRACTION POINT WHERE I CAN GET HOPE OUT.
"BUT I CAN'T DO IT HERE."
OPEN A PATH!

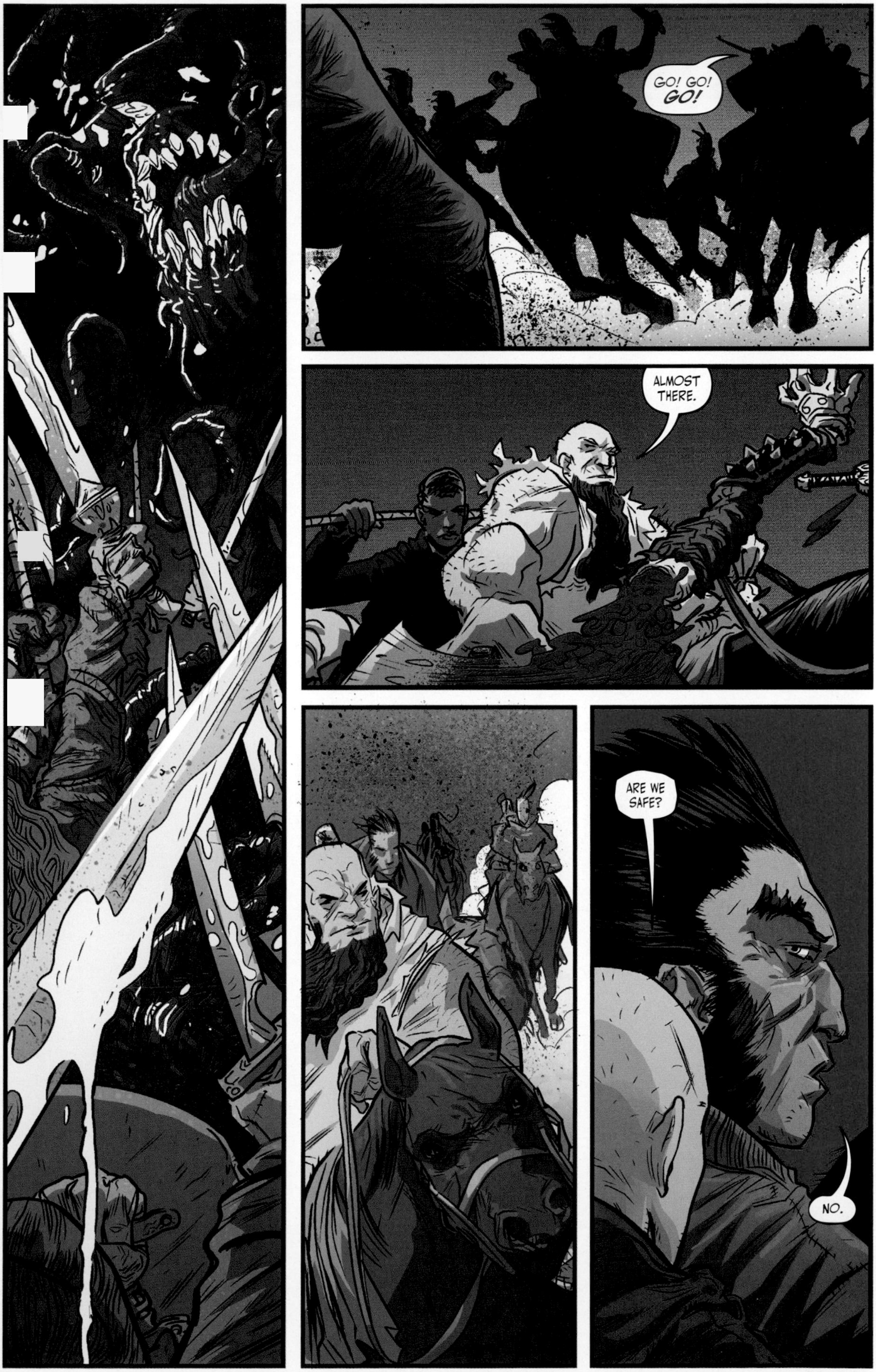
GO! GO! GO!
ALMOST THERE.
ARE WE SAFE?
NO.

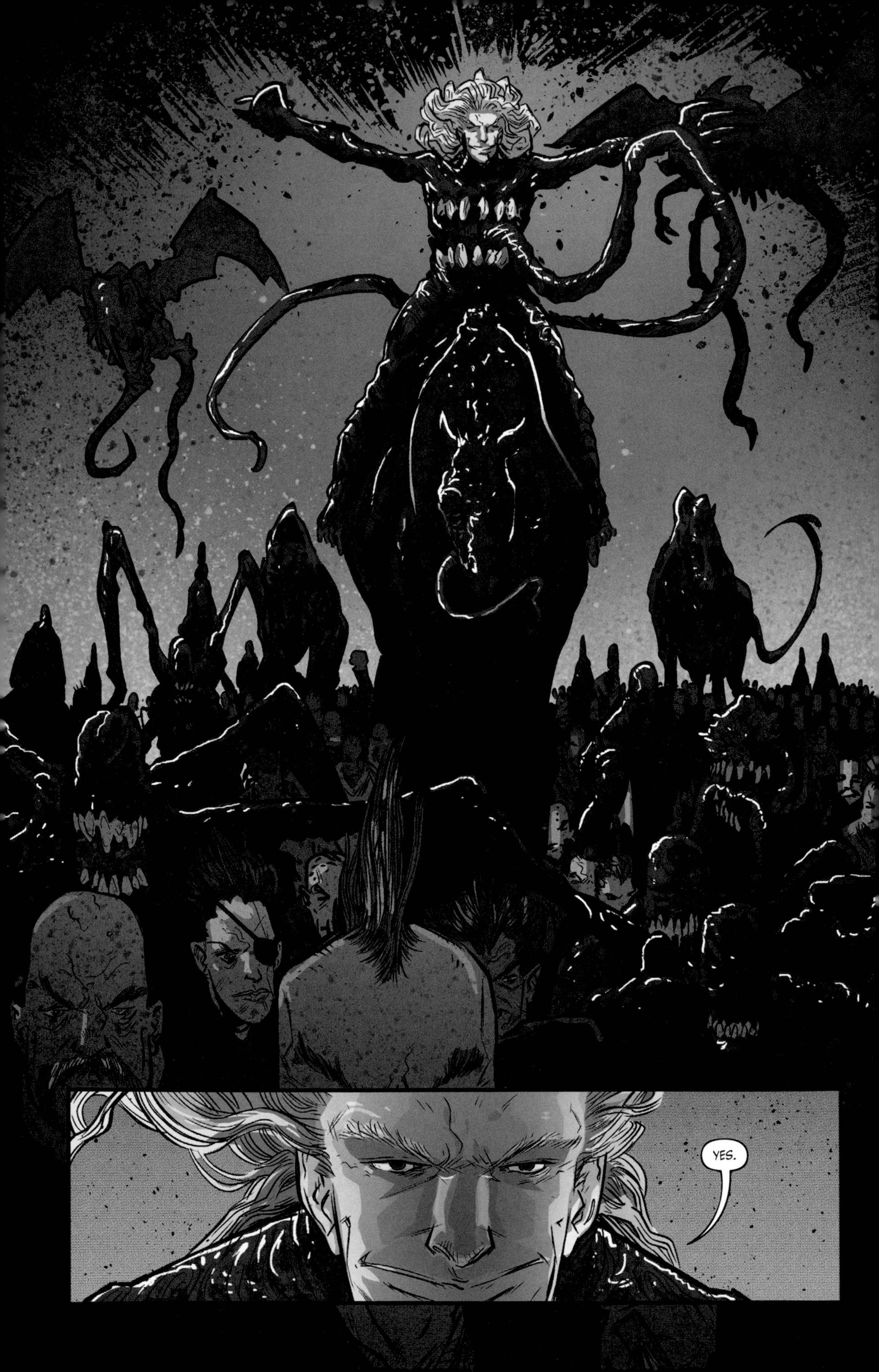
YES.

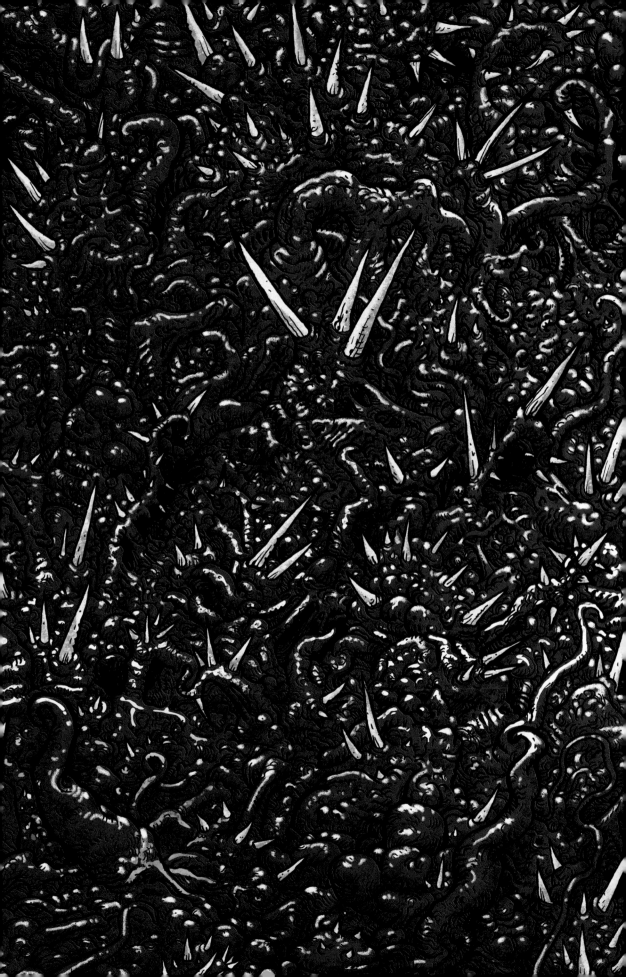

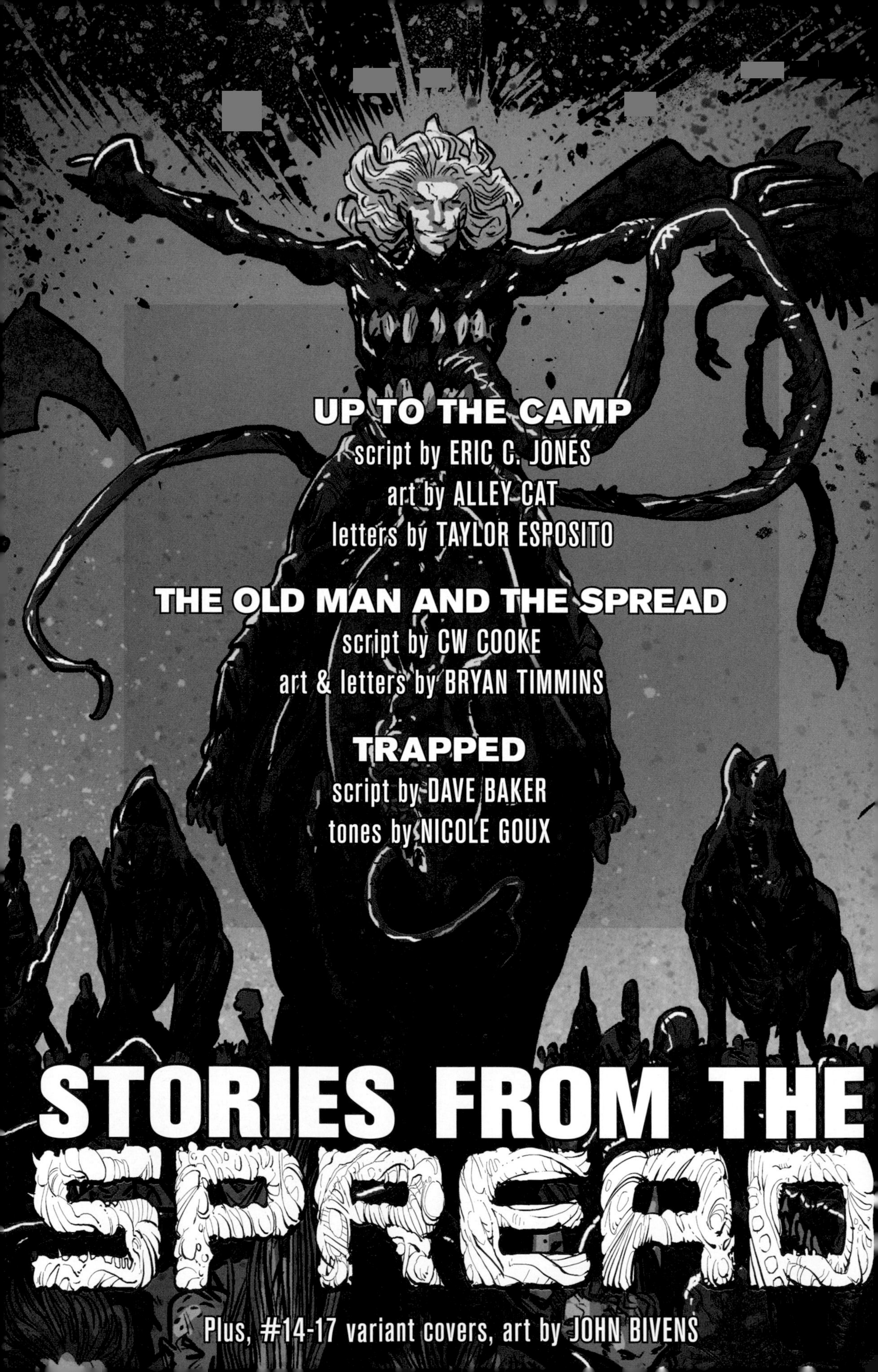
UP TO THE CAMP
script by ERIC C. JONES
art by ALLEY CAT
letters by TAYLOR ESPOSITO
THE OLD MAN AND THE SPREAD
script by CW COOKE
art & letters by BRYAN TIMMINS
TRAPPED
script by DAVE BAKER
tones by NICOLE GOUX
STORIES FROM THE SPREAD
Plus, #14-17 variant covers, art by JOHN BIVENS

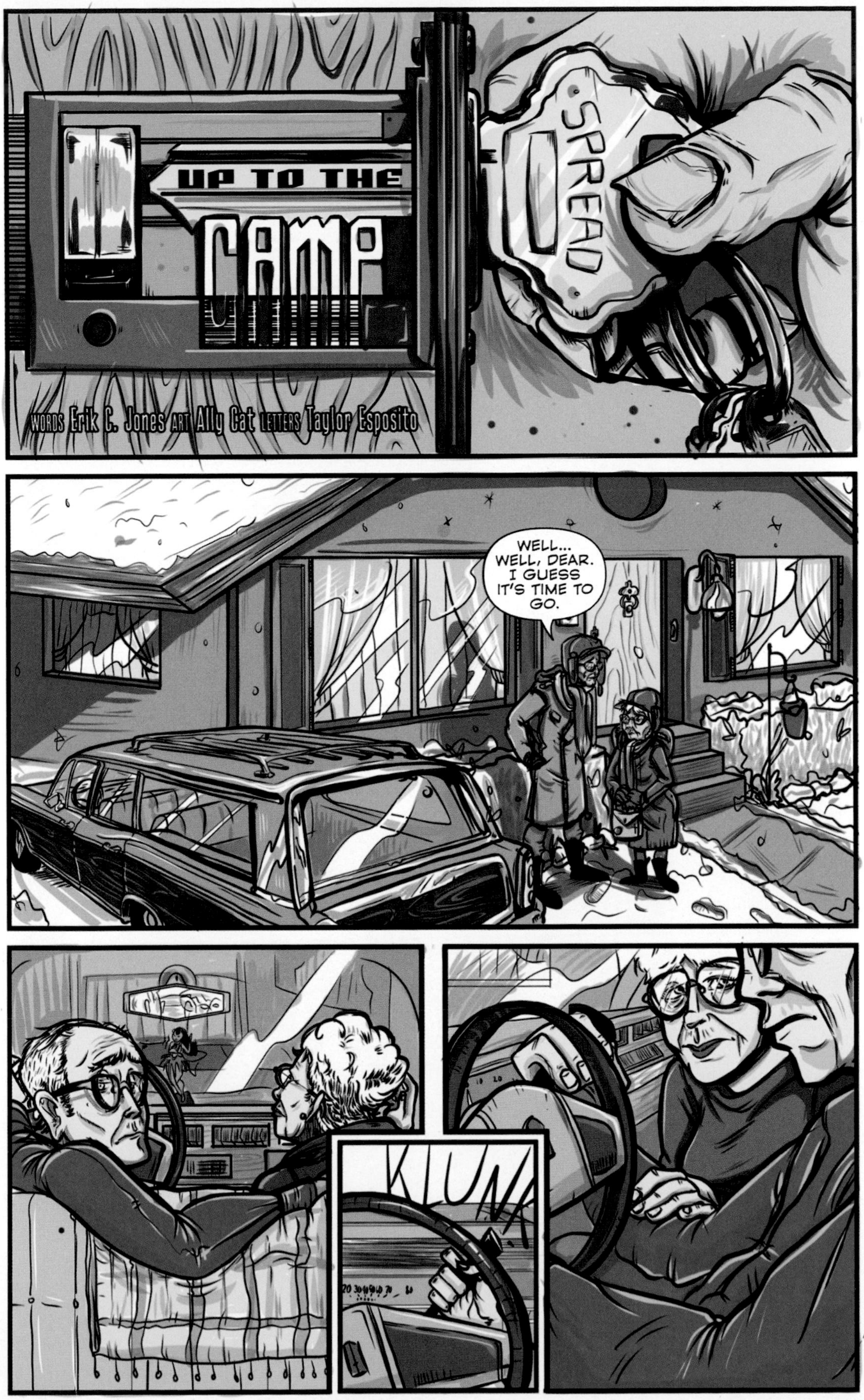
UP TO THE
CAMP
WORDS Erik C. Jones ART Ally Cat LETTERS Taylor Esposito
SPREAD
WELL... WELL, DEAR. I GUESS IT'S TIME TO GO.
KLUNK

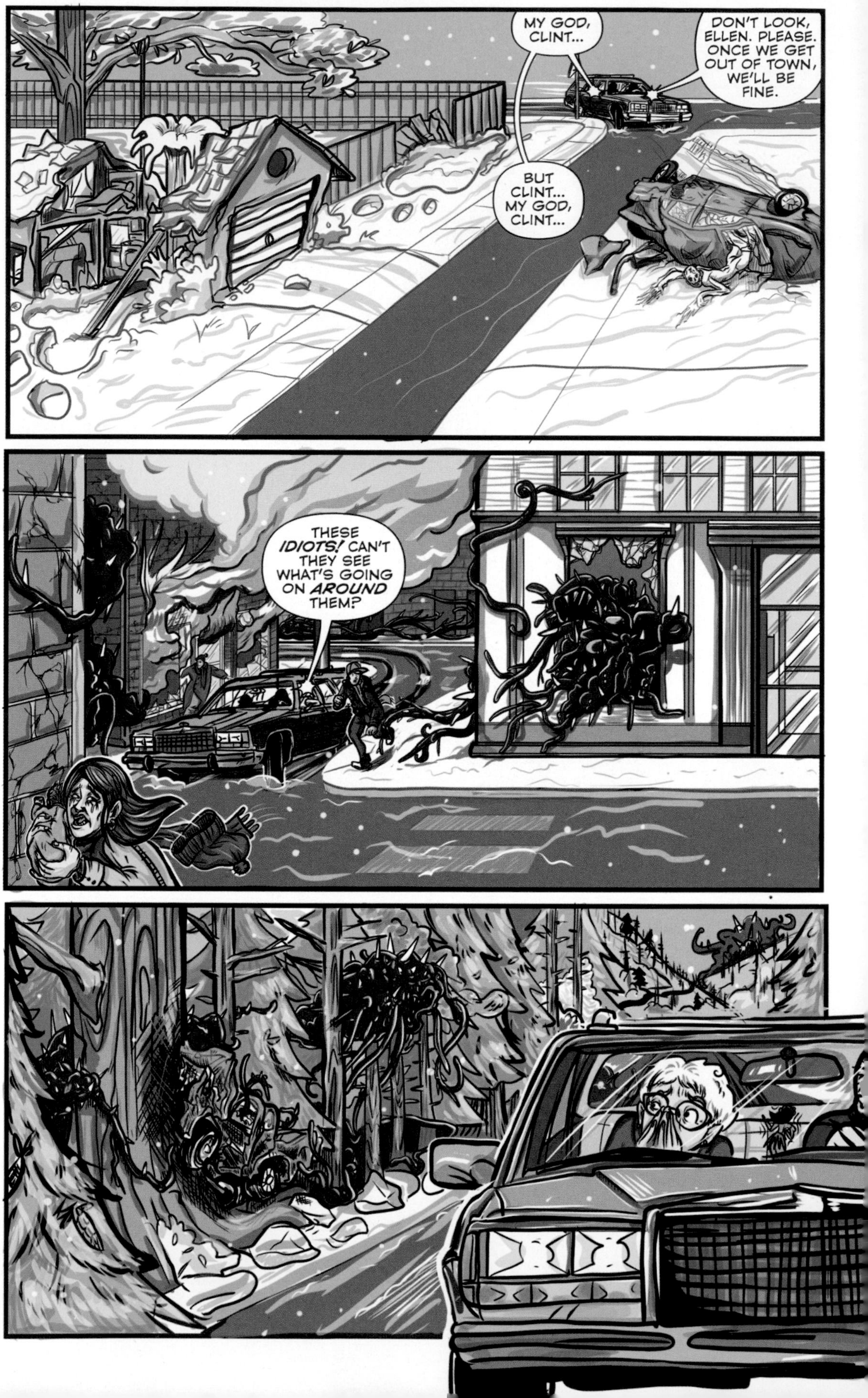
MY GOD, CLINT...
DON'T LOOK, ELLEN. PLEASE. ONCE WE GET OUT OF TOWN, WE'LL BE FINE.
BUT CLINT... MY GOD, CLINT...
THESE *IDIOTS!* CAN'T THEY SEE WHAT'S GOING ON *AROUND* THEM?

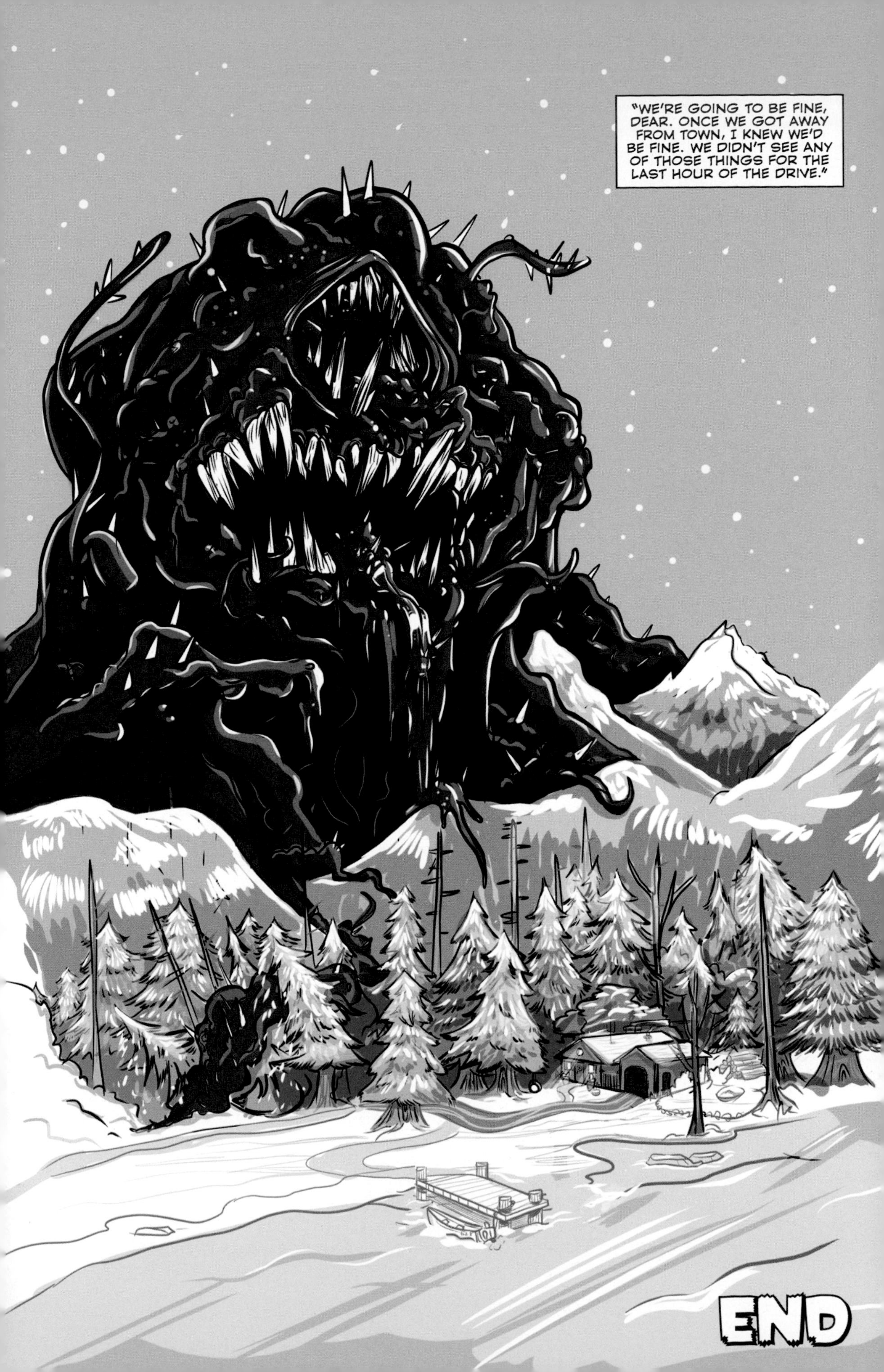
"WE'RE GOING TO BE FINE, DEAR. ONCE WE GOT AWAY FROM TOWN, I KNEW WE'D BE FINE. WE DIDN'T SEE ANY OF THOSE THINGS FOR THE LAST HOUR OF THE DRIVE."
END

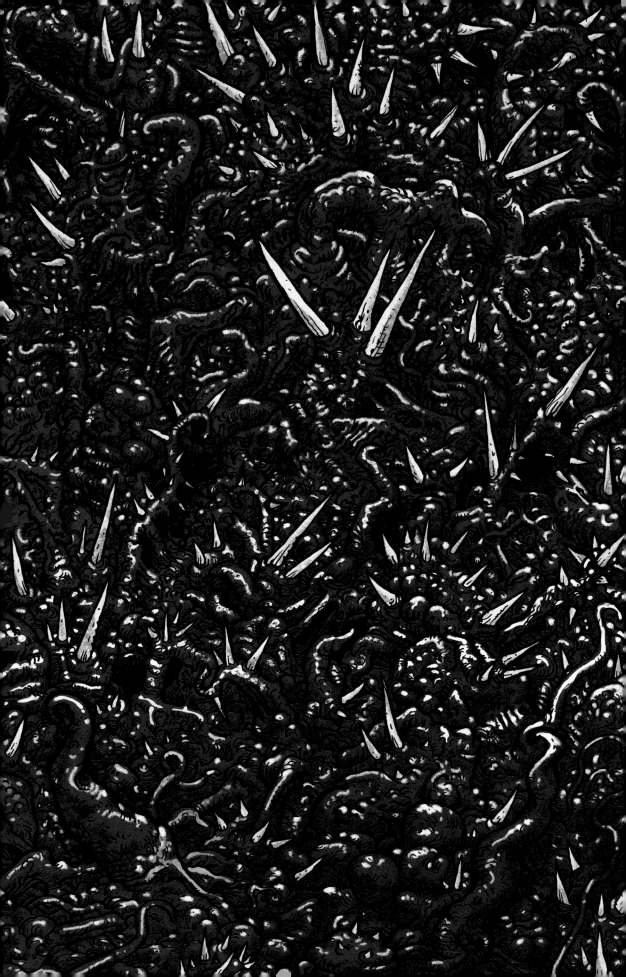

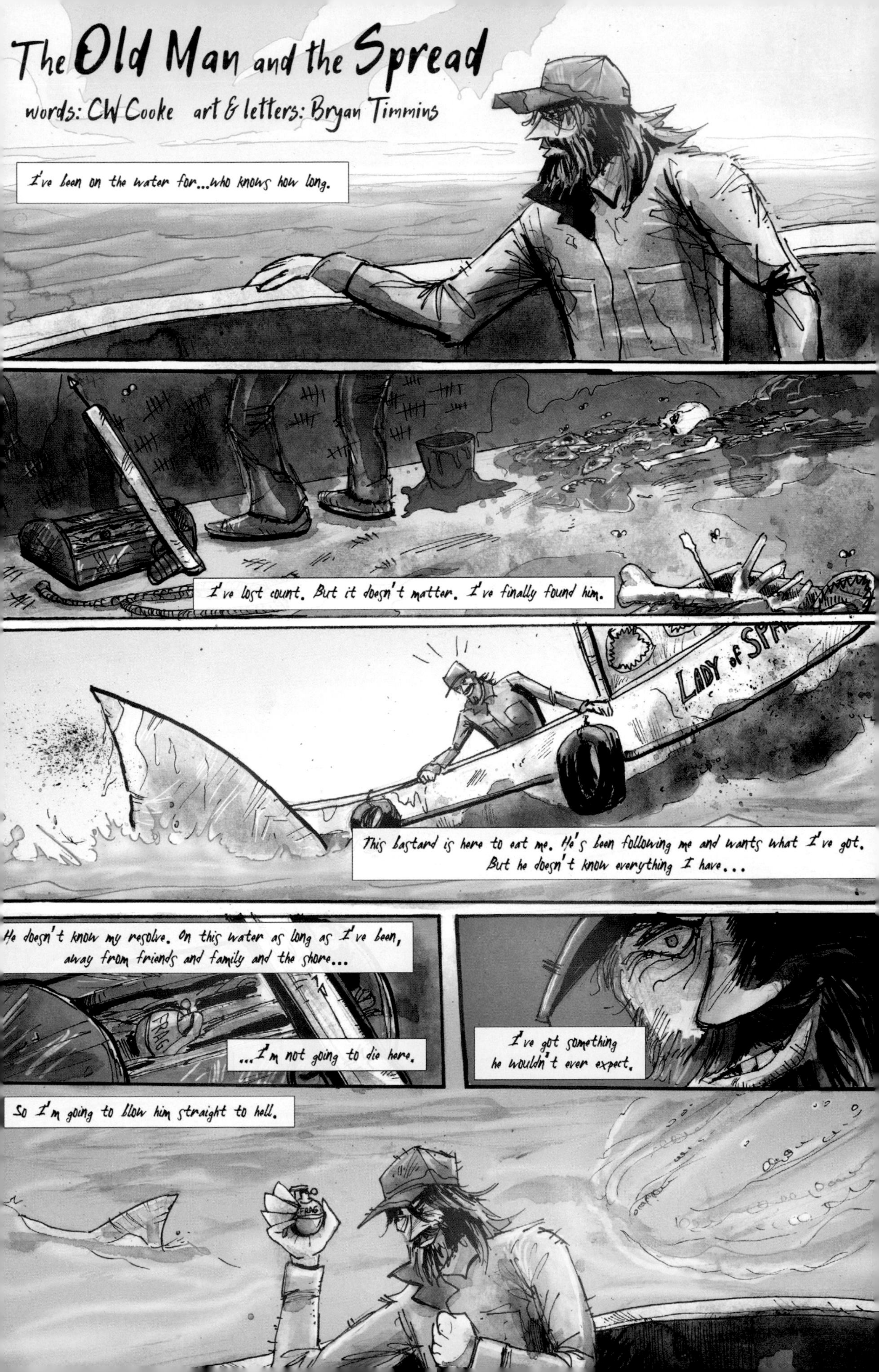
The Old Man and the Spread
words: CW Cooke art & letters: Bryan Timmins
I've been on the water for...who knows how long.
I've lost count. But it doesn't matter. I've finally found him.
LADY of SPR
This bastard is here to eat me. He's been following me and wants what I've got. But he doesn't know everything I have...
He doesn't know my resolve. On this water as long as I've been, away from friends and family and the shore...
FRAG
...I'm not going to die here.
I've got something he wouldn't ever expect.
So I'm going to blow him straight to hell.
FRAG

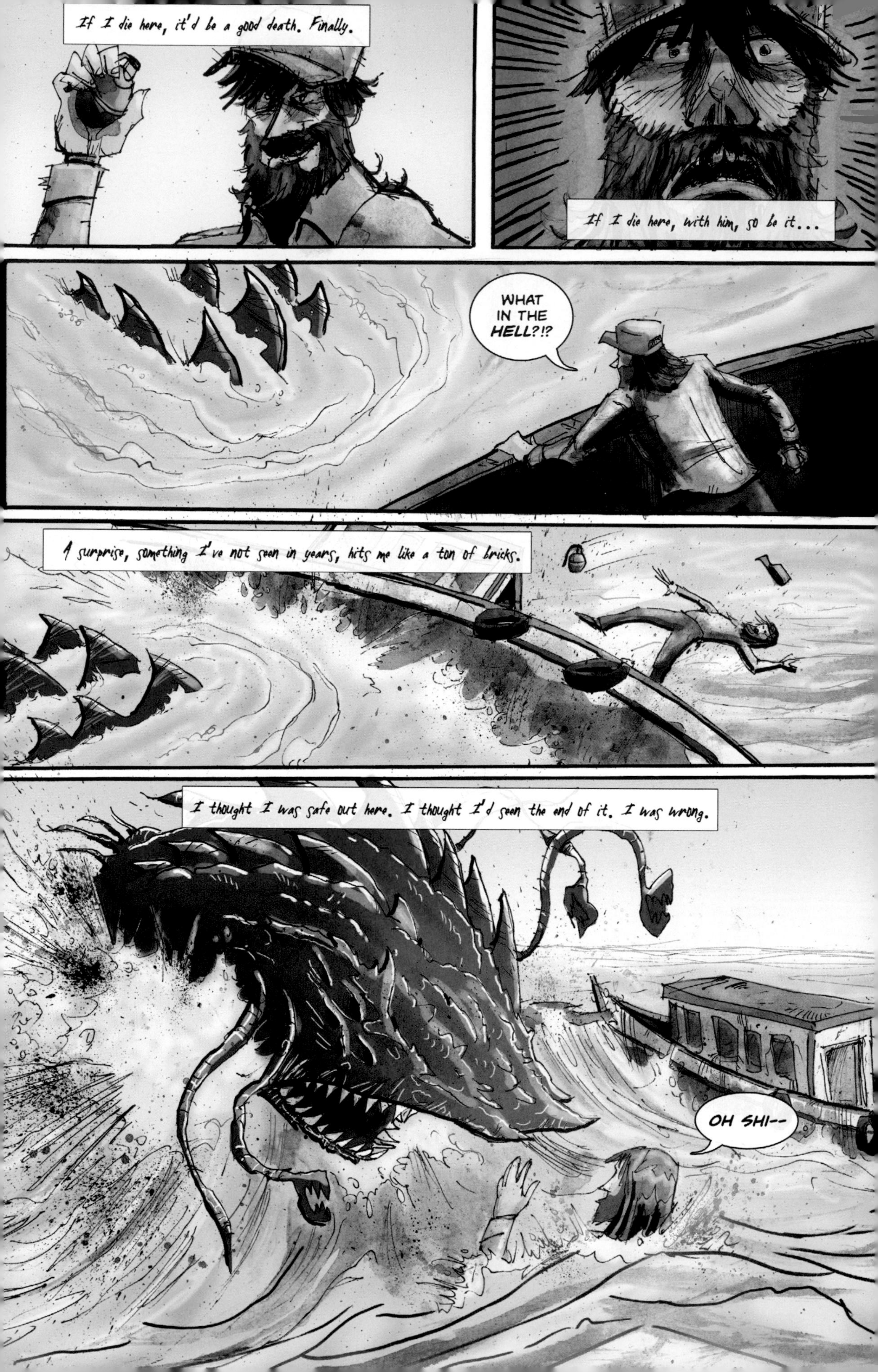

If I die here, it'd be a good death. Finally.
If I die here, with him, so be it...
WHAT IN THE HELL?!?
A surprise, something I've not seen in years, hits me like a ton of bricks.
I thought I was safe out here. I thought I'd seen the end of it. I was wrong.
OH SHI--

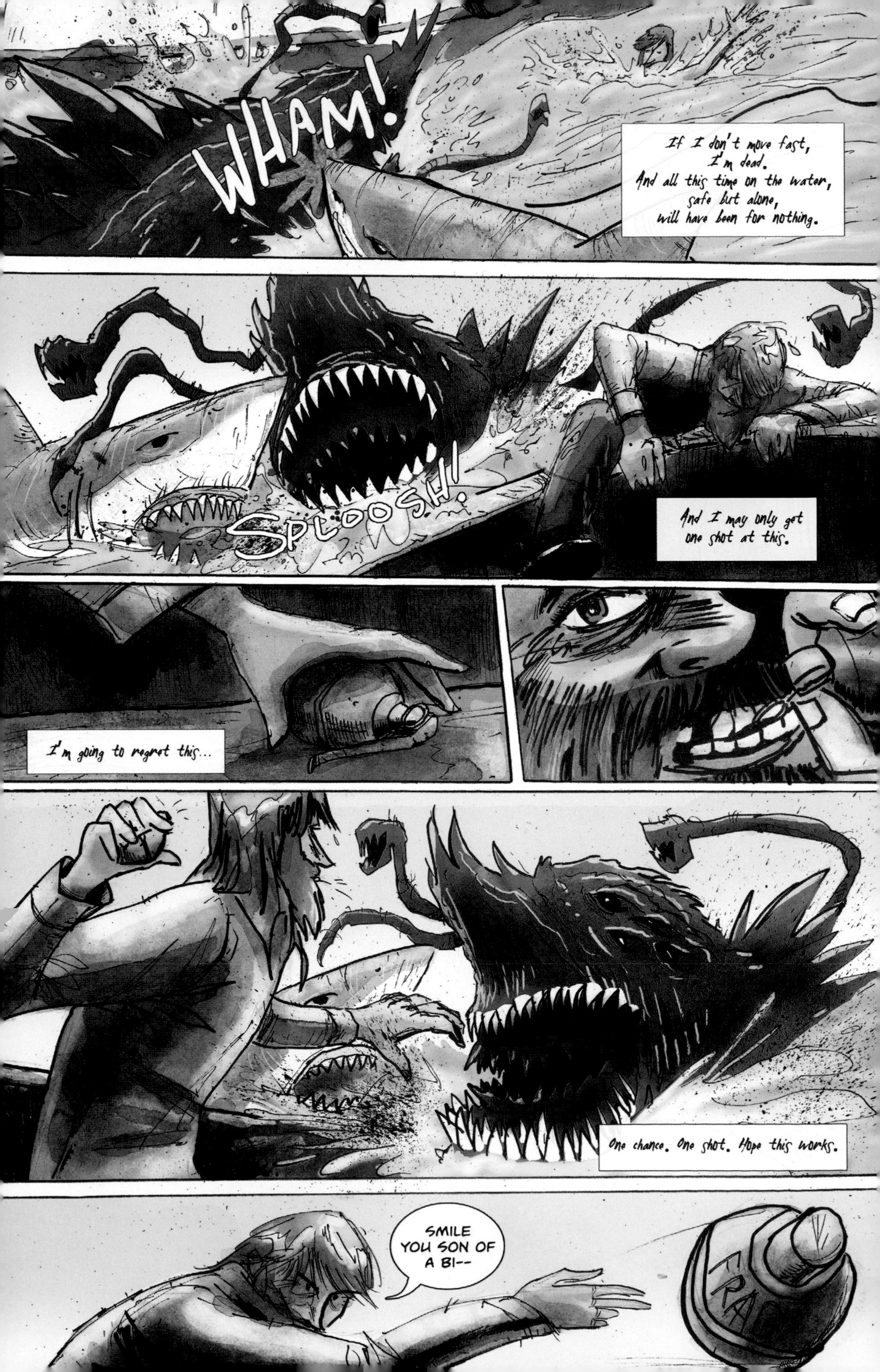
WHAM!
If I don't move fast, I'm dead. And all this time on the water, safe but alone, will have been for nothing.
SPLOOSH!
And I may only get one shot at this.
I'm going to regret this...
One chance. One shot. Hope this works.
SMILE YOU SON OF A BI--

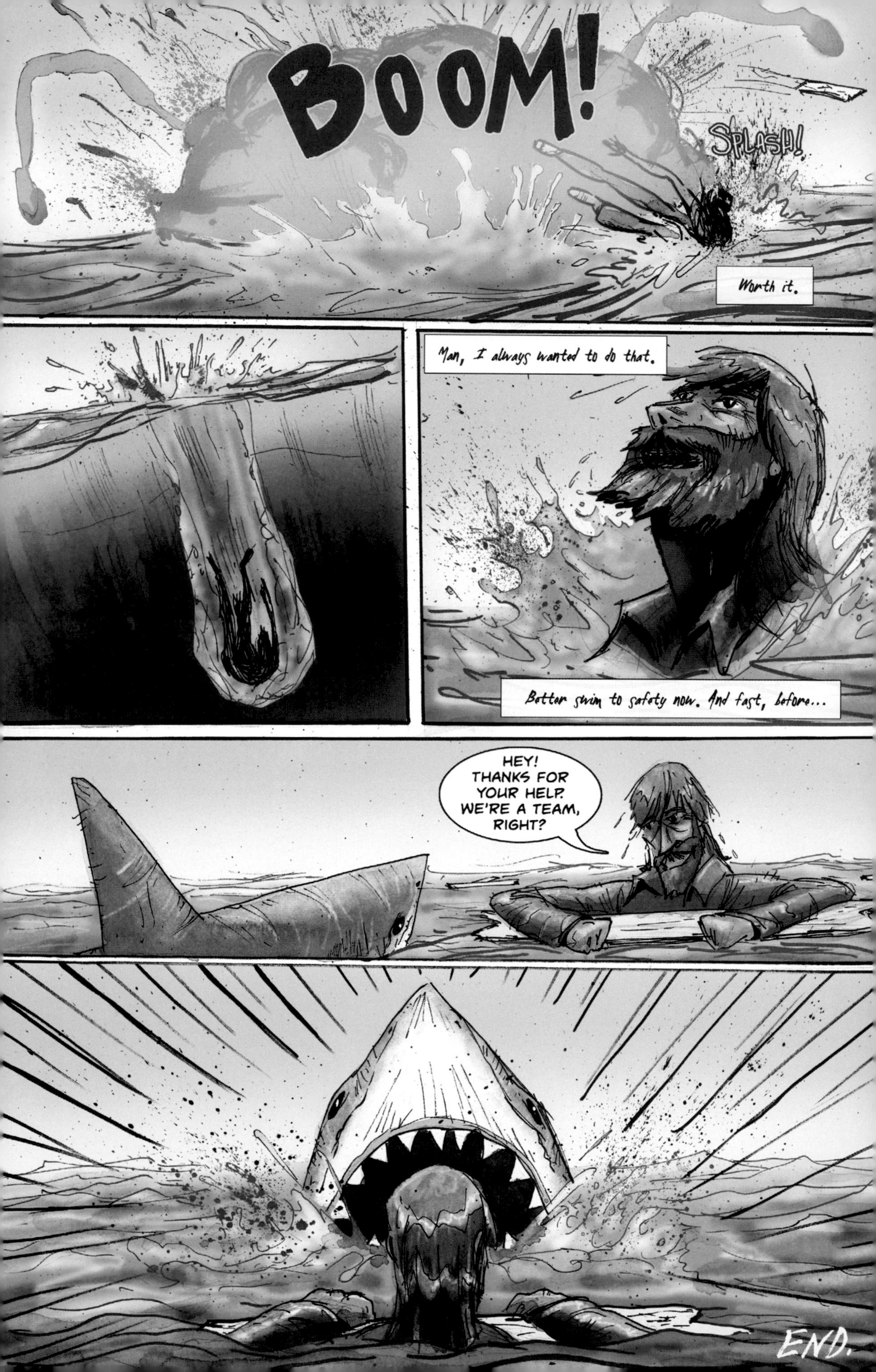
BOOM!
SPLASH!
Worth it.
Man, I always wanted to do that.
Better swim to safety now. And fast, before...
HEY! THANKS FOR YOUR HELP. WE'RE A TEAM, RIGHT?
END.

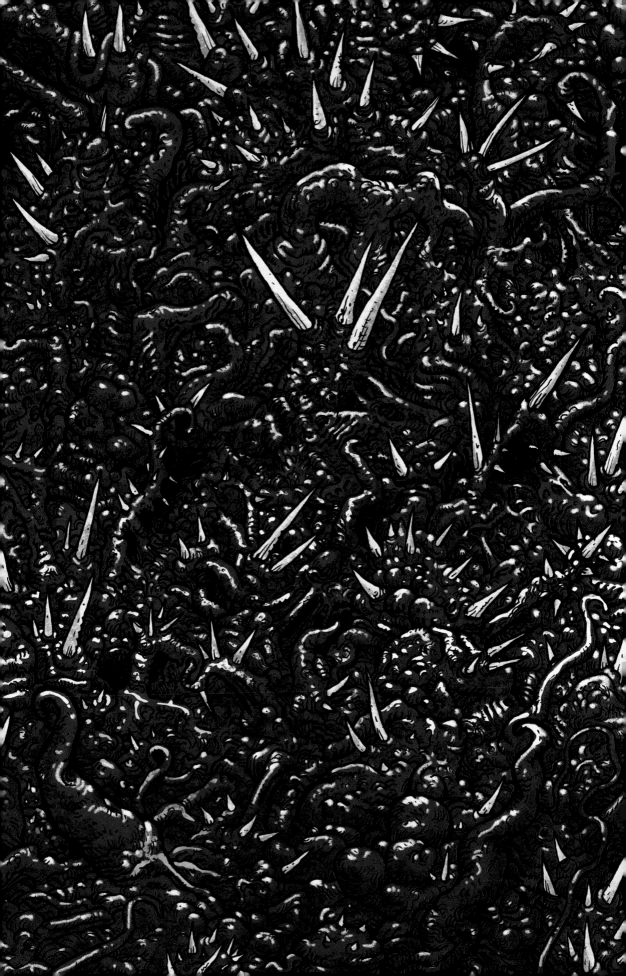

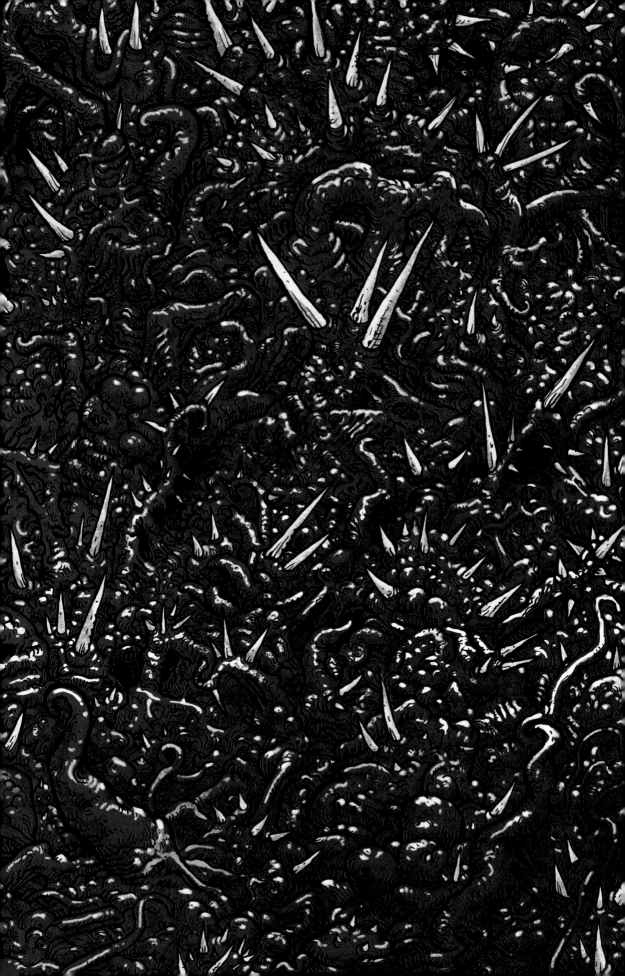

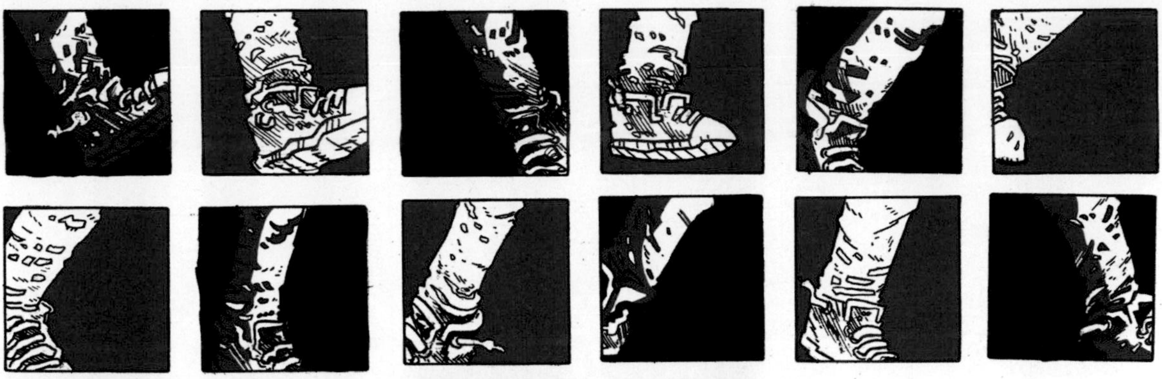

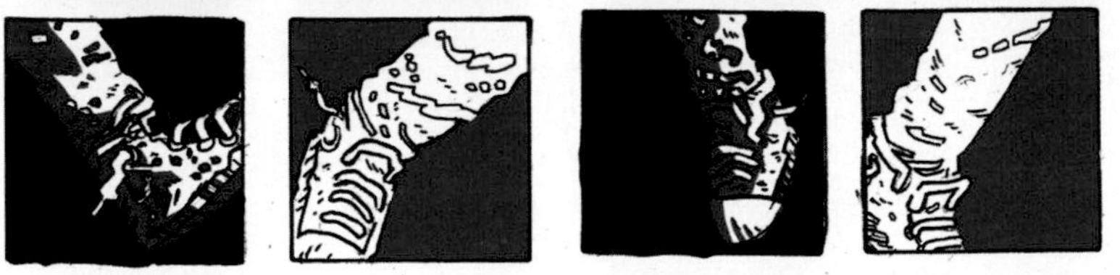

WRITTEN AND DRAWN BY

DAVE BAKER

TONES BY **NICOLE GOUX**

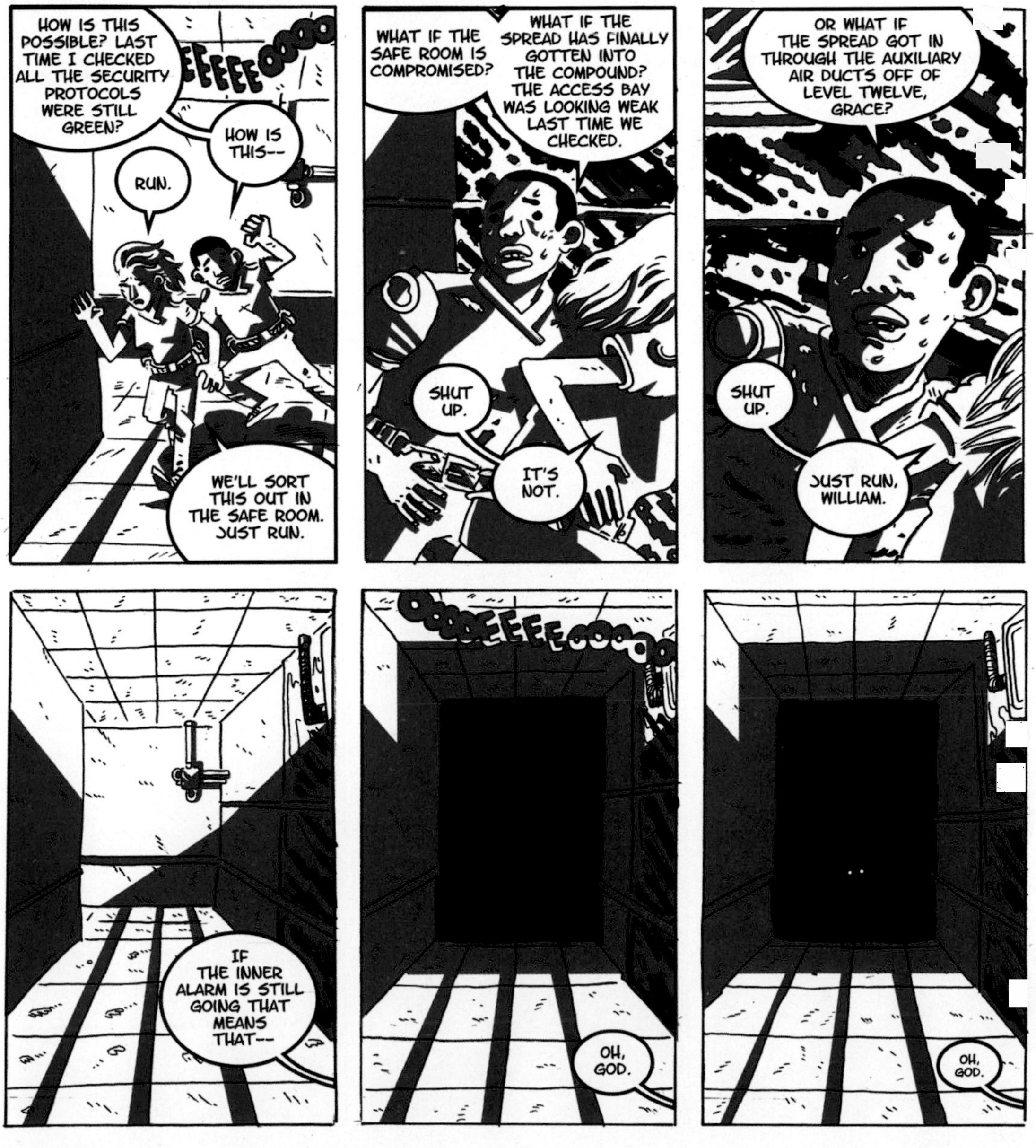

HOW IS THIS POSSIBLE? LAST TIME I CHECKED ALL THE SECURITY PROTOCOLS WERE STILL GREEN?
EEEEEEOOOOO
HOW IS THIS--
RUN.
WE'LL SORT THIS OUT IN THE SAFE ROOM. JUST RUN.
WHAT IF THE SAFE ROOM IS COMPROMISED?
WHAT IF THE SPREAD HAS FINALLY GOTTEN INTO THE COMPOUND? THE ACCESS BAY WAS LOOKING WEAK LAST TIME WE CHECKED.
SHUT UP.
IT'S NOT.
OR WHAT IF THE SPREAD GOT IN THROUGH THE AUXILIARY AIR DUCTS OFF OF LEVEL TWELVE, GRACE?
SHUT UP.
JUST RUN, WILLIAM.
IF THE INNER ALARM IS STILL GOING THAT MEANS THAT--
OOOEEEEEOOOOO
OH, GOD.
OH, GOD.

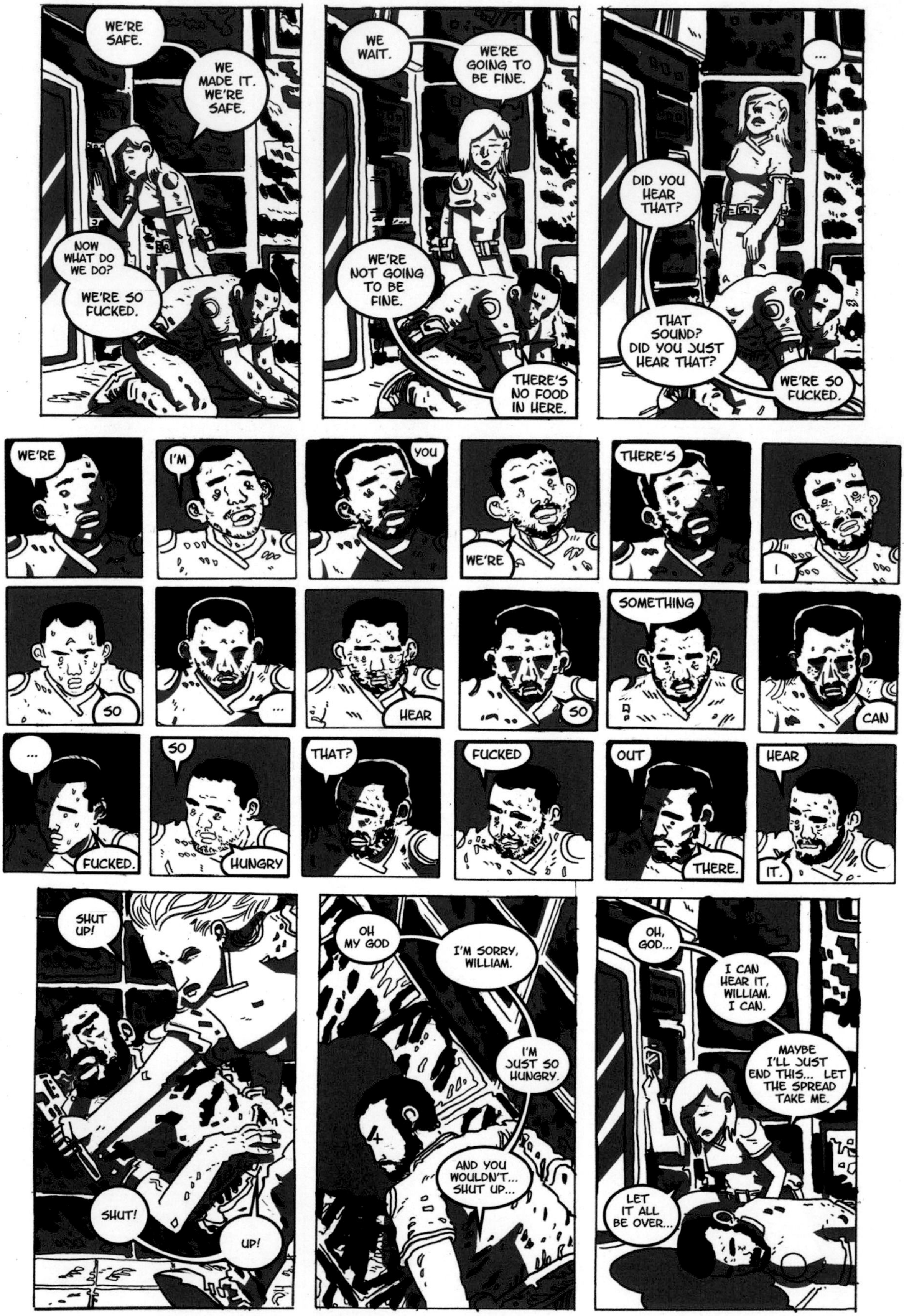
WE'RE SAFE.
WE MADE IT. WE'RE SAFE.
NOW WHAT DO WE DO?
WE'RE SO FUCKED.
WE WAIT.
WE'RE GOING TO BE FINE.
WE'RE NOT GOING TO BE FINE.
THERE'S NO FOOD IN HERE.
...
DID YOU HEAR THAT?
THAT SOUND? DID YOU JUST HEAR THAT?
WE'RE SO FUCKED.
WE'RE
I'M
YOU
WE'RE
THERE'S
I
SO
...
HEAR
SO
SOMETHING
CAN
...
FUCKED.
SO
HUNGRY
THAT?
FUCKED
OUT
THERE.
HEAR
IT.
SHUT UP!
SHUT!
UP!
OH MY GOD
I'M SORRY, WILLIAM.
I'M JUST SO HUNGRY.
AND YOU WOULDN'T... SHUT UP...
OH, GOD...
I CAN HEAR IT, WILLIAM. I CAN.
MAYBE I'LL JUST END THIS... LET THE SPREAD TAKE ME.
LET IT ALL BE OVER...

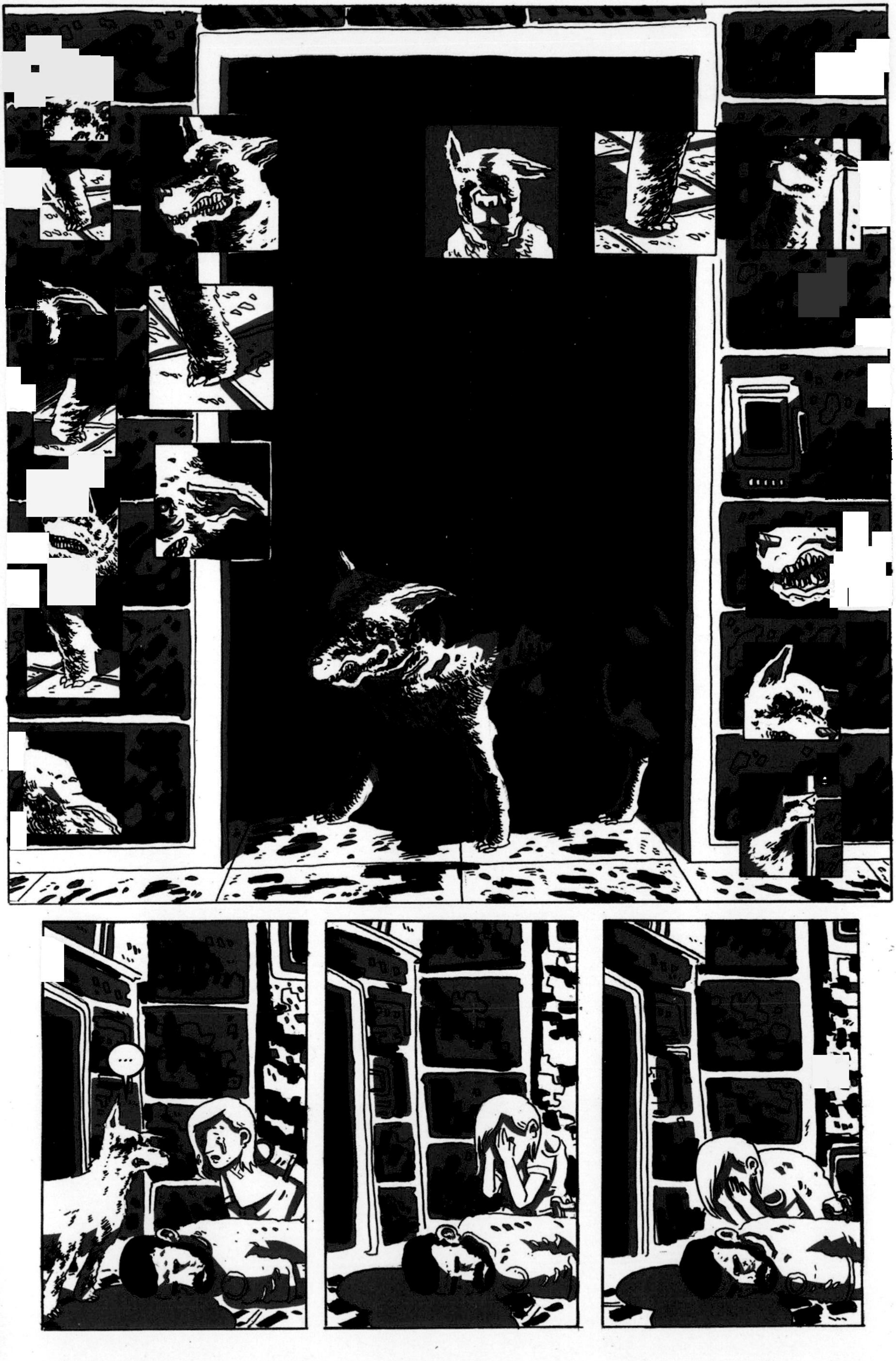
...

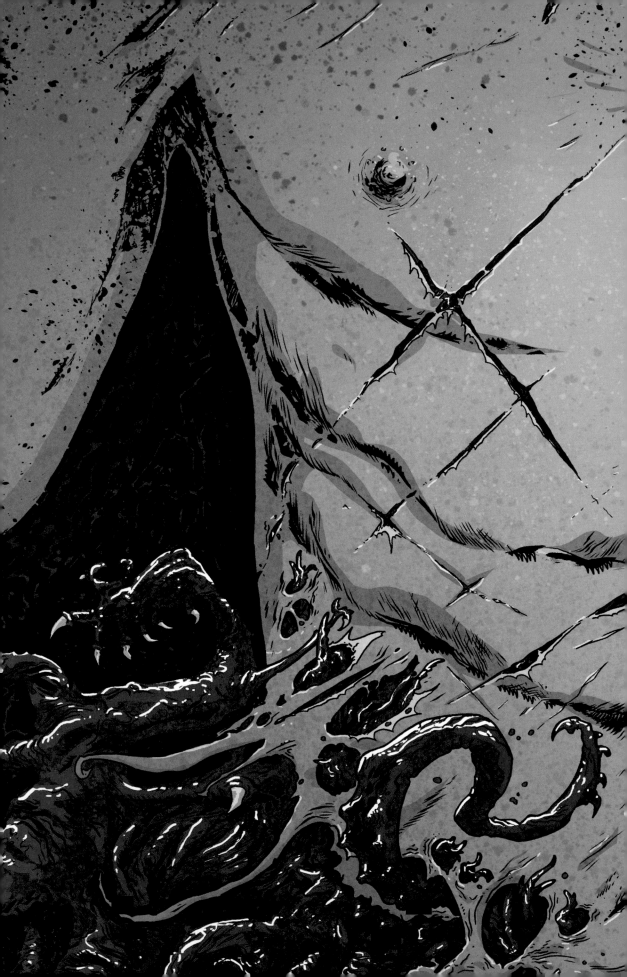

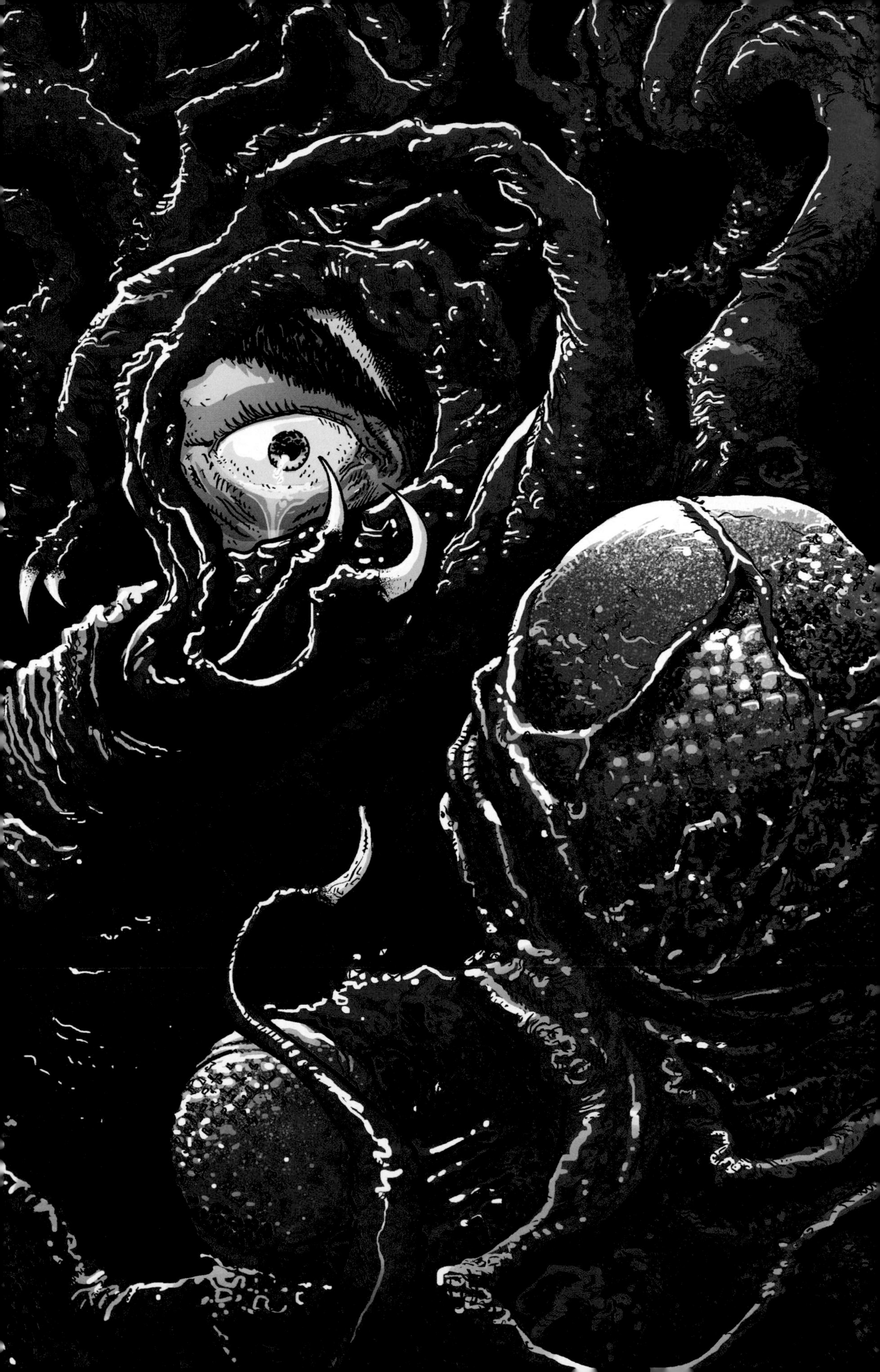

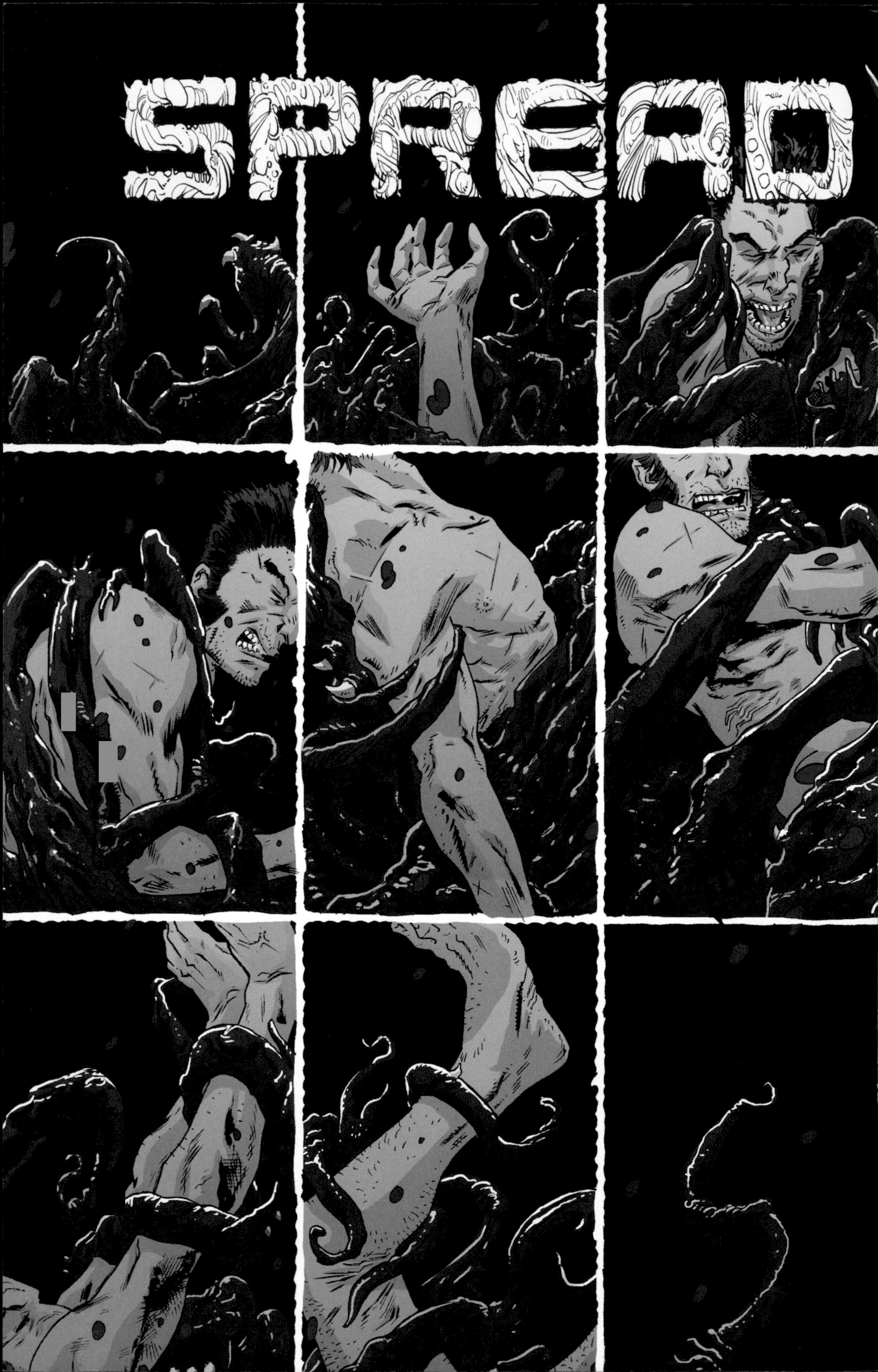
SPREAD

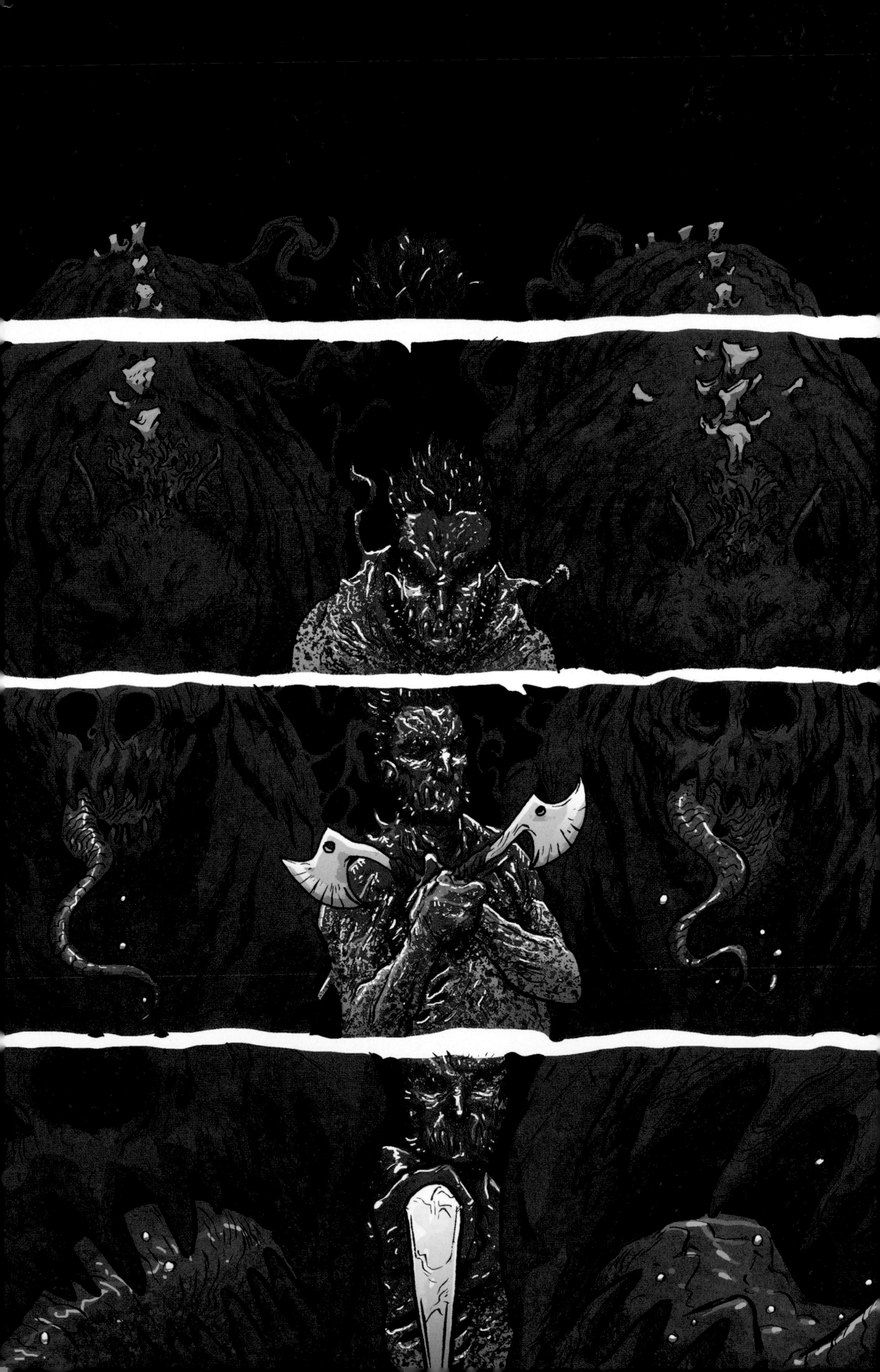

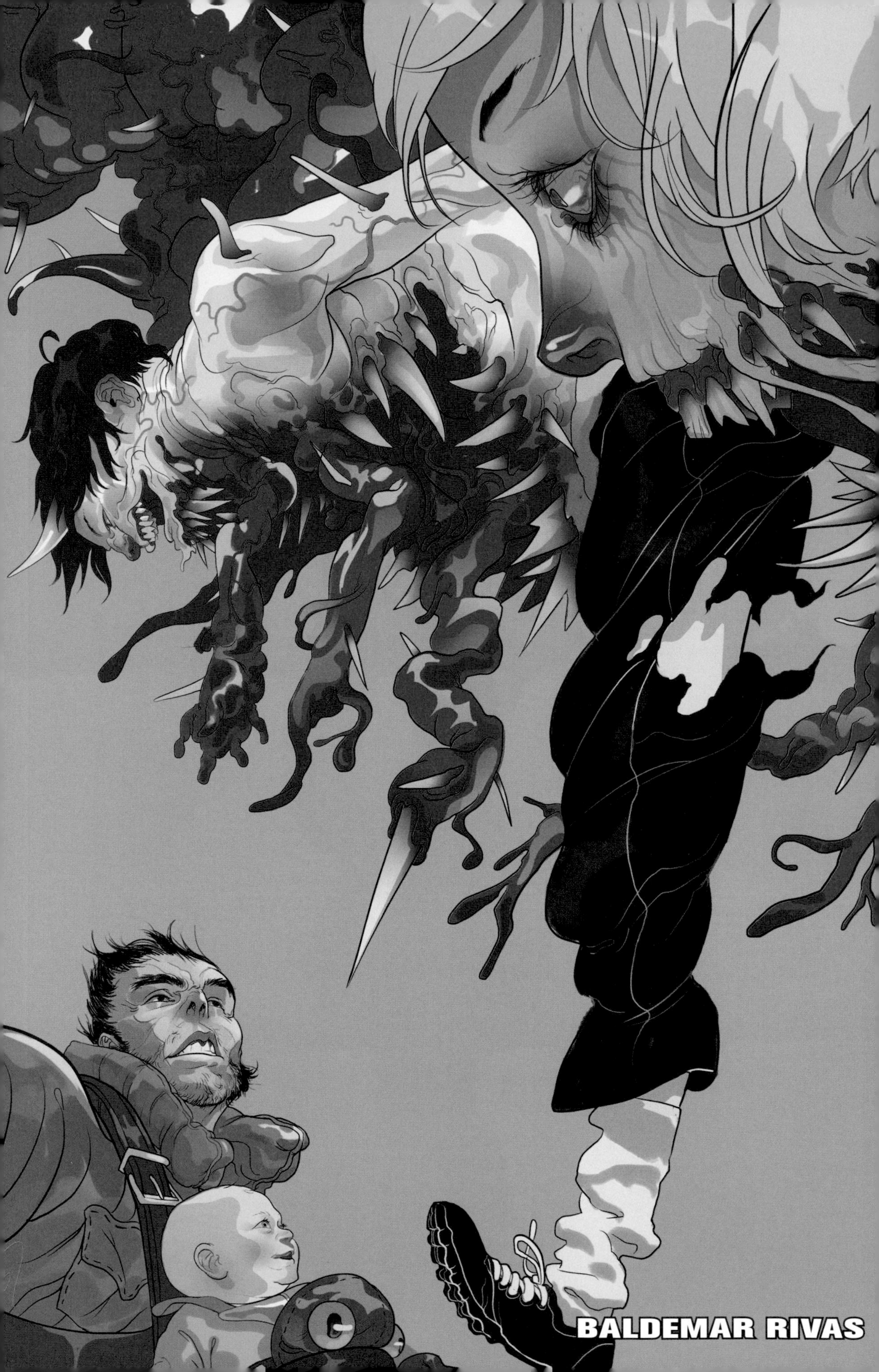
BALDEMAR RIVAS

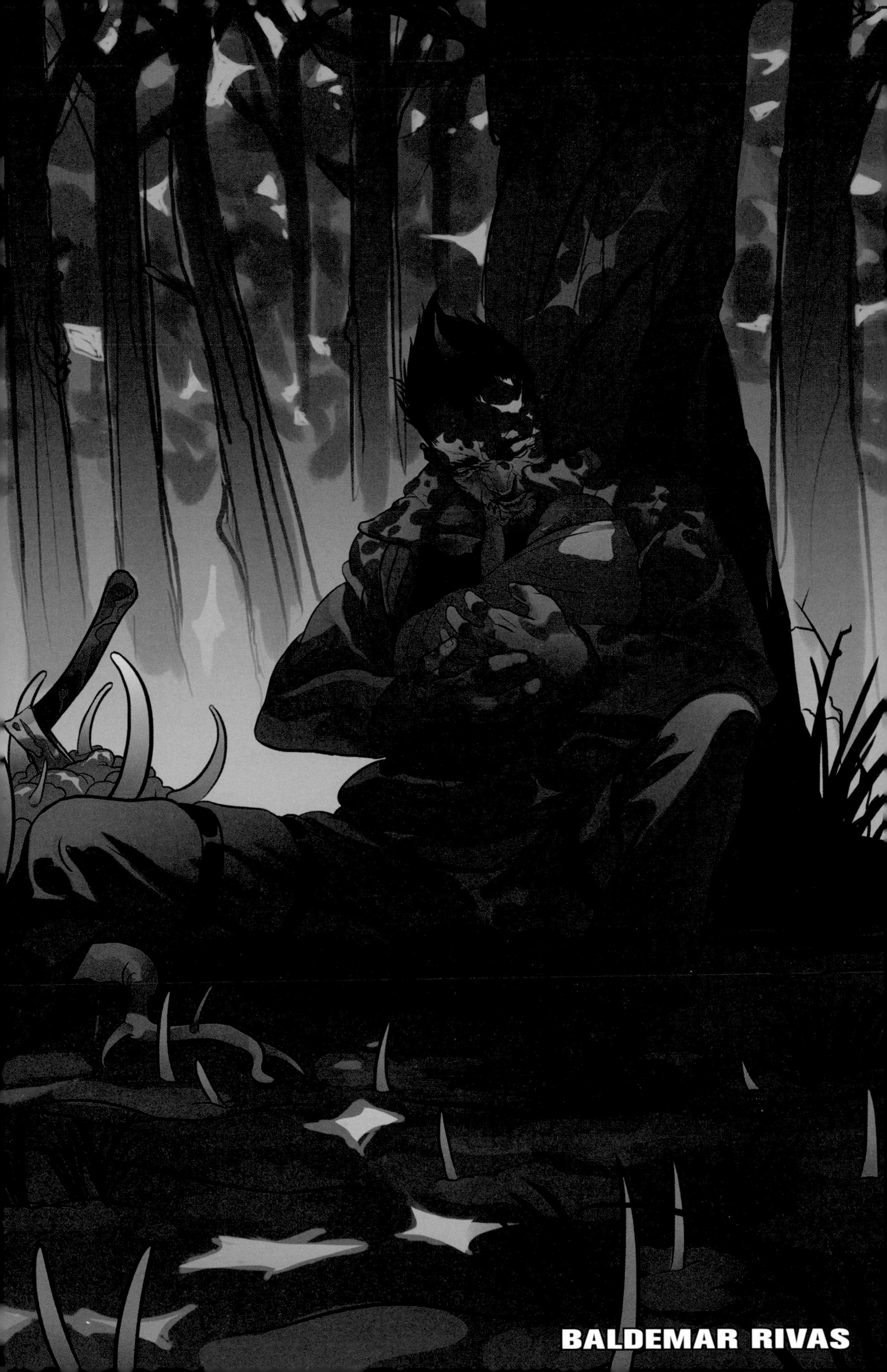
BALDEMAR RIVAS

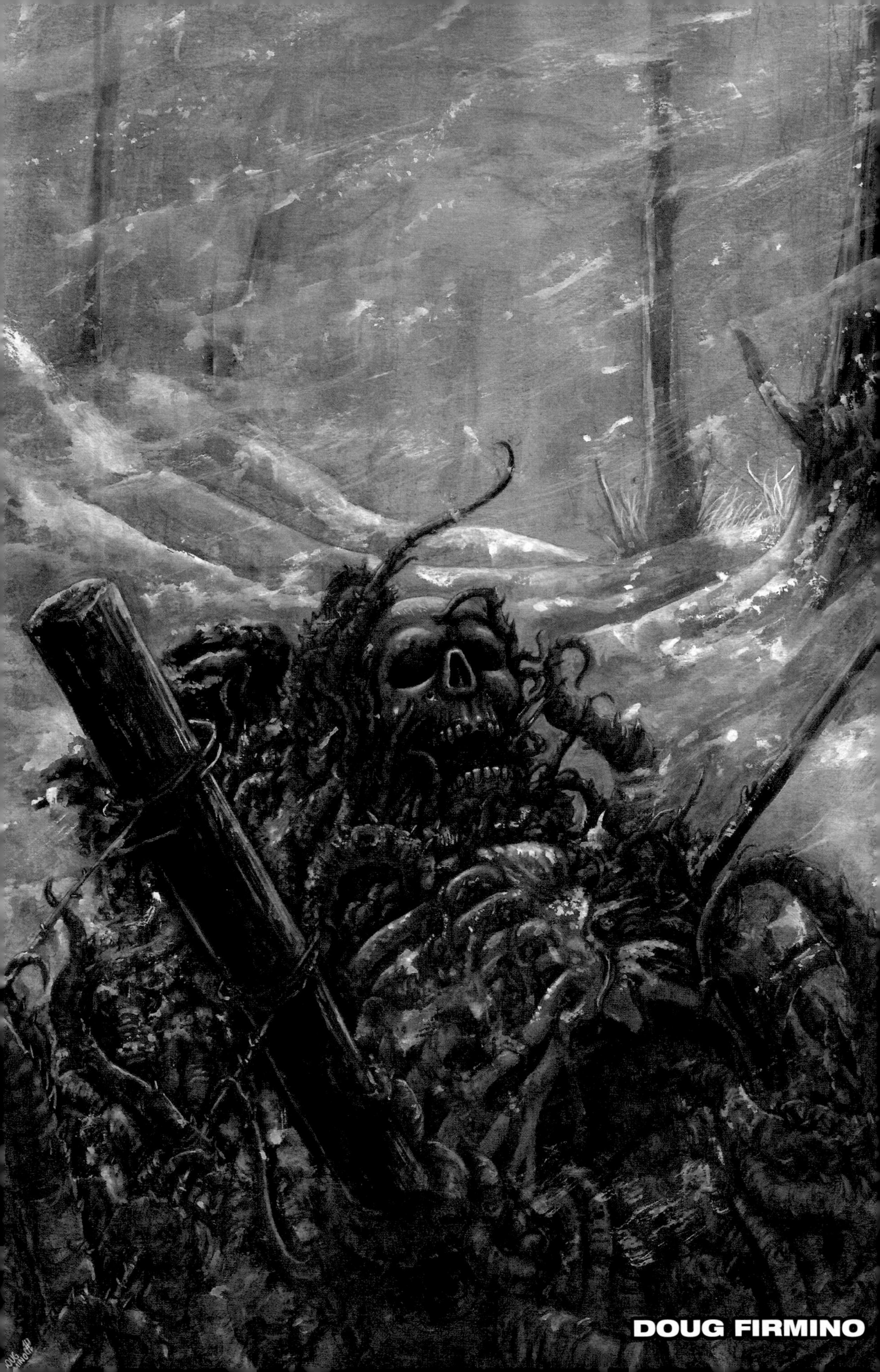
DOUG FIRMINO

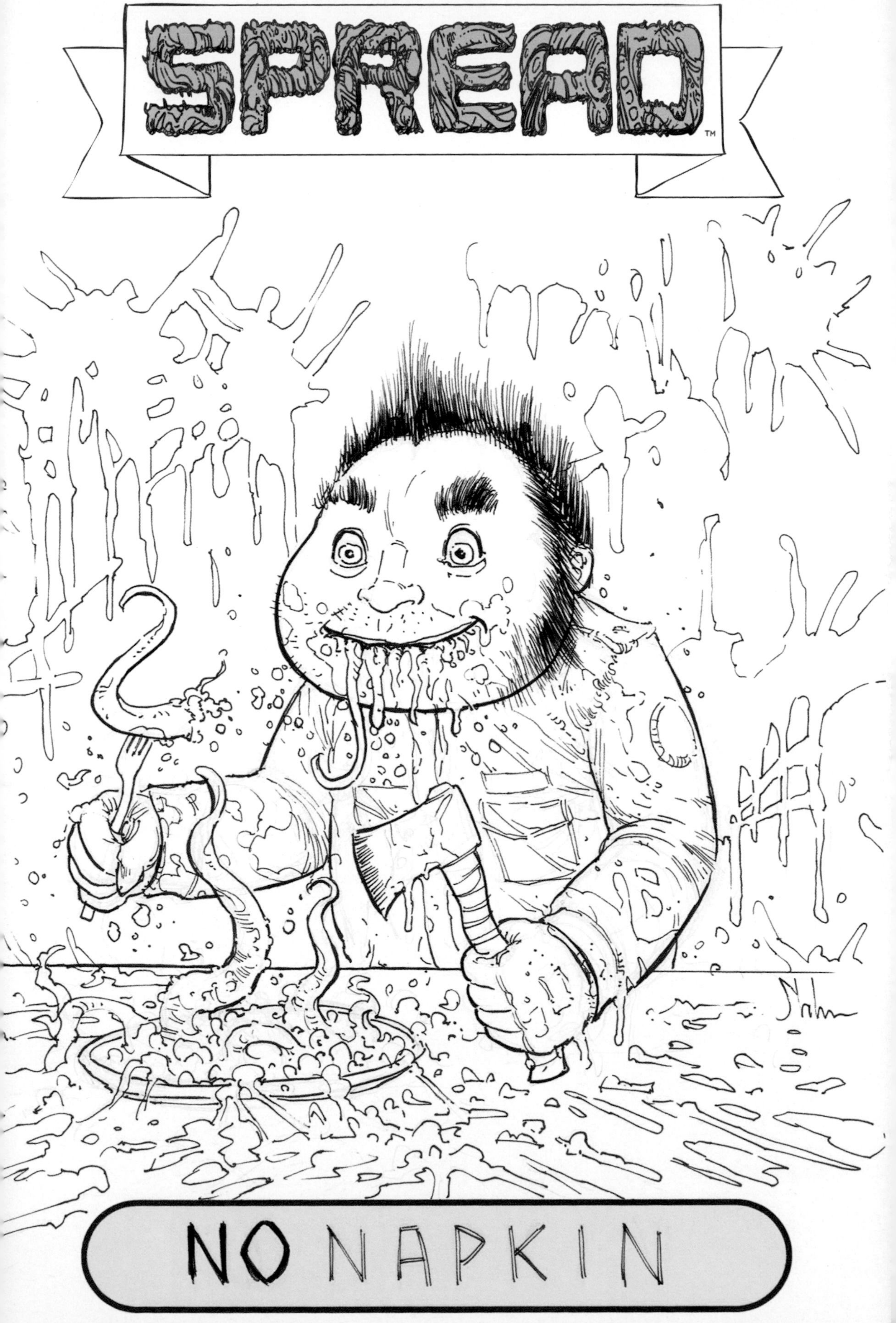
SPREAD™
NO NAPKIN

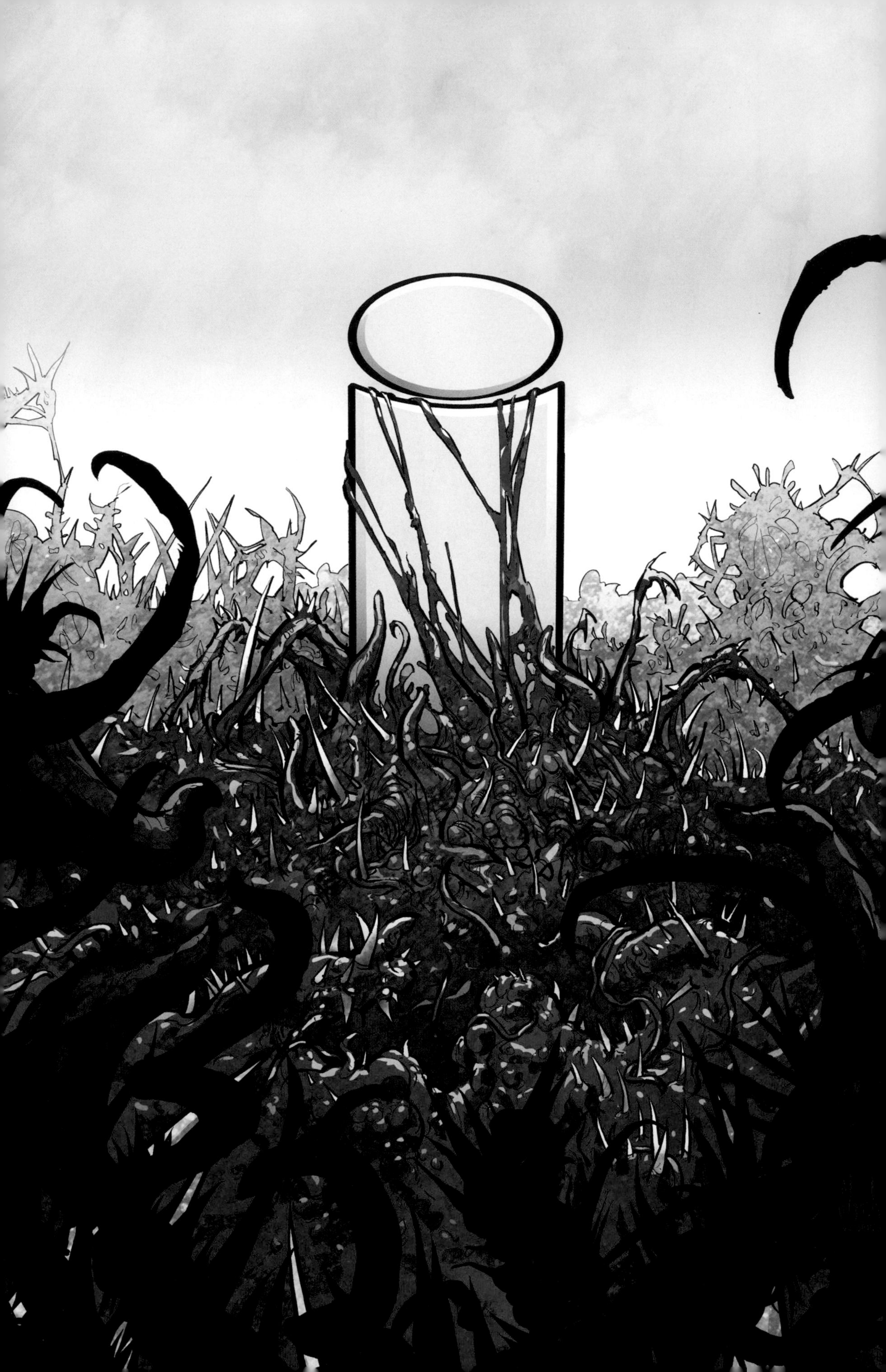

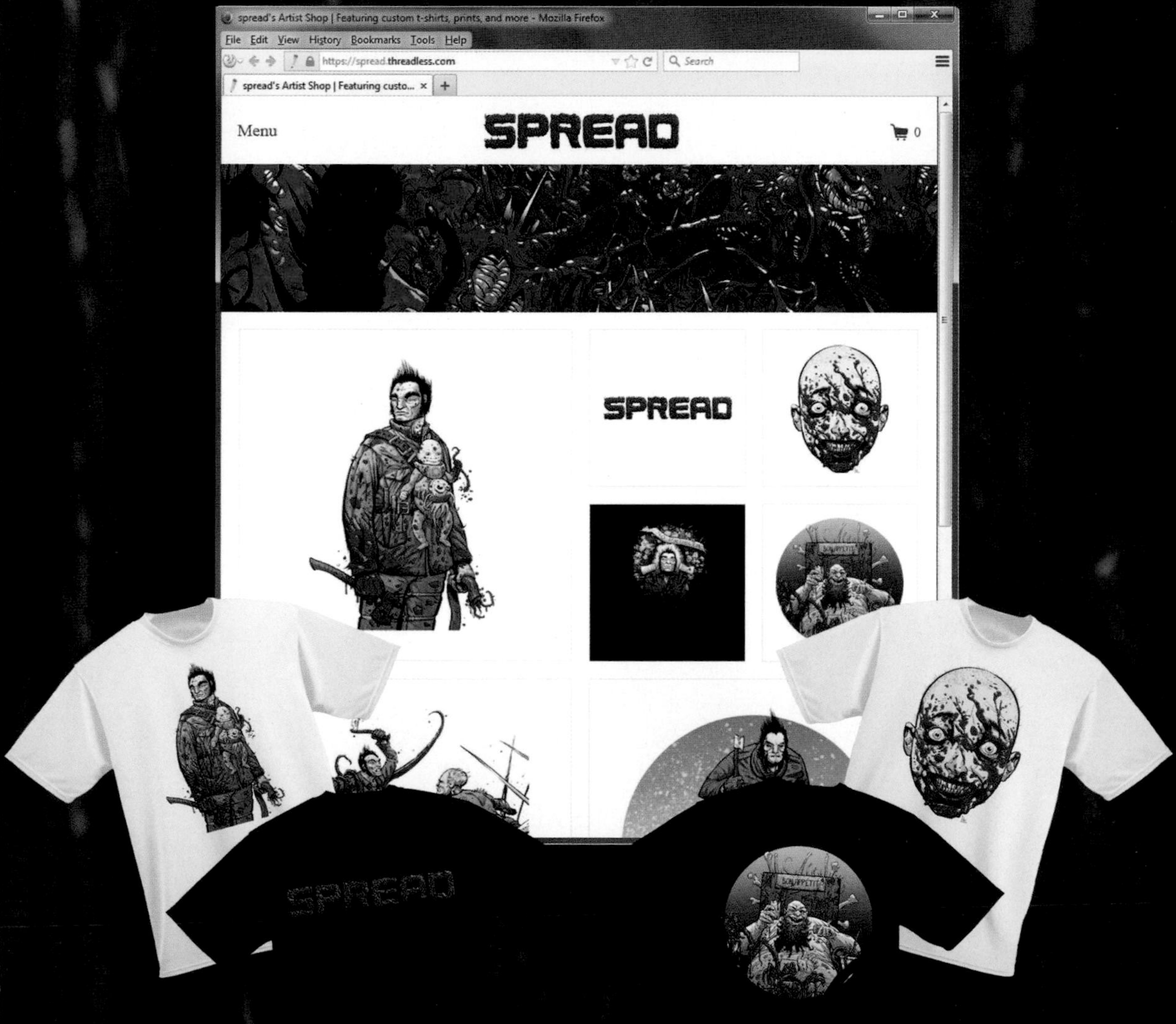
spread's Artist Shop | Featuring custom t-shirts, prints, and more - Mozilla Firefox
File Edit View History Bookmarks Tools Help
https://spread.threadless.com
Search
spread's Artist Shop | Featuring custo...
Menu
SPREAD
0
SPREAD
SPREAD

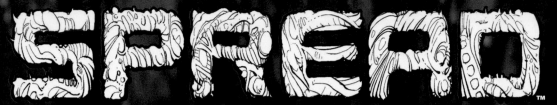

SO, I HAVE A PATREON...

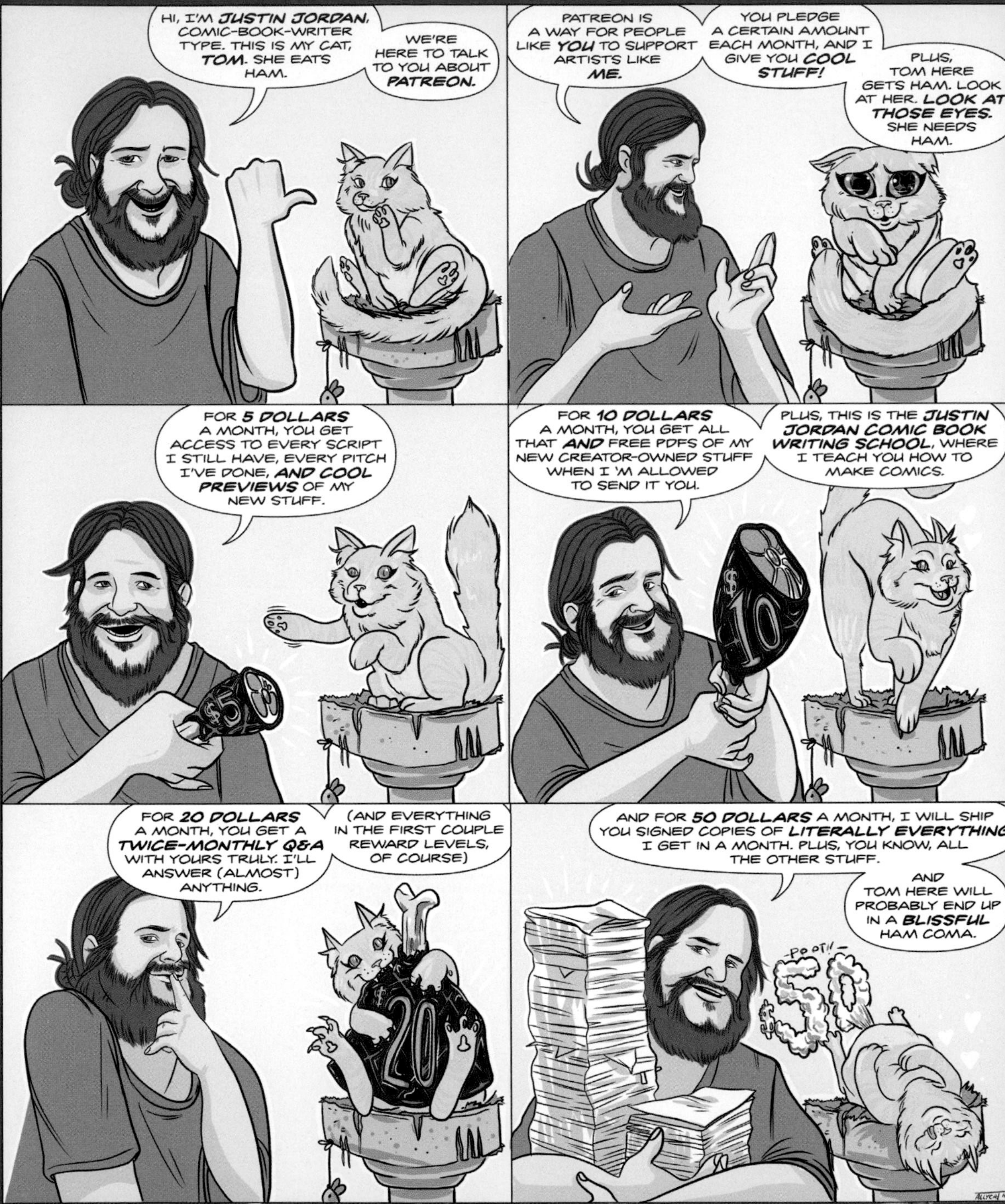
HI, I'M **JUSTIN JORDAN**, COMIC-BOOK-WRITER TYPE. THIS IS MY CAT, **TOM**. SHE EATS HAM.
WE'RE HERE TO TALK TO YOU ABOUT **PATREON.**
PATREON IS A WAY FOR PEOPLE LIKE **YOU** TO SUPPORT ARTISTS LIKE **ME.**
YOU PLEDGE A CERTAIN AMOUNT EACH MONTH, AND I GIVE YOU **COOL STUFF!**
PLUS, TOM HERE GETS HAM. LOOK AT HER. **LOOK AT THOSE EYES.** SHE NEEDS HAM.
FOR **5 DOLLARS** A MONTH, YOU GET ACCESS TO EVERY SCRIPT I STILL HAVE, EVERY PITCH I'VE DONE, **AND COOL PREVIEWS** OF MY NEW STUFF.
FOR **10 DOLLARS** A MONTH, YOU GET ALL THAT **AND** FREE PDFS OF MY NEW CREATOR-OWNED STUFF WHEN I 'M ALLOWED TO SEND IT YOU.
PLUS, THIS IS THE **JUSTIN JORDAN COMIC BOOK WRITING SCHOOL**, WHERE I TEACH YOU HOW TO MAKE COMICS.
FOR **20 DOLLARS** A MONTH, YOU GET A **TWICE-MONTHLY Q&A** WITH YOURS TRULY. I'LL ANSWER (ALMOST) ANYTHING.
(AND EVERYTHING IN THE FIRST COUPLE REWARD LEVELS, OF COURSE)
AND FOR **50 DOLLARS** A MONTH, I WILL SHIP YOU SIGNED COPIES OF **LITERALLY EVERYTHING** I GET IN A MONTH. PLUS, YOU KNOW, ALL THE OTHER STUFF.
AND TOM HERE WILL PROBABLY END UP IN A **BLISSFUL** HAM COMA.
-POOT!-

JUST HEAD ON OVER TO HTTPS://WWW.PATREON.COM/JUSTINJORDAN OR SCAN THE QR CODE AND CHECK IT OUT. I'D LOVE TO HAVE YOUR SUPPORT BECAUSE TOM REALLY LOVES HER HAM.

STRAHM

JUSTIN JORDAN

Justin Jordan lives in the wilds of Pennsylvania and writes comics. Lots of comics. Most notably the *Luther Strode* saga and *Dead Body Road* for Image.

Twitter: @Justin_Jordan
Email: JustinJordan@gmail.com
Facebook: www.facebook.com/JustinJordanComics/

KYLE STRAHM

Kyle Strahm lives and works in a house in Kansas City, Missouri, where he watches TV shows from back when they did it right and rearranges old toys like a crazy person. You might have seen his work published by Marvel, DC, Dark Horse, IDW, Todd McFarlane Productions and various others.

Website: www.kylestrahm.com
Instagram: @kylestrahm_art
Twitter: @kstrahm
Facebook: www.facebook.com/krstrahm

JOHN BIVENS

John draws stuff. Examples of this include the book you are holding now, *Dark Engine* (Image Comics), *Old Wounds* (Pop Goes the Icon), and multiple anthologies and such. He lives in Minneapolis.

Website: www.john-bivens.com
Instagram: @bivensjohn
Twitter: @John_Bivens
Facebook: www.facebook.com/ArtOfJohnThomasBivens
Tumblr: johnbivens.tumblr.com

FELIPE SOBREIRO

Felipe Sobreiro is an artist and colorist from Brazil. His work has been published, among others, by Image, Marvel, DC, BOOM! Studios and Dark Horse. He's the colorist of the *Luther Strode* saga.

Website: www.sobreiro.com
Instagram: @sobreiro
Twitter: @therealsobreiro
Facebook: www.facebook.com/fsobreiro

CRANK!

Crank! letters a bunch of books put out by Image, Dark Horse and Oni Press. He also has a podcast with Mike Norton (www.crankcast.net) and he makes music (www.sonomorti.bandcamp.com).

Twitter: @ccrank

SEBASTIAN GIRNER

Sebastian Girner is a freelance editor and writer who has helped creatively guide and produce comics for such publishers as Marvel Entertainment, Image Comics, VIZ Media and Random House. He lives and works in Brooklyn.

Website: www.sebastiangirner.com
Twitter: @SGirner

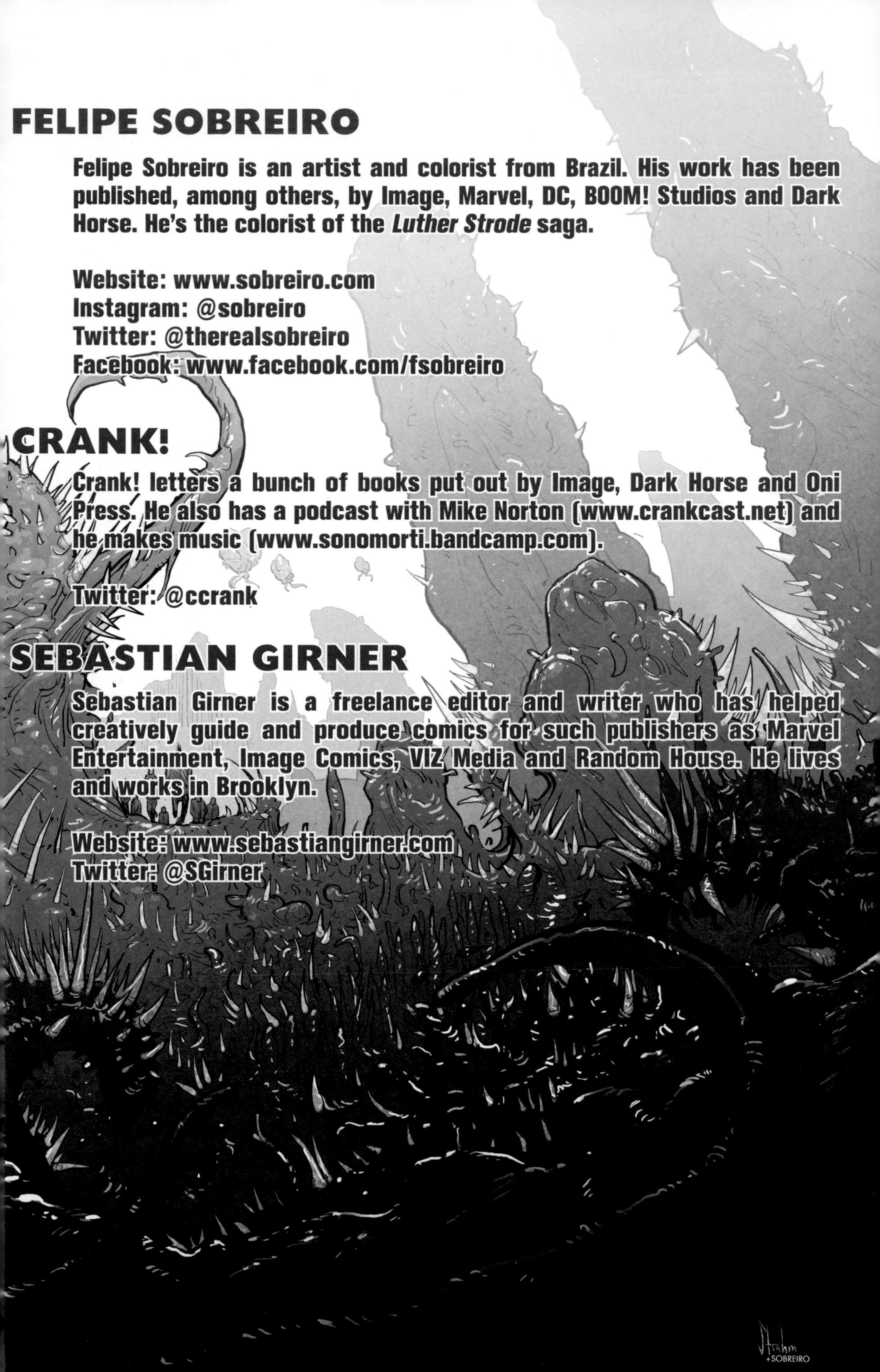
+SOBREIRO

SPREAD

WILL RETURN...

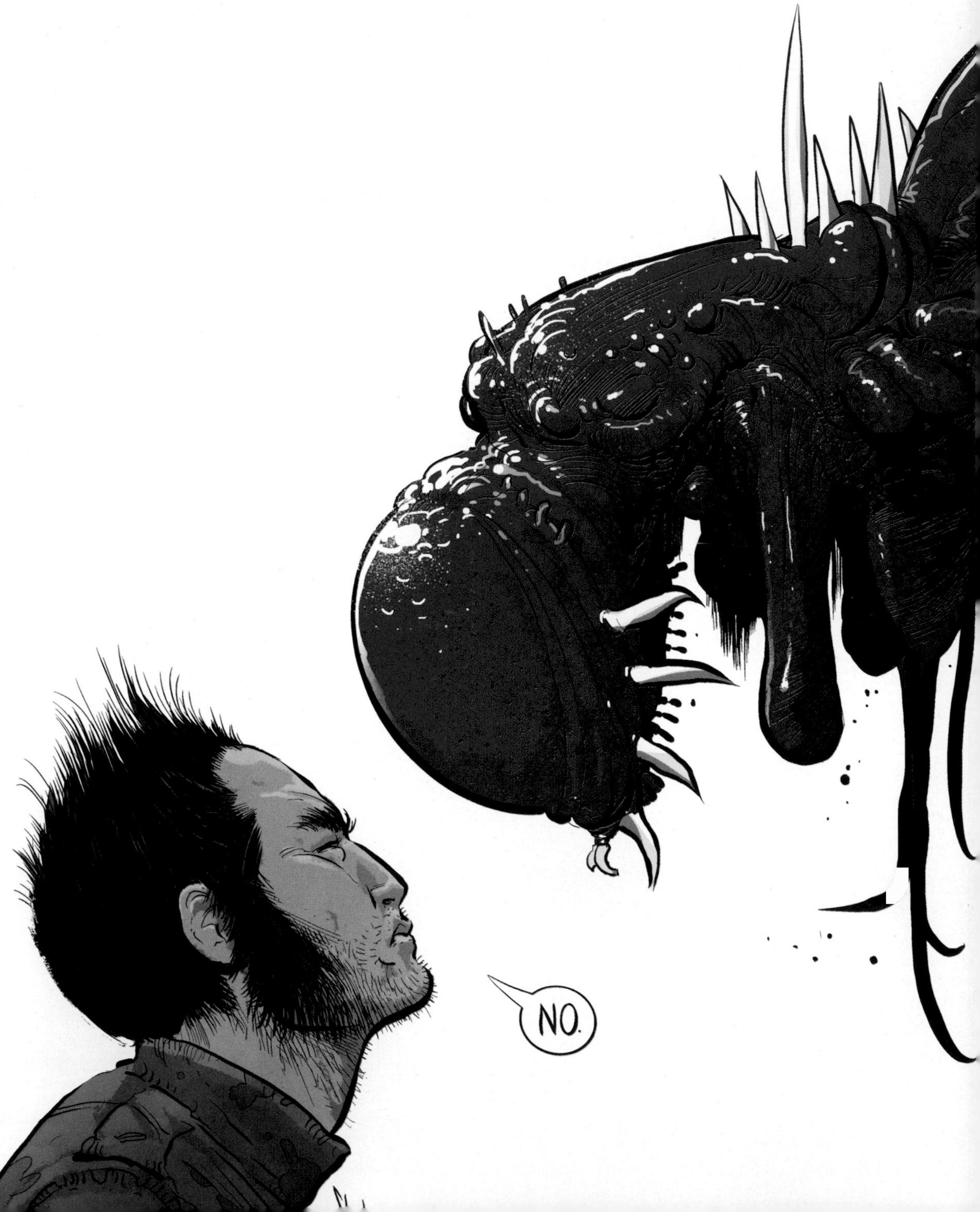
NO.